SENI GLAISTER

# MR DOUBLER
# BEGINS AGAIN

*Complete and Unabridged*

# CHARNWOOD
*Leicester*

First published in Great Britain in 2019 by
HQ
an imprint of HarperCollins*Publishers* Ltd
London

First Charnwood Edition
published 2020
by arrangement with
HarperCollins*Publishers* Ltd
London

A catalogue record for this book is available from the British Library.

ISBN 978–1–4448–4388–0

Published by
F. A. Thorpe (Publishing)
Anstey, Leicestershire

Set by Words & Graphics Ltd.
Anstey, Leicestershire
Printed and bound in Great Britain by
T. J. International Ltd., Padstow, Cornwall

This book is printed on acid-free paper

For my inspirational and
indispensable mother,
Penelope Glaister.

And in memory of

Mary Ann Brailsford 1791–1852
Marie Ann Smith 1800–1870
John Clarke 1889–1980

& the other unsung heroes
of the orchards and fields.

# 1

Doubler was the *second* biggest potato grower in the county. While it was true that his rival grew more potatoes than he did (by a significant margin), Doubler was unperturbed. Doubler's personal motivation was not quantity but *quality*, and the mere fact that his adversary had more land than he did had very little to do with their respective skills as potato growers.

Unlike his rival, Doubler was an *expert*. He understood potatoes in a way that potatoes had rarely been understood. He understood potatoes at least as well, he hoped, as that other potato great John Clarke. Mr Clarke, the infamous grower and breeder of potatoes, was Doubler's inspiration and Doubler sought his counsel often, asking questions out loud as he walked his land and finding the answers whispered to him each day as he worked on his notes, annotating his day's findings. Though they'd never met and Clarke himself had been dead for some decades, Doubler found enormous solace in their dialogue.

Recently, Doubler's experimentation had been going extremely well, and certain that he was close to securing his place in potato-growing history, he now carried within him (sometimes in his heart and sometimes in his stomach) a small, hope-shaped nugget of excitement. Doubler was not an optimistic man by nature, and the knowledge that he might soon take his seat among the most impactful potato growers of all time fuelled Doubler with a thrill of nervous energy, tinged by impatience but darkened by anxiety.

*To Doubler, his legacy was everything.*

But Doubler's legacy had attracted some negative attention. The most recent threat had arrived on his doorstep that morning. It had been packaged in a Manila envelope and addressed to him with a white printed label, suggesting a sinister professionalism on the part of the sender. The threat became more ominous still when combined with the two other envelopes, previously received. All three letters came from Peele, the biggest potato grower in the county, and together, this collection of three envelopes, now festering in the dark of the dresser drawer, had transcended from mere correspondence to a systematic *campaign*. Doubler dwelt on this, and what it might mean to his impending success, as he nervously inspected his land.

A brutal wind had stirred up the icy air from all of the surrounding valleys and had deposited it relentlessly on Mirth Farm, leaving almost everywhere warmer than Doubler's hilltop home, but despite this, Doubler did not hurry. Heading towards the farmhouse, he walked round the perimeter of the yard, stopping to check the angle of the new security camera and again to rattle the locks on each of the brooding barns. Even in happier days, when his wife had been with him, he had been a cautious man with a nervous disposition, but now, imperilled by this series of recent menaces, he had introduced new layers of watchfulness to his daily inspections of Mirth Farm, and his routine now incorporated a multitude of additional checks, which had quickly become mechanical, as if he'd followed them for as long as he'd followed the seasons.

Despite his nervousness, the steps he'd recently taken to protect Mirth Farm from his adversary felt empowering, so having hung up his coat and hat, he immediately turned his attention to the parcel that had arrived in yesterday's post in the hope that the contents would further bolster his defences. As expected, the package revealed a pair of brand-new binoculars, which he examined critically. He removed the lens guard and quickly replaced it, repeating this action a number of times, cautiously pleased with its certain fit. He planted himself firmly on the window seat, calming his breathing for a few moments before raising his new gift to his eyes.

He played slowly with the focal ring, moving the sight left and right with small, deft increments until the chaffinch on the bird feeder that hung from a twisted bough of the closest apple tree leapt into brilliant, dazzling clarity. Doubler paused for a moment to congratulate himself on the identification of the bird. 'Chaffinch!' he exclaimed, surprised.

Even a week ago, it would have been just another small bird idling away its time before it could clear the hedgerows of his fruit. This recently acquired knowledge, this sure-footed identification, gave him a flicker of pleasure he was unable to place, but it compelled him to linger on the chaffinch for a few moments more. The bird's bright eyes jumped into focus. Doubler was impressed. These binoculars were far superior to his last pair and would undoubtedly make his work more secure. Entirely satisfied, he now swung his attention to the right and refocused on a much further object: the entrance gate to Mirth Farm at the bottom of the hill.

Doubler recalled the feeling of the gate in his hands as he unlatched it and let it swing free. There had been a time when he had opened and closed that gate regularly, with barely a care in the world. He'd hung the gate himself and it had always swung open easily, without complaint or resistance. But there were no comings or goings for Doubler anymore: he was strictly a Mirth Farm man.

This was not something that had happened gradually; he had not taken a slow slide into solitude. He had decided, in fact, the moment his children left home, that he would never leave Mirth Farm again. If you never left, he had persuaded himself, there was no chance that you wouldn't return.

Doubler snapped back to attention as a car pulled into the bottom of the drive. It was only Mrs Millwood, and he had been anticipating her arrival, but he felt his muscles tense and the hairs stand up on the back of his neck. His anxiety was alleviated by the substantial weight of the binoculars in his hand and it gave him great comfort to train them on this arriving vehicle. He watched every movement as his visitor got out of the little red car, swung open the wooden gate, edged the car forward and once again clambered out of the car to close the gate behind her.

As soon as the vehicle was on his property, he was able to read the car's number plate and he made a note of it on the edge of the newspaper, intending to transfer it to a logbook that he planned to order specifically for this purpose. The car was making its way steadily up the hill, vanishing out of sight for several seconds at a time, then swinging back into view with each sharp turn. The ascent to Mirth Farm was a long, slow one, and Doubler observed that the quality of the vehicle probably had very little correlation to the speed of its approach — if anything, the faster the car, the slower the progress, as drivers of fast cars tended to be nervous of the ruts and bumps and the glinting edge of the flint that threatened the tyres with every turn. Doubler vowed to begin recording journey times to check this theory. He really didn't want to leave anything to chance.

# 2

Nine minutes later, Mrs Millwood let herself in through the kitchen door. The soundscape that accompanied her arrival never varied and Doubler listened attentively as she hung up her keys, removed her coat, tidied her bag away and changed from outdoor shoes to indoor shoes. She muttered noisily to herself as she eyed the overflowing compost bin spilling potato peelings onto the ancient wooden butcher's block. The scolding increased in volume as she came in search of Doubler, who was now standing to attention.

'Mr Doubler, you've been making an unreasonable mess in the kitchen again.'

Doubler inspected her as she flitted past, already patting piles into order, plumping, stroking and straightening. If Mrs Millwood were a bird, she'd be a wren he realized happily, as he watched her busying herself with the lightest touch.

'It's a bit of a mess, I know. I'm sorry.'

'It's a mess because you make it so. No need to apologize, though it would be better just not to make the mess in the first place.' She was already dragging a wooden chair to the edge of the room and, in a flash, she was standing on it, reaching up to put away the pile of unread books that had gathered mysteriously into her arms. It seemed, Doubler thought, that she put the books

6

away randomly, but when he inspected the shelves after she'd left, they always appeared to be in some sort of order. Before he could scrutinize her methodology, she was back on the floor again, a duster in her hand where books had been a moment ago.

'You've been at your potatoes again, I see,' she said with disappointment in her voice.

'My potatoes. Yes. I . . . ' Doubler suddenly wanted to share his concerns immediately rather than waiting until lunchtime. There were so many conflicting priorities in his head and he needed Mrs Millwood's pragmatism to work these into some sort of structure. He rose to his feet as if to take this matter firmly into his hands, but as the blood rose to his head so his thoughts bubbled into a whirlpool of disquiet and he fumbled with the words that threatened to break a decade and a half of routine should he prioritize their talk ahead of her housework. By the time he grasped the thread (a thread that when pulled would unravel to reveal his soul), she had gone, leaving a little trail of dust in her wake.

Even as he grappled to compose himself, he could hear the hoover being dragged into position above him and he knew he'd lost her for a couple of hours.

Doubler padded through to the kitchen, the disappointment of loneliness visible in the sag of his shoulders. The thick stone slabs were shockingly cold under his socked feet but kinder as he approached the Aga, and he paused there to warm himself up for a moment. To his left,

7

atop a deep block of wood worn rippled and smooth by the constant cutting and wiping of a long-dead butcher, sat three vast pans of dimpled tin, the type that Victorian cooks might have once used to make chutney or jam in large quantities. Each pan was draped with a generous square of muslin and he now peeled these back to examine the contents. Using a large wooden spoon to disturb the top layer of potatoes, he peered critically at them and then reached for the pan's corresponding clipboard. Each held a thick wedge of foolscap paper and was filled with Doubler's immaculate handwriting. In even-handed pencil, dates, measurements, numbers and formulae, sketches and diagrams filled the pages, and these themselves, without any further interpretation, already revealed something splendid about the study. But with the practised eye of an expert potato grower, the pages revealed a lifetime's ambition: research that was indeed groundbreaking. Aided by footnotes and appendices, the work amounted to the hopes and dreams of a man determined to leave a mark but conscious that time was against him.

With a steel fork, Doubler tested several spuds from each batch. From the pan that pleased him the least, he removed a number of potatoes and boiled them rapidly in salted water. He set these aside for his lunch.

Happy with his preparation, he set about writing up the morning's findings. To do this, he sat at the vast kitchen table, pale unvarnished pine in its origins but now marked with so many rings from water and scorches from scalding pans and polished so frequently with beeswax that it had the tint and the swell of a hardwood. He spread his paperwork out, frequently referring back to previous pages. The findings were consistent with his earlier conclusions and he remained certain that his research was irrefutable, but it gave him a sense of calm to add more dates, more affirmation, more proof as the days lengthened and the ground thawed, the slightest increments of warmth preparing the earth for a whole new generation of validation.

Doubler worked solidly for an hour: noting, refining, checking his work and underlining (again) his conclusions. With still no interruption from Mrs Millwood, he set out to do his second round of the land, a routine that he did, unfailingly, four times a day. He put on a thick woollen jumper, welcoming its scratchy warmth, and then zipped himself into a waxed jacket before pulling the flaps of his cap down over his ears to keep the wind out as he left the shelter of the farm buildings.

There was a quietness, a pause in the air that belonged uniquely to February and he loved it. The fields had been recently harrowed and the soil shone a warm chocolate brown in the weak winter sun, the pools of collected rainwater glistening brightly, creating a pleasing orderly stripe for as far as the eye could see. There were new birds today, scuttling across the fields in large flocks, bigger than the sparrows he could easily recognize but indistinguishable in their brownness to his still inexpert eye. He vowed to bring his binoculars next time he did his circuit.

Though bird identification had never been their intended purpose, he suddenly felt an urge to know who these newcomers were, pleased enough with himself to feel certain that they hadn't been here a week ago.

He walked slowly on, tracing the edge of the field, following the line of the twisted hedge, thick and impenetrable despite its lack of new foliage. He made his way to one of two vantage points, a small knoll from which he could survey the entire northern lay of the land. From here, he could sweep his gaze from field to field and run it quickly against his mental register. There was little to note at this time of year, though just a month later on in the season, when the risk of the heaviest frosts had passed, he would be meticulously checking the soil for the optimum moment to plant his seed potatoes. The winter offered an essential window to prepare the fields and maintain the machinery, but for now, it was enough to survey, acknowledge and simply honour the land, helping to lay the foundations of goodwill he'd rely on in later months.

Having walked the complete perimeter of the largest field, he climbed up the steady slope, matching each pace with the rise and fall of a furrow, mentally measuring the scope of his land for no other reason than the process gave him great comfort. Throughout the seasons the land grew and fell in height and potential as the crops sprang up and died down, the harvest succeeding or failing on the strength of that alchemical mix of science, skill and magic but dictated most omnipotently by nature herself, who always had the final say. While many factors dictated the strength of the growth upwards, the curtilage of the land itself didn't change. Providing his stride never faltered, then the count would always be the same, as it had since he bought the farm, nearly forty years before.

As he turned the corner back into the yard, the farmhouse in front of him once more, he again checked the locks on each of the barn doors. Several garages and outbuildings lay around the farm, but these were the three that delivered the greatest dose of pleasure and the greatest dose of stress. These, after all, were the structures that contained his legacy.

Each one of these buildings was sealed very convincingly with heavy chains strung between iron bars. He glanced up to check the camera angle and gave himself a worried little wave, which he would look for later on the monitor. Doubler had expected to find his security camera reassuring, but he had also found it to be surprisingly companionable and he took a curious pleasure in observing himself when he reviewed the footage each evening.

Doubler wouldn't return to inspect the two largest locked barns until the early evening. He liked everything inside to stay as dark as possible, so he never opened the doors in daylight. But he could sense the tingle of burgeoning life as he passed, and he could almost hear the new growth straining at the skin of last year's crop. The progress might be minuscule at this time of year, but multiply that by the thousands of spuds lined up on cool wooden racks and it was possible to imagine the effect of all that pent-up energy on the immediate environment. Or at least Doubler liked to think so.

The third shed, though inactive at this time of year, was Doubler's most treasured. If he could wrap chains round it like a giant parcel, he would. He had, instead, to content himself with the measures he had in place.

He glanced back and forth, checking that nobody could see him as he punched the code into the panel by the door to this the most secretive of his stores. He slipped in and closed the door behind him. Inhaling deeply, he took a moment to enjoy the unique scent that lingered long after the plant had been used. Potato, yes, to a practised nose, but also the more prominent tang of cleanliness smothering traces of sap and honey. It would be several weeks before this storehouse sprang to life again and he loved its emptiness and promise in winter. He savoured it for a few more deep breaths before flicking one low light on and inspecting the vast copper stills with their glorious pipes, funnels and gauges. Even in this dim lighting, the metalwork shone.

'Morning,' he whispered, with respect evident in his voice. To a layman, this equipment must look quite mysterious, daunting even. But to Doubler, every connecting piece made perfect, logical sense.

The apparatus had been there when Doubler bought the farm with his wife, Marie. He'd discovered it in the first few weeks of living there, once he'd started to assess the heaps of rusting equipment left behind by the previous farmer. (The farmer had died suddenly, fifteen years before he might reasonably have expected to, but even had he received some sort of warning, Doubler doubted he would ever have cleared this backlog of past misjudgements.)

When Doubler had first discovered it, this vast pile of metal-work beneath tractor arms, balers and rotting feed sacks, he had recognized the green hue as the oxidization of copper and knew it would be worth something if he found the right metal dealer. But then as he'd begun to painstakingly separate the wheat from the chaff, he'd recognized it as an old still, used for distilling vodka, and as a distraction from the trials of fatherhood and a diversion from a wife whom he constantly disappointed, he'd dared himself to investigate the equipment fully. He had tinkered at first, fixing a piece here and a piece there, wondering idly if he'd ever get round to restoring it properly, when, in a flash of inspiration he barely understood, he'd felt compelled to take the entire configuration to pieces, laying each of the component parts on the ground before stripping them down, cleaning and repairing each piece, replacing seals and valves, and then reassembling the entire structure, feeling his way part by part with the skill of a mechanic and the patience of an organ builder.

Now, he knew it inside and out, knew its sighs and moods, and he understood how to tune it to perfection, treating it with the respect that such an ancient piece of engineering deserved.

Doubler was well aware that modern techniques must surely have since outclassed this old thing, but the results it produced had its idiosyncratic imperfections woven into its fabric, resulting in the artisan end product that made it so distinctive and desirable — several bottles of which were now resting in the cellar.

His inspection complete, Doubler switched off the light and shut the door behind him, tugging at the handle twice to ensure it was locked securely. As he walked back into the yard, he looked up at the sun, which was now grazing the edge of the low kitchen wall, and hurried inside, confident that he had satisfactorily passed the time until lunch and could finally, carefully, share his worries with Mrs Millwood.

# 3

As Mrs Millwood bustled around the kitchen making a pot of tea for them both and setting out two places on the now tidy kitchen table, Doubler prepared his meal. From the dark of the pantry he fetched a couple of shallots, testing them between his thumb and finger, registering the lack of give, still, all these months later.

'So much superior to their cousin the onion,' he declared to Mrs Millwood, who watched him chop the bulbs into tiny cubes with a distrusting glance he could sense as he worked. 'Look at that! A delight!' The bulbs still glowed a pearlescent white and the pieces fell away crisply under his blade. These he scooped into a pan and softened for just a few seconds in butter before adding the potatoes and crushing them deftly with the back of a fork. 'Not mashed, mind you, just crushed.' He answered the unspoken question gleefully.

Grating black pepper with two sharp snaps of his wrist, he carried the steaming plate to the table.

Mrs Millwood was unclipping her Tupperware and removing the sandwiches that she prepared, with surprising variety, every day.

'What you want on that, Mr Doubler' — nodding in the direction of his plate — 'is a nice bit of melted Cheddar.'

'Cheddar? Melted? Heavens, no, Mrs Millwood. Why on earth would I do that?'

'For, you know, a bit of flavour. Or vitamins. You can't live on spuds alone.' This she knew was a provocative statement, but it wasn't spoken to provoke, more out of genuine and long-running concern over his nutritional intake.

'Oh, Mrs Millwood. I don't really need to tell you about the beneficial qualities of the British potato, do I? You know as well as I do that the potato produces more edible protein per acre per day than either rice or wheat.'

'But I'm not going to eat an acre of spuds, Mr Doubler. I just want something tasty for my lunch. Tasty and healthy.'

'Don't talk to me about healthy! The biological value of potato protein is better than that of wheat, maize, peas or beans. Potatoes are just as good for you as milk, and nobody would deny the health benefits of milk, now would they?'

'I know very well about the beneficial qualities of the British potato' — and indeed she did. Only last night she had enlightened the ladies in her knitting circle, who were amazed not just by this information but by the depth of Mrs Millwood's knowledge and the persuasiveness of her passion — 'but a bit of melted Cheddar for flavour wouldn't go amiss.'

Doubler put down his fork and looked sternly at his lunch companion. 'Mrs Millwood. Heat is the worst possible thing you can subject a Cheddar cheese to. All that would achieve would be to release the oils and destroy the flavour. If

16

you go to the trouble of making a decent Cheddar, there's only one way to eat it.' Here, he went to the pantry and produced a large parcel wrapped tightly in waxed paper and tied with string.

'Let me show you.' He demonstrated with exaggerated movements while never taking his eyes off his audience. 'You serve Cheddar on wood. Not pottery or porcelain. That's a rule,' he said firmly, placing the unwrapped Cheddar on the centre of a wooden chopping board. 'The natural oils and flavours in the wood are absorbed into the cheese, adding a quality that cannot be replicated by any other means. Secondly, wood is porous. It does not create an impenetrable barrier against the cheese, thus allowing it to breathe.'

Mrs Millwood appeared to be holding her breath.

'Allowing a cheese to breathe is another rule. Otherwise it sweats and that is not good. A sweaty Cheddar is never good,' said Doubler, unwrapping the parcel carefully.

Mrs Millwood shook her head solemnly.

'Next rule.' He counted this off on his index finger, suddenly aware that there were actually many rules when it came to Cheddar and he probably needed to keep a log. 'Just one cut, Mrs Millwood, or at any rate, as few cuts as possible.' He used here his penknife to make a sharp diagonal cut through the narrowest point until he could break it with his fingers. 'The Cheddar is a cheese of the fingers — it's a truly sensory experience. You breathe it in, you feel it, and you

17

taste it. The feel is the bit that can't be missed. By handling the cheese with your fingers, you prepare your brain for what to expect. You don't want any surprises. My brain already knows to ready itself for the sharp tang of good Cheddar because my fingers have already tasted it ahead of my mouth. You see?'

Mrs Millwood watched intently, her own sandwich hanging a little limply in her hands and a frown playing gently on her forehead.

'So, one cut with your knife and then break it with your fingers to get the full experience. You can serve it with an apple — probably a Cox's orange pippin is best, but I'm not a pedant, Mrs Millwood. And chutney. You're after a sweet chutney or something quite dry and sour. I'll give you a try of two I'd recommend, but chutney is a very personal thing — it's a matter of taste. Just so long as it's not pickle: the brine will compete with a good Cheddar, not complement it. You don't want competition on your plate. You're looking for harmony. Harmony and tone. Think of it as a piece of music and you're the conductor.'

Mrs Millwood looked at her own sandwich and took a cautious bite.

'Heat? No. I wouldn't even heat a good Cheddar on a cold day. Complete waste.'

'I'm sorry I spoke.' Mrs Millwood took a larger, more defiant bite of her sandwich, refusing to be ashamed of her sliced, evenly toned knife-cut cheese layered with supermarket ham, mustard, pickle, pepper and lettuce. 'Lovely,' she said, taking her biggest mouthful yet.

'I just thought it would perk up your lunch,' she added, washing her mouthful down with a generous gulp of tea.

'Well, yes, I'm not averse to a little cheese with my potato, but not in this context, and never with Cheddar. There are plenty of cheeses crying out to be melted. I'd put most of the goat family into that category,' thus dismissing the entire group with a wave of his hand. 'But I'm not after additional flavour. I'm working, Mrs Millwood, and what I want to taste is the potato.'

'And are you pleased with today's spuds?'

'Oh! I am, I am. I'm absolutely delighted. They are behaving themselves beautifully. There's little news to report, and that's a good thing. Just further validation.' Doubler lowered his voice a fraction, saying, conspiratorially, 'Once I have my findings confirmed by the experts — our friends overseas — I'm done.'

Mrs Millwood looked at him carefully. 'With your research? With your potatoes? What are you done with?' Mrs Millwood had concern in her voice. She'd known him when he was done before and it had very nearly killed him.

Doubler recognized the worry and set about reassuring her that his motivation, his zest for life and his appetite for continued research were very much unfinished. 'I can't imagine I will ever be completely done with potatoes per se. They are in my blood. What would I concern myself with if they weren't there to fill every working moment? But the detailed analysis, yes, I think I am probably finished with that. I cannot see any room for improvement or any questions left

19

unanswered. Once I receive validation, it will mark the end of a very long period of concentrated work. If I am right, and my research is formally recognized, then I suppose I shall have to think of another project, or dedicate my remaining years to ensuring my work is properly recorded for the benefit of future generations. It will be the most significant moment of my life, of that I am sure. Obviously, I'm still awaiting official word from the institute, and you can appreciate that I'm not finding the waiting very easy.' He sighed heavily, immediately undermining any pretence of confidence he had just delivered.

Mrs Millwood knew as well as he did that Doubler would not find the wait easy. She, too, was impatiently awaiting news. After all, since he had revealed his discovery to her, she had been instrumental in steering him through this convoluted course of action, which would, they both hoped, ultimately result in the scientific validation he craved. She had researched the options open to him fully and, without betraying any confidences, had taken the counsel of those comfortable in the areas of law, copyright, patent and scientific assessment, and in many respects these enquiries had been as meticulous and painstaking as Doubler's own endeavours.

The situation, as she had carefully explained to him over a lunch, was that during the decades he had spent as a potato farmer, the farming world had moved on and left him behind. It transpired that the science of potatoes was funded primarily by the *giant users*, those who stood to gain the most commercially from any significant improvement in the process. The big-label oven-ready chip producers were at the heart of research and development, and the fast-food retailers, too, had a considerable vested interest in blight. 'Who would have thought the oven chip had so much power, Mr Doubler!' she had exclaimed, before continuing with her lugubrious findings.

Despite his own significant production, Doubler had not struck deals with these commercial partners and so had never worked in league with them. Likewise, through the happy accident of his meticulous barn clearing, Doubler had found himself, most discreetly, in the vodka business, but never on any scale. So, while he was a much-valued and highly respected contributor to it, the vodka industry had its own specific regulations to navigate and its own endless legislation to challenge. Doubler was not of enough consequence either to those who funded research or lobbied on behalf of the potato growers, and he was certainly small beer for the beverage companies. Doubler simply did not move in the right circles.

Mrs Millwood had researched all of this carefully and had soon learnt an alarming amount about the duplicitous nature of corporate life. She had spent time talking to great legal minds, who all warned her of being too hasty in sharing her anonymous friend's findings until she had found a partner with deep pockets who could be trusted with the science. She should tread carefully, she had been warned, for an unscrupulous player further up the supply chain would not think twice about taking this research and presenting it as their own or undermining Doubler's findings. As one great mind had put it, 'Once they get wind of what he's up to on that farm of his, the big boys will simply chew him up and spit him out,' and so, instead, she had presented to Doubler over lunch one day a solution that would take a little longer but would have his work put in front of some of the most qualified and respected eyes in the world.

And thus, after much research, Mrs Millwood's solution was to seek a non-partisan validation from the Institute of Potato Research and Development in northern India. It was for feedback from this venerated institution that they now waited.

'Well, let's have a look.' Mrs Millwood rummaged in her bag for a little leather diary and flicked back through the pages. 'We posted your package just after Christmas, didn't we? Here we go. The twenty-seventh. Now, there will have been holiday delays and the like, but even so, that's six weeks.'

Doubler looked glum.

'But six weeks isn't that long if you think about it. That's overland post, not airmail, and I don't know what their postal service is like over there. Let's allow it four weeks, shall we? And then there's some processing time yet — two weeks? We don't want them rushing it. Four maybe? Four weeks to do a really thorough job. And we want a thorough job, don't we? Then four weeks back in the post. I think, Mr Doubler, you're anxious ahead of time. I think if you haven't heard anything back by the beginning of April, you can start to wonder if there's a problem.'

'What sort of problem?' Doubler's face was beset with a frown drawn from all sorts of unframed worries.

'Failure of the post to arrive. Administration error their end. Lost in an in-tray. Then there's the technical side. They don't think your work is important. They think your findings are wrong. They don't think it is worthy of a response.'

Doubler was alarmed by each one of these possibilities, but the sum of all the possibilities (why would he fail on one count when he could fail on so many?) had his head reeling.

Mrs Millwood smiled at him reassuringly. 'But do you know how hopelessly futile it is to worry about any of these issues? We can't worry about those things that are out of our control. You have your farm. You have your potatoes. You've made *break-throughs*, Mr Doubler. And they'll recognize that.'

Seeing her words land with little impact, Mrs Millwood reached for a more powerful weapon in her arsenal. 'Do you think your Mr Clarke floundered at the first hurdle?'

Doubler thought hard. He imagined his great hero working by candlelight, scratching out his own findings with the worn stub of a pencil. He thought about the many generations of potatoes that man must have grown with no clear goal in mind, just the burning desire to improve the spud for the benefit of all. He thought about the achievement this represented when undertaken by a man with no education. Doubler was ashamed.

'No, of course not. Mr Clarke overcame every obstacle.'

Mrs Millwood chuckled to herself. 'He did, didn't he? And here are you hanging your head in shame and you haven't had a single setback yet!'

'You're right, of course, as always. And poor Mr Clarke didn't have the benefit of a role model as I do. But, Mrs Millwood, you can understand my worries, can't you? This is my *life's work*. I've made some sacrifices along the way, too, and I want there to be some meaning, some purpose behind it all. I want my *legacy*.'

He stood up and went to look out of the window, clearing a small patch of condensation through which he could see the last of the winter sun as it chased across his fields.

'When I die, Mrs Millwood, this work is all that will be left of me. My potatoes are my bequest. I have devoted every waking moment to them, and my most useful days are now well behind me. I want to leave my mark; I want to show the world it was worth it. I want to die knowing I made a difference. Is that too much to ask? Am I being greedy?'

Mrs Millwood thought carefully before answering. 'Not greedy, but a little impatient perhaps. You have your health, Mr Doubler, and, what's more, you still have plenty of time left to make a difference. You should count yourself among the fortunate ones.' She paused, and Doubler, focused on the view from the window, missed the shadow of something fearful flickering across her eyes.

He turned to face her, looking at her quizzically as he waited for her to carry on. She shook her head a little sadly, a determined smile on her face, and she continued in a slightly different direction to the thought process she'd begun.

'We don't all get to do something of consequence, Mr Doubler, so you should be proud of everything you've achieved already. And who is to say this is your life's work done yet? That will be determined when the time comes. Now, a short wait for the postman to deliver your answer is a small price to pay. Others suffer substantially more for less of a legacy, Mr Doubler.'

Mrs Millwood bit into a Granny Smith with great relish and Doubler, grateful once again for her deep wisdom, and quite used by now to his housekeeper having a much greater instinct than his own for matters pertaining to life, chose not to comment on her choice of apple.

# 4

On the first Sunday of each month, Doubler's only daughter, Camilla, liked to visit Mirth Farm with her family. This had been happening for many years. It was a habit that had been initiated by Camilla once she had her own children, as if she might be able to teach her father the correct procedure to hold a family together. One or two such lunches established a precedent, a couple more sealed it as a tradition, and this was then upheld by Camilla with great diligence and worn proudly as some sort of badge of filial duty.

'It's lovely to know that my kids are part of Dad's life,' she said to her brother, Julian, with a barely concealed stratum of aggression-tinged superiority that she rarely found cause to exhibit in her brother's company.

Conversely, Julian, Doubler's only son, was ambivalent about his role in the family. His associations with both family and Mirth Farm were linked to his childhood and now, an adult with adult responsibilities, his main preoccupation at the weekends was the management, from afar, of his costly ex-wife and the ongoing provision for two expensive children who found little to interest them on a potato farm, having been exposed to the sort of infancy that valued lawn much more highly than soil. Even if they had clamoured to visit their grandfather, Julian would have found an excuse to resist. At Mirth

Farm, there was little escape from the immediacy of fatherhood and Julian felt exposed by this. In stark contrast, his own home provided any number of distractions and barriers that allowed the children and their father to coexist without confronting the enormity of each other's failings.

To date, Julian's involvement in his children's upbringing had given him very little fulfilment other than the satisfaction of completing numbers in a column of the ledger of his mind. Nevertheless, he wore his paternal responsibilities quite heavily on his stooped shoulders and never was this more apparent than under the gaze of his father and sister. He didn't quite understand Camilla's need to imitate a conventional family so regularly, but nor did he quite trust his own emotional response to try to change or influence the pattern.

Camilla, however, had a very certain sense of what these occasions should feel like to her offspring, and even though her own childhood had failed to live up to many of the obligations she liked to associate with the institution, she insisted on imposing her own needs upon all of them. She made sure that Julian and his children joined them at least four times a year, and this Sunday was one of those prescribed occasions when Doubler's son and daughter and his four grandchildren were due to visit Mirth Farm all together.

In his many years of voluntary isolation, Doubler had learnt to navigate the extremely narrow path that separates solitude from loneliness. One he sought; the other sought him. But never was he more certain that he would prefer to be alone than when his family descended upon him in this manner. Had Marie not gone in the way that she had, things would certainly have been different. Raising children was something that he and his wife had undertaken together, and he had no doubt that he would have approached grandparenthood with a similarly shared sense of commitment. But he had not sought the role of single parent with its double dose of duty and he eschewed all grandparental influence for fear that he would fall short twice. He deeply resented the additional pressure the seismic shift his wife's departure had imposed upon him.

And anyway, Doubler valued his time on his own. He relished the silence, and his intellect needed very little stimulation other than that provided by his potatoes, by his carefully stocked cellar and by his daily lunch with Mrs Millwood. In truth, he had come to dread these family occasions, but he knew that the more normality he was able to depict, the sooner he would be left to his own devices for the ensuing month. This meant interacting as well as he could, feigning interest in those around him, keeping off the subjects that tended to provoke conflict and never, ever letting any of his family realize that he had chosen to live life as a recluse.

Julian wasn't overly interested in the comings and goings of his father, Doubler knew that. But if Camilla had any idea of just how far, how conclusively, Doubler had removed himself from society, then she would be even more disappointed in him. As it was, Doubler felt his deceit had been reasonably successful, as his daughter believed quite vocally that her father was coping 'as well as could be expected under the circumstances'.

One of the greatest pretences that Doubler could enact to give the impression of lucid stability was to provide a flawless Sunday lunch. Increasingly he found great comfort in cooking well and these visits gave him an opportunity to put his skills into practice. He could produce a roast for eight people without any one of them even realizing there was expertise involved. To his visitors, lunch meant trays of piping-hot food sliding from the Aga at 1 p.m. with very little sense of the many significant decisions that separated a good Sunday lunch from a *great* one. His trick was to have completed the preparation long before anyone arrived — even the gravy was made. All he had to do as his family gathered in the kitchen bothering him with details of their small lives was to take the beef out, put the Yorkshires in and finish off the gravy by adding the meat juices while the beef rested before carving.

As for the next generation ('$f_3$', Doubler liked to joke to himself), he barely took a passing interest in his grandchildren. He was fascinated to see which, if any, of his own genetic characteristics had been passed on, but these could be observed with side glances as he went about his kitchen business. The trouble with humans, he had learnt, was that their life cycles were just too long to intervene in the genetics meaningfully. By the time the weak or undesirable traits fully emerged, the sample had probably already reproduced itself.

He suspected that Marie, had she not gone, would have been a very good, active grandmother, interested in their grandchildren's school progress, their extra-curricular choices, their loss of teeth, their new haircuts or the little triumphs that everyone felt necessary to discuss but that Doubler found dull. Marie would have *excelled* at grandparenting, so Doubler didn't dismiss his obligation altogether but nodded and listened and even made a small comment every now and then, feigning interest as best he could. What he was watching for in his grandchildren was something that might arrest his attention. A flash of genetic improvement that meant they weren't going to just be dull incarnations of their parents.

Julian's children, born to a generous portion of the same DNA as their cousins, had already been ruined by an expensive education. Though still small, they were haughty, just like their father, and their lack of stable family life meant they had quickly learnt to exploit their father's guilt to their own advantage. That is what their private education had taught them: to see a weakness in an adult and to monetize it. This manifested in a steady access to costly things: overseas cricket and skiing trips, expensive electronic gadgetry and a sense of entitlement that would guarantee them good careers later in life.

Meanwhile, Camilla's children were a little younger and it was hard to see who they might become in the years ahead. Doubler had some hope for them but expected their qualities to be presented to him like a gun dog's prize. He didn't yet like them enough to try to coax some good out of them or to shape the people they might become.

They arrived today in the usual flurry of coats and welly boots flung across the kitchen and Doubler, who prided himself on preserving some semblance of order within his home during the weekends, tidied up after them while putting the finishing touches to the lunch.

As they sat down to eat, Camilla smiled benevolently at all of them. 'Isn't this special!' she said, just as she always did. 'Being together as a family is what it's all about, don't you think?'

Her husband, a translucent man with thin lips that rested his face into a grimace, muttered some agreement, while Julian admonished his spoilt children, who were leaning over to help themselves to potatoes with their fingers. Scolded, they sat back in their chairs, growling their dissatisfaction and sharing that special camaraderie that unites siblings when they hate their parents.

Doubler carved, his heavy steel knife slipping through the beef and making light work of the task. Camilla served vegetables while Julian surveyed the room, assessing and valuing as he went.

'So, Dad, heard anything from Peele recently?'

Doubler stopped, his knife suspended in the air. After a pause of several seconds, he resumed the carving, watching with renewed pleasure as blood seeped from the joint beneath him.

In order to create a larger stage on which to star, Julian was rocking his chair back on its rear legs, a habit Doubler found alarming. He watched his son intently as Julian asked, feigning a polite interest, 'I heard he was considering buying this place off you?'

'Wherever did you hear that?' said Doubler, carving the beef with a deft movement.

'Oh, around and about. I can't recall. The golf course, I suspect. We're both members. Idle talk is golfers' talk,' said Julian with a smirk.

Doubler addressed the beef, not his son. 'I have not entered into any communication with Peele.'

'Oh? But I hear on the grapevine he's buying up everything left, right and centre. He's got most of the county apparently.'

Doubler shrugged. 'I have very little interest in Peele.'

'Well, that's not a bad tactic, I suppose. The longer you hold out, the more valuable this place will be to him. But don't leave it too long. There comes a point where it's just not practical you owning a farm in the middle of his land. At the moment, this place is valuable to him. But there will come a tipping point beyond which it is no longer valuable to anyone else.'

'My farm is not in the middle of his land. His farmland surrounds mine. And what he owns near me has little impact on me, providing he

32

leaves me well alone.'

'But will he leave you alone? I doubt it. Not once he's got his eyes on the prize. This could be the jewel in his crown.' Julian's own eyes were sparkling in anticipation.

'Potatoes?' Doubler asked the children scattered round the table. He gave the gravy a good stir before sitting down to contemplate the perfectly rare beef in front of him.

'As I say. I've got no interest in Peele.'

Julian peered at his father over the top of his specs. 'Well, Dad, if you ever need a hand entering into negotiation, I'd be more than happy to help. It can't be easy looking after this place on your own, and it's not the same, is it, since Mum . . . ' he hesitated to finish the sentence, 'went.'

Camilla allowed a small sound of exasperation to escape before addressing her brother with a sad whine. 'Julian, I don't know why you always have to raise the contentious issues just when we're having such precious time together. Let's talk about positive things, shall we?'

Julian answered in a quiet voice, in much the same way that a seasoned alfresco diner knows to keep still when a wasp is bothering them, 'I don't think a speculative offer from an extremely wealthy neighbouring farmer is exactly negative, do you? This place is bleak — look at it. There's ice on the inside of the windows, for God's sake.'

While it was true there were still traces of ice on the windows from last night's heavy frost, the house was snug. The fire was roaring and throwing out a huge amount of heat, adding the distinctive quality of light that can only be achieved from the flicker of flame.

'It's cosy,' said Camilla, looking for her father's approval. 'And anyway, it was our *home* — it was where we *grew up*. I don't see how you can be so unsentimental about it, Julian. I don't know about you, but I want my children to know this, to feel that they are part of it. We've got so many memories here.'

Julian looked unimpressed by this argument as he mentally flicked through a catalogue of recollections. Adulthood can have a strange effect on a childhood retrospective. He and Camilla had shared exactly the same experiences and yet they had very different associations. To Julian, it was black and white. His mother had been here and then she wasn't. Any glimpses of past joys had been obliterated with her.

'The land is valuable, Camilla. You're being naive. And who knows what will happen to it in the future? The train line could completely ruin the value of these properties. I think if there is a viable offer on the table, Dad would be very sensible to have a serious look at it.'

Doubler drew himself taller and said, in a clear and decisive tone, 'I'd really appreciate it if you didn't talk about me as if I weren't here. I am not selling the house, I am not selling the farm, and I will be here until the day I die. Please do not talk about matters that are none of your business, particularly if your conversation threatens to spoil the beef.' But this was said only in his head. In reality, he quietly began to eat.

'Spectacular food, Dad. Well done. Your

34

Sunday lunch is just super,' said Camilla, with a sad smile.

'I like the potatoes best,' contributed a small voice to his right.

Doubler examined the child, Camilla's youngest, with heightened interest.

'You do, do you? And why is that?'

'Because they're crunchy,' he said seriously. 'And they're fluffy.' He scrutinized the potato on the end of his fork. 'They're crunchy *and* they're fluffy.'

'You, young man, show some promise. That is exactly why they're good.' Doubler smiled, looking and feeling very much like a grandfather.

The small child, emboldened by his grandfather's warmth, continued, 'Mum's are oily. And a bit squishy. Sometimes they're hard, too.'

'Darling, that's not very kind,' said Camilla. 'Darren, tell Benj that's not very kind.'

'That's not very kind, Benj. Your mother's potatoes aren't as nice because we don't have an Aga. Your grandfather has an Aga, which is why the potatoes are nicer,' said Darren, without lifting his eyes from his plate.

Doubler was surprised by this information. Surprised that his son-in-law would have so much to say on the subject. It was a shame he was wrong.

'The Aga didn't cook the potatoes. *I* cooked the potatoes. A strong heat source is all it takes, and actually you can cook very good roast potatoes in most ovens, even those with an uneven temperature, providing you take a bit of extra care. It's in the preparation. You need to parboil them for long enough to ensure they're not hard in the middle. It's important that the outer layer of the potato just begins to break down so that it will absorb some of the fat you're cooking them in. Give them a really good shake in the pan when you've drained them, which will ensure you get a good mix of crispy bits. The fat's important, too. I use goose.'

'Gross,' said a voice from Doubler's left, the elder of Julian's children.

The younger of Julian's children stifled a giggle.

Doubler continued, 'The roasting is easy providing you put your parboiled potatoes into very hot fat. You can't go wrong. They need good seasoning, too. The seasoning is always important.'

'I don't know why you've never taught me to cook roast potatoes, Dad, if mine are apparently so substandard.' The hurt evident in her voice, Camilla directed the comment towards her husband.

'Because you only ever turn up here at lunchtime. If you want to see how I prepare the roast, you really need to be here around 9 a.m.'

'Fair enough, but what about when I was a teenager? That might have been more useful. It might have prevented me from a lifetime of cooking inferior potatoes for my family.' Again Camilla addressed the comment in the direction of her husband.

'Your mother cooked,' said Doubler definitively.

Camilla looked down at her plate and carried on eating.

Julian, uninterested in potatoes or their preparation, continued heedlessly, 'Arable land is worth a premium at the moment. Fifteen thou an acre on a good day, but with this strategic stronghold, it would be worth much more than that. And the house has a great footprint — you'd get a sizable premium from a developer. It might well be worth applying for outline planning now. If nothing else, that would get Peele to up his game.'

Doubler looked beyond his son to the view out of the window. He could see for miles at this time of the year, despite the frosted glass. In the summer, the view was curtailed by the wisteria that wrapped itself round the house, the vigorous new growth fighting with the honeysuckle and roses that entwined it. The foliage shaded the room, cutting down on the sunlight that crept in, and this, coupled with the thick flagstones, ensured the room remained beautifully cool. Doubler loved this view. He loved this room, hot and smoky in the winter, cold and shady in the summer. He was not a materialistic man; he was a man of the soil, but nevertheless he wondered whether he could love a house more.

Camilla was having a good look around her, too. 'Your daily is obviously doing a good job still: the place is immaculate.'

A small flicker of warmth enveloped Doubler's heart. Mrs Millwood! he thought to himself, but as quickly the thought of her dispelled. She had no place here; theirs was strictly a table for two.

37

'Mmmm,' he said non-committally.

'Is she still up here full time?' ventured Julian, doing a quick calculation in his head. 'Seems like a bit of an indulgence, Dad. If you had a smaller place, you wouldn't need all that help. Less to worry about at your time of life.'

'Seconds?' Doubler addressed the table.

'Really, Dad, you should get your head out of the sand. Opportunities can go just as quickly as they come. Think about how you will cope in five years' time, ten years' time. It's not going to get any easier.'

Doubler didn't feel old. He felt his years, but with these years came a host of benefits. He knew his body well, and he and it had come to a steady understanding. He fed it the fuel it required — not too much, not too little — and he maintained it to a good working standard. And in turn, it didn't let him down. Doubler felt that the mutual respect shared by mind and body might well mean that together they would go on for ever. But when Doubler's son was around, he felt different. Not older but much less *sure*. Julian made him feel fallible, and his impatience with his father if he were slow to stand to his feet or if he paused for a moment's reflection before speaking gave way to such obvious contempt and open hostility that Doubler became quite capable of doubting both his body *and* his mind.

'I'm not old,' he said, 'but goodness me, you make me feel tired.' This, he said to himself.

Plates found their way back to Doubler, and as he layered thin slices of beef on each and sent

38

the plates on their course for seconds of vegetables, he contemplated his son, who, somewhere in the background, was continuing to whine on about how old and incompetent his father would soon be.

That's me he's talking about, thought Doubler, somewhat abstractly. That's his old man's life he's wishing away. Now all he talks about is when I get old, when I die, what I'm worth. What he really wants to know is when he can bank some of my wealth in his account. I know what's on his mind. He's worried I might well fritter it away or do something stupid. Or give it to the animal shelter.

Doubler's thoughts drifted easily from the animal shelter to Mrs Millwood. Mrs Millwood volunteered at an animal shelter. Doubler didn't know much about the comings and goings of such a place, other than the tales he heard over lunch. And at their lunches, Mrs Millwood tended only to wield accounts of heart-warming kindness, designed to elevate his mood. But Doubler understood quite a bit about abandonment.

'There might be a need for some cash — you're right, Julian,' Doubler said, pulling himself out of his reverie, and experiencing a little thrill of anticipation at the knowledge that he was about to provoke his pompous son.

Julian looked up from his plate, surprised that his words had finally reached their target.

'Now you're talking, Dad. Go on . . . '

'The local animal shelter is doing a fundraising drive and I'm thinking of getting involved.

You know, lending a hand.'

'The local *what?*' Julian spat the question out, looking very much like a man who had swallowed an indigestible morsel.

'You know, the *animal* shelter. It's where they provide refuge to animals in need. They get all kinds up there, you know. You'd be amazed at people's cruelty when they no longer get any pleasure from an animal they used to be fond of. Particularly the old ones. The donkeys and ponies and the like. They're hard to house. And loads of older cats and dogs that have just been *abandoned*. It's really astonishing that human beings can be so selfish.'

'Dad. That is not what you need cash for. Do not do anything stupid. Camilla, Darren, back me up here. You don't want to see your inheritance buying straw for donkeys, do you?'

'Oh, Julian, they need a lot more than straw,' interrupted Doubler earnestly. 'They need grass all year round. Once I finish with the potatoes, this land would make great grazing for some donkeys in need. I've already suggested it to the folk up at the shelter.'

'You've done what?' Two spots of pink rose on Julian's cheeks and his eyes bulged, unblinking.

'I've just talked it through. The pros and cons. You know, what I would need to do to make a concrete contribution to the good work they are doing down there.'

'Jesus, Dad. By all means make a contribution. Put some money in the collection pot when you are doing your grocery shopping. Take the sticker. Goddamn it, *wear* the sticker! But that's

40

it. That's all they're getting from you.'

Camilla put her knife and fork down on her plate with a clatter. 'Julian, once again you really are taking a very hard line here. If Dad has a new interest, then I think that's just great. Go and volunteer, Dad. Go for it! Don't just put your loose change in the collection pot — rattle the collection pot! Go and join the troops in the High Street. Those volunteers can be extremely persuasive, too, and it's very rarely threatening, you know. I mean, sometimes it is just a little, well, daunting, if you're hurrying and you need your change for the parking machine and it's just there in your hand and you can feel their eyes burning into you as you rush past. You have to say something, don't you? You can't help but feel obliged. I often find myself apologizing to them as I pass.' Camilla's eyes darted round the table, searching for consensus among her fellow diners.

Darren made a rare interjection, interrupting his wife as she spoke. 'Volunteer. But I'm going with Julian's gut on this one. Don't sign anything.'

'Well, of course Dad's not going to sign anything, are you, Dad? I mean, not without talking to us first?' Camilla looked at her father for reassurance.

Julian, impatient with his sister's feeble enrolment to his cause, cut her off sharply. 'How long has this, er, relationship been going, Dad? How deeply have they got their claws in?'

He looked up at the three pairs of eyes watching him.

'Oh, don't worry. I shan't do anything daft.

I'm not at that stage yet.'

'Well, tell us when you are about to do something daft, Dad.'

'I did something daft when I allowed my genes to reproduce themselves,' Doubler said, to himself. And he continued to eat his food in silence.

# 5

Overnight, the thick cloak of disquiet Doubler felt after Sunday lunch with his family wrapped itself firmly round the seed of anxiety already generated by the three Manila envelopes lurking in the drawer. The envelopes hadn't been clamouring for his attention, but Doubler was painfully familiar with the impact of leaving one mouldy potato among a sack of sound potatoes and he feared the contents of the envelopes may well be festering and could perhaps become more volatile through lack of attention.

The weekends were always long, but he now only had a number of hours before Mrs Millwood returned to Mirth Farm. Doubler steeled himself, determined to pluck up the courage to ask for Mrs Millwood's assistance. There was nobody else in the world better equipped to help Doubler find the right solution and he knew that his first instinct, to ignore the threat altogether, was undoubtedly the most dangerous.

Despite his resolve, Doubler chose not to open the third envelope immediately. There would be time to read it, but there was an order to his day that needed to be adhered to. Leaving the envelopes in the dark drawer, their potency in abeyance for a little longer, Doubler prepared his tea.

Doubler warmed the pot while measuring out

a big scoop of his specially blended tea leaves. He drained the pot, added the leaves and then poured in boiling water, taking the pot to the still-boiling kettle and filling it at the Aga to ensure minimal loss of heat. Doubler believed the leaves should be allowed to mix freely with the boiling water to fully release the flavour so he didn't use any strainer inside the pot, choosing instead to strain the tea as he poured it. Part of his Sunday evening ritual was to mix enough of his blend to keep him going for a full week, preferring to leave the bulk packs of black tea in a cool, dark corner of the pantry and enjoying an inordinate sense of accomplishment when he had judged the week's requirement perfectly. His blend (equal quantities of Keemun, Assam and Ceylon leaves) provided him the versatility he needed from a tea: something light in colour with a smooth and mild taste whose well-rounded character suited both a morning and an afternoon cup.

His teapot, cup, saucer and milk jug set out before him, Doubler sat at the kitchen table and spread out all three envelopes, examining the contents in the order they had arrived. The substance remained consistent. Mr Peele wanted to buy his farm.

The first letter had arrived, conventionally, by post, and once he'd digested it, Doubler had paid it scant attention, tidying it away in the dresser drawer without too much further thought.

The second letter, however, was markedly different in both tone and manner of delivery. It had been hand-delivered, which meant that somebody had been to Mirth Farm in person.

It was this intrusion that had rung the alarm bells in Doubler's head and he swiftly responded with a proportionate stepping-up of his security. Doubler was fortunate that, while ostensibly a man with no friends, he had many people indebted to him and it was very easy to call in a favour, particularly as he leveraged this influence so rarely. Those beholden to him were eager to be of use and within two days of a brusque phone call, two men in a white van had arrived to install the security camera on the corner of Doubler's yard. This was the camera whose vigilant sweep now kept a watchful lookout for Mirth Farm trespassers.

Doubler worked meticulously through each letter, making careful notes in his journal of the most salient points, though these were sometimes difficult to extract from the ornate vernacular that intensified with Peele's mounting irritation. What struck Doubler was the very great haste with which Peele had crescendoed from a generous cash offer to an outright demand, but nothing had prepared him for the unveiled threats of the latest letter. Peele was clearly very used to getting his own way and, perhaps an impatient man, had been quickly affronted by Doubler's lack of response.

Should Doubler have responded to the first or second letter, even just to say a polite no? This was a question for Mrs Millwood. Mrs Millwood might not have a clue about property negotiation, but she had a very good instinct for people and she would certainly have an opinion.

The cash offer in the first letter was very good; Doubler had recognized this immediately. Even given the tiny sum for which he had originally purchased Mirth Farm and allowing for his lack of attention to rising property prices, he knew it was unarguably generous. In fact, it was hard to imagine that anyone should want to part with such a very large sum of money in exchange for his home. It was evident, Doubler deduced, that Peele was not trying to *steal* Doubler's farm or *trick* him in any way. But the size of the offer demonstrated to Doubler how very badly Peele wanted to own Doubler's property and he had made his determination abundantly clear by coming to Doubler with a proposal that was intended to be irresistible. And when Doubler had not even acknowledged receipt of the offer, Peele had accelerated the urgency by pointing out the reasons that Doubler might regret his lack of pliability.

The second letter swiftly introduced some legalese. The letter began with the words 'Without Prejudice', which in themselves were intended to be perceived as a threat. Doubler had already confirmed the definition with Mrs Millwood and so he knew that these words meant the letter could not be used in a court of law against the originator, but Doubler was not entirely sure why he and Peele might end up locked in a legal battle. Could Doubler be sued for not responding to the first letter? Was it an offence not to enter into a negotiation that you wanted no part of? Doubler didn't believe, logically, that this could be the case, but the very words 'Without Prejudice' were troublesome to him.

In his second letter, Peele used the language of courtrooms to forcibly suggest that Doubler must accept his generous offer within fourteen days or the offer would be withdrawn and Peele would thereafter be forced to pay fair market value. Doubler knew, logically, that this threat was nonsensical because he didn't want to sell his home at any price.

Doubler referred back to the earlier letter and glanced ahead to the third. They had not only accelerated in urgency, they'd accelerated in impenetrable speech. The first letter contained no 'notwithstanding's, the second contained two, and the third was riddled with them.

The gist of the third letter was one of unbridled intimidation, and Peele was very specific about the nature his threats would take. Peele insisted that he fully intended to increase his use of pesticides and warned that his liberal use of genetically modified crops might negatively impact on Doubler's own organic status and, therefore, his bottom line. This was a cause for grave concern to Doubler and he underlined the observation in his notebook. Doubler wasn't worried so much about his organic certification from an economic point of view: while his farming methods were indeed organic (he had begun his farming life not knowing any other way and he had failed to pay attention to progress so had failed to adopt more productive methods subsequently), his farming income did not depend on his organic certification.

But Peele was not to know that this threat was alarming for other reasons. Peele's land completely surrounded Doubler's and there was nothing to stop the insects that landed on Peele's fields stopping to inspect Doubler's. There was a very real concern that the purity of Doubler's potato experimentation could be compromised and that the data he had thus far gathered could be greatly undermined. What if the Institute of Potato Research and Development in northern India, the very body of excellence with whom Doubler was now in correspondence, got wind of this potential breach? Doubler was certain that he had allowed adequate set-aside at the margins of each field to pass the scrutiny of the organic inspectors, but would the country of India be so easily satisfied? Doubler's research, thus far, had relied on the absolute genetic integrity of each generation of potatoes, and now Peele was threatening forty years of work.

This was very vexing indeed.

And as if Doubler didn't have enough doubt and worry plaguing him, Peele went on to list yet another threat (as though he had an endless supply on which to rely upon in a purely non-prejudicial way). He had, apparently, 'excellent connections and relationships with influencers, government officials and local councillors' and these people might well force Doubler to sell his land under compulsory purchase order owing to proposed plans for the new high-speed rail link that was threatening to carve the chalky hills in two. Peele made it very clear that his own strategic alliances would put him in a strong position to deal with whatever was thrown his way but that Doubler, acting on his own, would find battling with the monsters of Westminster a very lonely and futile job.

Doubler sighed loudly and wondered whether Peele's apparent commercial success was because he dealt his blows in threes. The generous cash offer could be ignored in isolation. After all, what on earth would Doubler do with so much money other than find the ideal place to live and work, and this he already had at Mirth Farm? But dealing with an unsolicited offer from government officials was as vexing as the genetically-modified-pollen-carrying insects that Doubler now saw as little plagues of rogue militants dispatched in clouds by Peele's own men to undermine Doubler's life's work.

There was no denying it: Peele's threats had dealt greater blows than the perpetrator could have dared hope. The threat to Doubler's organic status paled into insignificance in comparison to the threat to his groundbreaking potato research. And the suggestion that officials might be invited to discuss the path of a new train and then accidentally stumble across the potato grower's business concerns was much more alarming to Doubler, who alone knew the true depths of his underground activity. Were the government to get wind of this other enterprise while routinely investigating resistance to a compulsory purchase order, then who knew what trouble lay ahead.

Doubler looked at his notes, the page divided

into three columns representing each distinct threat, and reeled at the sheer enormity of the attack. He had wondered, at the arrival of the third envelope, whether stepping up his security might be a disproportionate response, but now, when the words were distilled into a gradient of menace, he knew that war had indeed been declared. Yes, there was no doubt: he needed Mrs Millwood.

Doubler always looked forward to his housekeeper's arrival, but with such a clear agenda for their talk ahead, he was more restless than ever before. Ten minutes before she was due, he began pacing up and down by the window, looking constantly at the spot at the end of the drive and raising the binoculars to his eyes at every imagined disturbance.

As it was, he was fetching his notebook at the moment she came through the gate, but to ensure he was consistent with his diligent recordings, he noted the approximate time of her arrival as he watched the car pull forward on the drive. Scarcely able to contain his nervous energy, he wandered through the house awaiting her symphony of entrance, so it was a couple of minutes before he registered something different about the quality of sound of the engine on the drive. Mrs Millwood had a distinctive driving style. She kept the engine revs at a constant speed, taking the bends at a slow and steady pace that seemed to allow her to coast her way to the top. Although he had been absolutely certain that it had been her car he observed a couple of minutes previously, he was now not so sure. The car was revving up on the incline and then slowing to a crawl to navigate each turn, making the car sound strained and hesitant as it made its approach. Doubler stopped and held his breath to hear the small aural nuances of her arrival, listening carefully to the thud of the car door as she eventually reached the yard.

He stood stock-still, his ears trained on the kitchen door. When instead of it opening, the front doorbell rang, its noise echoing thunderously around the house, his heart leapt at the intrusion. There was no reason for Mrs Millwood to arrive at the front door — she never had done so before — so it was with great trepidation that Doubler made his way nervously down the hallway to see what Trojan interloper could possibly have made it as far as his doorstep. He eyed the doormat suspiciously, half expecting another one of the Manila envelopes to slide through the letterbox in front of his eyes, but the doorbell rang again, and unable to ignore it, he carefully undid the chain and turned the stiff key in the lock, his heart beating loudly in his ears.

As he opened the door hesitantly, a woman poked her head into the narrow space he had created. She was wearing a brightly coloured knitted bobble hat pulled down over her ears and some sort of duffle coat over jeans and wellington boots. He narrowed his eyes as he tried to process the threat.

'Doubler?'

'I am,' he tried, though he wasn't certain of anything at that moment.

51

'Hello! I'm Gracie's daughter.'

'Gracie,' he said, feeling even more nervous now she claimed to be somebody's daughter. He didn't know any Gracies.

'Gracie,' he said again, unsure whether he should yet betray the fact he knew nobody by that name.

'Yes. Can I come in?'

He didn't seem to have much say in the matter because she was already pushing on the door to enter his house. Her admission was almost forced, but Doubler was disarmed by her eyes, which were sparkling and bright, and there was a lightness in her look that he recognized and responded to. He stood back as she entered and walked ahead of him as if she knew the house.

'Shall I put the kettle on?' she asked as she made her way towards the kitchen. Her ease, her certainty became familiar. Gracie. Gracie must be the name of Mrs Millwood and this must certainly be her daughter. He shut the front door and hurried after her.

'By all means put the kettle on,' he said, perplexed, but by the time he had caught up with her, she was already filling the kettle at the sink as if she had performed this task a thousand times.

He sat at the kitchen table and allowed events to happen to him. He allowed this woman to feel her way around his kitchen as she assembled cups and saucers, and warmed the teapot, reaching for the tin of tea leaves as if it were second nature. He watched her and marvelled at the million little ways that identified her as her mother's daughter.

'Were you expecting me?'

'Not at all. I was expecting your mother.'

'Just as I thought. She was supposed to tell you, but she must have chickened out.'

'Tell me what?'

'Mum's poorly.'

She made this last announcement just as she sat down opposite him. She pushed a teacup towards him.

'Drink this.'

He tried to lift the hot drink to his lips but found himself quite unable to grasp the cup with enough force to raise it. He looked at Gracie's daughter.

'Poorly. What sort of poorly?'

'Oh, the worst you can imagine, I'm afraid.' She reached forward and spooned some sugar into his tea, stirring it, and then she sipped at her own. She smiled a small, sorrowful smile, one that, irrationally in Doubler's eyes, carried a trace of sadness for him as well as a multitude of sadnesses of her own. 'She's had it before, of course, but I'm afraid it's back again with sharper teeth.'

Doubler found himself unable to swallow, as if the disease's sharp teeth had sunk themselves into his own fleshy neck.

'When? When did she have it before?' he asked, once he had found his voice. This was all news to him. The first toothless episode and then the second, fanged one.

'A good while back. She was younger then,

53

much more able to deal with it and she's been well for such a long time now, we really thought she'd beaten it.'

Doubler imagined Mrs Millwood beating a sharp-toothed thing with a stick. Or a mop. Or a broom. Surely it wouldn't stand a chance. And he remembered, now, her absence. She had taken some time off and he had resented it enormously through a cloud of other resentments, and the combined force of his upset and all the other upsets had somehow obscured the reason for her absence. He had been at the lowest point of his life. He had settled into the routine of life without Marie, but nothing had made much sense to him still. He tried to remember how long Mrs Millwood had been absent for.

'How long?' he said. Using two hands, he lifted the cup unsteadily to his lips.

A sharp pain flashed across the face of Gracie's daughter and Doubler realized what she might think he was asking.

'Until she's *back here*, I mean. Back at work, until she's not *poorly* again.' The word 'poorly' stuck in his mouth like fluff, getting tangled there and drying his tongue and lips until he thought they might never work again. It had been the daughter's language, the daughter's choice of words. But of course it wasn't a big enough word to describe this thing with savage teeth.

Gracie reached across the table and took his hand in hers. 'Mum's really sick this time. We're taking it one day at a time. She is going to fight it, and the doctors are going to throw everything at it. But the treatment's going to be awful, so she'll feel a lot worse before she feels better. If she feels better at all.'

Doubler was horrified by his own selfish thoughts and yet all he could think of was the absence he would be left with. Not the threat of the ultimate absence (this, he hadn't even begun to process as a possibility) but the absence of the next few days and weeks. Without her visits giving his day some structure and purpose, he wasn't sure he would cope. He felt his stomach cave in.

'Will you cope, do you think?' Gracie's daughter asked, kindly.

Doubler was taken aback, completely, as if she had seen into his soul. He stumbled to find the words to express how utterly bereft he felt not to be sitting down for lunch with Mrs Millwood today, let alone the terror he felt when he tried to contemplate the bleakness of the horizon ahead of him.

'There's the day-to-day cleaning, I suppose. It'll probably be easy enough to find somebody to help you keep on top of that,' Gracie's daughter said, looking around her at the kitchen. 'I'm amazed she didn't want to talk this through with you herself. She may be poorly but she has you on her mind, you know.'

Doubler swallowed back his thoughts. To cope with the housework didn't even touch the surface of the loss he was feeling. And yet, somehow, a conversation seemed to be happening to him, around him, and Gracie's daughter was covering both sides.

'I tell you what. How about I find somebody to fill her shoes in the short term? I'd be happy to place some ads and do the first round of interviews if that would help. Shall I?'

Doubler nodded slowly, not entirely sure what he was agreeing to. He didn't want somebody to fill Mrs Millwood's shoes. Not in the short term, not in the longer term. He wanted her own outdoor shoes left under the bench by the kitchen door, and he wanted her own stockinged feet to slip into her indoor shoes, which she wore to dart around the house. The point of Mrs Millwood was that she barely wore shoes. She simply floated from room to room just above the surface. She only became substantial, a human form that might need shoes, when she sat down at lunchtime, and then they talked and talked. Nobody would fill those shoes; the footwear wasn't the *point*.

'I won't hire anybody until you've met them, of course. I'll just do the preliminary interviews and you can make the final decision. How does that sound? I think it will make Mum happy to know that somebody is taking care of things here. She worries a bit, you see, and I don't want her distracted. I want her mind firmly focused on getting better. She's strong in that she's vital and vigorous, but there's so little of her she's going to have to use every ounce of her physical strength to deal with the chemo.'

There. She'd said it. Doubler had known that the language of Mrs Millwood's poorliness would need to be upgraded to incorporate the technicalities of the practical. 'Poorliness' was too vague a word to describe her symptoms, and 'treatment' was too vague a word to tackle the solution. And here it was in black and white, a word that conjured up body-wracking drugs, tubes, needles, poison and pain. It didn't sound like a treatment; it sounded like a penance.

Gracie's daughter noticed Doubler wince and wondered, for the first time since she had arrived, whether Doubler was taking the news of her mother quite badly. She had assumed until now that his silence was born out of a taciturn nature, so she reached for his hand once more.

'We're all going to help each other through this. I need to make sure Mum has all the peace and quiet she needs to get better, so I'm going to shoulder her responsibilities. That means I'm here for you. You will do your bit, I'm sure, and it's just that none of us can know what that might mean yet. I don't, you don't, and Mum certainly doesn't. But I suspect you'll be there to support her if you're needed. Is that right?'

Doubler felt hope through the possibility of purpose. 'Of course. Anything. I don't really leave the house much. Certainly not since . . . not since Marie went. But, yes, I'll do what is asked of me. Tell her that, will you?' He closed his eyes briefly and allowed himself to imagine climbing into the car to leave the farm for the first time in years. 'Tell her I'll visit. She might be bored. She might like a bit of company.'

'Well, that's a very sweet offer, but I can't imagine she'll feel up to much — as it is, I'll be fighting to keep her friends away. Golly, my

57

mum's amassed a few of those along the way! There's the church lot, her knitting circle, the animal-shelter lot. Not to mention that gaggle of buddies she's known all her life. They're a good bunch, her school chums. They're always there for each other, but they're getting to an age where they have to offer this sort of support to one another all the time. They're a marvel, though, really, quite an inspiration actually. But still, that's a very nice thought and I will make sure she knows you offered. She'll be most touched.'

Doubler recoiled. He knew about the knitting circle. He knew she went to church. He knew she volunteered at an animal rescue centre. But he had assumed when she talked about these different pockets of interest that they were mere pastimes, mere distractions to avoid having to stare intense loneliness in the face the way he had to every single time he looked in the mirror. A *gaggle of buddies*? He scrolled back through countless lunchtime conversations. Jean? Her name had come up often. Dot? Was she part of a gaggle? Mabel?

'Jean? Dot? Mabel?' he ventured.

'Oh, Mum's told you about them, has she? Mum does like to talk.'

'She listens, too. She's an extremely good listener.'

'Hmm,' said Gracie's daughter, trying to imagine her mother listening, not talking.

'I mean really. She really is an exceptionally good listener. She's the type of listener who actually stops thinking while she listens to you.

58

That's rare in my experience. Most people in conversation are too busy thinking about what they're going to say next to truly listen well.'

'That's a very nice thing to hear about my mother. I'm you sure you must be right, and perhaps that explains why she's got such a wide circle of friends.'

A 'wide circle'. Doubler contemplated the phrase. A circle was a complete thing, with no breaks, no gaps. No room for another. How ludicrous that he had considered himself a friend of hers. On the other hand, she was clearly *his* friend. Perhaps his only friend. Doubler imagined himself a small bubble on the outside of her wide circle. Was it possible for those two certainties to exist in his mind and for both of them to be truthful? That she was a friend to him but that he was not a friend to her?

Gracie's daughter stood and began clearing away the teacups, taking them to the sink. As she rinsed them, she continued talking to Doubler, her back to him. 'She's got a week of intensive chemo, so we think she'll be in hospital for the duration and then, if all goes according to plan, she'll be treated as an outpatient thereafter. I'll keep you up to date with what is going on, how she's responding. And in the meantime, let's keep focused on some of the practical issues. I'll see if I can find somebody to give you a hand around here and I'll let you know how I get on. Anything particular you're after? Cooking as well as cleaning? Running errands? Shopping?'

'Not cooking. I cook,' said Doubler with a sharp bite of vehemence that surprised them both. 'Just the other things.' He went quiet for a moment, wondering how he could articulate his need for somebody who would sit with him and ask him just the right number of questions about his experiments. Somebody who cared almost as much as he did. Somebody who knew better than he did how to run his life but who never interfered, just trusted him to deal with it. Somebody who knew both his pre-Marie and post-Marie personas. Somebody who knew how far he'd fallen and how slow the climb up again had been.

'Just cleaning,' Doubler said, and he stood to dry the cups.

# 6

A heavy bank of cloud planted itself above the farm and rained relentlessly on Doubler's misery. The newly furrowed soil, dense and sticky, collected on his boots as he trudged round the fields, making each step heavier than the last. There was no glimmer of reprieve to suggest that this new pattern would ever be broken. Alone with the mud and his memories, Doubler had found the last few days intolerable, and by the end of the fourth, he was thinking of Mrs Millwood with rising resentment. His days had lost form and he found himself quite unable to fall into his usual routine without the additional punctuation Mrs Millwood's visits usually provided, and he blamed her for this interruption to his routine and his ensuing aimlessness. He started many jobs but finished few, and even those tasks that were essential felt lacklustre and without purpose. He pulled himself begrudgingly around the farm, but even this, one of his most joyous of routines, lacked urgency with no lunch companion to hurry home to.

The threat from Peele had paled into insignificance. Doubler wondered now why he'd even concerned himself with the written letters. Peele wanted to buy the farm; Doubler didn't want to sell it. That, as far as Doubler was concerned, was the end of the matter. He put the envelopes back in the drawer and buried them beneath a pile of paperwork. Peele would grow tired of waiting and turn his attention to some other prey. Doubler's research either would or would not be contaminated by Peele's farming methods. It didn't feel important anymore.

That morning, he had wondered whether he might stay in bed. If he didn't go downstairs, nothing would need tidying up and he then wouldn't be constantly reminded of her absence. He wasn't sad, he was irritable, and he wasn't concerned for her, he was overwhelmingly concerned for himself. Self-pity washed over him in waves, and as his mood darkened, he felt less and less inclined to give the day any of his attention.

When he finally dragged himself slowly downstairs, he'd found the tea caddy was empty. Briefly confused, he realized he didn't know what day of the week it was. He hastily made a new blend, carelessly tipping tea from each bag into the canister without weighing it and sweeping a mix of spilt leaves back into the first package he reached for. He took a sip and chided himself for his haste. It didn't taste right and he knew it never would unless he started afresh.

He left his tea unfinished and reluctantly forced himself out into the cold and damp morning, not stopping for a coat or hat. The wind burnt his ears and squeezed tears from his eyes as he made a cursory inspection of the bare land. He glanced at the barns, looking for signs of breach, and as he returned to the farmhouse, he stopped to glower briefly at the security camera. A bilious anger rumbling deep inside him, he flung open the kitchen door and pulled off his boots, pushing them forcefully with his toe under the boot rack. He made his way upstairs, now certain that his bed was the only place he could feel comfortable. As he reached the top landing, the phone rang in the hallway beneath him. Doubler grimaced, interpreting the intrusion as part of a conspiracy to ruin his life. The phone didn't stop. He turned round and padded down to the draughty hall below, where the telephone vibrated noisily on the small table.

His bad humour prepared Doubler for the worst and he was almost relishing the thought that it might be Peele calling him. As he reached for the telephone, he was already lining up a suitably sharp response, if it indeed were his rival having the audacity to disturb this precious time of quiet self-loathing. There was a small, disconcerting pause when Doubler lifted the receiver to his ear and into that pause swept a hesitation and uncertainty that Doubler felt echoing within the tiny space. He held the receiver more closely to his ear so that he didn't miss the unspoken words while he waited for the spoken ones.

'Mr Doubler. Where on earth were you? I timed my call in the certain knowledge you'd be in for your tea, but you took an age to answer the phone. I thought something might have gone awry.'

'Awry here, Mrs Millwood? No, all is quite in order, thank you,' boomed Doubler, projecting his voice in the general direction of the hospital.

His response was immediately cheerful, all traces of that earlier hesitation vanishing at the sound of her voice. He squeezed the receiver to his ear even closer but wanted, really, to hold it to his heart, as, much to his surprise, that was the piece of him that most wanted to hear her voice.

'How are you keeping?' she was asking.

'Me? How am I keeping? How are *you* keeping? That's the pertinent question.'

'Oh, not too bad, all things considered. I was supposed to be home, but the doctors, in their wisdom, want to keep me here. Some nonsense about my response to the treatment, when any fool could see it's my body's response to hospital that's the root of the problem. My next few days are therefore a little unpredictable, but everything is going as well as can be expected.' She paused and then launched into the reason for her call. 'Mr Doubler, I've got some worries on my mind and Midge seemed to think you might help.'

Midge! Doubler repeated silently to himself and then, in joyful recognition, Mrs Millwood's daughter! He congratulated himself on piecing this together for himself.

'Midge, your daughter. Well, of course I would be delighted. Anything.'

'Well, I'm a bit worried about my colleagues down at Grove Farm — you know, the animal shelter. I've left them in the lurch and I need my shift covered. Do you think you could manage it? It's only a couple of hours twice a week, and I'm sure they'll already be looking out for a more permanent replacement, but I think they'll be struggling for staff for the next month or so.'

Doubler's heart lurched, recognizing the threat in the words before his mind had a chance to process them.

'What do you mean by a 'permanent' replacement, Mrs Millwood? You're coming back to us, aren't you? I mean to the animal shelter and to Mirth Farm?'

'Oh, heavens, yes, but you know what these doctors are like. Once they've got their claws into you, they never want to let you go.'

*Claws.* All Doubler could picture were sharp-taloned fingers prying and poking, tearing at Mrs Millwood while she was at her most vulnerable. Those same claws should be attacking the monster with teeth, not Mrs Millwood herself.

'But it's all going according to plan, is it? A bit of treatment in the hospital your daughter said, then you'll be an outpatient. Is that still the plan? Home soon, right as rain?'

'Well, that's certainly *my* plan, but we'll have to wait and see. I don't want to promise anything as I don't like letting people down. I just want to make sure there's cover for me down at the shelter. I really don't want the added responsibility of worrying about them when I've got quite enough to worry about here.'

'What's troubling you the most there? Other than . . . the obvious.'

'Oh, they're wonderful here — I'm in great hands — but I'm parched most of the time and that blessed tea trolley taunts me. I can hear it as it makes its journey round the place. It's got a distinctive rattle. I swear it accelerates past me several times a day, only to slow right down again the minute it's snuck by my ward.'

Doubler beamed.

Mrs Millwood continued, 'I lie here dreaming of a cuppa, but it's running me a bit of a merry dance, to be honest.' Mrs Millwood paused. 'Mr Doubler,' she said sternly, 'I can hear you smiling. It's really not funny.'

Doubler bit his lip, trying not to let his joy escape noisily at the sound of her voice.

'You know the worst of it? If I'm sleeping when they come, they don't wake me! So I have to lie permanently alert just in case they pop their heads round the curtain. Sod's Law says I'll drift off or just close my eyes in a little daydream and that trolley is hotfooting it to the next ward. Practically mocking me it is.'

'Oh, Mrs Millwood! That sounds like my idea of hell. Tea needs to be on demand.'

'I'm lucky if I get three cups a day.'

'Three? Only three? That sounds like a *travesty*!'

'Quite. But other than that, no complaints. Shouldn't even complain about that really — what with them working flat out to save my life.'

'Your life, Mrs Millwood, shall be saved. By a combination of advanced medical techniques and *Camellia sinensis*. And if there are shortcomings in that area, just say the word and I'll be there.'

'Well, that's a cheering thought, but my main concern is the shelter. Particularly darling old

Percy. Would you be a dear?'

'It would be my honour. I'll give them a holler, shall I? Percy, is it?' Doubler registered with a stealthy hostility the use of the word 'darling'.

'Oh, heavens, no. Fat lot of good that'll do you. Speak to Colonel Maxwell — he'll be the one sorting the schedules out. He's not officially in charge, but he doesn't really know any other way. If he were a woman, he'd be called bossy, but he's not a woman, so I guess he's just called a natural leader.'

'Mrs Millwood?'

'Oh, sorry, Mr Doubler. Was I ranting?'

'No. No, not at all. At least, you were beginning to, but I like it. Rant away. That's all.'

'Has something got into you? Are you coping all right? You sound uncommonly cheerful.'

'I'm coping just fine. I've been a little out of sorts, but I'm feeling very much improved.'

'Good, good. Don't forget to call Colonel Maxwell, will you? I'll check in with you in a few days' time, shall I?'

'Marvellous, yes, do. Cheerio, then.'

Doubler held the receiver to his ear for a while listening to the conclusive hollow echo before replacing the receiver carefully with a smile, and he continued to smile as he went in search of a recent copy of the Yellow Pages. 'This is meant to be!' he exclaimed joyfully as he lugged the heavy book from the back of a cupboard. 'Julian will have the fright of his life!' Doubler said delightedly, plopping the thick volume down on the kitchen table. Grinning impishly, he flicked through the thin leaves until he found the number for the shelter, listed as Grove Farm Animal Rescue Centre. He drew a careful red line round it and wrote the name 'Maxwell' neatly in the margin. He carried the book back to the hall and positioned himself by the phone, a pen in his hand should he need to make any notes.

He stared at the phone and imagined himself making the call. The smile that had been on his face since he'd first heard Mrs Millwood's voice began to fade.

The minutes ticked painfully by, and the longer he stared at the phone, the less able he was to recall his previous sense of purpose. He frowned a little, thinking about who might answer. Would it be Maxwell himself or another of Mrs Millwood's circle of friends? Would *darling* Percy answer the phone? This unimaginable cast of characters must indeed be good friends for her to be worrying about them while she was undergoing unspeakable procedures in that place.

He imagined lifting the receiver and dialling the number. In Doubler's head, the abrasive shriek of the telephone would puncture a room full of laughter. The receiver would be picked up with impatience. Doubler would have to explain himself to a stranger and then to Maxwell, a natural leader no less, who would be compelled to ask what on earth Doubler could offer them. They were a close-knit circle of friends with years of animal care under their belts, and he was a nobody. He didn't even have a goldfish; he'd only ever cared for potatoes . . . and Marie.

And look what had happened to her.

Doubler folded the corner of the page in a neat triangle and returned the book to where he'd found it. He made his way slowly back to the kitchen wondering why he had felt so alive just a moment before. He lifted the lid on the tea caddy, inhaled deeply, frowned and closed the lid again, shaking his head. He studied his potatoes in silence, but finding no answer there, he returned to his seat by the window, raised the binoculars to his eyes and fixed his attention on the driveway with renewed anxiety.

# 7

Gracie's daughter was called Midge, as Doubler had learnt when Mrs Millwood had called from her hospital bed. Satisfied with this knowledge, he observed her arrival and noted the hesitancy with which she tackled the incline's sharper bends, but there was a degree of enjoyment to be taken in the observation of the differences between these two women, who were so clearly similar in many ways.

'Morning,' Midge shouted in a melodic voice as she tried the front door and, finding it open, let herself in. Doubler might have been offended by this rather brazen intrusion, but the days since her last visit had been long and empty, and he was glad for the company.

She had been christened Madeleine, but everyone had always called her Midge. Doubler was a little proud of his own nickname — it had been assigned to him by the butcher, and he liked it for its nod towards his considerable potato-growing skills — but, despite this, Doubler was naturally suspicious of nicknames. Midge, though, suited this spirited woman perfectly, so he had no hesitation in using it. Knowing her name endowed her with another layer of personality so that she was now so much more than just Gracie's daughter.

'Goodness me, Doubler. Is this the coldest place on earth?' Midge exclaimed as she unwrapped a scarf from her neck and hung up her coat on the peg.

Doubler looked out of the window at the scuttling clouds. 'This is nothing. I wouldn't say no to another proper cold snap, to tell you the truth. The earth likes it — kills off all sorts of unwanted visitors. And what's good for the soil is good for my spuds.'

Midge gave an exaggerated shiver at the thought of something colder. 'I thought I'd drop some groceries in to you — make sure you've got the basics for the week. I can't do this indefinitely, you understand, but Mum was worried and apparently she picks up your order once a week.'

Doubler hurried to help her unpack the brown-paper bags and was delighted that she had not tried to improvise but had simply collected his usual order from the farm shop. Cheese for the pantry, flour and fresh yeast for this afternoon's bake, some wintergreens and a dozen eggs.

'I'm surprised, I must say, that you don't produce some of this stuff yourself. Chickens would be nice company, wouldn't they? And pigs?' she said, eyeing the pile of potato peelings spilling out of the compost bin. 'Pigs would love that lot.'

'You're probably right, but it's just not practical. I'm not sure I could make the commitment. I look after myself and I look after my potatoes, but I wouldn't want to let anyone else down.'

'Why would you let anyone down? You barely

go anywhere, do you? You'd be just the right temperament, I'm sure. I'd keep animals at home if I had the space.'

'If I upped and went, I'd let them down,' said Doubler quietly.

'Where on earth would you up and go to, you daft thing?' Gracie's daughter threw her head back and laughed as she put the kettle on for tea.

'I don't know. But I'll die one day. And then who would look after the pigs and the chickens? The potatoes, well, they'll turn themselves back into soil eventually, but I don't like the idea of just abandoning a living creature.'

'Death? You're planning for your death? Dying can't stop you living, you know. Take a leaf out of Mum's book. You know what she's taken into hospital with her? Knitting wool and needles. She's starting a terrifically complicated blanket — I've had a look at the pattern. It will take her years to finish, years. I think that's a really defiant act, don't you? Death is going to have to want her pretty badly to take her and her knitting needles on.'

Doubler thought about this and liked the image. Perhaps she could knit herself a cocoon that would keep her safe, keep the teeth at bay.

'I suppose you're right. I think . . . I think . . .' He thought some more. 'I think if you make a commitment to something or someone, you've got to see it through. You can't just remove yourself from the scene without making provisions. Without making sure everyone is going to be OK without you. That kind of behaviour is irresponsible and causes all sorts of pain and

72

harm. I don't like to think I could do that.'

'But some hens would be great company for you up here, and you'd have the eggs. I tell you what. I'll make a commitment to you. If anything suddenly happens to you, I'll make sure any livestock you have is taken care of. How does that sound?'

To Doubler, it sounded astonishingly kind, this hand of help from a virtual stranger. But she wasn't a stranger, was she? She was Mrs Millwood's daughter and she was prepared to help him in one of the ways he needed the most help. To make a commitment to something other than his potatoes. To find love for something and to know that nobody needed to suffer as a result of that love.

'I'll think about it,' he said, already imagining the joy of having some hens to talk to in the morning. And it was true the potato peelings would certainly fatten a few pigs each year.

'And what about this produce?' asked Midge, resuming an air of practicality. 'Do I need to settle your account for you? Do you need me to drop in on the way back and pay for the groceries?'

'No. No, that's fine. There's nothing to pay. I'll settle up in April.'

'Oh.' Gracie's daughter shrugged. 'Fair enough.' And she took a big slurp of tea. In this, as with so many things, she reminded Doubler of her mother. She knew when to probe and when to leave well alone.

They drank their tea in companionable silence.

'I've placed an ad. Should have some candidates to interview in the next week or two. Shall I bring the promising ones up here?'

Doubler tried his best to compose his face into one of amenable cooperation. But it quickly crumpled.

'I'm not sure I'm ready. I don't want to inconvenience you or your applicants, but I'm not quite as adaptable as I lead people to think.'

Midge laughed at the idea. 'I don't think anybody would suggest that about you,' she said, looking around the kitchen and its stark lack of modern gadgetry. Copper pans gleamed on rusty nails, wedged into the crumbling gaps between brickwork. Pewter tankards hung on hooks, and large wooden sieves added a pleasing architecture to the shelves' contents. There wasn't a thing in the kitchen that couldn't have been there a hundred years ago. Or more, Midge mused.

'I just don't take well to change, so I think, if you don't mind, I'll cope on my own as best as I can. Until, you know . . . ' Doubler allowed the sentence to finish itself by looking hopefully at Midge.

'Dear Doubler, I rather admire your steadfast refusal to accept the serious nature of Mum's poorliness. You're nearly as positive as she is. But I think it would be healthier for us all if you stop assuming Mum is coming back to you. If she does come through this, it is going to be a long haul, and who knows if she'll even want to work again. She's probably earned herself a bit of a rest, don't you think?'

Doubler started to interject, shaking his head fiercely while forming the words that would not just stop Midge in her tracks but would cast aside her doubt and dismissal. He fought to form the words that had the power to reverse the conversation back to a time when the mother, not the daughter, was sitting across the table telling him off.

Midge silenced him with a stern wag of her index finger. 'No, Doubler, it's not healthy for you to put your life on hold, and it's not healthy for Mum to assume her life will continue as it was before this horrible, horrible thing got hold of her.'

Doubler drew a sharp breath and Midge softened. 'It's not disloyal to replace her. She will quite understand and so will I. This is a big place and you're rattling around on your own, so it makes sense to have somebody pop in and keep an eye on you while keeping on top of things.'

'I need nothing. I need nobody,' Doubler insisted, his voice cracking.

'Fine. As you like.' Midge reached out and held his hand, just as she had when they first met. 'Shall I pop up again later in the week?'

Doubler nodded furiously. 'That would be ideal. Lovely.' He regained his composure quickly and bustled around the kitchen rinsing the cups and looking, he hoped, very much like a man who needed nothing, nobody.

# 8

Thinking once again about calling the animal shelter, Doubler sought clarity by walking down to the bottom of the hill, using the driveway rather than following the field's own pathways. His feet slipped on the icy flint beneath him. There had been a heavy frost in the night and the wind carried a bite that threatened something colder still. It was going to be a late spring. He could hear a woodpecker drilling a tree in the distance, but other than the bird's persistent hollowing, the air around him was devoid of life. He mused, as he walked, on the possibilities that lay ahead. While making contact with Mrs Millwood's circle of friends filled him with a deep terror, the thought of Julian's anxiety should he get involved with a charitable organization at his time of life appealed to him hugely and he wondered if that might just outweigh the fear of leaving Mirth Farm. The walk cleared his head and he walked back up the hill, a little more slowly to match his breathing, wondering when he had become such a bad parent that the notion of challenging his son was motivation enough to jolt him out of years of isolation.

The telephone was ringing in the hall as he walked into the house and Doubler rushed to it, breathless and thrilled with himself for having timed his arrival back to the house to coincide with Mrs Millwood's hoped-for telephone call.

He snatched the receiver from the hook and reached for a cheerful 'Good tidings', which while he assumed might be an unconventional greeting, seemed to fit his mood.

'Dad?' The male voice at the end of the phone was puzzled and even a little affronted.

'Who is this?' said Doubler, wracked with a gut-wrenching disappointment he was unable to disguise.

'How many men call you 'Dad'?' said Julian, matching his father's tone with a barely contained disdain.

'Oh, it's you, Julian,' said Doubler, feeling simultaneously both let down and foolish. 'You don't often call.'

'Don't guilt me out, Dad. I'm calling you now, aren't I? And in my defence, I usually assume you won't be in to answer the phone. You're normally out with your blasted potatoes. But I thought I'd chance it today. I've been thinking things through since I saw you for lunch.'

Doubler felt tired. 'I'm not selling Mirth Farm, Julian.'

'I'm not talking about the farm. Well, at least not for now. It's about the car. That old banger of yours.'

'My car?'

'Exactly. I didn't see it at the weekend and it's normally on the yard. Are you keeping it inside?'

'Inside?'

'Dad, are you OK? You're sounding more vague than normal. You haven't had a turn, have you?'

Doubler just managed to refrain from asking, 'A turn?' though it was the most intelligible thing he could think of saying.

Julian was continuing to speak, his voice a little tinny and distracted, as though he might be doing something else at the same time. Doubler strained to listen to the noises surrounding the words and could hear the sound of a keyboard being tapped in sporadic bursts. Julian was working as he spoke.

'I'm wondering about the car. It's ancient and I don't think it's safe for you to drive it anymore. If the weather is bad and you should get stuck, you don't want to be relying on something past its best. It must be — what, forty years old?'

'Well, I suppose so, Julian. But I don't have much call for it, to be honest, and it doesn't let me down. What on earth made you think of my car?'

'Oh, I always worry about you in the winter. Seeing you up there reminded me how desolate it can be. I'm wondering if I should take the car off your hands. Swap it for something a little more practical? A Toyota Yaris perhaps, or a small Clio? If you're keen to keep a four-wheel drive, then there's a pretty handy little Fiat Panda that would suit you. What do you think?'

Doubler wracked his brains for a suitably grateful response. His son was showing an entirely unprecedented amount of interest in him.

'I don't know what to say. You've just said a number of words I don't understand. Yaris, you say? What on earth is a Yaris? And what were the other ones you mentioned?'

'Don't worry too much about the what, Dad. I'll do the research. I'll find you a good little runaround that will start first time, every time. Just let me know if you're in agreement in principle and I'll pop up and fetch the Land Rover.'

The Land Rover. Just the words made Doubler glow with warmth. Of course, his old banger was the Land Rover. He'd bought it new, soon after he'd bought the farm, and it had never let him down. As faithful as his potatoes really. Doubler thought back over that time span. Two-thirds of his life. Had anyone else been that reliable? Marie? Certainly not. The kids? Barely. On balance, they'd caused him as much worry as pleasure. That car, though, was as beautiful and sturdy as the day he'd bought it. It's dusty-green colour and its cream roof had seemed undeniably splendid when he'd first driven it home, but it had quickly become part of the landscape, camouflaged among the hues of the farm and as familiar to him as his own face.

Julian was waiting for a quick answer, impatient now as his busy day clamoured to reclaim him. 'Dad? Are you there?'

'Julian. Yes. I'm just mulling it over. I don't really think I need a new one, though it's jolly nice of you to worry about me. Other than running down to the lower fields, I don't exactly do much mileage. It sometimes needs a bit of bullying to start, but other than that, it's fine. I doubt there's anything much more suited to my lifestyle than that.'

'Dad, I'm trying to help you here. Don't put up barriers. I can find you something small and nippy that will get you in and out of town, and it will stop me having to worry about it. I won't hear another objection from you.'

Doubler looked at his watch and realized with horror that Mrs Millwood could be calling him from her bedside at that very moment. 'Julian? I am very, very touched, but I'm expecting another phone call, so I can't completely focus on what you're saying. Would you mind calling back another day?'

'Another phone call from who, Dad? You're acting a little strange. You've not done anything daft, have you?'

'Heavens, no. Chance would be a fine thing,' said Doubler, enjoying the sound of the echo down the phone just before he hung up with a resounding click.

The phone rang almost as soon as he had replaced the receiver.

'You were engaged. I wondered if you had left it off the hook. I thought I might need to send Midge up to check in on you.'

Doubler exhaled happily. 'You're fussing over me again, Mrs Millwood, when your energy is supposed to be focused on getting *you* better. And it's always a pleasure to see your daughter, but I'd like her to think well of me. I don't want her thinking I'm a burden.'

'Oh, I don't think she thinks you're a burden. I think she might see you as a mission, though.'

'A mission? What sort of mission?' Doubler's mind flicked through a mental Rolodex of images, scanning these for potential meanings, something he had started to do recently when words were being elusive. The word now triggered, in quick succession, a series of pictures of white men in heavy clothing wielding Bibles in hot countries.

'Oh, she thinks you're lonely,' said Mrs Millwood, dispelling the images in Doubler's mind. 'I believe she wants to sort you out with pigs or chickens. Or both.'

'Ah yes. Pigs and chickens. I probably wouldn't mind having a bit of a go with some livestock. I've been feeling a little more hopeful lately.'

'Well, that can only be a good thing. You're not exactly known for your optimism, are you?'

'I don't think I said optimistic — that might be pushing it a little far. But not devoid of hope, not quite so much in despair.'

'A lack of despair? Heavens! What do you think has brought that on?' Mrs Millwood joked, though there was probably some honesty behind the laughter.

'It's hard to say.' Doubler wondered which direction to take this; there seemed so many options. He settled for the truth, the veil of the phone making this feel more achievable. 'I think I was a bit troubled when you didn't appear. When I heard your news. The news that you were *poorly*. And I realized that I depend on our chats quite heavily. And then, bless you — you telephoned me. I doubt I've had another phone call in the last ten years! It's been quite a *tonic*.'

'Goodness me, well, perhaps I miss our

lunches, too. For the life of me I can't imagine why. When all you do is criticize me.'

'I criticize you? Heavens, no, I never have! Why on earth would you think that?' Doubler was horrified, his mind racing through their hundreds of conversations and finding no recollection of anything that might have been misconstrued as criticism.

'If it's not my choice of cheese, it's my bread. If it's not my bread, it's my apple,' Mrs Millwood was saying.

'I defy you to prove that I have *ever* criticized your choice of apple.' Doubler was certain here, though he was pretty sure he might have passed comment on her choice of bread on a number of occasions.

'Oh, it's not always the words, Mr Doubler; it's your eyes. Your eyes burn into my apple with enough force to combust the label clean off.'

'You're imagining it.'

'I am doing no such thing. Tell me the truth, Mr Doubler. Tell me if you disapprove of my Granny Smiths.'

Doubler hesitated. He so wanted to support *every* choice Mrs Millwood made. She seemed to have nothing but goodwill for him. But he was still feeling honest. 'You've got me there. I believe that you make an inferior choice in the matter of apples.' He waited. There was a moment of stillness and then a long sigh.

'But, Mr Doubler, I would like to think you can *respect* the choices I make, even when they don't coincide *exactly* with your own prefer-ences.'

'Indeed I do respect you, Mrs Millwood. I don't set out to criticize you. It is not your fault that you haven't had exposure to all of the opportunities I would wish for you. I would like to think that I might be able to educate you when the choices you make are simply ill conceived.'

There was a splutter down the phone and Doubler worried that he might have caused a seizure. 'Mrs Millwood?'

'I'm fine. Just laughing, Mr Doubler. You are a one. You are nothing if not certain of your superiority.'

'Actually, Mrs Millwood, I'm not certain about much, so when I am talking about a subject that doesn't seem to slip away from my grasp, then I like to be very, very sure indeed. Those subjects include potatoes. I know a great deal about potatoes.'

'And almost any other foodstuff.'

'Heavens, no! There are all sorts of foods about which I know nothing. Bananas for one. Are there even different types? I could name dozens of varieties of apple and hundreds of different potatoes, but I couldn't tell you the name of one single banana type. As far as I'm concerned, they just exist in two states: not ripe enough or overripe. And seafood. I know almost nothing about seafood. I could tell you what a lobster looks like, but I don't know what it tastes like. And I don't want to know.'

'What on earth have you got against the lobster?'

'I'm not overly comfortable with the consumption of a creature who has been boiled alive for my pleasure. I've never been tempted, to be honest, but if I had been once, then all thoughts were banished from my mind for ever when I read that lobsters are prone to suffering from anxiety. Who would boil an overly anxious creature alive, for goodness' sake? Us anxious types must stick together in solidarity. I eschew the lobster.'

'That seems entirely reasonable, Mr Doubler. That is a foodstuff that we can wholeheartedly agree upon.'

'Shall we vow never to eat lobsters again, Mrs Millwood?'

'Absolutely. I shall make a solemn pledge. Especially while I am in hospital. I shall speak to the cook at once and tell them to stop feeding me lobster with immediate effect.'

'Very good. I do so like agreeing with you, Mrs Millwood.'

'Feel free to make a habit of it, Mr Doubler. It would be a pleasant change. So, tell me, who were you on the phone to? I was surprised when I couldn't get through.'

'Nobody was more surprised than me. It was Julian. He called and appeared to have my best interests at heart. I can't quite fathom it.'

'Oh, don't be like that — he can't be all that bad.'

'Well, that's just it. He called to offer to help me and I can't remember when he last called at all, let alone to be so considerate. Normally it is Camilla who makes the arrangements when the family descends on me for lunch, but I very rarely hear from Julian from one visit to the next.'

'Well, that's progress, then. You should be happy. Take those little acts of kindness as a sign of his potential, perhaps? People do mellow with old age, I find.'

'Yes, yes, I suppose I must take it as a step forward.'

'What was he offering help with?'

'My car. He said he'd take it off my hands and swap it for a little runaround that I'd find a bit more reliable in the winter. I'm not remotely tempted. I'm very happy with my Land Rover, but at the same time, you're right. I shouldn't disregard an act of kindness, so perhaps I shall agree just so as not to be difficult. I don't want him to think I'm stubborn or impossible to please.'

There was nothing but silence on the end of the phone.

'Mrs Millwood? Are you still there?'

'Yes, Mr Doubler. I'm still here. Just thinking. Your Land Rover, you say. How old is it now?'

'Well, goodness, I must have bought it the second or third winter after I bought the farm and I've run it ever since. It's ancient, I'm afraid. Forty years old, perhaps?'

'That's lovely, Mr Doubler, just lovely that your son is thinking about your needs. But don't agree just yet. I am sure he'll let you have a little time to think about what's best as a replacement, won't he?'

'Well, he seemed quite keen to get the ball

85

rolling, but I can't imagine anything will happen in a hurry.'

'Good. Let me do a little research for you. My husband was a very keen mechanic; he knew an awful lot about cars, so we all picked up a bit of knowledge along the way. Let me have a chat with one or two people. You know how I like to research things properly to, you know, prevent mistakes made in haste. I'll do a little digging. It will help you reach the right decision.'

'Well, that's extremely kind, Mrs Millwood.' Doubler readjusted himself against the hall table and let out a small yelp of pain as his leg briefly gave way under him.

'Are you all right, Mr Doubler?'

'Oh fine, quite fine, thank you. Just getting into a comfy position. This might well be the longest conversation I've had on the phone and I've never thought to put a chair in the hallway.'

'You poor old thing. I had somehow imagined you in the kitchen or in the sitting room tucked up in front of the fire. It's draughty in that hall, too. Go and get yourself warm. I should probably stop my call now anyway. I'm getting slightly disapproving looks.'

'Very well, then, Mrs Millwood. Thanks for calling.'

'I'll call the same time tomorrow, see how you're doing, shall I?'

'Super!' said Doubler, any sadness at the approach of the end of the call vanishing at the thought of a guaranteed call the very next day. 'Cheerio.'

Doubler replaced the receiver and went to the

kitchen, where he sat very quietly while replaying the conversation in his head, smiling as he did so. He concentrated furiously, recalling it as accurately as he could because it suddenly felt extremely important to him that he held on to each and every word.

# 9

Later that afternoon, Doubler sat and watched the bottom of the drive with his binoculars. Sometimes his seat at the top of the hill made him feel invincible, but on other days he felt exposed up at Mirth Farm. The binoculars had become a vital part of his armoury and he liked the advantage they gave him.

Midge was unlikely to visit again until Thursday at the very earliest. If he was lucky. She had said she couldn't pick up his groceries indefinitely, but that implied she would pick them up again, at least this once. Which meant he had a visit to look forward to this week and next, he reasoned.

Even though he had chosen to shut himself off from the outside world, he had never really tested the theory of being an actual recluse. He had regular visitors; he only had to pick up the phone and any number of local suppliers and tradesmen would drop what they were doing to tend to his needs at Mirth Farm. Oil arrived; sewage left; wood was delivered to the wood pile; even the doctor, who had only ever been called out in Marie's time, ensured he paid Doubler a routine visit twice a year. These visits were, on the whole, brief and businesslike — the well-practised exchange of services that had played out comfortably for a long time — and though they offered little in the way of intellectual stimulation, Doubler felt no lack. Mrs Millwood had seen to that.

For five days a week the two of them had sat down and talked. And each day after she left, it wasn't long before he found himself having imaginary conversations with her in his head. This discourse was not in the same league as the advice he sought from Mr Clarke, the substance of which was rooted in the technical conundrums that their shared passion presented. From Mr Clarke, he sought inspiration of a very specific nature. The little observations he would store away for sharing with Mrs Millwood encompassed everything else that Doubler was capable of feeling, and even if this represented a narrow slice of an adult's emotional capacity, Mrs Millwood herself had a very developed range of responses from which to draw.

But what did he actually know about her? He now knew a bit more, that she had a wide circle of friends, but before that time, what had he known? That she knitted, yes. That she found great comfort in family and friends. There — friends again! That her husband had died, but not suddenly. He had lugged an oxygen tank around with him for several years. He had got thinner and thinner, more and more uncomfortable, before eventually dying of a massive asthma attack. It had been a *blessing*. Well, that had been a big difference between Mrs Millwood and Doubler. She had grown used to her husband gradually disappearing in front of her eyes. Whereas for Doubler, Marie had been there one day and not the next. No warning, no preparation. And there had been a choice there for Marie — that's what he couldn't forgive her for. Everything she had done, and how she had done it, was a choice she had made. And nowhere in that process had she thought once of him or the impact it would have on him.

Doubler looked around the room and imagined Marie there now. Would she be interested in his potatoes? Would she be proud of him? Would she even care? Perhaps Julian would be whispering in her ear suggesting early retirement and an easy life in a central-heated condo. That is almost certainly what she would have wanted. It was impossible to know now, but when he looked around the room, with his eyes narrowed, he couldn't imagine her sitting comfortably in any of the chairs. She'd be just getting back from somewhere, or just on her way out with a shopping bag slung over her shoulder and the hood of her anorak already pulled up to protect her from the elements. But she wouldn't be there, sitting still and talking. Or listening.

Doubler closed his eyes and remembered, as best as he could, Mrs Millwood telling him about the death of her husband, Bert. After a few moments of fierce concentration, her words came back to him and it was as if she were sitting in the room.

'It was a terrible thing to watch, the man you love dying in front of your eyes. There was so much pain and so much *inconvenience*. That was the unexpected thing. He was cross with himself and me. I was cross with him, too. It was impossible to live together: it was me and him and that blessed tank. But we talked about it; we talked to *death*. I was able to talk about why I was angry, and he was able to tell me how very furious he was that he had this terrible debilitation. But, my God, the sound of his breathing was heartbreaking. When he went, it was a *relief*.'

'Do you think you were better off knowing? I mean, if he had gone suddenly without any warning, that would have been worse?' Doubler had asked.

'Well, yes, I suppose so. But I'd have liked to have spared him the pain. That was bad. Watching him suffer was very tough. But we got to plan a bit for the future and we had no regrets. We'd said everything enough times. And even if he had suddenly dropped dead when I'd just told him I was sick to death of not being able to sleep at night because of the awful noise he made, then I'd still have no regrets because we'd have recently talked about our love for one another. We'd probably have talked about how we first met, or the arrival of our daughter. About how madly I wanted him and how madly he wanted me and how badly behaved we were when we first fell in love. We loved that, you know, recounting the really good bits. I'd never really tire of talking about that. Because, I suppose, all the bad bits towards the end could never really unstitch all the good bits from the beginning.

'I like to imagine our marriage was a little like a hand-knitted blanket. It was a glorious thing to behold, full of intricate pattern and a multitude of colours and so very beautiful to examine in detail. Towards the top, there were a few dropped stitches and a few holes, and maybe the colours weren't quite so bright, and maybe the needlecraft was a bit patchy, but it never *unravelled*. It still worked as a blanket. It was a lovely thing to look at, and it kept us warm, held us together. And it's so much better to look at the beginning bits and stroke the colours and talk about the love and the joy that went into creating it rather than to focus on the last few rows.'

'My blanket unravelled,' Doubler had said, tears pricking at his eyelids.

'I know. Our stories are not the same, Mr Doubler. Sometimes when you drop a stitch, you can't really patch it up — it just undoes. It's awful. It feels like a waste of time, doesn't it, to end up with a pile of loose wool where before you had something useful.' Mrs Millwood had looked thoughtful.

'But afterwards, when the pain stops, you can tidy things up a bit. You can't ever make that blanket again, not out of that wool, but what you can do is wind the wool up into a really neat ball — and that in itself takes time and patience and a degree of love and generosity — and then you can store the ball of wool away somewhere safe. And maybe just look at it from time to time.'

'I am so far from that time, Mrs Millwood. It is still just a knotted mess at my feet. It trips me up; it catches me out. I couldn't even find an end if I tried.'

'So don't. Do what you're doing. Walk around

it, step over it. Ignore it. Sweep it into a dark corner if watching it is causing you too much pain. But one day, you'll have the strength and the resolve to look for an end and then slowly, slowly you can tidy it away neatly. You'll feel some peace then.'

Doubler had carefully stored the image away in his memory and then asked, 'And the anger you felt when your husband was dying — did it go when he died?'

'In my case, yes. Because we'd said all our hurts and we'd said all our 'sorry's and I was just so glad he didn't have to suffer again and I was so, so relieved to sleep through the night. For the first week or so I just slept and slept. My daughter thought my doctor had medicated me, but, no, I was just catching up on the sleep that you can't have when you're caring night and day.'

'Ours *are* very different stories, Mrs Mill-wood.'

'They are chalk and cheese, aren't they? I bet when you're tripping over that mess of tangled wool, you can't imagine it ever made a blanket in the first place. But it probably did — the pain is just hard to see past. It can blind you, that kind of sadness.'

'I had no warning, no inkling. And yet she knew! She could have spared me the shock, couldn't she? She can't have loved me much if she didn't even think I needed a bit of gentle letting-down.'

'Love, Mr Doubler. It's a funny thing. True love doesn't go away, but the pressures of life can do things to people. Who knows why some people react so differently? Sometimes it's just an ageing thing. Like wine. Some wines are best drunk right away, as soon as the wine is made. And then no amount of keeping it and nurturing it will make it any better. Others aren't that great first of all, but they get better and better. But the really good wines, Mr Doubler, they're good when you first drink them and there's still room for improvement.' She had looked at him, puzzled then. 'Why 'chalk and cheese', do you think, Mr Doubler?'

'Well . . . '

Doubler blinked his eyes open and looked around the room, expecting to see Mrs Millwood bustling into the kitchen to put the kettle on. Had he told her where the expression 'chalk and cheese' had come from? Almost certainly — it was the kind of information he enjoyed being able to furnish. And she would have logged it carefully to relate to her friends at the knitting circle or, perhaps, the animal shelter.

There were people who knew Mrs Millwood at the animal shelter, people who perhaps missed her as much as he did. And surely there were animals, too, animals that might even be suffering as a result of her sudden departure. He had something in common with all of them, if only his sadness.

Doubler thought about the copy of the Yellow Pages he had tidied away in the cupboard and wondered from where Mrs Millwood drew her strength. She had been blessed with so much courage while he had so little. She certainly had enough for the two of them, but if he were to borrow some of hers, what on earth could he give her in return?

He looked at his strong and weathered hands. Mirth Farm soil was so ingrained in them that the fine lines formed dark contours and he wondered if he studied them for long enough, he'd find, drawn there, the topography of Mirth Farm itself. His hands were generously calloused, and Doubler was grateful for these hardened areas that gave him protection from the tools he handled daily. He ran the rough tip of his right thumb over the armour of his left hand, thinking how clever those skin cells were to form here where they were most needed, as if they had learnt lessons from every knock, every blister, every small wound. His heart, though, had taken some hard knocks of its own but had failed, he now realized, to similarly protect itself from future injury. If anything, it was more vulnerable to hurt now than ever before.

Perhaps, he wondered further, his heart had not hardened because that was not the place he suffered most when Marie went. It had been his head, not his heart, that had borne the brunt of the pain. His brain had ached with the inspection of her action and the replaying of the last months, weeks, days, looking for a clue, looking for a moment at which he might have changed their future. It was his brain that hurt from the constant examination and recrimination, and it was his brain that eventually stopped coping and had almost shut down altogether while he'd descended into the post-Marie chasm to escape the constant thinking. But the impact Mrs Millwood's absence had on him was a very different thing. It hurt deeply in his ill-prepared heart.

He thought of her in her hospital bed and wondered whether *she* was strong enough in all the right places to recover. She seemed to be so much more resilient than he would ever be. Here he was, physically as strong as an ox, being propped up by Mrs Millwood, an invalid no less. Somehow, he would need to find some courage. He headed out to the potatoes to think.

# 10

Having had no answer when she rang the doorbell, Midge rounded the farmhouse and crossed the yard, heading for the kitchen door, a bag full of groceries under each arm. Today, it was calm at the top of the hill, where normally the wind gusted, making it difficult sometimes to appreciate the silence that her mum so often talked about. She took a moment to inhale a lungful of hillside air and looked around her as she walked, observing her surroundings properly for the first time since she'd started to visit Doubler.

She popped the bags down in the yard, leaning them against a deteriorating stone wall. The yard was quartered by the back of the farmhouse itself, a locked garage and the first of some huge barns, which felt ominous in their stillness. The yard, nothing more than a turning circle really, was surfaced in gravel, and the bare fields she had driven through crept right up to each of the buildings so that, other than a briar-filled narrow flowerbed that circled the farmhouse itself, the grounds were devoid of anything that might be considered a garden. At the front of the house, to the right of the approach, there were a number of fruit trees — apple, she thought, and some others that might be part of an ancient fruit orchard — but their skeletal forms at this time of year lent little relief from the stark surroundings.

The roadside hill at the front of the farmhouse was quite steep for farmland but was furrowed in meticulous rows running the width of the fields. At the rear of the house, the field rolled more gently in all directions before dropping away to the boundary with that other big potato farmer Peele. Midge knew that the fields for as far as she could see were Doubler's, and these in every direction were a deep, rich brown. The hedges that separated them were largely bare at this time of year, and the occasional coppice or small stretch of woodland boasted little that was evergreen. Midge had noticed Peele's land as she drove past it on the way to visit Doubler and had acknowledged a discrepancy that she now realized she must enquire about.

As she stood looking, her sweeping gaze taking in the furthest reaches of the horizon as well as the immediate scenery, Doubler appeared from a narrow gap beside the first of the huge barns. Seeing Midge, he deviated from his planned circuit, hurrying across the yard towards her, waving cheerfully while briefly enjoying the thought that this warm interaction would be caught on film.

'Have you never thought of putting in a vegetable patch, Doubler? Seems such a shame that with all of this land you're having to buy in your vegetables.'

Doubler grinned in recognition. This trait of launching into a conversation as if he had been party to the preceding, unspoken thoughts in her brain was definitely a characteristic he recognized from Midge's mother.

'I agree it is a shame, but my potatoes occupy my day quite fully. I'm not sure I could give anything else my full attention.'

'But isn't it monotonous? The bare soil and stone? All those potatoes! I think I might go mad up here.'

'Here? Monotonous? Heavens, no. Barely two days are the same.'

'What you need here, Doubler, as I've told you before, are some nice hens pecking at the yard' — she nodded at the empty space around them — 'and there, perhaps, in the lee of that barn, a veggie patch. That's a great spot. It would be nicely sheltered.' She pointed at a corner of the nearest field that ran right up to the garage.

'I'm sure you're right. I have been meaning to be a bit more adventurous. But the day job keeps getting in the way. Perhaps in my retirement, eh?' he joked.

Midge picked up the groceries and they entered the house together.

Doubler nodded at the bags. 'I do OK, though, all things considered. These are probably grown locally, and I get by with the help of my friends.'

'Your friends?' Midge asked with an eyebrow raised and a hint of cynicism in her voice. The man in the farm shop had handed over the groceries without a word of greeting. Midge would have expected some sort of message of good wishes to pass on, particularly if Doubler hadn't been to the shop in person for a few weeks.

Doubler chose not to answer and busied

himself putting away the groceries.

When he returned from the pantry, Midge was already putting the kettle on.

'Right, you. Mum is pushing for a progress report.'

'From me? Well, nothing much to report and I spoke to her just yesterday.'

'Nothing to report? That's what we both feared. Have you arranged a time to visit Grove Farm yet? That's what she really wants to know.'

Doubler looked at his feet and wondered how best to reply.

Midge looked serious, her hands now on her hips. 'Have you even called them?'

Doubler shook his head apologetically, still unable to look Midge in the eye. 'I'm afraid not. I lost my nerve.'

'Oh, Doubler, that's such a shame! If you don't want to volunteer, I completely under-stand, but you need to tell Mum you've chickened out or you'll just be letting her down. She really was hoping you'd get involved and help them out. Help *her* out. Besides, they're expecting your call, so it will seem very rude.'

Doubler was appalled but unsure what he could do to right the situation, as recently he'd felt further away from making that call than ever before. 'I've been very busy up here — there's the normal workload to contend with, and I've taken on my domestic duties, too. There are already a great number of commitments to deal with. I'm quite *stretched*.'

Midge looked around at the immaculate kitchen. 'I'm sure you're doing a wonderful job keeping on top of it all, but I really don't think it's very healthy hiding up here all the time.'

Doubler protested, 'I'm outside most of the day and I provide well for myself. It's a healthy lifestyle — your mum would vouch for that.'

'I'm quite sure you are healthy physically. That's not what I'm concerned about. It's your mental health that worries me. You must go days without seeing somebody up here.'

Doubler bit his lip and looked embarrassed.

'Are you involved in any social activities? Golf? Bridge? A book club?'

Doubler shook his head and sat down heavily, resting his elbows on the table and putting his chin in his hands.

'And what about friends? Do you get many visitors to Mirth Farm?'

Doubler shrugged.

'When did you last go to dinner at a friend's house?' Midge still had her hands on her hips. She felt as combative as she sounded.

'Gosh, I can't remember. We used to go out a lot, Marie and I. She was very sociable. Drove me nuts, to tell you the truth. But after she went, I didn't really feel up to much, so the invitations soon tailed off. Not their fault. I probably said 'no' one too many times, so they eventually stopped asking.'

Midge, incredulous, came and sat down next to Doubler. 'But that was more than two decades ago! You're not telling me you've not eaten at a friend's house for all that time?'

Doubler immediately pushed his chair back to stand up, continuing with the tea-making process that Midge had abandoned in her shock.

'I suppose I haven't. Amazing how time flies, really. But it's not surprising. I've had my head down with my work, and your mum was always there to keep me company Monday to Friday. I never felt lonely.'

'But, Doubler, that is not good enough! What about trips to the town? To the shops? How many times a week do you actually leave this place?'

Again Doubler fell silent. He had deliberately kept his isolation a secret from his children, but he didn't think Midge would be so easy to fob off with a convenient version intended to pacify her. And besides, Mrs Millwood knew the extent of his solitary confinement, so there was little to gain by hiding it from her daughter. Still he hesitated, acknowledging his failure at life as if for the very first time.

She was insistent. 'Doubler, how many visits to town do you make a week?'

Doubler poured tea for them both, took a sip and concentrated furiously on the lip of his cup.

'A month?' Midge tried.

Doubler finally raised his eyes to meet hers. 'To tell you the truth, I don't leave here.'

'What, never?'

'No. Not since Marie went. I have an arrangement that covers me for groceries and it's quite satisfactory. Anything else I need is delivered to me here. I only have to pick up the phone. It lets me get on with the work I need to do. My potatoes are actually very demanding and even in the winter there is so much to do. I have very little help, you know — just a few extra pairs of hands for harvest. Most of it I do myself and I just wouldn't manage if I was always popping into town.'

'I'm not talking about *always* popping into town. I'm talking about once or twice a week, say, getting out and about, having a conversation with somebody, *anybody*. You're living as a recluse and that can't be healthy.'

'I'm OK,' Doubler said quite firmly. 'I don't need anybody much. I mean, of course I relied very much on my lunchtime natter with your mum. That I miss dreadfully.' His eyes filled up and Midge thought he might break down altogether, but he shook himself and drew himself up straight. 'But I'm coping without those even. Conversation is overrated, you know.'

Midge shook her head sadly. 'No, Doubler, it's not. And if I wasn't here trying to keep an eye on you in Mum's absence, I hate to think what would happen to you. I'm going to dial the number for Grove Farm myself, but you're going to do the talking — after all, you're a bright, interesting individual and you are more than capable of engaging with these people. You're going to volunteer immediately — and I mean immediately, tomorrow ideally. And just so you don't get cold feet, I am going to drive you there myself the first time. I can imagine the shock to your system could be immense and I don't want to feel responsible for you when your system goes into collapse because I've made you have a conversation with somebody other than my mother. Come on, I haven't got all day.'

She led him to the telephone, looked up the number on her own phone, dialled it and handed Doubler the receiver with a look of impatience that Doubler feared much more than the sound of a stranger's voice.

# 11

The phone rang just as Doubler was sitting down to lunch. He had still not got used to the silence round the table, which was so much louder than any conversations he'd ever had in there. Midge's insistence that his lifestyle was unhealthy had unsettled him, and the vicious hilltop wind that rattled at the windows and occasionally shrieked as it tried to find a way inside only served to exaggerate the stillness in the kitchen.

Doubler had propped himself up on his left elbow, his hand supporting his chin while poking at his potatoes with his fork, pushing them round the plate with a disinterest that was quickly turning into dissatisfaction. He wondered, as he chased a potato from one side of the plate to the another, whether he would ever enjoy eating again. Mrs Millwood might have been consuming an inferior lunch all these years, but she had been consuming an inferior lunch *with him* and that small distinction was now having a disproportionately large impact on the flavour of his own food. He added this new slight to the growing reasons to be disgruntled by Mrs Millwood's absence and he was so deep in this thought, crafting a list of complaints in his head, that he was shocked by the shrill ringing from the telephone.

He had just begun a quavering 'Hello' when

that perfectly familiar voice cut through his mumbled greeting. 'So, Mr Doubler, you know how you always sneer at my apple choice?'

'I do?' he asked, trying to force some indignation into his voice to compete with the warmth that was spreading from deep within him.

'My apples. You sneer. Don't tell me you don't.' Mrs Millwood paused, hearing a smile. 'My Granny Smiths?'

'Well, I suppose it wouldn't be my first choice of apple, it's true. Nor my second. Nor my third, for that matter. I doubt it would make it into my top ten. I doubt I could name a hundred apples, but if I could, I don't suppose the Granny Smith would make it there either.' Doubler luxuriated in the conversation, his mind casting itself out across the orchards of England. 'Cox's, the russets — all the russets — and, oh, I am *partial* to an in-season Bramley — '

Mrs Millwood cut him short, breathless with irritation. 'I didn't ask you for your favourite apples, did I? I didn't ask for a *lecture*. I just want to hear you openly admit that you find my choice of apple inferior.'

'I suppose you have a motive for this call, do you? There must be some very sick patients on that ward of yours and I don't suppose they want to hear you being confrontational for no good reason.' Doubler wondered, even as he spoke, whether he'd ever felt such intense joy.

'The thing is, Mr Doubler, I learnt something today. Quite by chance. It turns out, entirely unbeknown to me and without this knowledge

106

ever having influenced my apple choice, Granny Smith herself was a bit of a *trailblazer*. She reminds me very much of your John Clarke.' Mrs Millwood must have sensed an imminent interruption because she pressed on urgently. 'Now, I know you think he's special, but let's be honest, his father was a potato breeder before him, so it already ran in his genes, so to speak. But Granny Smith set sail for Australia back in the 1830s! She was a true *pioneer*. And to think how tough that voyage must have been in those days — I can only imagine what the boat would have been full of. Sickness and convicts, I suppose. But Maria Ann Smith — that was her name — Maria Ann Smith made the journey regardless and started an orchard way down there in New South Wales. Can you imagine such *courage*? She discovered her apple quite by accident. A chance cultivar from a seedling, would you believe it? I was shocked to my core when I learnt this. To my *core!*'

Doubler considered this information carefully. While the old lady might well fit the description of a true pioneer, he wasn't sure that he liked the fact that her entrepreneurship was being presented to him as somewhat superior to Mr Clarke's genetic predisposition to breed potatoes. He digested this brand-new information before forming his response.

'Ah, Mrs Millwood, I can see what you're getting at. You are proposing that your Granny Smith is an equal to my Mr Clarke. Is that it? Because I don't think that the chance discovery of a seedling bears comparison with years and years of painstaking potato breeding. A chance cultivar from a seedling sounds to me like a bit of an *accident*. Anyone can have an accident, Mrs Millwood.'

Mrs Millwood was clearly prepared for this response. 'Aha! But the chance wasn't the thing. The observation and the subsequent *perseverance* were the thing. She discovered her apple and then found it to have some excellent and unique properties.' Mrs Millwood was now talking really quite loudly, and quickly, as if competing with both background noise and other demands on her attention. Mr Doubler smiled at the image of the patient dismissing doctors and nurses with a wave of her hand. 'Her apple could be stored for a very long time, you see, which made it suitable for shipping around the world or for keeping through the winter.'

'That *is* interesting. But being a perishable good can be a blessing, too, Mrs M. One of the more interesting things about the potato, Mrs M, is that it *doesn't* travel well. It doesn't last! And why is that good, do you suppose?'

Mrs Millwood sighed loudly for dramatic effect. 'I have absolutely no idea, but I suspect you're about to tell me.'

'It means the potato can't be traded as an international commodity! Meat you can freeze and trade, other grains like rice will keep for ever, but the potato likes to be in the ground or in your stomach and it doesn't hang around in between.'

'And that's a good thing because . . . ?'

'That's a good thing because as soon as a

commodity is traded on the international market, it becomes a political *pawn*. Prices go artificially high; growers are squeezed out; quotas are imposed; sanctions are declared. It's not possible with the potato, so we all just get on with it and each country grows their own. It means that in times of hardship and economic turmoil, the potato remains affordable. You can *trust* a potato.'

'And you're saying you can't trust a Granny Smith?'

'No. I'm just saying that longevity isn't always a bonus.'

'If you're an apple, it's a bonus. A couple of world wars were fought and won with the help of the Granny Smith, I don't doubt. Imagine — no fruit, no veg for weeks on end and then somebody allows you to sink your teeth into a sweet, crisp, juicy Granny Smith apple as fresh as the day it was picked. You'd think your ship had come in.'

'A persuasive argument, I'll grant you that, but it still sounds a bit like luck rather than judgement.'

'Luck? You call that luck? A woman sets sail for the other end of the planet, plants an orchard by hand, has the presence of mind to observe the cross-cultivation of a common old crab apple and a domestic apple, and then nurtures it to establish a new variety. You call that luck?' Mrs Millwood turned from the phone to cough weakly, the first sign that she was in any way diminished by her hospital stay. Her coughing sounded distant and muffled, and there were other sounds, too — the noises, perhaps, of Mrs Millwood pouring herself a glass of water. Doubler listened, finding pleasure in the intimacy of the moment. When she returned to the phone, her voice was restored to its usual vigour.

'She was both a scientist *and* a pioneer. You know, you can't breed the Granny Smith apple today? If you try to, it reverts back to its components, a sour old crab apple or an undistinguished domestic apple. If you want a Granny Smith, you have to go right back to the original rootstock. Every single Granny Smith consumed today comes from that one chance seedling.'

'Well, goodness, I suppose that was an achievement, wasn't it? I wonder how many Granny Smiths are consumed these days?'

'A huge number. More, perhaps, than the Maris Piper, do you think?'

'Well, it would be a close-run battle, I suppose. Goodness, between them, my Mr Clarke and your Mrs Smith certainly knew how to leave a *legacy*.'

'My point is, Mr Doubler, I'd like you to be a bit more respectful of her, and her apple.'

'More respectful?'

'Yes. I mean, the way you talk about your Mr Clarke, you'd think he was the only unsung hero in the world. Think about the obstacles Mrs Smith faced! She was a woman travelling to foreign shores in the 1800s! And Mr Clarke might not have had much of an education, but that's only interesting to you because you assume all men *should* get an education. A woman in the 1800s couldn't assume to get any education whatsoever, quite frankly. All they were supposed to do was look pretty and breed.' Mrs Millwood paused briefly to breathe, before rushing on. 'And it seems that my Mrs Smith was good at breeding children *and* apples. She wasn't called Granny Smith for nothing. Though now I think about it, if it had been her husband who had made this groundbreaking discovery, I doubt they would have called the apple the Grandfather Smith, would they? Seems a bit *sexist*, now I think of it.'

'Oh, you have a point there. I think you're quite right. They'd have called it the Farmer Smith, perhaps?'

'In all likelihood. But couldn't Granny Smith have been Farmer Smith herself? I mean, the role of the farmer isn't assumed to be a man, is it?'

Doubler thought about the implications and wished there was a comfy chair to sit on in the hall. Instead, he leant slightly against the hall table for support, holding the telephone receiver tightly to his ear, as if he might bring Mrs Millwood closer to him.

She continued, 'Though that's an interesting one, isn't it? The term 'farmer's wife'. You never hear the term 'farmer's husband', do you?'

'Never,' agreed Doubler.

'Did your wife think of herself in those terms? As a farmer's wife?'

'Good Lord, no. She didn't really think of herself as having anything to do with the farm.

And to qualify as a farmer, or a farmer's wife, or perhaps a farmer's husband, the farm has got to be the first thing you think about when you get out of bed in the morning and the last thing you think about when you go to sleep at night.'

'And are those your first and last thoughts, Mr Doubler?'

'Well, in a manner of speaking, yes. But I don't think of myself as a farmer. I think of myself as a potato *grower*. And I'd like to be recognized as a potato breeder in time. I'm a *specialist*.'

'So your wife would have gone by the title of 'potato grower's wife'?'

'Ha!' snorted Doubler. 'She'd have loved that!' He shook his head sadly.

Mrs Millwood missed the sadness and laughed joyfully down the phone. 'Grandfather Doubler and the potato grower's wife! What a couple!' There was a silence, a muffled conversation and Mrs Millwood came back on the line, her voice an exaggerated whisper. 'I've got to go. I'm being scowled at.'

'Oh, righty-ho,' said Doubler, not wishing at all to end the conversation.

'I'll call you again when I've got an answer.'

'Lovely. An answer to what?' Doubler practically bellowed down the phone, so anxious was he to perpetuate this call. But she had gone. The dialling tone bleated at him.

He wandered back to the kitchen, to eat his potatoes with renewed enthusiasm. She'd left him so much to think about, there wasn't the possibility of silence getting between him and his work that afternoon.

'Why isn't there a word for a farmer's wife?' he said out loud, and resolved to think of one before he next spoke to Mrs Millwood.

# 12

It had taken nearly a week for Doubler to find a date that suited Maxwell, but now he was finally on his way, hunched in the passenger seat of the little red car, leaving the farm for the first time for years. In every version he had tried to imagine, he had been driving himself in the bumpy old Land Rover, but here he was, in the hands of Mrs Millwood's daughter, who was prepared to take no prisoners, with the exception, perhaps, of him. She had arrived punctually and then waited in the car at the front of the house, beeping the horn repeatedly while Doubler steadied himself, one hand on the door handle, one on the wall beside the door. Her insistence was the trigger he needed and soon they were turning out of the drive.

'So, what do we know about these people?' said Midge in a conciliatory tone, feeling a twinge of guilt for her inflexible insistence.

'Very little, other than the stories your mum told me. I've only spoken to Colonel Maxwell, but I do know that they're terribly short-staffed, so I've committed to covering your mum's shifts for the time being. Just till, you know, just till she's back on her feet.'

While Doubler tried to sound confident, adopting the tone of a man engaged in a normal conversation on his way to an un-noteworthy appointment, his shaky voice betrayed him.

Midge glanced at Doubler from the corner of her eye. His knuckles were white where he clung to the door handle, and he had pushed himself as far back in the passenger seat as possible. His eyes were darting all around him, as if he were trying to assess the landscape for an escape route.

'I know this is a big deal, Doubler, and I'm really proud of you. You're actually extremely courageous. But I feel very, very *good* about this. You're going to break some bad habits and start some good ones. Volunteering is really good news all round and I'm sure they're thrilled to have your help. I expect you've got skills that none of them have, so you might be able to help in all manner of ways.'

Doubler wondered silently to himself about his skills. He knew potatoes. If they needed somebody who understood potatoes, then yes, he could help. But other than that, he wasn't sure he had any skills as such. Still, there were always phones to be answered and notes to be made. Both of those things he could certainly manage.

Doubler watched intently from the window. His horizon at Mirth Farm was vast; from there, he could see for miles. His memories of his view were not defined by the breaking of dawn or the settling of dusk but the comings and goings of whole seasons as they swept in and rolled back, like the arms of a giant loom repainting the landscape around him. At the farm, his horizon calmed him.

From the car, down below his hill, among the landscape he thought he knew so well, the horizon was tiny and fractured. Flashes of field, barely visible between buildings, and trees vied for his attention, withholding their potential. He tried to hold the glimpses in his head before they were replaced by the next glimmer of view. The small world flickered by, and as hedges gave way to walls, his anxiety gave way to curiosity. The town had developed and grown in the intervening years, but Mrs Millwood had always had so much to say about each new change that the version he was looking at now seemed quite familiar to him.

After a fifteen-minute drive, much of it in silence, they turned onto a bumpy old farm track, ruts worn deep by heavy vehicles and a central verge that scraped alarmingly at the underside of Mrs Millwood's little red car. They had to stop twice to open gates and to close gates behind them, but they were soon coming to a stop in front of the farmhouse.

'I'll pick you up in a couple of hours, shall I?'

Doubler was startled. He somehow hadn't quite imagined the moment that Midge would abandon him. He had idly wondered if she might come in with him and introduce herself to her mother's friends, or perhaps she'd just sit in the car and wait for him. But no, no, of course she couldn't possibly do that.

'I'll be fine,' he said, in answer to a question she hadn't asked.

'Off you go, then.'

'Yes, yes. Off I go. Cheerio.' It took him a few more moments to find some courage and then he clambered warily out of the car, unsteady on his feet. As he made his way to the farmhouse door, he heard the whine of the little red car in reverse. Midge definitely wasn't waiting for him. The bark of a solitary dog, low and persistent, announced his arrival as he approached the farmhouse door. The noise came from some stables to his left and it was soon joined by a whole chorus of dogs, from a high-pitched yap to a much more alarming howl.

As the cacophony petered out, Doubler rang the bell and waited, listening to the distinct sound of somebody making their way to the front door. He wondered, in those moments, what he sounded like to a first-time visitor to his farm. The person inside was making quite a lot of noise, perhaps doing battle with keys and locks. He listened again, his ear cocked towards the door. Perhaps they were just going about their everyday business and hadn't heard the doorbell at all. Doubler hesitated while he wondered whether to ring the bell again.

'Yahoo! Doubler,' a deep voice called out from behind him. He turned to see a tall man stooping to climb down the three steps from the door of a tired-looking Portakabin. 'You must be Doubler, I assume? We're not in the main house. We try not to disturb Olive too much. Come on, let me give you the grand tour of HQ.'

Doubler apologized quietly to the closed door and hurried guiltily over to the Portakabin. Colonel Maxwell had turned to disappear inside again.

As Doubler poked his head in, the Colonel was already taking a seat and he waved his hand majestically as he greeted his guest. 'Welcome to our executive offices. I apologize in advance if you find our overwhelming grandness a bit intimidating.'

Doubler looked around. The chilly rectangular building housed a cheap Formica desk and two chairs (one on each side of the desk as if permanently prepared for a one-on-one interview). Separately there was a chipped tray on a small table set out neatly with electric kettle, mugs, a box of teabags, a milk bottle and a sealed glass jar full of sugar cubes. On the only shelf were a number of neatly organized box files. There was little else to observe.

'Most people call me 'Colonel', but if you're not an army man, you might rather call me Maxwell, or just plain old Max. As you like. At ease,' he said, motioning Doubler to the visitor's chair as if he were about to be interrogated.

While there was little to absorb, Doubler was struggling to take it all in nevertheless.

'Cat got your tongue, old man?'

'I'm . . . It's not quite what I imagined.'

'Sorry to disappoint, but we must make do. Limited resources and all that.'

'Oh no, not that. I mean, it probably does the job, doesn't it? I just expected a few more of you, for a start. Derek? Paula? Mabel? Olive? The team? Mrs Millwood talked extensively about *the team*.'

'Well, we're rarely all here at once, old fellow. We're volunteers. We take it in turns. We do our bit, cover our own shifts and leave notes for each other in the comms file. Not much to it, but I'll

118

show you the ropes.'

'And animals? I expected animals.'

'Well, of course you did. Not much good to anyone without animals, are we, old man? Another time, I'll give you a little tour of the ops, but I've got a busy morning so let's just get on with a sharpish debrief, shall we? No point hanging about.'

Doubler had wondered, when he first entered the office, whether he was experiencing a slight tinge of disappointment. It had taken a huge amount of personal courage to leave the farm and face some strangers, but he'd galvanized himself to do it in the unvoiced hope that he might make Mrs Millwood proud of him. But now, as the Colonel rattled through the handover notes, making it clear he would only stay for as long as it was required to settle Doubler in, any disappointment gave way to a huge surge of relief. He wouldn't have to interact after all. He was here, volunteering, making a difference and he would impress Mrs Millwood and Midge, but it would be no more taxing than sitting at home. And, he thought, as he looked around the sparse cabin, it was certainly a change of scenery.

Maxwell went through the daily procedure with him. There were only a couple of routines to memorize and there were concise notes written down to give guidance or instruction in any eventuality. 'What to do when you take a call about cruelty.' 'Procedure for rehoming.' 'Procedure for accepting an unwanted animal.' Doubler glanced down the points on each and felt he could probably manage all of these

119

scenarios without too much difficulty.

'Clear as mud?' barked Maxwell. 'Excellent. Carry on!' And off he went, leaving the Portakabin in a quite undignified rush as if Doubler might be about to change his mind. The Colonel climbed into a very old Renault 4, which took a number of attempts to start before it choked unconvincingly to life, and the pair of them were gone in a noisy and inelegant retreat.

Doubler sat at the desk watching the silent telephone. He thought he might wander out and take a look at the animals but didn't want to be away from his post if the phone rang or a visitor arrived. He sat quietly, forcing himself to wait for at least thirty minutes before he made himself a cup of tea. He wondered, as he twiddled a pencil between his fingers, what Mrs Millwood would do while it was her shift. He couldn't imagine her sitting still or quietly. In fact, he had instead imagined that he would be coming into a hive of activity in which Mrs Millwood would be the wise and rather magisterial leader, inspiring them all to rehouse and defend the weak, the sick and the unwanted.

Still the phone remained silent, so Doubler moved himself to the steps, where he could keep an eye on the farmhouse, look for signs of life other than his own breath in the air and listen out for the phone. He looked at the farm buildings around him and across to the farmhouse itself. He was tempted to go and explore, but unsure if he should abandon his post so soon, he went back inside to make a cup of tea. He opened the box of teabags and sniffed the contents suspiciously. Shaking his head sadly, he closed up the box. With mild disappointment evident on his face, he appraised the scant facilities available to him, finding no evidence of either a pot or a tea strainer. Sighing, he took from his inside pocket a small twist of paper. From his other pocket, he took a clean cotton handkerchief. While the kettle boiled, he carefully tipped the tea leaves into the centre of the handkerchief and this he knotted into a makeshift teabag. He poured the boiling water slowly into the cup, allowing the tea leaves to steep for the requisite three minutes before adding milk. He sipped at his drink slowly, while making a note in his pocketbook of the items he'd need to bring with him next time.

The minutes ticked by slowly, and after a long period of unbroken silence, he started to wonder whether there would even be a next time. It seemed to him that there was no point staffing the office constantly. Perhaps the drop-in clinic for potential new owners could just be a day or two a week. He thought about the inefficiencies of trying to run a charity that could not predict when they might be required. But just as he was beginning to think he would have to talk himself out of the role, he heard the rumble of an arrival and he hurried down the steps to see an old pickup truck pulling up, dragging a horsebox behind it.

Doubler walked out to meet the visitor, excited to be useful for the first time in his shift. To his surprise, a tiny woman with a headscarf knotted tightly under her chin slid out of the cab of the truck and bounced her way down to the ground, wincing with pain as she landed. She retrieved a walking stick from within the car and then used it to point at Doubler.

'You the new chap?'

'Yes, I'm Doubler.'

'Then you'll be expecting me.'

'Not exactly.'

'Should have been in the file. I'm here to pick up a donkey. Giving it a new home. You'll have to help me catch it, though.'

Doubler looked at her and the horsebox she was trailing, which to his inexpert eye certainly seemed like an adequate vehicle in which to safely transport a donkey.

Doubler cast his mind back over the notes he'd flicked through earlier, trying to recall the protocol and wondering whether there was anything else he ought to do other than express some gratitude and give her all the help and encouragement he could manage. This seemed like the best course of action, and emboldened by the series of changes he'd already undertaken in his life, he adopted the persona of a man comfortable in his own skin and with all matters pertaining to animal welfare.

'You're giving it a new home? How marvellous. We need more like you!' said Doubler, rather proud that this transaction was going to take place under his watchful eye. 'But I'm new here, as you know. So you'll have to lead the way.'

The woman, as yet unintroduced, looked a little hesitant but walked off, using her stick to steady herself over the deeply rutted farmyard. They passed through a gate into a small empty field and started making their way diagonally towards the next field, which was separated from the first by a thick hedge of hawthorn.

'My knee's playing up. You'll have to take it from here.' She handed Doubler a halter and rope, and turned to walk back to the farm, looking really quite sprightly.

Doubler watched her retreat. 'But I might need your help!' he called, worried that he'd never handled a donkey before and concerned, too, that he might not be able to identify the animal in a field of many.

She did not look back but shouted into the wind, 'I'll prepare the truck.'

Doubler didn't want to let anyone down so made his way cautiously to the gate, not knowing what he might find the other side. His immediate concern turned out to be completely unfounded. There was just one donkey there, a small thing with a beautiful thick charcoal-grey coat. Doubler opened the gate and held up the halter. The donkey looked at him nervously and started to back away.

'Here, boy. I've got some rather good news for you — you're going to a lovely new home.'

The donkey took some more steps in the wrong direction. If it could have glanced over its shoulder, it would have.

'Come on, you. I'm not surprised you've got the jitters. Probably been mistreated before in your time. That's what you're doing here in the first place, isn't it?'

The donkey responded to his low, gentle voice by locking his eyes on Doubler.

Doubler talked some more. 'But this is an exciting *new* chapter. A new home to go to, somebody to love you *for ever*. You'll never feel lonely again! Come on, boy. You know how awful it is, day after day after day with no prospect of love in sight. And here it is — another chance. Come on, boy. This is too good an opportunity.'

The donkey was lured by Doubler's patience and came slowly to him to investigate Doubler's outstretched hand. As he got closer, Doubler could see the fear in the animal's eyes, and signs of scars, nicks and tears pocked his old face. From afar, he had looked like a young animal, but up close, he looked quite worn out. Once he was close enough, Doubler gently leant forward and wriggled the halter over his nose and behind his ears, doing up the strap under his chin. The donkey submitted at this point and fell into an easy walk beside him as Doubler led him back towards the farm, being careful to close both gates behind him.

He led the obedient animal slowly to the yard, murmuring all the time of the many wonderful things that companionship might have in store for him and feeling rather proud that he had navigated a number of hurdles for which he was ill prepared. There was no sight of the woman, but the ramp was down on the trailer and there was a thick bed of straw inside that made the horsebox look very inviting. Doubler led the donkey carefully to the ramp, but with his front two hooves barely on the ramp, the beast then refused to budge. Doubler kept up his hushed monologue, giving the animal every little bit of encouragement, but the donkey was stuck firm. He wouldn't move forwards or backwards. Doubler was stymied and ashamed by his helplessness. He couldn't let go of the donkey: it felt irresponsible. He couldn't call for the new owner, either, as that might startle the donkey, who though rooted to the spot, was, at least, quite calm. But either with a tug at the halter or a firm shove on his hind, Doubler could not move him. He looked around anxiously, hoping the woman would appear at any moment to give him a hand.

As he waited, he heard the sound of a car approaching quite quickly up the drive. It was the complaining engine of the Renault 4 and it came to a grinding halt in the gateway, blocking the access. Colonel Maxwell jumped out.

'Schoolboy error. You didn't read the notes, old man!' said the Colonel. It was difficult to tell from his tone whether he was angry or not.

Doubler looked around him, both alarmed and perplexed, hoping to find support from the absent woman, who would be able to clear this up with a simple explanation. 'I read the notes. Did I miss something?'

'The addendum. We'll review it shortly, but in the meantime, let's get Percy back to his field, shall we?' Maxwell came and scratched the donkey behind the ears and led him gently away from the trailer. The donkey broke into a trot and happily headed into the long grass of the first field.

'We'll leave him here and sort him out later. He'll be absolutely fine for the moment. Right now, we'd better go and deal with the old dear, shall we?'

Doubler was baffled but found comfort in the Colonel's certainty. He trailed a couple of steps behind the Colonel, whose quick thinking by parking his car directly in front of the gate had ensured the visitor could not leave the yard. She was there in plain sight now, trying to heave up the ramp to the trailer all on her own.

'Don't struggle with that alone,' said Doubler, worry breaking out on his face.

'Oh, don't fall for that,' muttered Maxwell. 'She's as strong as an old ox.' He approached her, speaking sternly. 'Now, Mrs Mitchell. I'll say it one more time. *You can't have the donkey.* You haven't got any grass for him. He needs looking after, food and water, and proper care. He needs all of these things to live.'

The woman had wrestled the trailer closed and was now trying to scramble up into the cab of the truck as if to make a getaway. She reached in behind the driver's seat and tugged out a plastic milk crate, which she upturned to use as a step.

'Looking for these, Mrs Mitchell?'

Maxwell waved the truck keys, a weighty-looking bottle-cap opener acting as the keyring.

'You can't drive that truck any further. It's theft. But the owner has promised not to press charges if we return the truck and the trailer back to him in one piece.

'You'll never guess what she did,' said the

126

Colonel, turning to Doubler with a wry smile on his face. 'She stole it off the forecourt of the petrol station. The owner had gone to pay and the next thing he knew, she was driving it off at breakneck speed. As soon as the police took the call, they gave me a holler. Knew where she'd be heading.'

'She's done this before, then?'

'Oh, has she! Many times. The RSPCA removed the donkey from her care a long time ago. She was keeping him in her garage, would you believe it? And now she tries to steal him back at every opportunity. She doesn't even have a driving licence. She just waits to see an appropriate vehicle and commandeers it. Once, she turned up in a piano removal company's HGV. The piano was still in it.'

Mrs Mitchell was glowering at the Colonel but seemed quite uninterested by this discussion of her past misdemeanours. Nonplussed, she turned and leant against the vehicle, looking off in the direction of the fields beyond.

Doubler lowered his voice to ensure Mrs Mitchell couldn't hear their conversation. He nodded in her general direction. 'So why doesn't she come at night? She could probably just walk out with him, couldn't she?'

'Well, that's it — the donkey won't go to her. Won't go anywhere near her. She has to wait until she can rope in a newcomer or a stranger to give her a hand.'

They stopped as the sound of a police siren interrupted their conversation, but the siren faded as it passed the farm, racing elsewhere.

'Will they arrest her?'

'Heavens, no. No point. I'll take her home now and I'll explain to her all over again why she can't keep the donkey. She thinks he has been stolen from her. Gone a bit soft in the head, this one.'

Doubler looked carefully at Mrs Mitchell but could detect no softness in her scowl. Her elbows were askance, her pointed chin was jutting out beneath thin, pursed lips, and her eyes shot hatred in his direction. No, no softness, just hardness and angles. And yet, something tender spoke to him from beneath her frame because he felt a surge of pity and sadness wash over him, catching him completely off guard. Rather than feeling humiliated that she had compromised him on his first day at the job, he felt like he had glimpsed humankind for the first time in his life. He turned, confused and oddly ashamed, and headed into the Portakabin, leaving Maxwell, who clearly had a better grip on the situation than Doubler had, to return the trailer to its rightful owner and Mrs Mitchell to her home, where no doubt Maxwell would give her a stern rebuke.

As he was about to leave, with Mrs Mitchell safely buckled into his passenger seat, Maxwell returned to the Portakabin, poking his head round the door to address Doubler.

'We have regular get-togethers. Means we can have some off-the-record discussions — you know, keep each other abreast of developments. Avoid this sort of kerfuffle. Might be a good idea for you to join?'

'Well, of course. It would be my pleasure, and I'm very keen to meet the rest of the team.'

'Good. That's settled, then. We take it in turns to host — you can see the logic in that?'

'Yes, wonderful. Makes perfect sense.' Doubler was thrilled by the Colonel's conciliatory tone and was at pains to ensure his own was equally positive after such a poor start.

'So, next up is you. Would have been Gracie so it makes sense for you to take her place. Can't really deviate from the rota without all sorts of further repercussions. I assume that's fine?'

Doubler swallowed and nodded. 'Thank you,' he said, assessing the Colonel's brusque manner and deciding the request was probably issued as an honour.

'Don't thank me — thank Gracie. It was her suggestion.'

Doubler swallowed and nodded, processing several complicated feelings of gratitude and shame. A kind parting gesture from the Colonel rescued him from complete despair, but it wasn't quite enough to stop him wondering if he'd been made a fool of by not one person but two. 'Or three if you count the donkey,' he mumbled. He consoled himself a little with the knowledge that Mrs Millwood would surely find this story entertaining and he locked into his memory the finer details that would help bring the tale alive when they next spoke.

He listened to the sound of Maxwell's car retreat once again and the silence of the Portakabin surrounded him. His heart had been racing, he realized, and now he steadied his breathing in the silence. He replayed the last couple of hours in his mind. Three moments stood out in his memory: the Colonel's bombastic introduction, the donkey's terror and his own short-lived pride. But it was Mrs Mitchell's hateful glare that had wormed its way into his long-term memory and found a little unused pocket of his brain in which to fester and brood. And to top it off, he'd just agreed to entertain the whole team at Mirth Farm. Doubler sighed heavily and wondered whether this was what Mrs Millwood had in mind when she and Midge had coerced him into this nonsense.

# 13

Once again Doubler was pacing in the general vicinity of the telephone, having cut short his morning rounds for fear of getting delayed. This morning, for the first time in decades, he'd made his tea in a mug, without bothering to prepare a pot, and he'd eaten a biscuit standing by the Aga, unable to commit to sitting down for a break. He pounced on the telephone as it rang.

'So, how did you get on, Mr Doubler?'

Mrs Millwood sounded mischievous, as if she might already have heard of Doubler's misfortune, but he launched into his account enthusiastically, nonetheless.

'I think it would be fair to say it went as terribly as you could possibly imagine. An utter disaster.'

'Oh, Mr Doubler, I turn my back for one moment and it's complete chaos! What on earth could have happened?'

'I nearly allowed Mrs Mitchell to steal the donkey.'

'Nearly? But she didn't actually take him?'

'No, fortunately the Colonel returned in the nick of time and was there to stop her.'

'Well, then you didn't utterly fail. It could have been much worse.'

'That's a very generous and positive viewpoint,' acknowledged Doubler gratefully. 'But I don't think the Colonel was impressed.'

'It's not his job to be impressed,' countered Mrs Millwood. 'It's his job to impress you. And I certainly wouldn't worry about it: a close shave with Mrs Mitchell has happened to most of us. Consider it part of the initiation.'

'That does seem to be the case, though why the risk she poses isn't spelt out more clearly seems a bit of a mystery to me. There's a whole manual in the office dedicated to the fair disbursement and replenishment of sugar lumps, carefully worked out on the basis of numbers of hours volunteered. Effectively I am entitled, if I am to follow the manual to the letter of the law, to one sugar lump per hour worked, which if I were to take sugar in my tea, almost certainly wouldn't be enough.'

'Oh, you're making that up!'

'I am not — it's there in a file on the shelf. Sugar has its own ring folder. Believe me, I read every single word in every single file and Mrs Mitchell barely gets a mention. The Colonel's behind the sugar-lump legislation, of that I'm certain. It's just a shame he wasn't so thorough when it came to the welfare of the donkey or the threat posed by the utterly daft Mrs Mitchell.'

'Ah well, I suspect that's the crux of it. Is Mrs Mitchell actually mad? Clinically insane? Because nobody in the team would want to prejudice a mad person. We're all either a bit mad ourselves or we are capable of becoming so in the very near future. Perhaps we are all putting off the moment we contemplate Maddie Mitchell's mental state and therefore our own. I like to apply the mad, bad or sad rule of thumb.

I'd only be concerned about the 'bad'.'

'Well, I'm not really asking for a clinical diagnosis. I just think a notice on the wall — maybe *each* wall — saying, 'Under no circumstances give Mrs Mitchell the donkey,' would suffice. More useful than the 'Manual of Fair Sugar Disbursement'. Would have saved me and everyone else a spot of bother.'

'Well, it sounds like they left you to it, did they? If no one else was there to show you the ropes, then I don't think you can accept personal responsibility, can you?'

'That's very true, Mrs Millwood. I'm not a psychic. And I consider it a great shame that no one was there to show me the ropes. It would have been nice to meet the team.'

'Careful what you wish for!' quipped Mrs Millwood with a throaty chuckle.

'Really? Are there characters I should be wary of? Surely they must all be good types? Bad 'uns don't volunteer for that sort of work, do they?'

'Us oldies all have our own reasons for volunteering and you don't have to scratch very far below the surface to see the motives aren't always entirely altruistic.'

'What about the Colonel? He's a bit terrifying, but he seems a good enough chap. He's the only one I've met, mind you.'

'Well,' said Mrs Millwood, adopting her most conspiratorial tone so that Doubler could almost see her leaning in to him as she stirred her tea. 'The Colonel needs to be in charge of something, doesn't he, or he'd just drop dead of the shock. He's your typical 'leader-in-crisis

133

oldie'. He led a platoon, or a whole army, as far as I know — lots of responsibility, anyway, and lots of respect from the troops, the type of respect that is earned through years of effort but not necessarily by the people who are there to bear the brunt of his command. The new recruits just have to automatically respect him. That's a powerful thing to have on your CV, automatic respect. Could be intoxicating in the wrong hands. So then you retire and you go off home to civilian life and you've got your retirement mapped out, you know exactly how it's going to be, and you've worked hard for that relaxation. You are going to kick back and enjoy yourself.' Mrs Millwood paused, perhaps for a sip of water, perhaps to check who else might be listening in the ward.

She continued, 'But on the very first morning, your alarm goes off at 7 a.m., and by five past seven, you realize that you have absolutely *no* role to play. Your wife, who you assumed didn't say boo to a goose, has got the rest of the workday organized and she has absolutely no respect for you or your colonel-ing abilities. You try barking a few instructions and she silences you with one raised eyebrow. Her look says it all: 'That might have got you by in your last job, but I run the show here and you're going to have to start as a rookie all over again.'' Mrs Millwood laughed delightedly at the thought.

'And then, the real shock of it all is there is actually quite a lot to do and she does it all effortlessly as well as a thousand other things. You thought she was a stay-at-home wife, but

134

she just never seems to stay at home. In fact, she never seems to stay in any one place for very long. Everything happens with miraculous ease, but in the meantime, she's visiting the sick and the elderly, volunteering in the hospice, helping out at the local Women's Institute, improving lives immeasurably, and then there's your tea, magically, effortlessly on the table.

'And our Colonel? He's redundant. Defunct. Not only does he have no troops and no respect, he hasn't got a clue how to *do* anything. A lifetime of being in charge has meant that he has absolutely no capabilities whatsoever. You can make fun of the old gentleman staring blankly at the washing machine, entirely unable to decipher its codes, but it is actually very disabling to realize towards the end of your days that you are almost entirely incapable of fending for yourself. If your wife dies, you wouldn't be able to survive. So it's find someone or something to lead and leave your wife to her own devices or drop dead of the shock of it.'

Doubler roared with laughter, the sound restocking Mirth Farm with joy. 'What a colourful image you paint, Mrs Millwood! And that's how he came to volunteer?'

'Oh, very probably. I don't know the ins and outs, but he's representative of a million leaders who volunteer not to help others but to ensure they have some people to boss around. Without that, without some minions, they are nothing; they have no definition, no purpose.'

'But you're not going to tell me that you're one of Maxwell's minions? I don't see *you* as a

135

minion, Mrs Millwood.'

'I get his measure and for him to feel important is of greater value to his welfare than would be the equal and opposite act of me undermining him, so I go along with him. I let him feel important: it's good for his health. And it can't be easy for him. Adjusting to civilian life must be awfully lonely, and I expect admitting that is nigh on impossible for a man like the Colonel.'

'You're very wise, Mrs Millwood. So what can you tell me about the others?'

'Well, there's Paula. She and I would not be the best of friends in the real world; it's the animal shelter that's thrown us together. Let's just say she wouldn't exactly *fit* in my knitting circle.'

Doubler, who was used to hearing Mrs Millwood deliver accounts of the very best version of everyone, was rather enjoying her more salacious side.

'Go on.'

'She's a terrible *flirt*.' Mrs Millwood whispered the last word.

'She is?'

'Oh, incorrigible. It's always one disaster or another with her. She's forever looking for help when she's almost certainly quite capable of looking after herself. It's either her lawnmower or a wasps' nest or something else entirely that causes the latest crisis. She's almost incapable of coming into the office and putting herself at somebody else's service. Instead it's 'Oh, you'll never guess what's happened now' or 'I'm at my

136

wits' end' and the men are fussing round her like bees round a honeypot. One or other of the gentlemen will be hopping in her car to go and sort out her latest crisis before you know it.

'I've offered before, you know. She came in looking all forlorn because her cat had brought a mouse in and it was alive under the kitchen cupboards with her cat pacing up and down, and she didn't want to flush it out into the jaws of her cat, but she didn't want it to make a home there feeding on crumbs and electric cables, so she needed one of the *brave men* to go and deal with it.' Mrs Millwood paused to catch her breath. ''Honestly!' I said. 'Oh, come on, Paula, a mouse? Really? Let me come and deal with it for you,' and she gave me a look, Mr Doubler, a look that I've never quite forgotten.'

'What sort of a look?'

'A look that was there at its most basic level to silence me, but it was just much more complex than that. A look that suggested I might be somehow betraying the whole of the female race — that somehow if I let on that women could actually take care of something for themselves, then men might never fall for her simpering charm again.'

'Golly, that's a very complicated look to convey.'

'Yet it was *unmistakable*. She sort of narrowed her eyes but managed to make them bulge at the same time. Most disconcerting.'

'So why does she volunteer, do you think?'

'Oh, most definitely for the social opportunities. She likes to be around men, and she likes to make herself vulnerable for them.'

'So she hasn't got a husband or a partner?'

'No. I don't quite know what's going on there because I'm sure she could. She's a little on the large side, but that can be quite fetching, I think, when you reach a certain age. No one wants a woman who might snap. The men certainly seem to find her fetching, at any rate.'

Doubler sensed her possessiveness, which in turn sent a little vial of jealousy coursing through his own veins. (Whose attention was Mrs Millwood trying to guard? Why would she resent the attention that Paula seemed to be getting? Doubler's mind raced.)

'But then, I suppose people like Paula make people like the Colonel feel like they have some sort of purpose, so perhaps she's performing a greater good.'

'Well, we all need somebody to make us feel purposeful,' ventured Doubler uncertainly.

'Oh, Mr Doubler, not you. I've never known a man so driven.'

'Are you mocking me?'

'No! Your work is *vital*, and what's more, no one else can do it because no one else has your vision. And you're working to the most important deadline of all.'

'April?'

'No. The *ultimate* deadline. No one else is going to finish your work off for you when you're dead and buried. It's a race against time, isn't it? If you die and the Great Potato Experiment goes unrecorded or unrecognized, that's your whole life's work down the drain. Whoosh.'

138

Doubler reeled at the significance of his own undertaking. He felt something akin to vertigo grab first at his knees and then somewhere deep in his belly as he saw his own imminent death and his eternal damnation, where his failures both taunted and haunted him. But even as he felt himself plummet, his brain registered another sensation, a glow of satisfaction that clamoured noisily for recognition, because, surely, hidden beneath the possibility of failure, the compliment he had been paid was unmistakable. He packed away both responses to examine at a later moment, fearful Mrs Millwood would lose her momentum.

'And what about the others? What about Derek, or Mabel and Olive?' he pressed on, hoping to cement her to the phone.

Mrs Millwood was not so easily detained, though. 'I've got to go. I'm being frowned at. I'll give you a tinkle tomorrow.'

'Right you are, Mrs Millwood.' Respectful of the time she had to chat, he let her go, but rather than rushing out to his potatoes to deliver his promise, he wondered at the choice of Mrs Millwood's words. She had called his work 'vital' and 'important'. She didn't seem to think that growing potatoes was menial. He wondered whether he could allow himself to imagine she even *admired* him for his sense of purpose.

Doubler felt a new emotion, one he had buried many years ago. Doubler felt proud.

# 14

Grove Farm, where the animal shelter was housed, occupied an inconsequential dip within a peaceful valley. The farm was separated from Doubler's land by the town, an alarming new bypass, a supermarket and pet superstore, and the burgeoning swathe of land owned by Peele, the potato baron. Grove Farm had once been much more significant in farming terms and could even claim prosperity, but over the years the scale on which a farm might trade profitably had shifted and there had come a time when the worth of the land to a bigger concern was disproportionately valuable in comparison to the decreasing living that could be scratched from the soil. Olive and Don, the farm's owners, had sold the vast majority of their land to Peele, thus cementing his position as the biggest potato farmer in the region and consigning Olive and her husband to live out their days as hobby farmers. This transaction could have represented a perfectly choreographed final dance, removing many of the strains of farm life while providing a comfortable nest egg and keeping the happy couple's feet firmly planted in the soil for their latter years. But, as many farmers will testify, things don't always go to plan. Don had dropped dead, leaving Olive to stare at a very blank canvas featuring one hundred acres of effort, a farmhouse riddled with regret and a future saddled with grief.

Don had been a good man and he had lived a good life. He had exhibited exactly the right blend of practical skills and sensitivity to be both an excellent farmer and a caring husband. Olive shared these qualities, which meant that the couple had been blissfully harmonious. It also meant that she refused to go to pieces on his death and coped admirably, except on those days when she was crippled by sadness.

Grove Farm had been home to the animal shelter for a number of years. It had begun as an entirely symbiotic collaboration, dreamt up and executed by Colonel Maxwell. The shelter used the stables, grazed the fields and gave the farm purpose. The arrangement distracted Olive from her heart-wrenching loneliness and gave her some shape to her week, which she desperately craved. But over the last twelve months or so, Olive had been called upon less and less, and now she couldn't quite shake the feeling that she was being ostracized on her own turf. The only regular interaction she had with the shelter these days was every Friday, when Maxwell and perhaps Derek or one of the other team members would visit to brief her on the week's activities. As the only contact she could rely on, these short meetings had become inordinately important to Olive.

Now, Olive answered the door to Derek and Maxwell as she did at the end of every week. On this and every other occasion, her heart raced a little as she rushed to let her visitors in, a small charge of adrenaline surging through her veins in anticipation of something unfamiliar to break the monotony of the day. Each week, as now, she felt herself deflate as the Colonel brushed past her impatiently, looking like a man who was performing a slightly repugnant ritual he barely had time for.

'Reporting for duty,' said Maxwell, taking off his flat cap and doffing it grandly.

Derek hung back by a couple of paces but was careful to look Olive in the eye as he shook her hand and smiled sympathetically. Derek was in awe of the army man and his commanding manner, but he was simultaneously embarrassed by the relentlessness of the Colonel's need to deploy it. In order to show respect to the Colonel while signalling affinity with Olive, Derek set his face somewhere neutral, right at the centre of the range of emotions that struggled within him.

Inexplicably, Olive was terrified of the Colonel and was so keen to please him that her vulnerability rendered her completely powerless in his company. She felt no need to impress Derek and liked him instinctively but paid scant attention to the development of this friendship, though it would have required very little effort on her part to turn it into something valuable. This was a grave oversight, as Derek had the disposition to offer Olive all that she required from a friendship. As it was, the Colonel's compulsion to be at the centre of the lives of all of these people prevented those in his orbit from ever quite feeling the tug of each other's gravitational pull.

The Colonel accepted a glass of squash and helped himself to a couple of custard creams from the biscuit tin while refusing the seat he had been offered. He examined the biscuits with contempt and was unable to disguise the fact he believed them to be paltry payment for the extra time he took to debrief Olive at the end of each week.

He rocked back and forth on his heels while sifting through the week's news to distil only the facts he thought were relevant to Olive. 'There is a new face on board. You'll see him around, I'm sure. He's the temporary replacement for Gracie. Quiet chap, Doubler the potato farmer. Doubt you'll even notice he's here.'

Olive recalled the moment earlier that week when Doubler had knocked on the door and the regret she'd felt when she missed opening the door to him by just a few seconds. 'Yes, I'd heard he was to join us and saw him arrive. He's supposed to be a fascinating man. It will be a pleasure to meet him. I really don't mind the interruption at all, of course — I like the company, and I'd welcome the diversion.' Olive loathed herself for looking at the Colonel quite so beseechingly but found it quite impossible to otherwise convey the depth of her feelings in the short time she was allocated. She heard herself whimpering and liked herself even less.

'Fascinating? Is that how they describe him? Hard to say what's fascinating about him. You won't get much out of that one — he likes to keep himself to himself — but between you, me and the gatepost, there's no real point getting to know him. I'm not sure he would have been my first choice, but I took him on as a favour for Gracie. Seemed important to her. But I doubt he'll be around for too long. I definitely get the impression he sees himself as a temporary fix, filling in for Gracie until we can get ourselves a more permanent solution.'

'How's Gracie doing? What do you hear?' Olive looked to Derek, knowing the two were close, but the Colonel was quicker with his response.

'Not good, I'm afraid. Didn't take to the chemo — her system rejected it entirely apparently — so they're keeping her in a while longer until they get to grips with the situation. Gather they're deciding on the best course of action. Poor prognosis, I fear. When the men in white coats are simply waiting for you to get well enough to send you home with no further treatment, that can't be good news.'

Derek was quick to interject when he saw Olive's crestfallen face. 'It's really not that clear-cut — we are waiting to hear more news, and you know what a fighter she is. I'll see her at the weekend, so I'll send your best, shall I?'

'Do, please. Gosh, I do hope she isn't feeling too miserable. I just wish I could help.'

The Colonel was checking his watch and rattling his car keys in his pocket. He was already making moves to leave.

Olive was not yet ready to be plunged back into solitude. She choked on her words in her desperation to tether the Colonel to the kitchen table with them. 'How are the animals? What's the grazing like? Is there anything major to be done before the spring?' The wretchedness was evident in her voice. She so wanted these men to sit down, to talk about their work at the shelter, to consult with her. She wanted to contribute, to suggest changes, to even make some decisions perhaps. But more than all of that, she wanted a conversation that lasted beyond ten minutes on a Friday.

'Got it all under control, I think. Animals are much the same; it's a shocking time of year for placements. But the week wasn't entirely dull. Damn near lost the donkey!'

'Percy?' Olive's hands shot to her face. 'Is he OK?'

'Oh yes. Doubler, the new chap, nearly handed the poor blighter over to Mrs Mitchell. Within an hour of being on the job!'

Olive laughed. The thought of Mrs Mitchell getting the better of the new man appealed to her and this new development immediately blotted out her earlier feeling of despair.

The Colonel was less amused. 'Can't leave this place for a moment without near calamity bestowing us. Wish I had a better team of men sometimes — they're just not adequately trained.'

'That's a little rich, Colonel.' Derek knew he was one of the men the Colonel was talking about and knew, too, that the Colonel distrusted him and wouldn't have had him in his team in the army, either. 'We're volunteers, giving our time freely. I think we do a reasonable job under the circumstances. And we are all very keen to learn.'

'Volunteering does not excuse you from meeting high standards. If anything, it expects more of you. We won two world wars on the strength of our volunteers. You wouldn't catch those fine men handing over a donkey to a stranger.'

'But at least those soldiers had some training,' said Derek, who felt defensive and affronted. Surely if the Colonel was going to appoint himself as their leader, he should be responsible for their shortcomings too? Derek appealed to the Colonel with as much force as he could muster, keen not to be put down with such contempt in front of Olive. But even as he spoke, he wondered who he was defending, himself, the rest of the team or the new chap.

'Quite, quite. Well spoken. Leadership. Always comes down to that. And resources.' The Colonel shook his head, dismayed by the paucity of both the leadership and resources he had available to him. 'Got to be off, Olive. Plenty to be done.'

Olive knew that by prolonging their stay she was prolonging her agony, but the thought of the empty days ahead of her were more terrifying still. The desperation she so despised in herself was there on her face and in her voice, yet she couldn't stop herself. 'We must be due another get-together surely? It was Gracie's turn to host us next, wasn't it?'

'Yes, shame. Tended to put on a passable spread. Damned shame that won't be happening.' The Colonel looked at his watch again, as if the passing of time only added to his regret.

146

Only a minute or two had elapsed since his last glance at the time.

'Perhaps I could host you all here? I'd be very happy to.' Olive looked hopeful and allowed a tremor of excitement to creep into her voice.

'No need, no need for that at all,' said the Colonel. Nonetheless he briefly reappraised the space around him as a potential venue and, fixing his attention on the disappointing custard creams, quashed the idea as quickly as it has evolved. 'New chap is taking it on. Nothing like throwing him in at the deep end.'

Olive's face lit up. 'Oh, at Mirth Farm? Lovely. I've always wanted to go up there. The view must be amazing. You can probably see all this land, I expect.'

'Of course, you would be welcome to join us, but don't put yourself out. It's a bit of a trek, and I know you're not a confident driver, so somebody would only have to sort your lift out. Why not wait to see if he's a stayer? Could be that he doesn't stick around for more than a week.'

The trouble with the Colonel, thought Olive begrudgingly, was that he was cruel but usually right. Somebody might well have to give her a lift and then she would be an inconvenience to one of the other volunteers. And it was true that the new man was unproven yet. Her enthusiasm faltered.

'I could go another time,' she said sadly. And then she remembered some gossip she had heard at the butcher's quite recently. 'Though I heard that Mirth Farm is to go up for sale soon. Peele is to buy it apparently.'

The Colonel stopped his excruciatingly awkward shuffle towards the front door, genuinely interested in something Olive had to say for the first time since he'd arrived. 'Is that right? Well, Peele is buying up everything, so that's not a surprise, but Doubler didn't mention any change of plans. How reliable is your source?'

'It was Ernie who told me, and he knows most of everything that goes on around here. Certainly in the farmers' circles.'

'Yes, that butcher has a knack for picking up knowledge ahead of the crowd. Mind you, he doesn't hold onto it for long. He'll readily wrap a half-pound of sausages in gossip.'

Olive managed a small smile and knew she had been defeated. 'I'll never get up there once Peele owns it. That might well have been my last chance.'

Derek, exasperated, intervened even though he risked irritating the Colonel.

'Don't be silly, Olive — I'll pick you up. Come along to this next one, of course you must. It's nice to see the whole gang together, and who knows who will be around in a month's time. I've never been more certain that nothing's certain.'

Olive looked at Derek and nodded her thanks. She was grateful to him, of course she was. He was kind to look out for her, and he often did, even if it meant standing up to the Colonel. But it was the Colonel whose approval she sought and it was from the Colonel that she really

wanted an invitation. She was suddenly irrationally irritated with Derek for stopping the Colonel
from extending the invitation himself. Now she
had to go with or without his consent. She
turned sharply away from Derek, whose kindness
still hung in the air.

'Well, Colonel, I suppose that's that. I shall
come with Derek and join you after all. Perhaps
then we might have a bit more time to discuss
the plans for next year. You're always in such a
rush.'

'Never more than today, I'm afraid. Frightful
hurry. Come on, Derek, let's be off. Enough
dilly-dallying.'

Olive went ahead to open the door for them,
smiling a brave smile as the Colonel pushed past
and waving softly to Derek. She shut the door
behind them both and, leaning heavily on the
closed door, squeezed her eyes tightly shut to
stop the tears forming.

# 15

Doubler's optimism was continuing to flourish, bolstered by his regular conversations with Mrs Millwood and the curious intimacy that the telephone had brought to their relationship. He had enjoyed a perfect morning. He'd made a round of the farm, his binoculars slung on one shoulder, noticing details he'd never stopped to examine before. Spring was already fighting the elements, wresting itself through the hard ground, bursting out in small frenzies of noisy clamour. Doubler usually only focused on his potato crop, discounting all other signs of life as irrelevant to his cause, but his heart was full of a renewed energy that perfectly matched the deadened hedgerows' determination to flourish once more.

On his way back to the house, Doubler popped into the distillery and stood in the half-light for a minute or two, breathing in the scent of the darkness. Enlivened by his morning's walk, an unbidden thought popped into his mind, first as an idle whim but almost immediately evolving into something the shape of a plan, with definitive edges and weight to its structure. Closing the door behind him, he switched on the light and crossed in front of the distillation equipment to the storeroom beyond. In there, against the far wall, were half a dozen ancient oak barrels, darkened with the stains of their past use. He moved some boxes aside and examined them more closely, running his thumb across a hoop and pressing his nose to the cask, inhaling deeply. The heady amalgam of wood sugars and toasted char was still there, preserved within the staves.

'Barley,' he said, addressing them. 'I wonder.' He stayed there for a few more minutes, allowing the thought to develop further before carefully locking up behind him and crossing the yard, stopping only briefly to gesture towards the security camera with a confident thumbs-up as he passed.

He had taken his time this morning, so he had barely brewed a pot of tea before the phone rang. He left it, stewing, beside the Aga and hurried to the hall.

'So, where were we?' Mrs Millwood asked as he put the receiver to his ear.

With an indulgent sigh of happiness, Doubler leant against the wall, steadying himself for a lengthy conversation.

'We'd got to the bottom of the Colonel,' said Doubler, ticking off the volunteers from a mental list.

'That, Mr Doubler, is not an image I want to dwell on.'

Doubler chuckled. 'And we've had our fill of Paula the flirt.'

'Well, quite. We've said all that needs to be said about Paula the flirt. So it's time to tell you about Mabel.'

'Is she a terrible flirt, too?'

'Oh no. Mabel is far too busy fixing the

world's problems to flirt.'

'So she's a bit of a do-gooder, is she?'

'Oh my goodness, yes. They invented the term for her. And to make her even more insufferable, she *always* has an answer.'

Constantly wary of criticism, desperate for praise and vigilant for either from Mrs Millwood, Doubler felt a jolt of concern. *He* always had an answer: he'd been told that enough times in the past. But he always assumed that was a statement of fact, not a criticism. 'Like *me*, you mean? I think you've accused *me* of that, haven't you?'

'No. You only have the answer to the things you know. The things about which you are very certain. She has an answer to everything. There is literally nothing she doesn't know.'

'Literally?'

'I mean it as the word intends. Literally. She knows something about everything and she normally has personal experience, so she can relate to any issue imaginable. Her uncle or her brother or her neighbour or someone always had the exact same thing but *worse*, so she knows exactly what you're talking about.'

'She's an empathizer.'

'Worse. She's a *compulsive* empathizer.'

'She sounds like a hoot!'

'Well, rather surprisingly, she's actually quite a useful person to have around sometimes because the truth of the matter is, she really does know all these people and she has had all this relevant experience. And if it sounds implausible that a woman whose whole life has been spent in a benign market town should be quite so well endowed with knowledge and experience, then I think I know why.'

'Why?'

'Because she makes absolutely everything her business. She's in people's houses at a whiff of scandal or intrigue. 'Let me pop in and make us a cup of tea, shall I?' Code for 'Tell me everything you know while it's still fresh in all its gory detail.' Then she takes her newly harvested gossip and she drip-feeds it to her circle at her own pace. She's the self-appointed disperser of scandal and human tragedy. 'Now, that's very interesting that your son-in-law got caught in bed with the interior designer, but don't go telling everyone — they'll only gossip,' she'll say. And then the next week someone will say, 'Oh, I'm thinking of booking that nice Dionne the interior designer,' and she'll drop her voice to a whisper and say, 'I wouldn't if I were you . . . ' and you're left wondering whether it's the curtains or the character you should be concerned about. But you won't get the full story, not until you've got some gossip of your own that's worthy of a trade.'

'I'm going to mind my manners around her . . . As you know, I'm nervous enough of fuelling the tittle-tattle already.'

'What's interesting, though, Mr Doubler, is that people do sort of open up to her. Even though they know she's in everyone else's business, too. It's like she hypnotizes them and then extracts their darkest secrets.'

'But you say she has her uses?'

'Oh heavens, yes. Someone drops a cat off, trying to be a bit discreet, saying it belonged to a deceased neighbour. Most of us will just take the cat and get them to sign the disclaimer, but Mabel will have them crying into a handkerchief within minutes. It's quite an impressive skill. And it's *never* the neighbour's cat, you know. Normally it's the subject of a bitter custody battle.'

'I had no idea there was so much going on in that Portakabin. Perhaps I got off lightly with my Mrs Mitchell incident.'

'That poor Mrs Mitchell,' replied Mrs Millwood passionately. 'As far as I can tell, no one has ever worked out what makes that woman tick. She's a genuine enigma. Cruel to animals, no doubt about it — what she did to that donkey was just shocking — and yet there's something that seems to make it almost *forgivable*. I just can't put my finger on it. We've all tried talking to her, but she's got a poisonous tongue on her. Maxwell says she cannot safely be engaged in conversation.'

Doubler tried to imagine the Colonel engaging anyone in conversation. 'Maxwell is an army man. I'm not sure conversation is one of his specialisms.'

Mrs Millwood sighed. 'You might be right, I suppose. I know he has our best interests at heart, but I can't help wondering if a different approach might uncover a quite *different* Mrs Mitchell.'

'What sort of approach did you have in mind,

154

Mrs M? One where I arm myself with a cattle prod?'

'No. Actually, quite the opposite. I think we're probably all guilty of responding to cruelty with more cruelty. We don't like what we see, so we're quick to judge, and blinded by our righteous indignation, we believe our own response is appropriate. But maybe we just don't ask the right questions.'

'Such as?'

'What if Mrs Mitchell's cruelty to the donkey is a response to cruelty she's been shown? What if *she's* responding to cruelty with cruelty? And then, jumping to conclusions, we do the same to her, and so the cycle continues? What if somebody then sees us being cruel to *her* and they then judge *us* and treat *us* with cruelty? Cruelty could spread like a disease, couldn't it?'

'Like a human blight!' agreed Doubler enthusiastically, understanding exactly how cruelty might spread. 'If you don't stop it in its tracks, it will spread from the leaves to the stems, from the stems to the tubers, from the tubers to the soil, Mrs M.'

'Exactly. And back again, Mr Doubler. From the soil to the seeds.'

Doubler spent a moment contemplating blight in its perpetual motion of destruction. He'd spent most of his adult life thinking about how to break that cycle, but the remedies he had to hand weren't suitable for Mrs Mitchell. 'I understand *potatoes*, Mrs M. I think I'm possibly in a unique position to comment on *their* diseases. But I'm less experienced with people. How do we stop the *cruelty* disease spreading?'

'Perhaps we could interrupt the cycle with kindness?' Mrs Millwood suggested.

Doubler frowned as he pictured it and then shook his head. 'Kindness? It wouldn't work with potatoes, Mrs M.'

'There's nobody kinder to potatoes than you, Mr Doubler. If you showed yourself as much kindness as you show your potatoes, you'd be a substantially happier man.'

Doubler filed this thought away for later inspection, asking instead, 'Have you tried responding to Mrs Mitchell with kindness yourself?'

'I've talked to the Colonel about it, but he says we'll only get caught in friendly fire.'

Doubler could hear the frustration in Mrs Millwood's voice and wanted to banish it as much as he'd ever wanted to banish the blight from Mirth Farm. 'I will certainly give it a try, Mrs M. I can't imagine getting another chance to speak to her myself — I doubt she'll be back for the donkey on my watch — but I'll keep the idea up my sleeve. And in the meantime, you'd advise me to avoid Mabel, do you think? Not get hypnotized by her?'

'I don't think you have anything she wants. So feel free to mingle.'

'I'm quite offended. I have plenty of dark secrets, I'm up to my ears in intrigue, and I've got more than my fair share of skeletons in my closet.'

'But she doesn't *know* that. And besides, you

rarely trade in speculation. You're a fact merchant these days.'

'A fat merchant?' Doubler looked down at the way he was leaning against the wall and drew himself a little taller, breathing in and checking he could draw his stomach with him.

'A *fact* merchant. *Fact.*'

Doubler was perplexed. 'I am?'

'You deal in facts. You only speak when you know what you're talking about.'

'Ahh,' Doubler agreed. 'That's probably true. I'm not a big fan of speculation. Terrible waste of time and energy. And often I've found it to be a huge source of grief and unnecessary anguish.'

'Yes, I don't imagine you're much of a speculator. You're exactly as I described, a fact merchant.'

'Most gossip is merely somebody else's speculation.'

'And most speculation is merely someone else's gossip,' countered Mrs Millwood.

'So I'm of no use to her now, but what if Mabel got a whiff of my shady double life?'

'It's not going to happen. You're a closed book. Nobody will think you have anything remotely interesting to contribute.'

'But I do! I have interesting views on many interesting subjects,' Doubler exclaimed, partly in jest, but also with a desire to be held in slightly higher esteem by Mrs Millwood, who might just have described him as boring.

'You don't have views; you barely have opinions. You assume when you speak that not only do you speak the truth but you speak

157

everyone else's version of the truth.'

'That's because I will have spent a great deal of time considering the options and will only offer an opinion when I am absolutely certain of its veracity.'

'You are a very certain man.'

'But I wasn't, was I? There was a time when I knew nothing. At least, I'd bumbled happily along and then, post-Marie, my world flipped and the people closest to me, the only significant people I had in my life as such, behaved with such unexpectedness that I felt unable to be certain of anything.'

Doubler considered this some more, while Mrs Millwood waited patiently, allowing him to recall and give name to the heartbreak. 'Climbing out of the dark chasm was a rebirth. By the time I was able to function, I had made myself forget everything I had ever known because, really, the memories I had of my pre-Marie or my post-Marie life were no longer reliable. I could not count upon them as a true reflection of things past.'

'Because you didn't see it coming?'

'No, I didn't see it coming. It meant that everything before was a lie and that every happy memory was incorrectly recorded.'

'And when you climbed out of the chasm? What happened then?'

'Well, I was in the chasm for a while, wasn't I? By the time I came out, I had pretty much erased those memories. I was like a newborn baby. And from then I just dealt with certainty. This potato is better than that one. There's no opinion, no subjectivity. I had scientific data to back it up.'

'So now you're a closed book, which has its advantages. Nothing for Mabel to extract.'

'I don't know how I feel about that. I think you're making me sound rather *dull*.'

'Who wants to be *interesting*? Nothing good ever came from *interesting*. You should be satisfied with dull but *good*. I'd certainly settle for that.'

Doubler would have liked to have put the conversation on hold while he decided what she meant by that. Did she mean she would settle for those qualities within herself, or did she mean she'd settle *down* with somebody able to demonstrate those qualities? But there was no time to interrogate the meaning further, no time to push her for clarification. Mrs Millwood was already continuing at her usual rapid pace. 'And besides, dull is good if you want to protect yourself from the likes of Mabel.'

'But you don't think I'm dull, Mrs Millwood? You'd settle for — '

'You dull? Heavens, no! I know the dark secrets your cellar holds. I know all about the shady double life you lead. And I know about your past and your rebirth.'

'This is all quite true, Mrs Millwood. You do know me well. You're possibly the only person on the planet who knows all of it.'

Mrs Millwood snorted down the phone, a sound that reflected her disbelief. 'That sounds like you're putting all your eggs in one basket, Mr Doubler. And this basket definitely isn't up to holding something as delicate as eggs. I think you need a contingency plan. What about the kids? How open are you with them? They know what you went through, and they know about your business matters, I assume?'

'Of course not! They have their own version of their childhood. They haven't had to rewrite it, so they know their past, not mine. And as far my gradual infiltration into the murky underworld of business, they know absolutely nothing of that. Both children are very satisfied with their dull father and his dull potatoes. They don't need to know anything more than that. Julian particularly thrives on the knowledge of my pitiful life. It helps him to feel successful. The less he thinks of me, the more he thinks of himself.'

'That is a rather sad outlook. The thing is, Doubler, by not being honest about all you have achieved, they don't really understand how *extraordinary* you are. You are not only at the forefront of scientific breakthrough but you're an *entrepreneur*! Are you not tempted to bring them in on your secret?'

'No. Camilla would be horrified. I think it would offend her morals: she makes it quite clear that I've let her down enough as it is. And Julian would find an opportunity to exploit it. Once he got hold of the information, I bet he would find a way to suck the joy right out of it.'

'And it does bring you joy, does it?'

'It does. Creativity is good for the soul and my business enterprise is the means through which I have been able to explore my creativity. I'd never have had the patience to be a watercolourist, or the talent for that matter. But making something special from my potatoes on the side? This is something I can do that is *consequential* and people seem to really quite appreciate it.'

'But you'll never get any recognition for it! It will always remain a dark secret. And your children will never appreciate you for your brilliance. That does seem a *shame*.'

'Haven't I done enough for my children to value me? I've built this life here. I *raised* them. I carried on raising them long after their mother decided to give up on them. Do other dads have to jump through hoops to earn the respect of their children? Isn't it enough for them just to be tied by blood? I don't believe I should have to prove myself to them. And I don't need recognition in other circles — my potatoes will be my legacy.'

From the tiny sounds of displeasure down the telephone, Doubler detected Mrs Millwood's dissatisfaction. He adopted a more conciliatory tone, seeking to reassure her that he was an ambitious man. 'The minute I receive confirmation from the Institute of Potato Research and Development in northern India, I shall write up my findings formally, with their accreditation attached, of course, and I shall submit it to all the periodicals while simultaneously applying for the registration of the genus and its trademark. I very much hope that is only a matter of weeks away. But the other thing? No, that's not my legacy, but it is something that gives me an enormous amount of satisfaction.'

Mrs Millwood remained unsatisfied with this

161

response. She was displeased by the lack of effort Doubler was prepared to go to in order to secure the respect of his children. But she knew Doubler well and she recognized that his tone betrayed not anger but sadness. She let the silence gather around them before Doubler broke it.

'And besides, this conversation wasn't about me, was it? You were supposed to be filling me in on the rest of the team. So what can you tell me about Derek, then?'

'Derek, oh, you'll meet him soon enough.' Mrs Millwood sounded like she'd lost interest in the conversation, but Doubler wasn't ready to let her off the hook.

'But what *about* him?' said Doubler, insensitive to her quietness and relishing another character assassination embellished with salacious gossip that rendered each of the volunteers as mere extras in the feature starring Doubler and Mrs Millwood.

'You can make your own mind up about Derek. I'll see that you meet him. I'll make sure he's there when you're next in the office. He'll make sure there's no funny business with the Colonel and the rest of them. Derek's a steady pair of hands.'

'I shall certainly look out for him, but I'm not sure you can influence the rota from your hospital bed, can you?'

'Of course I can. Derek calls in to see me most days. I'll simply ask him to make sure he drops in to see you when you're next there.'

Doubler felt himself unable to swallow. But

the overwhelming sensation, greater than all the emotions swirling round his brain like mercury in a concrete mixer, was one of nausea. He thought he might throw up right there in the hallway.

He exhaled steadily, calming himself until he managed to find his voice. 'Derek visits you in the hospital? Midge made it quite clear to me that you weren't receiving visitors and that you were not to be disturbed.'

'Oh, well, Derek is something different. I consider him part of my palliative care.' Mrs Millwood spoke softly and Doubler strained to hear any frivolity in her voice: she was quite serious.

'I'm a little tired, Mr Doubler. Would you mind if we carried on tomorrow? I need to rest.'

'Of course. Quite so. Get some sleep and we'll talk again.'

Doubler was trembling as he replaced the receiver, and wearied by the very same things that excited him just minutes before, he walked slowly to the sitting room and lowered himself into his chair, where he sat quite still and allowed the day to grow quite, quite still with him.

# 16

Midge rang heavily on the bell and Doubler hurried round the corner of the house, having just finished a circuit of the farm.

'I saw your car — you really don't have to ring. Use the side door and make yourself at home. It's always open.'

'I wasn't planning to pop up today, but Mum insisted. She asked me to pick something up from the shops for you.'

'She did?'

Doubler and Midge headed out of the cold into the kitchen together. In a synchronized ritual that pleased Doubler very much, they both bent down to wriggle out of their wellington boots, standing both pairs side by side before heading towards the Aga and, still in unison, turning to lean back against the old range for warmth.

'How is your mum doing, Midge? Will she be out of that place soon, do you suppose?'

Midge looked worn out as she answered. 'The thing about my mum, Doubler, is that she is terribly resilient. She always has been. I hear the doctors say one thing, but I look into my mum's eyes and I see something else. My mum is fuelled by stubborn determination. I've always believed in her and I don't see any purpose in doubting her now.'

'So she's on track, would you say? She'll be home soon?'

Midge studied Doubler's face carefully. His baseless hope was of equal weight to her mother's belligerence. She shook her head briefly and, ending the conversation, handed Doubler a plain white plastic bag. Cautiously, he peered inside.

'There's not a pig or a chicken in here, is there?' he asked, looking at a brown, unlabelled box, as long as a shoebox but about half the width.

'It's a *gift*, I think. Well, I'm rather hoping you'll know why Mum wanted you to have this and why she seemed to think you needed it so urgently.'

Doubler continued to peer at the featureless box, enjoying the thrill of anticipation while craving a moment of privacy to examine the contents alone. This was not just *any* gift but an *unasked-for gift*. And it wasn't just an unasked-for gift; it was a gift from Mrs Millwood, who was thinking of his needs while lying in her hospital bed. It didn't really matter what was inside. He already loved it.

Midge watched him eyeing up the box. 'Go on, open it up. It won't bite.'

Doubler removed it gently from the plastic bag and placed it beside the Aga. He folded the plastic bag carefully in half, smoothing it out. He put the plastic bag away in a drawer on top of a pile of equally neatly folded plastic bags.

'Come on. I know what's in there and I'm intrigued to see if you knew you needed it. Do get on with it. I haven't got all day.'

Doubler took his penknife from his jacket

165

pocket and with meticulous precision he painstakingly sliced the Sellotape that sealed each end. He peered in and then shook out the contents. They were a snug fit, so it took a few vigorous shakes to release them. A tightly wound bundle of cable and two plugs tumbled out onto the work surface. Doubler scratched his head but refused to look at Midge for help. Puzzled, he stared hard at the coil, thinking carefully. Then its significance dawned on him. He smiled, and picking it up, he hurried to the hallway and connected it in place. He removed a plastic twist that held the coil tight and he allowed the lead to unfurl fully as he carried the telephone with him into the kitchen.

'Well, I'll be damned,' he said. 'Who'd have thought it?' He took the phone to the table, sat down and picked up the receiver while pretending to dial. 'Well, this is a turn-up for the books, isn't it? Revolutionary, I'd say.'

'Revolutionary indeed, Doubler. This has propelled you right into the twentieth century.'

'It certainly has. I'm at the cutting edge. Look at me — I've got a mobile phone!' He stood up and carried the telephone carefully with him, retracing his steps into the hallway but this time turning into the sitting room. He allowed the lead to trail behind him once again and went and sat by the fire. He placed the phone on the table next to him and looked at it, as if he expected it to ring right away.

Midge watched him from the doorway and smiled. 'Little things please little minds, Doubler.'

Doubler was now smiling even more broadly. 'It might seem little to you, but I can honestly say this is a vast life improvement. I'd go as far as to call it a game-changer. I can have the phone by the fire or in the kitchen, which is exactly as your dear, dear mother must have envisaged it. That woman is a wonder. Sometimes I think she understands me better than I understand myself.'

Midge studied him carefully before laughing and shaking her head. 'It's not exactly a hi-tech solution, you know. I think this technology has been around for as long as the telephone. What on earth took you so long to get an extension lead?'

Doubler thought hard about this and looked at Midge earnestly. 'I suppose I've had no call for the phone until now. It never occurred to me that the phone was for anything other than relaying short messages, and I was quite capable of standing in a draughty hall for those. But I'm spending more time on the telephone these days. I'd never quite appreciated what a wonderful invention it is, to tell you the truth. Oh, granted, I've always been aware of its value in an emergency, but for day-to-day living? It's only just revealing its potential to me.'

Midge laughed. 'Now, while I'm here, Mum also asked me to take a quick look at your Land Rover. Would you mind?'

'Good heavens, no, I don't mind in the least, but why everyone is suddenly taking such an extraordinary interest in my car I simply can't imagine. Let me show you the way.'

They left the house, reversing the ritual as they replaced their boots and coats. Doubler led the way, picking up a big bunch of keys as he left. 'Thanks for coming up today, Midge. You didn't need to do that.'

'It was important to Mum. She's happy I'm keeping an eye on you.'

'Hmmm,' said Doubler, wondering out loud. 'And are there other people you're, you know, keeping an eye on for her?'

'Other people? Like who?'

'Derek? Has your mum asked you to keep an eye on Derek? She's very *fond* of Derek.'

'Golly. I lose track. Which one is Derek?'

'Never mind,' said Doubler, mollified by this response. He was aware that he was fishing, and not wanting to build any greater significance for Derek by alluding to him further, he changed the subject. 'You know something about cars, do you?'

'Yes, a fair bit. It's what comes of having a mechanic for a father and no siblings. Dad absolutely loved cars. Was always under the bonnet of one pet project or another. It was the old stuff he liked the best. Always maintained that the fewer parts to go wrong, the better the car.'

'I feel a bit like that about telephones. Come to think of it, I feel a bit like that about life. Here she is.' Doubler opened the garage door.

It took Midge a while for her eyes to adjust to the dark. But once she could take in the car, she let out a slow whistle of appreciation.

'What a beauty,' she said, running her hand along the bonnet.

'She gets me from A to B. I don't have much call for her, but she's never let me down. Sometimes the old ones are just so much more reliable.'

'I couldn't agree more. These were built to last, these were. And, of course, they were supposed to be workhorses. Tough as old nails.'

'Well, she's certainly been worked hard, that's for sure. In the past, she had to put in the effort, so she's earned her rest now.'

'And she's never given you any problems?'

'None at all.'

'Never been to the garage for repairs?'

'Nope, not that I recall.'

'She's as she was when she left the factory?' Midge asked this with rising excitement evident in her voice.

'May I?' she said as she climbed into the cab of the car and stroked the steering wheel appreciatively. She adjusted the mirror as if she were about to set off on a long journey and then peered at the dashboard. The dim overhead light gave her very little help in the dark interior of the garage, so she flipped on the torch on her phone and pointed it at the milometer.

'I thought you said she worked hard!' Midge exclaimed, squealing now. 'She's practically brand new. She's got less than thirty thousand miles on the clock.'

Doubler peered into the car, looking behind the steering wheel, examining the dashboard as if for the very first time. 'Thirty thousand? As much as that? You surprise me. I suppose it all adds up.' He swung the driver's door shut on Midge with a very pleasing clunk of metal on metal and then walked round to the passenger's side, where he climbed in next to her.

Midge looked at him. 'Doubler, you really can't have used her much at all!'

'Oh, but I did. Back in the early days, she was used an enormous amount. Not too much on the road, mind you. Marie had a biggish car that we used for outings and such. She wouldn't have been happy driving this. Hated it, in fact. Wouldn't even go in it as a passenger. I bought it soon after I bought the farm and it was a hefty investment, getting myself a proper farm vehicle fit for purpose. It was pristine, as good as new and with barely any miles on the clock. Bit naughty in hindsight. Reckless, even. Can't think what got into me. Golly, Marie wasn't happy.' Doubler smiled wryly at the memory. 'I suppose it sent out a pretty strong signal that I was committed to life as a farmer. Perhaps it was the first time she realized what she'd signed up to. A lifetime of potatoes.'

Midge sat still with both hands on the steering wheel. Doubler leant back in his seat and strapped himself in. Above them, the cab's interior light faded and then switched off altogether. Finding the darkness of the garage the perfect environment for honesty, Doubler prepared himself to speak. Midge sensed this and probed gently. 'It can't have been easy for her.'

'No, I'm sure it wasn't. But I swear to God I

never made any pretences. I never promised her anything other than this, you know. Mirth Farm was never a *whim*.'

'Did she ever love it here?'

'Love? That's probably too strong a word. But maybe when she was a young mum, it wasn't too hard on her. Plenty of space for the children to run around and near enough to the town for her to escape quite easily. The house is big, and it offered a healthy lifestyle with plenty of fresh air. And we never went hungry. We did rather well, actually, though perhaps by accident rather than by design. The money came in, better than for many who work the land, so I thought I was doing her proud. I actually believed I was giving her a lifestyle that may have been better than expected. She was always off shopping and I never complained — it gave her something to do. It took her mind off it.'

'Off what?'

'Well, off the potatoes, I suppose. The dreariness of it all. I think there was a tipping point when she realized that it didn't really matter how successful we were, I was never going to be interested in the trappings and I couldn't really afford to take holidays. She could — she took plenty — but you know, time-wise, leaving the farm was difficult for me. I'd started my research by then and I knew I was onto something big. I had a mission, but I immediately resigned myself to the fact it was going to be a long haul. Groundbreaking work doesn't come overnight. Not in the potato field. You need the seasons to pass and you can't hurry them: you can't force nature to work at a pace more convenient to your wife.'

Doubler looked sad as the memories came flooding back. 'I think I recall the straw that broke the camel's back, so to speak.'

Midge continued to stare straight ahead, letting Doubler talk in his own time. 'I remember when she said she'd had enough: enough of the winters, enough of the mud, enough of the potatoes. The kids were growing up and they didn't need her quite as much, so she was feeling a bit low, I think. A bit like her life was going to flash by without any variation. And I agreed with her. I agreed so readily. I held her hand and said yes, we could move on. Yes, we could finish up here, but I was onto something important and I needed a little more time.'

Doubler paused, dredging up the exact words from two decades of suppressed memories. ' 'How long?' she said. 'How much more time do you need?' 'Ten years,' I told her. 'Fifteen max.''

Midge let out a low chuckle. 'Another decade of doing something you hate? Gosh, Doubler, you weren't exactly throwing her a lifeline.'

Doubler was crestfallen, devastated by the ease with which Midge had been able to see Marie's point of view. 'I was being honest. I couldn't hurry this work up. I had made a lifetime commitment to it, to carry on for as long as it took. I was beginning to realize my experimentation had the potential to make a difference to potato growers around the world. It was work of tremendous importance, but it was never going to happen overnight.'

Midge turned to face him now. 'You did the right thing. Being honest was good, Doubler. Don't doubt yourself now — making false promises would have been worse in so many ways.'

Doubler hung his head in shame.

'But I wasn't being honest, was I? When I gave her a deadline often to fifteen years, I only did so to buy myself a bit of time. I never had any intention of leaving here. Not before my work was done and not afterwards. I know that now and I probably knew that then.'

They both climbed out of the car. Midge closed the door behind her, speaking loudly to Doubler across the width of the car, her voice echoing pleasingly in the garage. 'Come on. Don't be glum. Your work here is important work, and sometimes work just does come first. It's very rare that progress is made without personal sacrifice. But not many people have the courage of their conviction to see it through. You're a brave man, Doubler.'

Doubler started to lock the car door, but Midge stopped him.

'Could I?' she asked, motioning to the bonnet. 'Would you mind?'

Doubler shrugged. 'Be my guest,' and he opened the bonnet up, propping it on its metal support.

Midge flicked her phone's torch back on, passing the beam back and forth over the engine and making admiring noises.

Doubler watched her curiously. 'So your dad knew a thing or two about engines, did he?

Would you say, Midge, you're *genetically disposed* to like cars?'

'If you're asking if it's in my blood, possibly. But it's probably much more nurture than nature. My dad absolutely loved cars. Cars were his livelihood, but more than that, they were his passion.'

'Like potatoes for me!' Doubler exclaimed.

'Indeed. And isn't it nice when those two things coincide? Dad spent most of his free time tinkering around with old cars, I liked spending time with my dad, so it meant that's what I ended up spending some of my free time doing, too. Dad was happiest at work, you know, which isn't that rare. We are often at our very best when we're doing what we are good at. But we don't always get to see our parents at work, so we don't always get to see them at their best.'

Doubler pondered this. 'I wonder if my kids think I'm at my best when I'm at work. I'm not even sure they think there is a 'best' version of me. I'd love them to take a bit of interest in what I do, but I suppose that's unlikely. Not as long as they hold me accountable for what happened with Marie.'

'Your kids have every reason to be extremely proud of you. But you might have to work a little harder on your PR.'

She waited while Doubler carefully locked up the car and then the garage behind him. They walked to Mrs Millwood's car. She had linked her arm through Doubler's, holding him close to her as they walked.

'Well, the good news is, your car is an absolute beauty.'

'Oh, I'm glad you think so. It's sometimes hard to recognize the underlying qualities in a bit of old farm machinery, but I certainly like to think I appreciate it.'

'Well, actually, her beauty goes beyond that. I'll do a little research when I get home, but I think what you have there is worth an absolute fortune.'

'Really?' Doubler allowed a small chuckle of astonishment to escape. 'Somebody would pay good money for her, even after all these years?'

'Particularly after all these years. Your wife might have resented it, but you made an incredibly prudent investment. If the car's what I think it is, then it's very, very valuable indeed. It's worth a great deal of money. And particularly now, as they've stopped making them. They've become highly collectable anyway, but yours is very, very special.'

'Well, I never. That's a bit of a surprise, I must say.' He shook his head, incredulous. They'd reached the little red car by then. 'Is it worth more than one of these newfangled things?' he asked, waving a hand towards the old red car.

Midge laughed. 'Mum's old jalopy? Gosh, yes, a lot more! You could buy a fair few brand-new cars in place of yours.'

'Well, I'd better tell Julian. He will be surprised. And he ought to be very thankful to you. You've saved him a bit of embarrassment no doubt. Imagine his upset if he'd swapped it for some little bit of modern rubbish and then he'd found out what he'd done. He'd have been *mortified.*'

'Oh, Doubler!' said Midge sadly.

Doubler assumed it was the biting wind that caused her eyes to fill with tears. But then she took him in her arms and hugged him tightly to her.

'Mum's right. You're a lovely, lovely man,' she said. She pulled herself away abruptly and jumped into Mrs Millwood's car, starting it and closing the door in one swift movement.

Doubler watched her pull out of the yard and then walked thoughtfully back to the house, wondering if perhaps it wasn't the wind making her eyes well up like that; perhaps it was something else entirely.

# 17

Doubler had walked twice as far as he usually would on an average morning. He'd been restless all night and had awoken long before dawn. Unable to fall asleep again, he had become tired of waiting for sunrise so had dressed hurriedly, grasped his stoutest walking stick and stumbled out into the dark, making his way down to the bottom of the hill. While he walked, he dwelt on the revelation that Derek was a frequent visitor to Mrs Millwood. With each step he examined his turmoil, teasing out the conflicting elements and trying to make sense of the waves of jealousy that occasionally swept over him, catching him off guard.

In some ways, it made perfect sense for Mrs Millwood to have a special friend at Grove Farm. Why else would she have had the animal shelter on her conscience when her mind should have been solely focused on recovering in hospital? Feeling the complex flashes of jealousy more often associated with a teenager, Doubler began to simultaneously condemn and condone the special relationship that flourished between Mrs Millwood and Derek. Doubler wondered if each time Mrs Millwood had hung up the phone at the end of their calls, it was because Derek was arriving and he became enraged by his own foolish vanity that had allowed him to contemplate his own special relationship.

Doubler walked furiously down the hill, careless in the dark, unbothered when his boots landed clumsily on the sharp flint stones. He used his walking stick to catch himself on a number of occasions as he strode on with a confidence the darkness shouldn't have afforded him.

Yes, thought Doubler, certain now that his agitated mumblings, some out loud, some just a hiss in his wildly whirring head, were helping him to come closer to the truth. A special relationship with Derek, to be protected and cherished, would explain Mrs Millwood's uncharacteristic hostility towards both Paula and Mabel. Clearly neither was to be trusted while she languished in her hospital bed. Doubler felt vicariously disgusted by any potential betrayal.

He stopped and looked all around him to get his bearings. He'd reached the end of the drive and turned left, following the footpath at the far boundary of his land, a path that tracked the country lane for a while before cutting in and marking the edge of his own land. Now, to his left he could look back up to the top of the hill where his home sat, almost out of sight. The driveway snaked down the steep gradient, the chalk and flint making it easy to pick out in the dark against the inky fields, their rich dark brown hues turned to black by the pale moonlit night. To his right now was a wide corridor of set-aside land, a margin of abandoned ground that he'd allowed to grow wild with thickets of brambles and thorn, which caused an almost impenetrable barrier before a good area of woodland that separated his fields from those of Peele.

As he stood at these edge-lands, he allowed his brain to settle into nothingness. It was still dark. He stopped and listened. A bird sang from a hazel branch not far from him. The pure sound cut through the dark and distracted Doubler from his quandary.

'Hello, robin!' Doubler said, under his breath for fear of disturbing the gutsy singer. 'It's a bit early for that racket, isn't it?'

The lone, tentative voice was almost immediately joined by another flute-like refrain from just behind him. The birds had sensed the dawn before any trace of the new day had become obvious to Doubler. These birds, the robin and perhaps a blackbird, were soon joined by several others and now, after just a few moments of listening, the chorus was beginning in earnest and it was impossible to separate one song from another. Together, this competing cacophony should have jarred, but instead it united to form a harmonious ensemble that appeared to be led by one unseen conductor.

'Is that you, you brave chap?' Doubler asked of the robin. 'Are you responsible for this orchestra? What a talented little thing you are!' The robin continued wistfully with his complex mix of long and short notes.

Doubler had followed the driveway down the western-facing slope so that the sun, when it did rise, would be on the far side of the hill. He realized now that rather than getting up early to greet the dawn, he had unintentionally delayed the day by walking in this direction, and this suited him grandly, because he really wasn't ready for the day to begin: he didn't quite know what to do with it. For a man who only dealt in certainties, he found himself in a quagmire of doubt. Why did he even care this deeply about Mrs Millwood's admiration for Derek? he reasoned with himself impatiently. After all, she was only his housekeeper, who, at best, had poor taste in both cheese and apples.

But despite Doubler's proclivity for irascibility, the birds' optimism and their ability to take the day for granted, celebrating it before they could definitively count on it, sparked a glimmer of optimism in his own heart. They weren't waiting for the day to prove itself before rejoicing in it; they were going to start their song regardless and sing the day awake if necessary. Doubler wandered on a little, and though the complete darkness had faintly softened to a paler version of itself, he was still picking his way carefully along the footpath, barely able to see and stumbling occasionally. Joined now by the rousing encouragement of, it seemed, every possible bird species in the region, he realized he was beginning to enjoy the danger of exploration as he found himself reaching for some emotional courage through his physical bravery.

He stopped at the sound of a sudden splash and turned to peer into the darkness to make out a small dew pond nestled among the hazel trees, only just visible in the moonlight. A mallard drake had landed clumsily next to a female and they now circled their tiny patch of water in a happy and noisy duet of flapping wings, hoisting themselves almost upright in the shallow water.

This pleased Doubler. The dew pond, full enough to host a pair of courting mallards, was a visual reminder that the intensive work he had put in during the months since the harvest had paid off. He had heavily ridged the land across the slopes, preventing run-off, and to work these steepest slopes, he had methodically ploughed these ridges again and again to ensure that his hard-earned fertile soil wasn't washed downhill in the winter rain. As well as three substantial ponds, big enough for a heron to call home, there were a number of these small ponds dotted around the circumference of his land, which filled naturally from rainwater and several small underground feeds. If they were full of water as spring approached, rather than bunged full of soil and silt, it proved that the extra-deep furrows he ploughed were working effectively. An occasional inspection of these ponds was a great discipline, and seeing the ducks playfully welcoming spring reminded him to take this walk more often. It had needed the ducks' noisy clamour to signal the health of his farm, and with his spirits a little lifted, he turned to head back up the hill, where he would be able to witness dawn in all its glory.

His mind wandered in a different direction as he retraced his steps, more determined, less defeatist. He thought, instead, of how to explain to Mrs Millwood that he depended on her in so many ways that she (or Derek) couldn't possibly understand. And he knew now, in the calmness of the early morning air, that it wasn't her fault if she had not responded to him or invited him to visit her in hospital. He was not a noisy mallard crashing into her pond. He'd been a timid coot, watching from the sidelines and allowing other more brash and gaudy species to splash and encircle Mrs Millwood. He wondered whether a more direct approach might at least allow her to welcome him into her circle of friends.

He wandered through the house, making himself useful in a number of small ways. He picked up a couple of books and idly wondered whether he might read them. As quickly as he'd considered the idea, he rejected it, leaving them on a pile by the fireplace. Now that the phone could sit quite casually on the occasional table beside his armchair, Doubler could allow himself to be close to it without having to commit so fully to waiting for it to ring. He found that he could busy himself with any number of jobs that would have been almost impossible to replicate in the hallway. He could sit on the window seat and look at his birds; he could train the binoculars onto the gate and watch for unwanted visitors; he could even sit by the fire and have a go at the crossword. While he had some nagging doubts that were plaguing him as he went about his chores, he only had to look at the trailing cord of the telephone to admit that there were some areas of his life that had improved immeasurably.

He began to dust the bookshelves. The housework was therapeutic and he came to the certain conclusion that while he wasn't very knowledgeable in matters of the heart, he knew Mrs Millwood. He would let her tell him about her feelings for Derek when she was good and ready. This conclusion made him feel less anxious as the impending confrontation receded from his immediate horizon.

When the phone call came, he let it ring four times as he allowed his breathing to steady before picking up the receiver and saying, quickly but in a measured tone, 'So, what about Olive? What do you know about her?'

Mrs Millwood didn't hesitate. It was as if she too had prepared herself to pick up the conversation as they'd left it before, with no acknowledgement of the intervening twenty-four hours. 'Ah, Olive. Now, she is terribly interesting. She is one of those straightforwardly good people. She's been quite extraordinarily generous to the shelter. She's given us use of her land and her outbuildings, and she has undoubtedly relinquished her privacy and solitude. She allowed the Colonel to erect the Portakabin we use as an office right outside her home, which let's face it is a bit of an eyesore. I'm not sure I would have gone that far. And, from what I can see, she gets *nothing* in return. She doesn't interact socially, so she's not in it for the company. She's not on any charity committees, so she's not in it for the kudos. She just leaves us to it. That's the mark of a truly *good* person, isn't it?'

'Selfless giving, you mean?' Doubler was immediately drawn into the conversation, with any trace of his earlier resolve diminishing in the reality of this more pressing conversation.

'Yes, don't you think? Doing something without expecting anything in return is an *irrefutable* mark of goodness, surely? Olive doesn't appear to want any acknowledgement, or any recognition. Even our simplest acts of kindness usually have a streak of selfishness to them, don't you think?'

'I suppose it depends on the scale of the gift. Giving over access to your farm, that is a pretty substantial contribution. But what about putting money in a collection pot — you know, outside a supermarket? That's an anonymous gift, and you're not looking for any acknowledgement, are you? That might be a smaller scale, but that's selfless, surely?' Doubler was giving this conversation all of his attention, determined to honour the gravity that Mrs Millwood had decided to afford it.

'Well, you'd be pretty disappointed if the collector with the bucket outside the supermarket ignored your gift entirely, so I expect you're probably looking for thanks at the very least. But beyond that, you do it for the impact you make on the people around you when you stop to put your money in, don't you? To send out a little signal of superiority? I mean, you see the people who are rushing past with their heads down and their hands in their pockets, or looking at their watches to signal their supreme busyness, and you think, I'm going to stop and put a coin in that bucket because I'm better than them . . . '

Doubler was genuinely quite taken aback. He thought of his daughter's own response to the charity collectors, and how she found the process so intimidating. He thought of the days he would regularly visit the supermarket and wondered what sort of person he'd been then. It had been so long that he couldn't quite recall, and he wouldn't have trusted his memory to be truthful anyway.

He answered thoughtfully. 'That's quite cynical, Mrs Millwood. Gosh, I hope that's not how people think. It's been a while since I ventured out to a supermarket, but I think I used to put a bit of loose change in the pot to make the person collecting feel better, less futile.'

'So what you're doing there is making a small gift while exerting a little bit of power or influence to make yourself feel superior? That's not entirely selfless.'

Doubler reeled a little. Mrs Millwood always understood people so well. Had he ever met another person who could commit so fully to the most trivial of conversations? 'Maybe. But I wouldn't want to stop giving to a charity just because I am unable to entirely extract my selflessness out of the action. Nobody wins then.'

'But what I'm saying is that Olive is a *thoroughly* good person. If giving a home to the animal shelter made her happy, then that would be a reason, wouldn't it? But it seems to me she's pretty miserable regardless.'

'Is she lonely?'

'Almost certainly. Up on her own in the farm all the time? No family as far as I know. Who wouldn't be lonely? We come and go, tending the animals and running the shelter, but she doesn't interact with us. The loneliness must be *crippling*.'

Doubler was quiet. Today the telephone couldn't offer the release he needed. If this were a conversation he was having at the kitchen table, over lunch, he could break it now. He could stall the progress by standing up and putting the kettle on. Putting the kettle on was the best possible way to freeze time. But that wasn't an option: he had to press on or the conversation must end. It couldn't exactly continue without him.

'So, it's *interesting*, Mrs Millwood.'

'What is?'

'Are we all simply the product of our relationships? The Colonel volunteers because he has been demoted to second in command on home turf and his ego cannot stand it. Paula behaves the way she does because she wants a husband and nobody can see her in any other light; she's just a woman in want of a partner. I'm here, let's face it, alone in a farmhouse, not unlike Olive, because of my own wife's actions. You, Mrs Millwood? Your character, too, must have been formed in part by your husband?'

'Or by his absence, yes.'

'Yes, or both. A combination of the two things, a lifetime spent happily together followed by the ache of his absence. You must be the product of those two chapters.'

'You mean he made me what I am, but I am now reduced to one half of a couple?' She trailed off, sounding distant, but Doubler pursued the thought nonetheless.

186

'Yes. Quite. Are any of us . . . Is anybody at all capable of just being themselves? Not ruined or completed, not bolstered or outshone? Just a being?'

Mrs Millwood paused before answering, carefully, 'I think the content person, all alone, is probably a very rare thing.' She thought a little more. 'Perhaps a holy person? Somebody seeking solitude in search of God, that kind of thing?'

Doubler was quick to dispute this, as though he had already thought through this argument and dismissed it. 'Well, no, then God becomes the partner, the other person in the relationship. That holy person isn't lonely; they're communing, aren't they? And an admission of loneliness would be an admission of the absence of God.'

'Yes. Yes, you're quite right, of course.'

'But suppose Olive gave the outward appearance of being happy. Could we believe she is happy, really happy, in her farmhouse all alone?'

Mrs Millwood snorted briefly, an indication that she and Doubler would shortly be in disagreement. 'Well, why look at her? Why not look closer to home? What about you, Mr Doubler? You're all alone in *your* farmhouse. Can you be happy all alone up there?'

'Happy? Me? Heavens, yes! Some of the happiest moments of my life have been in solitude. And they're not rare; they occur *often*. I've had my moments when I've despaired, you know that. But I have had my moments, probably several each day, when I am extraordinarily happy. That is to say, I'm entirely content.' Doubler thought a little more. 'There are *triggers*, I expect, things I see or notice that remind me how very lucky I am.'

'Like what?'

'When the kindling baskets are piled high and the log store is full to groaning and I lay a good fire. I mean a really good fire. A fire that takes just three twists of newspaper and one match. When I hear those first crackles that tell me it's the wood that is burning not just the paper, and I know I will have heat in a matter of moments, I'm truly happy.'

Doubler smiled at a realization. 'When my potatoes don't just behave themselves but they *over*-deliver, when they do exactly what I expect of them but that behaviour has never been achieved before, by any other potato grower, then I'm truly very happy.

'But my happiness doesn't just come through personal success. My potatoes constantly deliver me happiness. When one day the soil is bare and the winter feels relentless and unforgiving and the next day there are a thousand green shoots and they are so small and so faint you can barely see an individual sprout and yet they combine to form visible lines of green, then I am the happiest man on the planet.'

'You're not then a product of your wife's absence,' Mrs Millwood said solemnly.

'No, then I am a pioneer full of purpose and promise.'

'A pioneer full of purpose and promise!' repeated Mrs Millwood, delighted with the sounds of these words. 'Who could wish for more, Mr Doubler? So, you've answered your own question: of course we can be happy on our own, and of course we can be more than an absence, more than an addendum.'

'But there are other types of happiness, and when you get a glimpse of these types of happiness, then the others can lose their shine.'

'Like what, Mr Doubler?'

'You know when you've cleaned the sitting room from top to tail, and you've polished the windows to a gleam? Suddenly, the sunlight finds a way in, and its beam picks up all the dust, showing the particles dancing in the air and you can see that you've not cleaned well after all. The sitting room is nothing more than a swirl of dirty particles, but without the sunshine, you'd never have noticed them ... It took the light to highlight the dark.'

'You're talking in riddles, Mr Doubler. It does unsettle me when you do that.'

Doubler took a deep breath, aware that his metaphor had not quite opened the door to the conversation he wanted to have. 'Well. Take this phone call. I don't believe I've ever felt happier than right now. When the phone rang and I knew it would be you and I knew you'd hang on while I dragged the phone to the sitting room And I was dragging the phone while it was ringing in my hand, marvelling at the joy of my new extension cable, and I was grinning from ear to ear because I knew that we were about to sit down for a really long chat. Well, that's a very pure form of happiness.'

Mrs Millwood burst out laughing. 'You daft brush!'

Doubler was undaunted. 'But. But there's a flip side. If the phone stopped ringing, if I knew it couldn't be you or that you'd never ring again . . . ' He trailed off, feeling that familiar shatter of his heart when he contemplated a pain he didn't want to name.

'Why?' yelped Mrs Millwood, alarmed. 'Where have I gone? Where am I in this scenario? Why am I not calling you?'

Doubler shook his head dramatically, exhaling slowly. 'I suppose you are either dead, Mrs Millwood, or you've eloped with Derek.' Doubler winced, furious with himself for having mentioned Derek when only a few moments ago he had resolved not to.

But Mrs Millwood was already responding. 'Derek?' she shrieked. 'What on earth have I done that for? That's a truly terrible idea!'

'Well,' said Doubler sadly, 'you haven't eloped with the Colonel, so it has to be Derek, I'm afraid.'

'Derek or dead? It's not really my day, is it?' There was warmth in Mrs Millwood's voice, but Doubler had borne his soul and it hurt.

'No. It's a bad day all round,' he agreed. 'But worst of all, not only will our telephone calls cease for ever, but I will never, ever be able to take pleasure in any of those other things again.'

'The fire, the well-behaved potatoes, the first new shoots of spring?' said Mrs Millwood, echoing his sadness.

'No, I'm afraid not. Nor clean, crisp bed linen on Mondays. I will be back in the chasm of despair.'

'Well, honestly, I feel terrible, just terrible. I'm sauntering around with Derek and you're *languishing* in a chasm of despair. Poor old you!' Mrs Millwood laughed heartily.

Doubler sat up in his chair, mildly affronted. 'Well, you don't sound quite as sad as perhaps I meant you to be.'

'Oh, I am *so* sad for you! Really. I'm *mortified*. That my absence could send you into that horrible chasm. And the worst thing is, my poor Derek, who I actually love to pieces, is miserable too.'

A shock of pain seared through Doubler, whose imagined loss was indeed sending him at least very close to the edge of the chasm of despair, even if he hadn't quite hurtled into it yet.

'What does he have to be miserable about? He seems like the winner in this scenario.' Doubler felt a visceral hatred for Derek and briefly contemplated the image of a large fireball hurtling towards him from space, obliterating him entirely. This brusque vision gave him almost no relief.

'Derek is miserable because he doesn't *want* me! I'd be the last person on earth he'd want to elope with!' Mrs Millwood was still laughing openly.

Doubler resented the laughter while wanting to increase the pain he could inflict upon Derek. It was impossible: he had already taken the punishment to the furthermost reaches of his imagination. 'Well, I doubt that. You're beautiful. You're accomplished. You're wise. And you love him, apparently, 'to pieces', which sounds quite destructive if you ask me. He'd elope with you in a heartbeat. Just try and stop him.'

Mrs Millwood, through her laughter, spluttered her response. 'Derek is gay, Mr Doubler. He's a homosexual. I'm not exactly his *type*.'

Horrified, Doubler banished his previous, violent imagery from his mind, immediately ashamed of his draconian response to jealousy. He softened but remained on alert, suspicious of the love Mrs Millwood had expressed. 'Oh. Well. Yes. I can see that might be an obstacle. Still, he'd be very lucky to have you.'

'No, no, no,' said Mrs Millwood vehemently. 'He'd be the saddest man on the planet to find himself with a female wife when all he probably wants is a male husband.'

Doubler was overjoyed at the news of Derek's sadness. He exhaled again, though he hadn't consciously inhaled once in the intervening conversation. 'So, you're dead, Mrs Millwood, which was always a very viable alternative,' he said, with resolve in his voice.

'Well, my death is much more *sound* under the circumstances. Let's bury me instead of dumping me on Derek, shall we?'

'Let's!' clamoured Doubler exuberantly. He thought for a while, recalling his earlier train of thought and remembering now that despite his victory in winning Mrs Millwood from the clutches of Derek, he was all alone again. 'But I'm back in that chasm now you're dead. Do you see? So I have simultaneously the ability to be a pioneer full of promise and purpose and the

192

perpetual potential to enter the chasm of despair.'

'But you've been in the chasm before, Doubler. You've shown that it's not the end of the world.'

'No, not like this. This is a totally new threat.'

Mrs Millwood was insistent, excited by the recognition. 'No, you have. I've seen it. When Marie went, you leapt into that chasm and you buried your head in the dark silt of its coldest, deepest point. And yet you *still* climbed out.'

Doubler recalled the ascent. 'But not without your help, Mrs Millwood. You extended your hand, Mrs Millwood. You reached in and you helped me climb out. Day by day, lunch by lunch. If it weren't for you, I would never have ascended. I'd have died down there.'

'I'm not sure you're accurately remembering this, Mr Doubler. You're certainly not giving yourself enough credit. I was there to witness your elevation, and perhaps I stopped you from falling back in again, but you definitely climbed out of there yourself. You had your *purpose*, you see. It was your *purpose* that got you out. Thank goodness. There were times when I wondered if you almost enjoyed it down there, anyway, wallowing in self-pity. My job was to stop you enjoying yourself down there so much that you wouldn't even *try* to climb out.'

Doubler thought back to the darkest days, the days when he didn't want to breathe anymore because it hurt too much. 'I hated it. I was desperate. I didn't enjoy it down there in the least.'

'I think you did. I think by keeping yourself in the chasm you found a weapon to punish Marie and the kids. That's how you fought back. Other people might have gone out and played bingo or learnt ballroom dancing, but you chose to banish even a glimmer of happiness from your life. You were angry, Mr Doubler. You were so very angry.'

'But what if I fell back into the chasm? Where could I possibly find purpose again?' Doubler was still contemplating a life in which Mrs Millwood didn't exist, but he didn't want to give name to her death anymore, not with her languishing in her hospital bed while they spoke. Not now her other exit route had been closed off. Death seemed too inevitable now.

'Oh, while you've still got your potatoes, you've still got your purpose.' Mrs Millwood was chiding him, much in the way she would have done all those years ago when Doubler had wanted nothing to do with the conversation she had offered him over lunch. His sadness had been so compelling then.

'And there's some more good news, Mr Doubler.'

Gloomy, despondent and depleted, Doubler could barely raise interest in his voice. 'What's that?'

'I'm not dead!'

He shook himself, horrified that he'd taken this self-obsessed journey with her on the phone, nearly leaving her behind. He wanted to be the mallard. He needed to crash noisily into her pond.

Doubler grinned. 'No, you're not, though I killed you off there for a moment.'

'And,' said Mrs Millwood, hearing the note of lightness in his voice, 'while I seem to be rather unsuccessful at negotiating my way out of this place, I have absolutely no intention of kicking the bucket yet. I've got a blanket to knit and it is fiendishly complicated.'

'That's *your* purpose!'

'Yes, it is. It's tricky beyond belief, this blanket. Sometimes it's hard to see where I'm going with it. There are these different threads, you see, that must somehow magically come together to complete the pattern, but after wondering whether I have the capability or the patience, the will, if you like, then suddenly I'll have a bit of a breakthrough and . . . whoosh! Just a few rows further and I get a glimpse of it in all its glory. I get a flash of the future and I like what I see. That kind of vision, the knowledge that it will be done, makes me feel better than all this poison they're pumping into me.'

'Perhaps you never want to finish it, Mrs Millwood. If it's the blanket that is keeping you going.'

'Oh, it's not like that. I'm not going to cast off literally and then immediately cast off meta-phorically. I do want to see this one through, though. I want to know the ending, that's all.'

Doubler thought he might like to know the ending, too.

'I'd better be off now. I'm a little tired. All that talk of death, Mr Doubler. I blame you.'

'No hurry. It's been a great conversation, Mrs Millwood. The best. In fact, I can't remember a better one in all my time. Shall we speak again tomorrow, Mrs Millwood?'

'Oh yes, we have unfinished business, Mr Doubler.'

She chuckled the low, throaty laugh that made Doubler's heart ache and she hung up.

'Cheerio, then,' he said happily to himself as he replaced the receiver.

# 18

Doubler had not had much notice to prepare for the shelter volunteers' visit, which was probably a good thing, as he would undoubtedly have found an excuse to cancel if he had dwelt on the prospect of the impending visit for more than a couple of days. Instead, he had set to work preparing the house, the kitchen and the contents of his pantry to the very best of his ability.

Now, the moment was just about upon him. Doubler looked around the kitchen and noted the time. He had a half-hour to wait. He had wrestled with how best to proceed, having no real precedent for receiving visitors other than the imposed visits by his family and the sorely missed daily visits by Mrs Millwood. After much deliberation, he had decided that being a good host and making a positive impression was more important to him than a temporary suspension of security at the farm, so he'd driven down the hill and latched the gate open, allowing his visitors easy access. He didn't know whether they'd car-share and arrive all at once or if they would make their own way to Mirth Farm individually and he didn't like the idea of his guests being inconvenienced by the gate.

He checked the oven and took a tray of scones out, sliding them easily onto a cooling rack. He set out cups and saucers on the kitchen table, warmed both teapots, put the fruitcake on a plate, placing it initially in the centre of the table and then, after frowning a little, moving it to the far end of the table, where it didn't appear to try quite so hard. He took a walnut cake out of the fridge and confirmed that the butter icing had set satisfactorily. He put this next to the fruitcake, adjusting both slightly to avoid any suggestion of contrived symmetry. Finally, he popped a couple of loaves into the coolest oven of the Aga to let them warm gently. The table looked beautiful; the house looked welcoming; the kitchen smelt delicious.

Doubler felt proud of his achievements but was still anxious that he hadn't gone to enough effort. He had no idea how formal these meetings were or how much trouble the other hosts would go to when it was their turn and he felt predisposed to inadequacy. He had, however, prepared two further cakes: a lemon drizzle and a Victoria sponge, layered with homemade jam and dusted with icing sugar. These were stored out of sight in the pantry and Doubler resolved to bring them to the table only if his guests looked underwhelmed or disappointed. He wondered whether he should have ordered some clotted cream for the scones, whether butter and jam would be enough, but there was no time for regret or last-minute decisions now as his guests would arrive any minute.

They were punctual and very quick to make themselves at home. Their arrival passed in a haze, with Doubler feeling very much like an actor playing the role of host. One by one they filed into his kitchen, appreciative, Doubler thought, but by no means overwhelmed by his effort. Maxwell, clearly in charge, introduced him to Derek, Paula, Mabel and — much to Doubler's surprise — to Olive from Grove Farm, who said very little but appeared fascinated by Mirth Farm and everything within it.

Doubler had no doubt that he gave the impression of an overly anxious host. He felt unqualified to join in with the conversation, yet was eager to impress, which made him a busy but silent bystander. The instinct he had fought with for days was to run and hide, to abandon the whole idea of entertaining strangers at Mirth Farm, but this had been countered by an even greater desire to please Mrs Millwood and to do whatever he could to fill her shoes while she recovered. Now he listened attentively, storing away phrases, looks and asides, and the little currents of tension that zapped among his guests. Doubler was determined to observe and record it all accurately for future dissemination to Mrs Millwood, so while he absorbed it all, he spoke barely a word.

Two pots of tea had been made, both with Doubler's special blend. He had thought briefly about making two different types of tea, his own and something more pedestrian, but he reasoned that there was little point in serving something substandard. After all, it had taken him years of painstaking trial and error to create a perfect blend, so if he could contribute to his guests' education by serving them the best tea available, then they would surely leave more than satisfied.

Tea had been poured, and cakes had been sliced and enjoyed, with Doubler joining the table for brief moments of inescapable conviviality interrupted by almost constant fetching and carrying, serving, slicing, while all the time acknowledging praise only with a quiet, self-appraising nod of the head. With no fanfare, he'd produced the lemon drizzle cake from the pantry and sliced it the minute he saw the other cakes beginning to disappear.

Now, with everyone full, the guests had pushed their chairs back a little and were talking not just of the animal shelter but also of other idle gossip that affected them all in one way or another. Doubler knew nothing of these subjects, but he did his very best to memorize the detail where he could. He followed the talk carefully, training his eyes on each speaker, observing their accepted protocols and manners, and studying each one, to prepare himself for his own moment of contribution, whenever it might arrive.

It arrived shortly after the teacups had been drained and thirds had been refused. The sudden turn of conversation came as a surprise to Doubler, as well as to his guests.

Mabel had been telling a story that had amused the other guests greatly. It concerned, as far as Doubler could tell, a rather unpopular man from the town who had apparently been passing off shop-bought eggs as home-supplied free range, which he sold on at a premium. Doubler was confused by the hilarity round the table. He was sure they were condemning this neighbour and were appalled by his audacity, but they were laughing openly, which Doubler found baffling. In Doubler's eyes, if the deed were to be considered serious, it should be met with appropriate gravity.

While he was dwelling on this and trying to follow the conversation, Derek, roaring with laughter, slammed his palm on the table, saying, 'If I know Mabel, this will just be the start of it. We'll begin with the minor offences and she'll soon be telling us who's up to *serious* mischief. Brace yourself, everyone — we're going to need something a lot stronger than tea!'

Maxwell quickly agreed with very little trace of amusement. 'Too early for whisky, mind you. Though whisky is undoubtedly the drink of conversation. Frees the tongue, but rarely in a regret-table manner,' he said, looking into the bottom of his empty cup as if discerning the future.

'It's far too early for anything stronger than tea, surely — it's barely five o'clock!' said Mabel, looking alarmed by the very thought.

Maxwell interrupted her protest impatiently. 'Good God, woman, it's not a workday. You wait for six o'clock on a workday, or any day you've got responsibilities. But on a holiday? Heavens, no. There are some conventions that are adhered to far too rigidly. Back in the day, we'd think nothing of pouring a good bottle of port at midday or mixing an old-fashioned at four. My last CO would pop a cork at breakfast without a by or leave. Earlier you drink the better. Much better to drink when you can still enjoy it, rather than in the last few moments before you fall asleep.'

Doubler cleared his throat after a short silence. 'By your leave,' he said, testing the sound of his voice in his full kitchen.

'Excuse me?' said the Colonel, who had been quite content with Doubler's lack of contribution up until this point.

'It's 'without a by *your* leave'.' Doubler's tone was good-natured, but the immediate silence round the table acknowledged the suggestion of confrontation, which in turn made the attendant guests immediately uncomfortable.

'Don't think so, old man. Nautical term. Think I'd know.' The Colonel drained his empty teacup for dramatic effect.

'It's not a nautical term. It's Medieval English, and the phrase is most definitely 'without a by your leave'. It's a common mistake.'

'Heavens,' mumbled Paula, made anxious by the will of the Colonel being challenged. In her book, Maxwell tended to be right. She swerved the conversation back to the previous one. 'If I drank in the daytime, I would soon be flat on my back. Can't imagine it.' She cast around the table for approval while doing a very good job of looking like she was prepared to imagine it if they were.

'There are plenty of drinks that seem to me perfectly acceptable to drink in the day,' said Doubler from the far end of the table, unaware of any potential hostility he might have evoked.

'What would you recommend?' This was from the Colonel and was widely regarded by the other guests as a ceasefire. They all looked to

Doubler for a similarly conciliatory response.

Doubler, often completely incapable of reading the subtleties of conversational interplay, had correctly deduced from the Colonel's immediately attentive repositioning that Maxwell might well expect Doubler to pour him a drink, so Doubler thought very carefully before he spoke.

'I find half a pint of cider goes particularly well with a working lunch. A farmer's lunch, mind you, or a potato grower's lunch at any rate. Not, perhaps, an office lunch.'

'And what about five past five? What then would you recommend?' There was challenge in the question, but Doubler was preparing to answer it literally.

'Gin and tonic. Gin and tonic goes rather well with tea. Surprisingly well with cake.'

The Colonel smiled broadly and the others relaxed. 'What an excellent idea, old man! Thank you. But you surprise me. I certainly wouldn't have had you down as a G and T man.'

'Oh, I know quite a lot about the subject.' Doubler raised his eyebrows and, nodding, looked at all of his guests, pleased that he had found such sure footing after a conversation that had been, for the most part, bewildering.

But as soon as he'd spoken the words, Doubler sensed an exchange of glances between his guests and was quite sure he could detect the lightest suggestion of a smirk on Maxwell's lips. He felt embarrassed but was entirely unsure why. He stood and began the process of washing up, turning his back on his guests and wondering whether they thought him a fool.

'Go on, then, tell us what you know,' urged Maxwell.

Doubler turned to face them, a little pink-cheeked. They were all looking at him expectantly, a single smile shared among them. He had been right: they were mocking him.

'Why are you mocking me?' he asked, his genuine curiosity outweighing his anxiety. After all, these were not his friends. He had not invested anything of himself in these relationships other than a little baking, and once they had left, he never need see them again.

'Oh now, you're being a little sensitive. 'Mocking' is a rather strong word. Gracie warned us that you are a bit of an expert on food and that you have some rather strong opinions on quite a lot of subjects.'

'Did she? Do I? I have certainly never claimed to be an expert on food. I am an expert on very few subjects. Though I might consider myself a leading expert on potatoes. And I know something of the subjects I have studied carefully, but I'd say those subjects are rather limited. I know much about a few things, and almost nothing about almost everything else. I know about bread, because I have spent a lifetime working with it. I know about cheese, but only the English ones. Similarly, I know about English apples. And I know a very *great* deal about gin.'

This might have been a little more than he intended to say on the subject and to claim expertise in this area was potentially dangerous, but the ego is a difficult beast to tame, even if you've kept it suppressed for much of your life. Doubler had found himself challenged not just by these people round his kitchen table but by the absent Mrs Millwood, who had potentially spoken quite uncharitably about him. Something complicated happened in his mind and he quickly found himself keen not only to give a good account of himself but to win them over entirely.

The Colonel was amused by the intensity of Doubler's conviction. 'You do, do you?'

'Yes, I know a *vast* amount.'

'Well, come on — share your knowledge and let's make it a practical interrogation, shall we? Perhaps you should pour us a little something and let's see what you know about the subject.'

Doubler, without saying another word, left the kitchen to go into the pantry. Much to the surprise of his guests, he shut himself into the small room, leaving them looking at the closed door and listening to the effort being made by Doubler on their behalf. Inside the pantry, Doubler had pulled on the light switch in the corner and was now shifting some bags of flour away from the floor to allow access to a heavy wooden trapdoor beneath him. He hadn't closed the door for privacy but for practicality, as he needed to rest the trapdoor on the closed door to the kitchen. He was very conscious that he was drawing considerable additional mystique and intrigue to something he should really have downplayed.

Nevertheless, he had committed to showing off, so he clambered down the wooden steps and, guided by pinholes of fading light from an airbrick at ground level, made his way to the shelves in the furthermost corner, passing rows and rows of neatly stacked unlabelled glass bottles. Once he'd found what he was looking for, he returned with his prize.

Part of him regretted being so bold, but it was too late now, and having claimed expertise, he felt certain that he needed to back up his claim with hard evidence. Once he'd closed the trapdoor, he felt in the wire rack for a firm lemon and helped himself to a large bottle of tonic that had stayed nicely cool on the stone floor. Leaving the pantry, he passed his guests, his head held high knowing that they were observing him both carefully and silently.

He fetched a jug of ice from the freezer and laid down all the components on the table in front of him, like a surgeon laying out his tools in preparation for a particularly tricky procedure.

'Tradition,' he said confidently, in a voice that would have been very familiar to Mrs Millwood, 'is overrated in the matter of gin. Because gin undoubtedly is evolving and the multifarious ways of serving it have advanced hugely our understanding of the spirit and the pleasure we can take from it.

'I am, however, not going to overwhelm you. I expect you're all very familiar with the G and T, the ice and a slice. And that is what I shall prepare for you because I want you to notice the gin, not the accompaniments. Some gins lend themselves to this classic treatment. But it is very possible to tease out the flavour of a gin by the addition of other flavours. I am not a gin pedant — in fact, I would go as far as to consider myself more liberal than most.'

While Doubler spoke, he cut the lemon into thin slices, allowing the scent of citrus to fill the room.

'All gin makers use a mix of botanicals to flavour their spirit. We all know and love juniper berries, and this is, of course, the flavour that we associate with the spirit. Indeed, it is essential to qualify as a London dry gin, as I'm sure you all know. But, depending on the distillery, you might find notes of any number of spices, herbs, plants or other flavourings — for example, coriander, angelica, orange peel, lemon peel, cardamom, orris, cinnamon, nutmeg, cassia bark, almond, liquorice or cubeb. When you're mixing a drink yourself, it is advisable to accentuate the flavour of the botanicals that have been used to craft it, so a gin that has used rose and cucumber to enhance its flavour might well benefit from the addition of a slice of cucumber or a couple of freshly picked rose petals. If there are no citrus notes at all, you should steer clear of lemon or lime.'

'Well, I never!' exclaimed Maxwell, who had spent a lifetime travelling the world and drinking in clubs and pubs with both rulers and rogues but was certain he had never heard of anything so outlandish.

Paula and Mabel were both staring at Doubler open-mouthed, as if he were speaking another language.

Doubler was enjoying this moment of

controlling his audience. He continued; his voice was measured and calm. 'Others, particularly from the more delicately nuanced end of the botanical spectrum, might benefit from a sprig of rosemary or fennel. There is a degree to which you can experiment, try flavours with flavours, but then there are, of course, some basic rules that must be adhered to.'

Doubler adopted an even more serious tone, as he was getting close to pouring his guests their drink. 'This gin we are about to drink is terribly good. The addition of lemon is not there to mask the flavour or indeed to add a flavour, but the citrus will introduce a welcome layer of complexity and the palate will enjoy the interplay. In an inferior gin, of course, the lemon is essential because it *becomes* the flavour.'

Doubler wasn't sure if he had his audience with him, but they were mercifully silent as he filled tall glasses to the brim with ice and poured a double measure of gin over each, filling the glass to the top with tonic. 'Use plenty of ice. The more ice you use, the more slowly it will melt. You don't want to dilute the drink with water. Disaster.'

He passed a drink to each guest, swilling each a little as he handed them over. 'We'll drink them long, shall we? It better befits an afternoon tea. This gin is good enough to drink neat and is excellent sipped from a very cold glass after dinner. I'd heartily recommend it, but, in the meantime, cheers.'

Doubler raised his glass and took a long slug, allowing the flavours to dance on his tongue and shutting his eyes in order to let his mouth alone make the assessment.

Derek was the first to respond. He, too, closed his eyes and allowed the flavours to reveal themselves. 'Well, I must say that's rather good. Not quite what I'm used to, mind, but I'd say that was very good indeed. More . . . '

'Floral,' offered Mabel tentatively.

'Yes, exactly and . . . '

'Herbal?' suggested Paula, taking a second hearty swig.

'Mmmm. And . . . '

'Complicated?' piped up Olive, looking for affirmation round the table.

'Yes,' agreed the Colonel. 'Couldn't have put it better myself.'

Mabel sipped hers self-consciously, looking for other flavours she felt ill equipped to detect but very much enjoying the surge of cold alcohol after the hot tea and rich cake.

Paula continued to gulp at hers greedily and was clearly delighted by it. 'Strong, is it?'

'Forty per cent. A good strong gin. About right for a drink that is in all probability going to be diluted.'

Maxwell was rejuvenated by his drink but also felt that he might have lost a small amount of control during this unexpected turn of events. He steered the conversation swiftly towards a subject he knew rather more about. 'So, I must say I find it rather surprising that gin is one of your topics. If you feel this strongly about gin, then I expect your views on whisky are very forceful indeed. Water or no water?'

'I don't care,' Doubler said, examining his gin carefully.

'Good God, man, everyone cares. Wars have been fought over less.'

Doubler looked up at the Colonel. 'Well, of course I care how *I* drink it, but I don't care how *you* drink it. Whisky is a uniquely personal drink. I doubt it even tastes the same to me as it tastes to you, so how could I possibly begin to prescribe a right or wrong way? Add some water, don't add some water, I really don't mind.'

'But what about you? How do you take yours?'

'Highlands, never lowlands. Equal measures of peat and smoke. Single malt, not blended. No water. No ice. Crystal glass.' Doubler drained his gin, pleased with the account he'd given of himself.

Maxwell roared with laughter and took another generous slug of his own drink. He genially swilled the half-glass of liquid round the ice, enjoying the sound. 'Rather perfect after-noon drink, I have to agree.'

Doubler felt proud that he'd held his own and that they all seemed to be appreciating the gin. 'Oh yes, quite definitely. Winter or summer. After food or before food, but ideally never with food. You want to be able to really explore the notes.'

Doubler looked deeply into his glass and took another sip, aware he now held his audience. 'The interesting thing about gin is that the flavour is never accidental. It's not so much about a good year or a bad year. The basics of any gin are essentially the same. Though it helps if you begin with a decent vodka, of course.'

'Vodka?' Paula squealed and looked at her glass in horror, as if to say that while she might condone the occasional afternoon gin and tonic, vodka was simply out of the question.

'Of course! Gin is merely flavoured alcohol.' Doubler was enjoying enormously the many pairs of eyes fixed upon him. 'Vodka is the obvious choice as a base spirit for gin because it is produced in very great quantity and to varying degrees of quality, so it is commercially cost-effective to use it. Anyone can make gin by simply buying a bottle of vodka and then adding their own botanicals.'

'Good heavens,' said Maxwell, contemplating his own drink with renewed respect.

'This is very basic knowledge. But there are many different schools of thought beyond this. I believe, quite strongly, that in order to make an exceptional gin, the quality of the vodka is of paramount importance. The better the vodka, the better the gin.'

'And what do you suppose makes a good vodka?' asked Derek.

'Good potatoes, of course.'

'Potatoes? Ahh, so now we're getting to the root of your interest,' said Maxwell with a pantomime wink.

'I'd be a rather poor potato grower not to investigate properly and thoroughly the many end uses of my crop. Don't you think?'

'Well, yes. I suppose it's like growing grapes and not drinking wine,' proffered Derek.

'No, not exactly. I could become very interested in grapes as a fruit, in their inherent qualities, and I could trust a vintner to make the wine and never think twice about it. But a potato is a far more interesting crop because its uses are so very diverse. If you're a commercial potato grower, you need to be pretty sure of your end market before you plant a single seed potato, and it helps if the potato you grow can serve more than one purpose — gives your business a level of robustness in times of uncertainty.'

'So you use your potatoes to make vodka? I was told that you're a bit of a dark horse. Is that your big secret?' Maxwell asked.

'Well, that's not a secret, no. I've always made vodka here for one particular vodka label. They are *very* discerning. Vodka made purely from potatoes is not cost-effective. It probably costs around thirty times more than a standard base spirit.'

'So,' asked Derek, 'why on earth would anybody pay the price?'

'You wouldn't unless you care deeply about the quality of your vodka, and there probably aren't many of those people around. But I have just one customer and they've bought my entire production since very early on in my potato-growing career. Plenty of people really don't mind what their vodka tastes like — what they want is something cold, something cheap and something that will mix well in cocktails. If you were going to drink your vodka mixed with orange juice from a carton, you certainly wouldn't drink Mirth Farm vodka. But if you're going to sip it after dinner, then, yes, you'll consider the price well worth it.'

'Well, thank you, Doubler. We've had an excellent tea and we've learnt a lot, too. So where can we get our hands on some of this delicious gin?' The Colonel picked up the bottle to examine the label. There wasn't one.

'I'm afraid you can't. The gin is a . . . It's a hobby. It's not for sale commercially. I make it to my own recipe for a number of special clients.'

'How about a number of special clients and the occasional special friend?' said the Colonel with a greedy look in his eye.

'We'll see. I make very little and it's allocated very strictly. But if I decide to increase my production, I'll let you know.'

The Colonel frowned, sensing he had been fobbed off, but returned to his glass, content for the moment to contemplate the flavours and allow the gradual release of alcohol to cushion his natural instinct for combat.

When Doubler's guests came to leave, there was a sense of celebration in the air, though Maxwell was a little more contemplative than usual. As he turned to leave, he patted Doubler on the back thoughtfully. 'You're a good sort, old man. You've earned your stripes this afternoon.'

Paula was a little flushed as she leant in to kiss Doubler goodbye. Doubler hadn't anticipated the attempted peck and instead stuck his hand out to shake her own, causing a small dance of clumsy ineptitude. Paula stumbled and fell heavily into his arms.

Maxwell immediately looked a little sternly at her and took her quite firmly by the elbow. 'Come on, old girl. Let's be getting you home.

That's quite enough of that.'

Meanwhile, Derek shook Doubler's hand vigorously. He seemed relieved, as if Doubler had passed some sort of test, and that a successful outcome had been as vital to Derek as it had to Doubler. Olive was the last to leave; indeed, she had appeared to be the most reluctant.

Doubler saw her to the car. She had been assigned a space in the rear of Maxwell's small Renault. Just before she folded herself into the cramped seat, she shook his hand decisively, but her voice was barely audible over the sound of the engine as the car warmed. 'Thank you for a delicious tea. You really are a very talented baker and a remarkable teller of stories, too.'

Doubler held her hand between his, basking in these words and realizing with a jolt that they were the first words he'd ever heard her utter.

Doubler leant into the car, still grasping her hand in his. 'I'm partial to baking, Olive, and I really don't have much of an audience, so if you ever feel like popping in any day between three thirty and four fifteen, you can be sure of a treat or two in the cake tin.'

Olive glowed as Maxwell slammed the driver's door shut, beckoning Paula to take her place beside him. Doubler stood to watch them leave and marvelled at the sheer volume of whirring thoughts these visitors had left him to process. He couldn't wait to share the news with Mrs Millwood and wondered if she'd be proud of his previously unexercised powers of hospitality. He so hoped she would be. He had felt dangerously exposed at times, but the memory of that discomfort was already fading with the anticipation of the smallest praise from Mrs Millwood.

# 19

When it was time for his next shift at Grove Farm, Doubler mustered as much confidence as he could and used it to propel him towards the animal shelter before his courage failed him.

Doubler was fortified by a sense of purpose and this had enabled him to lock up the house, guide the Land Rover carefully down the drive, unhook the gate and leave Mirth Farm behind him. As he neared the farm, he realized that the anxiety he had felt that first time had been replaced by a much rarer thrill of anticipation. He knew he was probably being silly and he couldn't possibly expect as much action as last time — after all, how often could he hope to be an accessory to a crime? His last visit had marked the end of his life as a recluse but on this visit he was determined to make it memorable through action at Grove Farm. He rather hoped he would even achieve something of note that might be considered a contribution.

Since his last visit, the sadness of that donkey had haunted Doubler, but he wondered whether, as Mrs Millwood had hinted, the real tragedy was the plight of Mrs Mitchell herself. Doubler was determined to get to know the animals and he was determined to get to know more about Mrs Mitchell's story. Mrs Millwood had told him she believed there might be more to her than met the eye — and Mrs Millwood had a very good instinct for these things.

And much to his surprise, Doubler had also enjoyed Olive's quiet presence when she'd visited Mirth Farm, and though he didn't want to intrude, he wondered whether he may be able to engineer a chance encounter with her while he was visiting Grove Farm.

As he passed the farm shop that regularly delivered his groceries, he idly thought about pulling in to pick up some carrots for the donkey, but though he slowed down and indicated to turn in, he hesitated and drove on. He wasn't ready to compromise their current arrangement. Boxes of food found their way to him and he paid his suppliers regularly, not in cash but by delivering them a generous order of his Mirth Farm gin. He and his suppliers barely knew each other, and though clandestine, the arrangement had worked very peacefully for years and he didn't want to jeopardize that relationship now, particularly as there was so much change in the air. He instead resolved to add carrots to his weekly order. This donkey needed not just the friendship of the animal-shelter volunteers but a consistent kindness he could rely upon. This was a relationship that Doubler felt he might be able to commit to. Perhaps then poor Percy could start to trust in a bond with a human once again.

Doubler arrived at the Portakabin, helped himself to the key from under the mat and let himself in. He wasn't sure if heating was rationed with the same strictness that sugar cubes appeared to deserve, but he switched the heating

217

on high and flicked the fan switch to ensure the cold room warmed up as quickly as possible. He picked up the comms file and read through it carefully. Little had changed since last time, other than the arrival of a large number of ex-caged chickens, the return of some cats from the neuter clinic and a hastily scrawled reference to Mrs Mitchell's attempted kidnapping of the donkey. He noted the terse entry and wondered whether it was up to him to file an unexpurgated report.

Doubler was excited by the amount of responsibility he had all of a sudden. Here he was with a key to an office and a report to write, but he knew his shift would stretch out uncomfortably for him if he didn't pace himself. He decided to have a wander round the yard and acquaint himself with the animals. On the desk, ready for his perusal (a yellow Post-it note told him just this), was Mrs Mitchell's file, which the Colonel had thoughtfully left out for him to read. To understand the donkey, he had to understand his backstory, but anticipating untold depths of despair and loneliness within the pages, he concluded that he hadn't quite built up his strength for that yet so resolved to read it carefully upon his return.

Before heading towards the stables, Doubler went in search of Percy. He couldn't find him where he had been on the day of the breakout attempt, but he quickly found him in an adjacent field. He was grazing happily in the company of a number of shaggy-haired goats, who were browsing the hedgerow, thoughtfully helping themselves to a smorgasbord of hawthorn, young elm, blackthorn, willow and hazel. Necks stretched taut to reach the few tender leaves the winter could offer, the goats were systematically clearing branches as if they were working to a deadline. Doubler wasn't sure he had ever witnessed such intensity of mastication. The donkey wasn't much more interested in his visitor than the goats, though even with his nose in the grass, he maintained a wary eye on Doubler.

Doubler chatted to them all self-consciously, finding his voice alarming in the quiet field. With a promise to return soon, he retraced his steps and went in search of the dogs, cats and small animals he knew were housed in the stables. These buildings occupied three full sides of a large courtyard. It was ideal. Doubler supposed that once the farm had offered a livery service, because there were enough stables for more than a dozen horses and, really, what farm needed more than one? But now Olive had loaned the space to these poor dejected and rejected creatures, and this space, he hypothesized, was pure luxury compared to the lives they must have come from.

Doubler had no specific brief to care for the animals while he was there: a team of students took it in turns to feed and water them on their way to college in the morning, and the same team stopped by at the end of the day to exercise and muck out the animals. While he was here, however, he felt they were in his care, and even if he didn't have to do much to keep them alive, he bore the weight of responsibility upon his shoulders, and after trying out this new burden as he walked around, he decided he liked it.

The first stable was divided into several small sections, some empty and some home to a few bored-looking cats. They barely looked up at him as he went from cage to cage. He thought of the few cats he'd known over the years, farmyard cats with the scent of prey forever urging them from place to place, backs arched in anticipation of sporadic human contact. He thought of the skilled solitary hunters patrolling their territory with watchful concentration occasionally masked by feigned nonchalance. These cats were different. Resigned to their fate, with nothing left to fight for, they slumbered wearily, taking as little interest in each other as they were taking in their visitor. Just one cat raised its head to fix Doubler with a look of contempt and he was reminded, uncannily, of Mrs Mitchell. He left the stable guiltily.

We all reach a time in our life we're no use to anybody, he thought. I wonder what on earth compels our hearts to continue beating?

He opened the latch to the second stable and peered in. It was empty. He inhaled deeply. The newly laid straw smelt clean and sweet, as if it had just been prepared for a new intake. The thought overwhelmed him with sadness. A new intake could only come from someone else's wretchedness — from a sudden, unplanned departure or the felling of something that had once been strong and vigorous. How many deathbed promises were not being fulfilled that these animals would end up here? he wondered.

There were more than ten stables yet to explore, but his heart felt tight in his chest and his memories were conspiring to remind him of the most painful of abandonments. He stumbled a little as one image after another flashed before his eyes, merging in a medley of nonsensical confusion. His wife, Marie, not as he saw her last but prowling, fiercely alert; Mrs Millwood lying pale and thin not in a clean hospital bed but on a nest of straw; a donkey's baleful glower.

A cockerel crowed loudly, setting off a chain reaction from the hens around him. Doubler listened to the noise to reassure himself that the mayhem wasn't ominous before turning back and hurrying towards the Portakabin, as if reminded he was late for an appointment by the rooster's call.

He headed back, sat down and opened Mrs Mitchell's file, greedy for information. But to his surprise, and mounting disappointment, only a few pages of scrawled notes served to tell her story. He read them once quickly and again more carefully, but he knew nothing other than the scant facts provided. Dates and incidents were recorded, as was her address, but there was very little detail and certainly nothing to suggest a more in-depth investigation into Mrs Mitchell's background.

One thing he was certain of was that Mrs Millwood's instincts were to be trusted. She was sure to be right: nobody had yet asked the right questions.

# 20

Maddie Mitchell's house was one of a number of identical houses in a neatly kept close. Each had a porch, a brightly painted door, a single garage and a thick laurel hedge separating it from its neighbour. Doubler knocked several times before Mrs Mitchell opened the door to her tidy but unremarkable home.

Doubler nearly didn't recognize her. Not only had she lost the walking stick, the headscarf and the exaggerated limp, she had also lost the wild glint in her eyes. She wore a white shirt, closed at her throat with a large silver brooch, a long cream cardigan over a brown corduroy skirt and neat loafers on her feet. She was subdued, meek almost, as she inched the door open. The defiance returned, though, emboldened by a flash of hostility, when she recognized her visitor.

'Oh, it's you,' she said. 'The new man.' Mrs Mitchell did not have any intention of inviting him inside — this much was clear from both her contemptuous tone and her tight grip on the barely opened door.

'Good morning, Mrs Mitchell. Can we talk?'

'No,' she said, not even attempting to disguise the disgust she felt for him. 'I don't think we can. I've heard what you've got to say and you're wrong, wrong, wrong. All of you.' She started to close the door, but Doubler put up his hand and attempted to disarm her with a submissive tone.

'I don't know what's been said before — like you say, I'm the new man — but let me come in and let's talk. Maybe we can clear this mess up.' Doubler took a step back from the door, allowing some space to open up between them. This had the effect of softening Mrs Mitchell's stance, but she was still deeply suspicious of Doubler's motives.

'It's a mess for sure. That's exactly what it is. They stole my donkey from me, took him away with no consultation, and unless you can get him back, there's nothing much to talk about.'

'I am not going to promise anything, but I am going to listen. I'm going to listen to your side of the story. I've read your file from start to finish and I learnt absolutely nothing. I know the facts from our side, though nothing much more than the dates of each incident and the action taken. But nobody's recorded the facts from your side, and as far as I can tell, nobody seems to have asked the basic questions, like *why* this keeps happening. Please may I come in?'

'If you do listen, you will be the first.' She assessed him for a few seconds and then shrugged. Resigned, she stood aside and let him in before turning to lead the way silently. Doubler followed her down a corridor to the sitting room. The house was sparse but immaculate. Somehow, despite the scant information he had found in her file, Doubler had imagined a more chaotic lifestyle for the woman.

He took a seat, and once he had accepted that

223

there was unlikely to be any tea or biscuits on offer, he began to ask her questions as they occurred to him.

'Do you want to start from the beginning? How long have you had the donkey? How do you fill your days?' Each question was punctuated by a lengthy silence.

Mrs Mitchell said nothing in reply to Doubler, so, instead, realizing he had a captive audience and nothing to lose, he began to talk about himself.

'I have a hero, Mrs Mitchell, and his actions guide me every *single* day of my life. His name was John Clarke. He was born in the late 1800s and lived to be an old man. He was a man of great principle, an honest gentleman with an incredible work ethic and a burning, selfless desire to improve the world.'

Though he got no response, Doubler was certain that he had her attention.

'You know what he gave the world?'

There was still no sound from Mrs Mitchell, but she had set her head on one side and had fixed her eyes on him with the calculating stare of the magpie.

'He gave us the Maris Piper.' Doubler paused for effect.

'You'd think his name was Maris, wouldn't you? Or Piper. But no, nothing so grandiose. He was a humble man, you see. Just plain old Mr Clarke. He had no formal education, left school at twelve and dedicated his working life to improving the world's potatoes. That man has fed millions and millions of people. And nobody even knows his name. There's not even a statue to honour his memory anywhere in the world, as far as I can tell. Nowadays you can be a global phenomenon for just about anything. Eat a cricket live on telly and you're known in all four corners of the earth. It puzzles me.'

'Why on earth would anyone eat a cricket?' Now Mrs Mitchell was interested, and she edged forward in her chair, her bright eyes locked on her guest, baffled by the turn the conversation had taken.

'Well, that's the right question to ask, Mrs Mitchell. Why on earth would they? And will the world be any better for it?' Doubler shook his head at the perplexity of life. He looked around the room, his systematic sweep taking in the empty bookshelves, the lack of personal effects, not even the trace of a scent of cooking coming from the kitchen.

'Forgive me if this observation seems like an intrusion, but I'm guessing, Mrs Mitchell, that you must be very lonely.'

Mrs Mitchell sighed heavily. 'I suppose I must be. But this isn't about me. He's so lonely it's killing him.'

'Do you think so? I think he's probably in the best place. He's very well looked after. Surely you can trust in that at least?'

'Oh, that's what they all say. You're just no different from the rest of them.' Mrs Mitchell stood up and left the room. He could see glimpses of her through the hatch in the wall busying herself in the kitchen, opening and closing cupboards, but there was still no sign of a boiling kettle or the reassuring rattle of a biscuit tin.

'But you can understand, can't you,' he said, raising his voice to continue their conversation, 'the practical difficulties? You can see why everyone thought he might be better off elsewhere?'

She appeared at the hatch, poking her head through it and shaking it with force. 'Actually. No. No. No. I just can't accept that.'

Doubler chose to respond with calmness, adopting a gently cajoling manner rather than entering into combat. 'But he's got needs, and you can't possibly look after him at this stage. I know it's tough. On you both. But you can visit, can't you?'

'Yes, yes, I can. And I do. But I find it so very hard. I try to be strong, but I just cry and cry and that upsets him. He doesn't really understand.'

'It must be very, very hard on you. I'm so sorry. I take it you were very close.'

'Close? Well, of course. As close as two beings can be.'

'And how long did he live with you?'

'Live with me?' She thought for a few minutes. 'Gosh.' Mrs Mitchell frowned and then smiled as her eyes flicked through a back catalogue of memories. 'We'd have been celebrating fifty years just about now. Coming up for it.'

'Fifty years! Goodness me! I had no idea!' Doubler shook his head in disbelief. 'Fifty years! Imagine! What's that in donkey years?'

'You're right.' Mrs Mitchell nodded sadly,

making her way back to the sitting room to take her seat opposite Doubler. 'Donkey's years.'

'Well, no wonder you were traumatized by the separation. I'm beginning to understand the depth of the relationship. But *nonetheless*. You simply can't keep him here!'

'Why ever not? That's what I don't understand. It's a big house, you know. Two bedrooms. And a dining room. What do I need a dining room for, for goodness' sake? I'm not exactly throwing dinner parties. I eat in front of the telly most nights. Alone. I could have him in the dining room if he couldn't manage the stairs.'

'Oh, but you just can't, Mrs Mitchell. That's the problem. Do you realize what a ludicrous proposition that is?'

'But why? Give me one good reason why not. There's nobody better qualified to look after him than me. Nobody that would take better care of him than me.' Mrs Mitchell cried out her appeal and it was clear to Doubler that this was something she'd had to do many times before.

'I don't doubt your good intentions, but it's not possible. That's the thing you've just got to get into your head.'

Mrs Mitchell scowled, rose to her feet, planted her hands firmly on her hips and said with palpable disgust, 'You can see yourself out.'

'Now, now, Mrs Mitchell, don't be like that. Let's see if we can find some middle ground. I'm here to help.'

'You can't help. Your mind is made up. You're no different from the rest of them.'

'I *am* different. I *can* help you.' Doubler

looked at the woman before him, the slackness of her shoulders, the despair in her eyes. Once again she took a deep breath, the gulp of a woman who might be drowning.

'This is the deal. You give me one good reason why he can't live here with me and I'll listen. But you'd better make it good.' The fire in her eyes returned and she folded her arms in challenge.

'There are plenty of good reasons, but I'll start with the obvious one. Because, Mrs Mitchell, he needs plenty of grass to graze on.'

'He needs *what?*'

'*Grass*, Mrs Mitchell. You do understand that, don't you?'

Mrs Mitchell looked him up and down, a range of emotions playing across her face. Disgust, shock, anger, puzzlement. And then a pause while Doubler shifted uncomfortably in his chair. She sat down slowly and leant forward, scrutinizing him carefully as understanding began to sweep across her face, replacing the bafflement that had been there just a second ago.

'Oh my,' she said, a broad smile breaking out and wiping decades of pain away. 'Oh my, oh my.'

Doubler swallowed, unsure what might follow.

'I'm not talking about the donkey, you daft oaf. I don't miss the *donkey*. I haven't been in a *relationship* with the donkey for fifty years, you foolish, foolish man. I'm talking about my *husband!* It's Thomas I miss!'

Doubler looked at her in horror. 'Your husband? You have a husband? He's still alive?'

Mrs Mitchell leapt to her feet. 'Of course he's

228

alive. Very much so,' she said, a little indignantly, and then, under her breath, 'but I bet he wishes he wasn't.' She sat down again.

Doubler raced through their conversation, pulling scraps to the front of his mind, trying to work out what he had learnt and what he hadn't from the visit. If they had been talking at cross purposes throughout, then he knew very little indeed.

'We grew spuds,' said Mrs Mitchell, as if in answer to Doubler's earlier conversation around the development of the Maris Piper.

'You did? You and Thomas, Mrs Mitchell?'

'Me and my hubby, yes. And please, call me Maddie. We grew cabbage and broccoli. Sprouts, too. Didn't bother with the lettuce and such, but we liked our brassicas a lot. Brassicas and roots will see you through a winter.'

'True that, Maddie. You had a bit of land, did you?'

'A bit? More than we could handle. We didn't have a patch, you know — we had a *farm*. A smallholding some would call it, but it didn't feel small when you were responsible for everything that you put in the earth or took out of the earth. It didn't feel small when it was your soil to dig, or your weeds to remove, or your animals that would die if you didn't take proper care of them. We never stopped. We worked ourselves hard, but I wish ... ' She paused, uncertain of continuing this train of thought with a stranger.

'You wish what?'

'I wish we'd worked ourselves harder. I wish we'd worked ourselves to death. It would have

229

been so much better if we'd both died of digging.'

Doubler allowed Maddie to compose herself, waiting until her chest had stopped heaving in emotion before asking, gently, 'What happened to Thomas?'

'He didn't die. More's the pity. He's still very much alive. Technically. But he's definitely retired from living. I wish he'd died and that's the truth. And I wish I'd died with him. He had a heart attack. That was the start of his decline. They said the farm was too much. They forced us to sell it, insisted we had to downsize. Then he had a stroke shortly afterwards and they put him in a home. They used the money from the sale of the farm to keep him alive. Ironic.'

Doubler nodded, the sound of his son's voice ringing in his ears. 'It's not an unusual story. I hear this time and time again. But it doesn't make it any easier to swallow. I'm truly sorry for your loss.'

'We should never, *ever* have left the farm. Never. It would have been so much better to just be there, even if we had let it go a bit. But *they* had other plans.'

Doubler watched her carefully. Although the subject was obviously distressing, he could sense her beginning to unwind a little, as if just the act of telling him her story was therapeutic.

He kept his voice calm, coaxing more from her through gentle probing. 'Who are 'they'? These people you're talking about? The social workers?'

'Heavens, no! The social workers have been pretty good when you consider the runaround I give them. No. My sons.' Mrs Mitchell bowed her head in shame.

'Oh, Maddie. I'm so, so sorry.' The pain in her eyes etched sharp lines around her face and it was easy to see where the pain and the anger had blurred and become inseparable.

'Tell me about the runaround you give the social workers. What do you get up to?'

'I don't quite know. I'm doing fine. I can go a few days just right. And then I get this terrible, terrible darkness and I just want to break him out of that place. He's unhappy, I'm unhappy, and so I make up my mind to go and bust him right out of there. But it all gets so confusing and I work myself into a state and I, somehow — I'm damned if I know how — go and break that blasted donkey out instead.'

Maddie paused for a moment to dab at the corner of her eyes with a handkerchief. 'They took away everything. Percy was my Tom's love, you know. He was the one thing that didn't really have to do a day's work on the farm and nobody resented it. The chickens had to lay eggs or they went in the pot; the cats had to catch mice or they'd starve; the veggies had to produce or they be dug right back in. But not Percy. Lord and master he was. It sometimes felt like he was running the place. Had his pick of the best grazing. Had carrots *grown* for him! Can you imagine? But Thomas loved that donkey, said there was something a little bit holy about him.

'When Thomas went into that place, he begged me to look after Percy and I didn't quite know what to do. I was still grieving from the

231

end of my world as I knew it, the end of the Thomas I knew. I wasn't really strong enough at the very moment when I needed to be strong to resist all of this horrible change that was being imposed on me. It's hard to describe just how ghastly that time was. A nightmare. It was poor Thomas lying there in hospital, but I was the one that was treated like I was brain-dead. Nobody told me *anything*. My sons sold the farm, bought me this place. They thought they were doing what was best, I suppose, but I don't ever remember them asking my opinion.

'Soon after I moved in, I had the rather brilliant idea of bringing the donkey here to live with me. I was almost unbearably lonely and it seemed like a marvellous plan. Defiant, even. The donkey had been left at the farm and I suppose they knew somebody would tip up and collect him one day, so I did. Nobody even questioned me. I popped a halter round his neck and walked him down the bridle path. We had the loveliest walk, the two of us. Several miles of chatting and then, bold as brass, I brought Percy here and made a stable for him in the garage. I know it was wrong. It was *terribly* wrong, but I thought then that Thomas might come home to me and I couldn't bear not to have Percy ready and waiting.

'I kept him as best as I could. But God, they don't half make a mess. You don't really appreciate it when they're out in a field, but keep them inside and for every barrow load of food you give them, they produce three barrow loads of muck the other end. It overwhelmed me a bit.

And it's heavy stuff to move. So for a while I did what I could to get it in the bin for the collection each week, but the more I shovelled, the more the donkey produced. It was like a story I used to read my children about a bad man and a magic porridge pot and the porridge spilt over from the pot, into the kitchen, then the house. There was a terrible, terrible picture of the porridge escaping from the front door and threatening to drown the whole village. That's what it felt like — that me and Percy were going to suffocate in a mountain of manure.'

Doubler tried to imagine the scene and couldn't help smiling a little at the image of this fierce woman shovelling donkey manure into her wheelie bin. He was also delighted at the ease with which she had told him the tale; in fact, he was beginning to wonder if now she had started to talk, she would ever stop. But she'd paused and her eyes looked troubled as she remembered the mounting manure, the mounting panic.

'What happened next?' he asked gently.

'The neighbours got wind. Got wind! Get it? Oh, they certainly did get wind! The smell of it must have had the whole close wondering what I was doing in here.'

Maddie was suddenly delighted by the memory.

'I suppose it must have been the stench or the rats. I'll never know which gave the game away, but social services knocked on the door first, and then the RSPCA turned up and they lectured me like I was some kind of animal abuser. Which I'm *not*. I just wanted the donkey to be here when my Thomas comes home. And I suppose I still do.'

'Is he ever coming home? Your husband, I mean.'

'Yes. No. I don't know. He is poorly. Not in his body so much now, but his mind has gone. I don't think he'd like it much here: there's nothing he'd find familiar. But he *hates* it there. I know he does and I can't bear it. He wouldn't hurt a fly, that man. He worked so hard and he gave what he could to anybody that needed it. And he was a good, good dad. He didn't deserve this ending.'

Doubler frowned. 'And what about the donkey? Obviously that was a bit of a mess you had to sort out. But do you miss him, too? Is that why you keep going back for him?'

'No. That's the joke. Having the donkey here was terrible. *Just terrible*. But I look at that donkey in the eye and I just see Thomas. I can't seem to separate the two in my mind. On a good day, I can, of course, but on a bad day, I don't really know which way is up. I just feel so alone and so confused and so betrayed.'

'Who betrayed you?'

'My sons for sticking me here, for not respecting my choices. I looked after them all their lives, I sorted their problems out, and I was always there for them. But the minute I needed them, they did what was most convenient for them. So yes, they definitely betrayed me. But most of all, Thomas. His betrayal was the worst. We had a pact. We were in it together. It was a marriage. And he left me.'

'Aren't you being a bit tough on him? I mean, it doesn't sound like he had much of a say in the matter.'

'But he promised! He made a commitment to stay with me for richer or poorer, for better or worse, and he gave in to *them*. He let them decide what was best.'

'Your sons?'

'Yes. I don't know when he became so weak in his spirit. He so wanted them to grow up to become good men that he was blind to it when they weren't. Anything they did he thought was brilliant, so when they told him how things were going to be after his heart attack, he just sort of succumbed to them. He didn't want to admit that they might not have his best interests at heart, so he just agreed with everything they said.'

'And you felt this betrayed you?'

'Of course it did. But they're *my* kids, too. No one wants to admit that their kids aren't very nice people. To raise unkind people is the biggest failing you can make as a parent. But to acknowledge out loud that they're not nice is taken as a sign not just of bad parenting but, apparently, of your mental decline.'

'Is it? I think I'm able to admit that my son is a bad sort. I'd be a bit soft in the head to think anything else. But is that my failing? I don't think so. Aren't some kids just predisposed to be not very nice? Does it always have to be somebody's fault?' Doubler thought about Julian as if for the first time, shocked that his son might be a product of his own making.

Maddie was emphatic. 'Yes. Somebody has to take responsibility. Or at least admit that they managed to breed an awful human being. But pretending they're better than they are just because they're your own flesh and blood is pretty weak, pretty delusional, don't you think?'

'Gosh. I've never thought about it. My son doesn't appear to have any values. Or perhaps he has values but they don't coincide with mine. Right now I'm trying to think of a single redeeming feature and I can't.' Doubler stopped and thought, images of his son's deeds flashing in front of his eyes.

'Nope. Not one. He is not evil, you know; he's not a psychopath. He's just not somebody I'd particularly choose to spend any time with. Is that my fault? I think it's a straightforward case of genetics.' Doubler paused again, searching for an image to help him illustrate his point. He found one. 'Take a potato. Two spuds that *look* identical when you put them in the water to boil. There's a chance that one will go brown when you cook it and one won't. There's no way of knowing which before you put it in the water and yet the occurrence is entirely predictable. While that gene exists, there's a one in four chance of it happening, regardless of outward appearances. It must be the same with us. If niceness is dominant and unpleasantness is recessive, then it doesn't really matter how you are as parents — you have a twenty-five per cent chance of having an unpleasant child.'

'Not very good odds.'

'No. And maybe you think you can nurture

and educate that child into becoming something other than its true destiny. But no, that unpleasantness is inherent and will probably pop up in the next generation as well.'

'So you raised a bad potato, too?' asked Maddie, her relief palpable. 'I don't think I've ever met somebody else who admitted that. Normally people are falling over themselves to tell you how great and accomplished their children are. You read some of the round robins I get at Christmas and you'd think they were handing out Nobel Peace Prizes like Smarties.'

'Ah, perhaps that's because they are doing exactly what you're guilty of — taking responsibility for them and thinking their children are an absolute reflection of themselves, when in fact they're just a sequence of DNA.'

'I wish I'd had this conversation years ago. I should have persuaded them not to reproduce themselves. Too late, sadly.'

'Well, that's definitely not the answer either, is it? Because there's a seventy-five per cent chance they're going to produce a kind child. Although, I've got a few grandchildren and I've got to say the jury is still out.'

'So you have one bad apple. Do you have any others?'

'I have just the two children. There's Julian, who's my bad apple, and there's Camilla, who is just like her mother.'

'And what *about* your wife? Does she dote on your children like my Thomas does?'

Doubler hesitated. 'She's . . . she's not with us anymore. I was devoted to her, you know. But I don't think I was able to be the husband she needed. She wanted me to be somebody else and I didn't notice soon enough. I thought she had fallen in love with me, but I think she perhaps fell in love with the person she hoped I would become. Does that make sense? Maybe if I'd noticed sooner, I could have had a go at being the husband she dreamt of and maybe things would have ended differently. But I had my potatoes, you see. I've blamed myself for a very long time, and the children blamed me, too.'

Doubler thought about Marie, thought about the changes he would have had to make to satisfy her. 'I don't really like to speak ill of her, but perhaps she was a bit selfish as well.'

'Well, it's very easy to bestow the ones we've lost with great qualities they never had. That's common. So perhaps coming to terms with some of your wife's faults makes it easier to let her go?'

Doubler looked at her, as if to speak, but then silenced himself.

Maddie tried to interpret the sadness in his eyes and weighed it up against her own. 'Or perhaps not. Perhaps the memories whether good or bad are all just distilled pain when you can't rewrite the ending.'

'It's very complicated, Maddie, but you and I aren't so different. In fact, we're remarkably similar. We're both blighted.' Doubler softened. 'But your husband, Thomas, he didn't really betray you. He was bullied by his kids, that's all. And he probably hates that feeling as much as you do. It's probably tormenting him a bit.'

Maddie shook her head sadly. 'I just don't

know. Sometimes he doesn't even recognize me when I visit. He just asks for them, over and over again. They don't visit much, of course. He probably thought that if he submitted to their wishes, he'd get more of them, but he gets so much less. They seem to be able to forget about him the minute they leave.'

'It must be terribly confusing for him.'

'And hurtful for me. If we'd stayed put, stayed up at the farm, then Thomas might have gone a bit downhill, he might even have lost his mind, but it would have been gentler. Mine's gone too, so we could have muddled along together, knowing just enough between us.'

'Perish the thought! You'd have had to put Percy in charge!' Doubler joked, masking a surge of emotion threatening to engulf him.

'Well, yes, I should have thought of that myself. It's about time that donkey did something to pay us back for a lifetime of soft living.'

They sat in comfortable silence before the loud rumbling of Doubler's stomach interrupted their thoughts. 'Goodness me, Maddie. Do you happen to have a biscuit? I have one of those constitutions that needs constant refuelling or I turn pretty ugly.'

Maddie looked crestfallen. 'No, none. I'm so sorry. I don't get visitors and there's just not any point keeping a tin for myself. I could pop out to the shops? I could be there in twenty minutes. Back in under an hour?'

Doubler tutted and went to the kitchen, talking loudly to Maddie as he went. 'Do you have flour, butter and sugar?' He was opening the fridge and peering into the cupboards, extracting packets and jars as he spoke.

'Probably?' said Maddie, uncertain of when she last stocked up.

'Well, if you've got flour, butter and sugar, that's even better than a biscuit tin. Come and give me a hand — let's get your kitchen smelling of a kitchen. I can whip up some shortbread much quicker than you can catch a bus. And while the shortbread bakes, we can work out what on earth we're going to do about you and your donkey.'

'And Thomas?' asked Maddie, with hope in her voice.

'Why not? Let's sort your husband out too while we're at it.'

Maddie, less bewildered now, handed Doubler a stripy apron and assessed her kitchen as if for the very first time.

# 21

Doubler recounted his visit to Maddie Mitchell to Mrs Millwood. She listened attentively and didn't interrupt until Doubler had relayed every last detail, right down to the delight on Maddie's face when she tasted her first bite of the buttery shortbread, fresh from the oven.

'You did a good job, Mr Doubler. It sounds like she just needed to be asked why she's so sad.'

'That was the right question,' agreed Doubler.

'And she's sad because she and her husband don't deserve to be alone and confused. They deserve to be together for their last years, muddled but complete, even if that might be a bit inconvenient to the people trying to care for them.'

'That's it, Mrs M. Together they could face all of the difficulties of life, even death.'

Doubler listened to Mrs Millwood's silence as she thought about this for a few moments.

After a while, she asked, 'Do you fear death, Mr Doubler?'

Doubler thought carefully. 'Yours or mine, Mrs M?'

'Your death, Mr Doubler. Do you fear your own death?'

He wasn't shocked by the question, but nor did he feel equipped to answer it from the enveloping warmth of his most comfortable armchair. He stood up and carried the phone with him to the window seat, where he sat down again before answering cautiously.

'When I wake to a heavy mist, it often clears up here at the farm before it clears down below in the valley and then it might as well be just me left on the planet. It's most dramatic in the late spring or summer, and it's exquisitely beautiful. I'm alone at the farm sitting here with a sea of thick white cloud beneath me. My view is obliterated, just blue sky above, and the only thing I'm sure of is my little hilltop island, nestled in this foamy white sea, and it's *astonishingly* quiet. It's eerily silent. I have no idea what the birds think is going on. When that happens, I can't help imagining that I'm alone, the last person alive. The rest of the world's global population could have been wiped out by a fireball or some devastating disease and I wouldn't know.'

'How does that make you feel? Lonely or frightened?'

'Neither lonely nor frightened, strangely. It feels calm and entirely natural. I feel isolated up here anyway and I'm comfortable with that notion, but when I can't see anything else, it's a little like death. Just me on my floating island, and I *like* it. I *love* it! Which must mean, I suppose, that I am very at peace with the prospect of my physical demise.'

Mrs Millwood made a noise down the phone that Doubler was now very familiar with. The noise was part snort of disgust, part exclamation of disapproval and, combined, it served as a precursor to an expression of outrage. Smiling warmly, Doubler braced himself.

'Well. I shall certainly remember that, next time it's foggy down here. I shall be sure in the knowledge that you're basking in the sunshine above, not imagining at all with sorrow or regret that I and everyone else down here might have fried in a fireball or withered away at the hands of some devastating disease.'

'Oh no, Mrs Millwood. That's not what I meant at all. I don't want *you* caught in the path of the fireball. I want you up here above the clouds, safe with me on my island.'

Mrs Millwood was not easily cajoled. Her outrage unabated, she continued, 'But I've got *friends* down here, Doubler. I have *family* too. I don't think I want to leave them to their grisly fate while I gloat up there with you. I'm not quite as callous as you are, apparently. I have *responsibilities*.'

An unlikely image of a fireball racing towards Mrs Millwood while she shielded Midge flashed fleetingly in Doubler's mind. 'Perhaps I didn't think this through,' he conceded. 'I wasn't really thinking of the end of the world in the context of you and your friends and family. Rather, I was thinking of my removal from all of you, and that sitting up here on my own either in a suspended state of semi-death or an actual state of death doesn't seem to fill me with fear. And when I'm here above the clouds, I'm not really thinking at all. I'm just able to enjoy the peace and the quiet and the whiteness beneath me. The knowledge that it is just me up here is one of comfort, not fear. That's all.'

'Well, it's nice to know where I stand,' said Mrs Millwood with only the slightest hint of humour in her voice.

'But the knowledge that you're down there, begrudging me, does change things a bit. I mean, I am not as comfortable being the sole survivor of a global wipeout in the certainty that somewhere below you're writhing around in pain or at least a tiny bit cross with me for enjoying my solitude. I seem to be substantially less at peace all of a sudden.'

'I should jolly well hope so, Mr Doubler.'

She was quiet for a few moments before exclaiming, with passion, 'Oh, I do *know* those mornings, Mr Doubler, when you open the curtains and the sky is the colour of old bed sheets. But I suppose even if the mist has crept right up to the windowpanes, you still need to be aware of the possibility of a far horizon to be able to appreciate the beauty of an impenetrable fog. If all you're missing is a handful of wheelie bins and a garden fence, then perhaps there's less beauty in the whiteness?'

'I beg to differ. How do you know, in a thick, thick fog, what you're missing? Wheelie bins? I doubt it. Could be anything out there.'

'I suppose you're right. I shall see what I think I'm missing next time the weather closes in. I do like it, though, when it's misty down here in the town and in the surrounding countryside, and I think I might enjoy it even more now I know you'll be sitting up above us all, somewhat godly.'

'If I had godly powers, Mrs Millwood, I'd use them to whisk you away from that place. I'd make you well and hearty, and I'd soon have you sitting in the clouds with me.'

Mrs Millwood thought about this before answering seriously, 'It's a funny thing, Mr Doubler. There are other mornings, aren't there, when it's quite, quite clear down in the town but there's a little cloud covering at the top of your hill and shrouding Mirth Farm in its own little hat of despondency. We'll all be down here below and enjoying a fine morning and I'll look up towards the farm and see you're in cloud. That's always made me feel sad for you. What's that like, Mr Doubler, being alone in your own cloud and knowing the rest of the world is bathed in sunshine?'

'I'm often in cloud up here and I don't mind a bit. You must *never* feel sad for me. When it's cloudy up here, I have to admit I rather assume it's cloudy everywhere. It has never occurred to me to think very much beyond my own local climate. But I shall from now onwards. I shall think of you bathed in sunlight and shall hope you're sending me a cheery little wave in my direction. I should like that a lot.'

'Well, I'm glad you cleared that up! I shall certainly do my best to wave. But I do find it interesting, Mr Doubler, that when you've been alone on top of your cloudy hill and I've been overwhelmed with sadness for you, you've barely thought about anything beyond your immediate surroundings. I feel a bit of a fool, quite frankly.'

'But when I'm in the chasm, Mrs Millwood, I can't *see* anybody else, let alone *empathize* with their feelings. I can't see anything, even on the clearest day. In the chasm, Mrs Millwood, I am a very self-centred man, and I probably only survive by assuming everyone else is in their own version of the chasm, unable to think or feel or empathize. If I imagined a happy world continuing despite me, I might find life unbearable.'

'But were we talking about the chasm, Mr Doubler? I thought we were talking about a literal cloud, not a metaphorical one.'

Doubler squeezed his eyes tightly shut in order to see well. 'Yes. No. I don't know. It's hard to separate the two, the cloud from the chasm. Perhaps I imagined that when I'm in the chasm, it could be seen from the valley below as the little hat of despondency you described earlier. Either way, in cloud or chasm, my own world becomes very much smaller.'

'But you've been more cheerful of late, Mr Doubler, or is that me imagining it? You sound rather thrilled with yourself most of the time.'

'I'm not thrilled with myself, Mrs Millwood. I'm thrilled with you.'

'My illness has cheered you up, has it?'

'Heavens, no. Your illness has the capacity to destroy us both. But by missing you, I've felt so *alive*, more alive than I've felt for years. Missing you has made me remember the possibility of loss mattering.'

'This is all quite complex, Mr Doubler, and hard to fathom from my hospital bed. But I think you're paying me a compliment. Is that right?'

'I don't know if being admired by somebody like me could ever be considered a compliment.'

'Goodness, you're exhausting. Can you stop talking in riddles? I feel so overwhelmed when you do this. I have to be in the mood for your games and I'm just not. Was there or was there not a compliment buried beneath your riddles?'

'Well, if by compliment you mean — ' Doubler began, desperately trying to buy some time, but Mrs Millwood was impatient and exasperated.

'Mr Doubler!'

'I *admire* you, Mrs Millwood.'

'Excellent,' said Mrs Millwood with a smile in her voice. 'That's what I thought you were trying to say.'

Doubler remained silent, chewing his lip, unwilling to interrupt the silence with an unworldly response.

'And I admire you too, Mr Doubler. Mostly I admire your *courage*.'

'My courage?' asked Doubler, immediately questioning Mrs Millwood's sincerity. 'I don't have many qualities that are admirable, but I would imagine my dedication to my purpose would probably be ahead of my courage. And my abilities with potatoes. That would probably top the list.'

'You're a brave man, Mr Doubler. You're getting on a bit, you're set in your ways, but you're still prepared to do things that make you uncomfortable. Having the folk from the animal

247

shelter up to visit Mirth Farm took courage, Mr Doubler. So did climbing out of the chasm. So did raising your children on your own. So does taking on the potato giants.'

Doubler fell silent. Midge had called him brave, too. But Mrs Millwood thought he was kind *and* brave. Doubler wondered if it might be possible to become those things just through her belief in him.

Eventually Mrs Millwood spoke. 'Shall we talk tomorrow, then, Mr Doubler?'

'Let's do that. We don't have to talk about death, though. We can be a bit more cheerful if you'd like.'

'I found our chat about death very cheering, Mr Doubler. Very cheering indeed.'

Doubler murmured goodbye awkwardly, and when he'd hung up, he put the phone down gently, stood up slowly and did something he'd possibly never done in his entire life. He danced a little jig of happiness, right there in his sitting room, in plain view of the walls and furniture, the books and rugs, and without a care for what it might look like to the many birds who could be flitting by at that very moment.

# 22

The phone rang early, as Doubler was preparing his breakfast. His heart lurched with joy at the thought that he might be the first thing Mrs Millwood thought of when she woke; she was certainly occupying the front of *his* brain in every waking moment. Instead the voice on the end of the phone was terse, unhesitating and male.

'So, old man. I'd like to place an order for some *you know what.*'

'Who is this?' said Doubler, recognizing the voice immediately but feeling the need to buy a bit of time. 'Is that you, Maxwell?'

Doubler dragged the phone cord behind him and made his way to the window seat, watching the wind play with the boughs of an apple tree as he listened to the Colonel.

'Of course it's me. Can't get the damned stuff out of my mind. I'd very much like to place an order for a substantial quantity, if you can see your way to it. Wouldn't want to face a *drought*, if you get my drift.'

'If you're talking about the gin, that's simply not possible. I'm sorry.' Doubler felt Maxwell's sharp intake of breath as he said the word 'gin' and realized that Maxwell believed he was embarking on something illicit, perhaps for the first time in his life.

The Colonel lowered his voice to a loud

whisper. 'What do you mean, it's not *possible?* I know you sell it — you said as much yourself. And I'd watch your tongue. Little pitchers have big ears,' he said, somewhat obliquely.

'I don't think anyone can hear our conversation, and yes, but on the whole I don't *sell* it; I *trade* it. I *sell* vodka to make my living, but I *trade* gin to enrich my life.'

'Fine. I'm happy to trade your gin for some crisp ten-pound notes. And your secret will remain absolutely safe with me. Though,' the Colonel said, dropping once again into a conspiratorial tone, 'you might want to heed some advice, man to man: best not to share your deepest and darkest unless you're committed to keeping on the right side of your colluders. I'm not suggesting my mood is going to turn ugly anytime soon, but you wouldn't want to test that theory.'

'Maxwell, there's no conspiracy here, and threatening me is not going to change my mind.'

'Good. So how about it? I'm not going to be greedy. A case would tide me over.'

'A case? You'd be lucky to get a bottle. I haven't got any spare.'

'What, *none?*'

'No. I've got a few bottles for my own purposes, but I don't have a single bottle left available for new customers. I'd let you have a bottle if I could spare it, but I need to keep a permanent record of previous output.'

The Colonel sounded deflated. 'Disappointing. Very disappointing. I'd quite set my heart on it.' Maxwell fell silent for a moment, though

Doubler could hear him breathe quite heavily down the phone while he thought. 'I can pay more. I can pay a premium. Anything is for sale at a price, they say.'

'Well, I would be delighted to sell it to you if I physically had it. And as it is, I already trade it at a premium. Mirth Farm gin fetches two and a half times the price of the average supermarket own brand.'

'Two and a half times?' The Colonel did the maths very quickly in his head. 'Still, that's probably reasonable for the quality. Can't quite shake the memory. Very, very good. Excellent job, if I might say so. Probably worth every penny.'

Doubler was pleased to hear this. 'I like to think so. Each year I look at the average cost of a seventy-centilitre bottle of supermarket gin and I use a two and a half times multiple to determine the price I will trade mine for. It means I don't have to worry about what else is going on in the supply chain. I am confident mine is two and a half times as good as the average bottle.'

'Only that? Honestly, it was extraordinary. I'd say it was *ten* times as good.'

Doubler considered this seriously for a moment before dismissing it. 'That's not possible. The qualities on which you can judge a spirit are *finite*. I scrutinized the numbers quite methodically. Obviously, you can further improve on the base liquor by serving it in a specific way or embellishing it with specific accompaniments, but centilitre by centilitre, I'd say I can comfortably state that mine is two and a half times as good as the average.'

The Colonel thought about this and, undeterred, continued in pursuit of a deal. 'So, when do you make your next batch? Can I reserve a case or two?'

Doubler surveyed the weather from the window seat and wondered whether another storm was brewing. 'It's a little early to be certain, but I can't be far off my spring distillation. It should be late April or early May, depending on the conditions over the next few weeks. But I'm afraid to say that the spring batch is already spoken for.'

'All of it? Every last damn drop?'

'Yes. But I can put you on a waiting list. A couple of my customers are quite old ... ' Doubler trailed off, allowing the Colonel to realize the significance of this without further elaboration.

'You are joking. I had no idea this was going to be so difficult.'

'I'm not trying to be difficult. I just don't make very much. I make a thousand bottles in the spring and a thousand bottles in the autumn. The two distillations are quite different. It is always my recommendation — in fact, I feel quite strongly about it — that you drink the spring distillation in the autumn and vice versa.'

'Interesting. Which were we drinking the other day?'

'Autumn,' said Doubler emphatically, as if that should have been obvious.

'Marvellous. Bloody marvellous,' said the Colonel, remembering the taste.

Doubler cleared his throat and asked, a little tentatively, 'How did it make you *feel*?'

'*Feel?* It made me *feel* like I'd had the best bloody G and T of my life. And you're talking to a man who's sunk a few of those in officers' messes over the years.'

'Yes, yes. But beyond liking the *taste*, how was your mood impacted when you were drinking it?'

The Colonel thought back. 'Well, it's rather hard to articulate. I might need another to crystallize the feeling. But I'd say it made me recall some of my most glorious days. Is that possible? Is that overstepping the mark?'

Doubler was very pleased with this as a response. 'No, that's more or less what I would expect.' Doubler hesitated before continuing with uncertainty in his voice, 'We're friends, aren't we?'

'Yes,' answered the Colonel quickly, 'if it means you count me in when you keep a few bottles back for your nearest and dearest.' Maxwell guffawed loudly. When Doubler didn't respond, Maxwell added, sincerely, 'Of course, old man.'

Doubler continued, 'The fact that I blend a very good gin is no accident. I start with exceptionally good vodka and I use superior botanicals. Making gin is a *science*. It uses a certain skill, the nose of a chef, the molecular knowledge of a chemist and the eyes of a botanist. And I like to think I've come close to perfecting that science. And' — he could hear Maxwell clearing his throat as he prepared to interrupt him — 'I'm certainly not about to divulge the ingredients. The recipe will almost certainly go to my grave with me. But let me share a few thoughts with you.'

The Colonel grunted in agreement.

'I insist that my autumn distillation is drunk in the spring and that my spring distillation is drunk in the autumn. My customers respect this. When I make gin, I like to create memories and promises in equal measure. I will make a thousand bottles soon; they're all spoken for. I will ship those in the autumn for the lucky recipients to drink as the days shorten and the year's final flora heralds the dying days of the season. Those bottles that I have just shipped are from last year's autumn batch. That's what you sampled. I have a theory that by drinking the gin 'off season', I can broadly put the drinker into one of two categories: nostalgic or hopeful.'

'How do you figure?' Doubler could tell from the Colonel's tone that his interest was piqued.

'I believe the drink will make you dwell on your autumns past or look forward to the autumns your life yet has to deliver, depending on your outlook.'

'So I am . . . ?' wondered the Colonel, uncertain what verdict might be delivered.

'I suggest you're probably of the nostalgic persuasion. You think your best days are behind you.'

'Well, that's a bit of a blow.' The Colonel tried to sound light-hearted, but it was hard to disguise the disappointment in his voice.

'Oh, I don't think it's a *bad* thing! It's statistically *likely* at your age that your best days are behind you. But if you can look back upon them with pride and happiness, then that is a very *positive* attribute. It doesn't mean you haven't got some autumns to look forward to, but you should certainly think about making each one *count*.'

'Golly. I called to buy some gin. I didn't think I was asking to have my fortune read.'

'Ha! Yes, I suppose that does make me sound like a fortune teller. But the response doesn't lie and it's there for us all to consider, even me, after so many years. For instance, I noticed when I drank my gin with you up here at Mirth Farm recently that for the first time in my memory, the drink made me imagine the future rather than dwelling on the past.'

Doubler dragged the telephone back with him to the kitchen, and planting it on the butcher's block by the Aga, he set about boiling the kettle. He turned to lean against the range, continuing thoughtfully, 'I took a sip and wondered what the seasons would have in store for me. I wondered whether I might try my hand at some bramble jelly or whether it would be a good year for the crab apples. I imagined myself with a *companion*, well and strong and gathering the year's final burgeoning harvest, by my side. It made me feel *hopeful*.'

The Colonel made a noise as if he were about to interrupt again, but Doubler was finding himself able to voice a gradual realization and he didn't want to lose his train of thought. 'Where perhaps until recently I'd worried that I'd never again feel that sense of fellowship, I realized

255

instead that I could see *two of us* tramping round the perimeter of our shared life. And once I'd seen that image, I knew then that it could materialize. It made me not just hopeful but *confident* about the future.' Doubler sounded surprised by his own revelation, but he'd been carrying this image with him and had found the more he examined it, the more he believed in its possibility.

'And you got all of that from a sip of gin?' The Colonel's excitement was rising; he was now even more determined to get his hands on some of this spirit with its magical soothsaying properties.

'Yes. The botanicals are straightforward. They are an autumn hedgerow captured and suspended in the alcohol. The vodka I make is the perfect vehicle for holding those flavours, those *feelings*, if you like, and releasing them directly into your brain as soon as the liquid hits your tongue. I believe that your brain must then analyse the flavours and will invite you to imagine your future autumns or inspect those that have passed.'

The Colonel was not at all sceptical and did not make Doubler feel foolish. Rather, he sounded enthusiastic about these unimagined properties. 'All sounds feasible. The drink shook me up. Made me think. Now I reflect on it, it made me remember the happiest days of my life. Perhaps that's why I'm so keen to get my hands on some more.' He paused. 'You know, Doubler, I was *somebody*. I was a *leader*. I had men looking up to me, taking my word as the final say. Nobody doubted me or questioned my authority. One word, one nod and they'd follow my command. It was a wonderful feeling and one I know I will never recapture.'

Doubler heard the truth in the Colonel's words and was quick to reassure him. 'I can understand what a shock the change must be, but it really needn't be a sadness to you. Take those years as your glory years and relive them. Know that you lived a life you can be proud of. Take that knowledge to your deathbed and you will die a happy man. Not only did you live a fulfilling life full of purpose, you are cognisant of it now. No regrets, just great memories. That's an enviable state to achieve.'

The Colonel sighed, unconvinced. 'I suppose so. I think it's hard to adjust, though. To realize that you are no longer of consequence.'

'I am sure you've plenty yet to offer. And we are all capable of change, you know. Even me. I've spent so many years concerning myself with my potatoes, but Mrs Millwood made me realize that anything I've learnt from them I might perhaps be able to apply to myself. I never even knew I was a kind man until she told me I was kind to my potatoes. I didn't know kindness to potatoes counted. But I'm very grateful to her. She made me feel more courageous and more responsible, more capable. And, Maxwell, one bad season — even several bad seasons — can be followed by an exceptionally good one. Just as bad cycles can be interrupted with kindness. I suppose we're all prone to blight, but for most of us, it's most likely just in our leaves, and

257

providing it's not yet rotted our core, we can probably stop it doing any further damage.'

Doubler realized by the prolonged silence that he had lost the Colonel at the first mention of potatoes. He turned his attention back to his subject and pressed on. 'You might not be leading an army to war, but you needn't waste the next few years wallowing in self-pity. Trust me, I've dedicated my latter years to just that. It's only a suggestion but I don't think that paying close attention to those you depend on will mean you waste the rest of the time you have on earth.'

'I don't know quite what to feel, old man. I called to buy some gin and now I feel quite *unsettled*.'

'Retiring must be hard on you. But remember it's probably hard on your wife, too.'

The Colonel sounded ruffled. 'Goodness, I don't think so. I think she's been very much looking forward to our retirement. I led a very busy life, you know, so she was probably frightfully lonely, twiddling her thumbs and waiting for me to get home. Being there for her now is one of the few benefits.'

'I am sure it is. But don't forget to be the husband she needs you to be, Maxwell. Notice what she does for you and for everyone else within her orbit. It's not enough to wait for the regret that comes as a side-serving with loneliness, and I am beginning to understand that true love doesn't count if you can't express it with commensurate action. If you can do that, I'll see if I can find a spare bit of capacity for you. Who knows, perhaps I'll make an extra case of the good stuff just for you.'

'You'd do that for me?'

'I think you've got goodness in you, Maxwell. You just need to find some means of showing it. Goodness left inside you, unshared, is worthless.'

The Colonel's response was lost to the kettle's noisy exclamation as it reached its boiling point in a rush of steam. Doubler hung up the telephone and set about making his tea.

# 23

When Mrs Millwood next called, Doubler answered the telephone with an enthusiasm that a few weeks ago would have been unprecedented.

'You'll be glad to know that while you're idling your time away in that hospital you seem so partial to, spring is getting on with being spring, and it seems there's no stopping it. Mirth Farm is bursting with life; it is *burgeoning*.' Doubler was pleased with himself, revelling in his own jollity and buoyed by his own delight, which soared in ever-increasing escalations of elation.

'That's nice,' said Mrs Millwood quietly, unable to match Doubler's joy.

'And the pond — you know the small pond, nearest the gate? — it's got a pair of *mallards* on it. I'm rather delighted. I'm not sure we've had ducks there before. That's a sign of something good, a positive omen, wouldn't you say?'

There was an almost imperceptible sigh on the other end of the phone. 'There are ducks there every year,' Mrs Millwood answered in a dull monotone.

'No, no, on the *little* pond, the dew pond nearest the gate. There's a pair of ducks *there*.'

'I know the pond you mean and there is always a pair of ducks there. They've hatched ducklings by that pond before, and I quite often see them walking along side by side. They cross the drive and make their way slowly back to their home, looking like they're completely lost in conversation.' Mrs Millwood sounded wistful, but Doubler still failed to hear the dissonance above his own ebullience.

'Are you sure? I'm not sure *I've* ever seen them.'

'Yes, I'm sure, Mr Doubler,' she snapped a little. 'Just because you don't stop to look at it, it doesn't mean to say it's not happening. Throughout the dark years in that chasm of yours, the daffodils still flowered, the ducklings still hatched, the pussy willow still burst from bare stems overnight — it's still all there. Spring gets on with it regardless, Mr Doubler. It doesn't need you to notice it.'

Doubler had been so excited to share his news that it had taken him a while to register the deflation in her voice. But he stopped now, as he noticed the irritation creep in.

'Are you all right, Mrs M? You sound a bit out of sorts. Are you fed up?'

'Yes, I'm fed up. Of course I'm fed up, Mr Doubler. I'd like to be on the mend and I'm not.'

Doubler felt his heart thumping painfully in his chest as his mind raced through the possible reasons for her decline. 'You're supposed to be in hospital to get better, Mrs M. What on earth are they doing to you in there?'

'I'm not sure they know anymore. I'm a bit of a puzzle to them, apparently.'

'But they're going to fix you. They're going to give you your treatment and get you up and about in no time, aren't they?'

Mrs Millwood was quiet for a while, but her voice was bright and strong when she spoke again. 'Yes, Mr Doubler, that's the plan, and I'm not in the mood to be told otherwise, but I do miss my own bed and I'm so very, very *tired*.'

'Oh heavens, shall I leave you be, let you rest?'

'I wish it were that easy. I need to sleep, but sleep doesn't come. I suppose it is all this inactivity. My mind doesn't seem to want to shut down when I've given it so little ammunition with which to exhaust itself.'

'Well, yes, of course, inactivity can be utterly draining. I remember that only too well from my days in the chasm. Sometimes I was so depleted of all energy I could barely get myself out of bed in the morning. So, let's have a think. Is there anything you can do there to tire yourself out?'

Mrs Millwood didn't even attempt to make light of the question. 'Here? You're joking.'

'I could visit?' he asked tentatively, knowing he would be in the car racing down the hill in a heartbeat. She only had to say the word.

'I have plenty of visitors, Mr Doubler. They're the wrong sort of tiring.'

'I see.' Just as she hadn't disguised her despondency, he failed to disguise his jealousy in those two small words.

She registered his disappointment and immediately moved to rectify it. 'You really don't need to visit — trust me, I'm doing you a favour. The wards are noisy at visiting time and, understandably, the staff can be quick to lose their patience. They're good with the sick, but they just haven't got the time for the healthy, and in my experience the healthy can be very, very demanding. And the car park? It's a joke. You take your ticket when you enter the car park and then, if you're lucky, it takes an hour to find a free space. Meanwhile you're paying a king's ransom for the privilege of not being able to park. By the time my visitors get to my bedside, they are often seething piles of rage and they quite forget that I'm lying here *longing* for an adventure as thrilling as a race for a space in a car park.' She paused for breath and then said, quietly again, 'These calls are perfect, aren't they? They're every bit as good as our lunches. Do you remember our lunches, Mr Doubler?'

'Of course I do! How could I not? We had lunch together every day for fifteen years! Those lunches *saved my life.*'

'That's funny. I was thinking about our lunches just the other day. I was never quite sure if we were having lunch together or just having separate lunches near each other.'

'Oh, we were most definitely having lunch together. I'd go as far as to say we communed.'

'But we didn't eat the same thing.'

'I might have thought the same, but since you've been gone, my potatoes don't taste quite *right.* I'd go as far as to say that I'd choose to eat one of your dreadful sandwiches with you over eating my home-grown potatoes on my own.'

Mrs Millwood laughed, delighted. 'There's an admission, Mr Doubler. I knew you'd been eyeing up my lunch all those years.'

'Oh, I wouldn't go as far as that. But I don't

think you need to eat the same food to commune. Our lunches weren't about the food, were they? And anyway, we're sticklers, you and me. You liked your sandwiches and I liked my potatoes, but we still ate *together* every day.'

'Communed. I like that. It sounds holy.'

'It *was* holy, Mrs Millwood.'

There was a long silence while they both contemplated this.

Mrs Millwood spoke first. 'Would you do something for me?'

'Anything! Your wish is my command. What can I do for you?'

'Would you read to me? Not now, but when I call tomorrow. I'd like something that isn't *this* to think about. I can't seem to shut the world out on demand and listening to something other than the nonsense in my head might just help me find some peace.'

A surge of pride raced through Doubler. He tingled at the thought of sharing something as *intimate* as a book. 'Of course. It would be a privilege. What would you like me to read?'

'Anything. You've got thousands of books up at the farm, so there must be something there that is just right. You know me well enough — we've been communing for the best part of fifteen years.'

'It's been the best part, Mrs Millwood. Our lunches have been the very best part of the last fifteen years.'

'Are you getting sentimental, Mr Doubler?'

'A little.'

'But not maudlin?'

'Good heavens, no! You can't be maudlin as a potato grower. You can't grow much if you're maudlin. I'm chipper. You can definitely be chipper as a potato grower.'

'You're funny! That was an extremely witty riposte, Mr Doubler.'

'Jolly good. Glad you thought so.'

Mrs Millwood let her smile run out and continued, anxious once more, 'But I don't want a chipper book to be read to me. Chipper wouldn't do.'

'Nothing maudlin, nothing chipper, I promise.'

'Something reflective. Poignant. Something that will make me think long after the reading has stopped.'

Doubler's mind started frantically racing through the book-shelves of his mind. 'Goodness. I've got my work cut out. Leave it with me and I'll find just the right thing.'

Doubler headed to the bookshelves as soon as he'd hung up. The enormity of the task was daunting, but the honour was unmistakable and he was determined to find exactly the right book. The book that would help Mrs Millwood sleep *and* make her think. The book that was neither maudlin nor chipper. The story that would become part of their own story.

He stared at the tightly packed shelves in the sitting room, knowing there were still more books along the length of the upstairs landing. He regretted never putting them in some sort of order, though he'd often meant to. He ran his fingers across the creased spines, loving the

265

bumps and folds that told their own tales, quite separate to the words inside the covers. Each evoked if not a memory, a frame of mind, and he realized for the first time how immensely telling his books were. They occupied every spare inch, lying horizontally on top of the upright books to completely fill the gaps between shelves.

His fingers stopped moving as he came across a large section of pristine spines. There were books here, within this section, that were noticeably *unread*. He took a pace back and looked at the wall as a whole, trying to interpret the pattern that was beginning to emerge.

He shook his head slowly and peered more closely at these books. The titles were familiar and they too evoked a frame of mind. But he hadn't read them. Puzzled, he looked further, his eyes scanning from top to bottom, from left to right, wondering what they were telling him. The section furthest to the right of these were less densely packed and were titles that he had read and reread, battered and bruised and bearing all the qualities of books well loved, well read, books that he had fallen asleep with, that had slipped to the floor, that had come outside to the picnic table on a summer's day, that would reveal, if opened, the telltale signs of crumbs and sweat.

Startled, he realized exactly what he was looking at. The chronology of his life, marked out in meaningful chapters. He had applied some logic in the filing of his books after all, and Mrs Millwood had continued the pattern, of that he was sure. His books had been placed in the order in which he had read them, from top to bottom, left to right, forming orderly pillars of time. And all the care and all the indifference he had shown them now reflected back to him the biorhythms of his life. He checked the unread section once more. This was certainly a shelf full of books that had built in the post-Marie years. He remembered now that he had been unable to read while in the chasm; perhaps it was just too dark in there. He had certainly tried, he was sure, and he'd still been given books, had opened them, had made a *pretence* of reading them, but each one had let him down, unable to pull him out of the quagmire. Each one had failed in its duty and as such was destined to remain unread, unloved, with only the fragments of a sad secondary story to tell. And, somehow, he had forgotten to pick his books up again.

Were these books he should revisit? Doubler tilted his head and examined the titles and their authors. Some of his very favourites were there. He wondered whether they might get a second chance to deliver now what they had failed to deliver then. He looked at the spaces yet to fill in the furthest corner. These spaces were his future, but there wasn't much room left. He needed that space for the books that were going to be read in the coming months and years. And he'd have to choose them very carefully because these were the books that he must be prepared to fall in love with.

# 24

'*He was an old man who fished alone in a skiff in the Gulf Stream and he had gone eighty-four days now without taking a fish.*'

'Oh heavens, I'm not sure I have the strength to cope with this. What's it about, Mr Doubler?'

'It's about an old man and his *struggles*,' said Doubler, impatient to continue reading.

'What sort of struggles?'

'Can I just read, Mrs M?'

Doubler carried on, his voice melodious and measured. '*The old man was thin and gaunt with deep wrinkles in the back of his neck. The brown blotches of the benevolent skin cancer the sun brings —* '

Mrs Millwood interrupted him again. 'Oh Lordy. Is it a book about death and cancer, Mr Doubler?'

'No. Of course it's not. It would be very inappropriate to read you a book about death and cancer, Mrs Millwood. This is *The Old Man and the Sea* by Ernest Hemingway. It's a book about *fishing.*'

'A book about fishing? I definitely don't want to listen to a book about fishing. I think I'd rather hear a book about death and cancer.'

'The fishing is a *metaphor.* You don't need to worry about the fishing.'

'Of course I must worry about the fishing. It sounds very much to me like fishing is the *point.*'

'No, the *struggle* is the point. It's the struggle of an old man to demonstrate that his life still has purpose. He's had a run of bad luck, but he catches a huge fish, the most magnificent fish, though he is going to have to use all his strength to land it.'

'Does he land the fish?'

'I can't tell you the ending, but make no mistake, Mrs Millwood, the old man is very *tenacious*.'

'I think the metaphor sounds more interesting than the fishing to me, but I'm not sure I'm looking for a book about an old man looking for purpose as he nears death. Read me *The Little Prince*, Mr Doubler.'

'That's for children!'

'Oh, but it's not. It is a book of great profundity. It is a book, I think, about remaining capable of seeing what's important in life despite the great pressures of adulthood. It's a book about life and love and the *broadening* of your horizons.'

Doubler was not convinced. 'But it's a very short book. My fishing book is perhaps too short as it is. *The Little Prince* is even shorter.'

'Short is good! A short book where I have a satisfactory ending within my sight is exactly what I need. What we both need.'

'No, I think we need to commit to a project that's going to keep you engaged for a long time to come, Mrs Millwood. We need something that will make you think about the journey and not the destination. My book is not very long, Mrs Millwood. But it is very *dense*. It is a book where each word counts for ten or more. It will make you think and it is certain to provoke conversation, Mrs Millwood.' He flicked the pages to the end of the book. 'I think that is more suitable for our purpose, don't you?'

Mrs Millwood laughed a little as she began to understand Doubler's reasoning. 'Do you think I'm preparing to die, Mr Doubler? Do you think this is my last book?'

Doubler swallowed. 'That thought had crossed my mind, yes.'

'So you deliberately picked a slow story?'

'Well, yes, but a very poignant one. I made sure it satisfied all your other criteria, too. It is not a chipper book, Mrs Millwood. And I don't believe it is maudlin, either. Ultimately, the old man defeats some sharks and lives to go fishing again. In fighting his physical demons, he overcomes his metaphorical ones as well. Quite uplifting, I'd say.'

'I like the sound of your book, Mr Doubler. You may read it to me. I wouldn't want to wait for all those pages for the old man to come home empty-handed. I'm not sure I'd want to commit the time to *that* story. But now I know it's uplifting ultimately, then I'm happy to embark on your fishing trip with you.'

Doubler was glad. He settled comfortably in his chair, turned back to the beginning of the book and began to read.

# 25

Doubler had just pulled his muddy boots off with a grunt when he heard the sound of a car. 'Used to be that nobody came up here, but I can't get a moment's peace these days,' he muttered as he tugged his boots back on to go and investigate.

Much to his surprise, it was excited anticipation rather than anxiety that flooded his nervous system as he rounded the corner. He expected to find Midge hopping out of the little red car so flinched when he found, instead, an unfamiliar vehicle, a long brown station wagon of some sort, though as he got closer, he realized that mud obliterated most of the paintwork and it could have been any colour underneath all that muck. The driver was already out of the car, dealing with something in the car's boot and therefore obscured from sight. Any instinct to fear a visit from Peele was immediately quashed, for he felt confident that this was not a vehicle that would convey the biggest potato grower in the county.

The boot slammed with a jarring clunk and Olive appeared from behind the car, waving a little nervously at him. She was dressed in a rather fine tweed two-piece suit of khaki and beige tones, and was wearing her steel-grey hair in a neat twist at the back of her head. The shoes on her feet were flat, laced, leather and very sensible.

Doubler reached her with his hand outstretched. It was a beautiful day, cool still but clear, and there was the smell of new in the air. He felt cheerful, and welcomed his visitor warmly.

'Well, this is a surprise, Olive. I didn't really expect you to take me up on my offer.'

'I do hope you don't mind me dropping in unannounced, but I decided to dust off my driving licence. The suggestion of a piece of cake from your tin was too good to resist.' Her voice pierced the afternoon air, ringing out quite shrilly. Doubler relaxed. The woman he remembered from the last visit had been so painfully coy and her visceral vulnerability had made him anxious. Olive today was a much more sure-footed version of herself.

'Heavens, of course I don't mind. I wouldn't have suggested it if I did. Come in and get out of the cold.'

'What a lovely spot you have up here, Doubler.' She stopped to admire the view and her sweeping gaze also took in the locked barns, the neat yard and the lack of farmyard clutter that characterized her own home.

Doubler opened the front door for her, allowing Olive to make her own way into the warmth of the kitchen.

'It's hard to know what to expect when you come up here. No dogs barking, no chickens pecking on the drive. No sign of life in the dead of winter. Just bare earth, and that can be a bit *sullen*, can't it? And yet when I came before with Maxwell and the others, I thought that this was one of the most welcoming homes I'd ever been into. It could have been devoid of all human life and I'd have still felt embraced.' She stopped to breathe in the scents of the kitchen, allowing her senses to wallow and explore.

Doubler flushed with pride. 'Well observed. Mirth Farm very much likes to receive visitors. Unfortunately, its current incumbent hasn't always been quite so hospitable.'

'Well, as long as I'm not intruding.' Olive had already hung up her coat and removed her neat shoes, and was now sitting at the head of the table in a wooden armchair, looking very much at home. She picked up jars of jam, examined them and replaced them, while also looking around the room, taking in the detail, frowning at the small puzzles and irregularities that were so much part of Doubler's personality and nodding in recognition at those things she both identified with and approved of.

Doubler was delighted. Whistling softly under his breath, he put the kettle on and busied himself in the pantry, selecting a handful of scones to reheat and unwrapping a big slab of date and walnut loaf.

'You're in luck, Olive — I've been in a baking mood this week.' He laid two places at the table and set out the food in front of her.

'I don't think I've ever met a man who bakes as you do. I've seen them on the telly, but I've never met one in the flesh.'

'Oh, I'm sure we're not uncommon. Baking is

a rather satisfying blend of science and art, so it very much appeals to me. It's not the same as other aspects of my life — you can't get too experimental, you need to learn the formulae, but once you've grasped those, you can innovate and personalize to your heart's content.'

'Well, your gin is certainly experimental.'

'Indeed, no two batches are the same. The gin depends very much on the season, the weather and what the hedgerows have to offer. I grandly call it single-estate botanicals, but that just means I don't leave home very often.'

'Don't you get lonely here? I have to get myself out and about from time to time or I think I'd die of wretchedness.' Olive barely paused as she squared herself up to the tea in front of her. 'I was a keen baker myself back in the day, but I was more of a bread person than a cake person. I haven't got much of a sweet tooth.' As she spoke, she leant forward, and angling her scone to the rim of the jar before her, she swept a healthy covering of jam onto it.

'Marvellous!' exclaimed Doubler, with genuine admiration in his voice. 'That takes real skill!'

Had the praise been open to interpretation, Olive failed to notice. 'Yes, I probably spent the best part of twenty years mastering it, but there's no point baking just for me. I wouldn't get through enough and I don't eat much these days.'

Doubler watched her as she spread jam onto a second scone. He considered her plight and imagined his own life devoid not only of human company but of all home comforts. 'I'm very happy to bake for myself. There's nothing I like more than the smell of the dough as it proves or a cake as it cooks. And I suppose it's possible that the pleasure might be greater if it were shared, but I can't deny myself it altogether. I'd wither. I've always thought it is quite important to pursue some pleasures just for oneself. Baking is one of those. The process soothes me and the results sustain me.'

'I'm sure you're right. I miss it. There's something uniquely satisfying about it, yes. That feeling when you knead dough well and it just begs to become bread. It springs alive in your hand and nothing will stop it taking its form. Perhaps that's the attraction, the knowledge that you're never quite in control, so each success is a little miracle. There's so much to go wrong in the process; there's so much potential for disaster. But when you get it right and you know it is perfect, there's nothing better.' Olive took another big bite of scone and chewed thoughtfully before washing it down with a gulp of tea.

She continued, talking to the plate in front of her rather than to Doubler directly, 'But it isn't a joyful thing for me, baking, not anymore. Too many memories of a big, full, happy house are wrapped up in the fear of an uneaten loaf.'

Doubler stopped what he was doing and sat down at the table to join her. 'Where's your family, Olive? Why are you living in that big farmhouse all on your own?'

Olive met his eye with a challenging look. 'I could ask you exactly the same.'

'My situation is quite straightforward. But I

rather got the impression from Maxwell that you're a loner by choice.'

'A loner? Isn't that a bit disparaging? I am *alone*, certainly. But I'm not sure it's by choice. It's circumstantial. As for Maxwell, I don't fully understand what he's up to.' Olive stopped and appraised Doubler, as if deciding whether to trust him or not. Whatever she saw, she decided she liked it and she continued on, her words almost colliding in their rush to be heard.

'He was the one who made the approach to use my farm for their animal shelter. He was terribly persuasive — I don't remember having much say in the matter — but it did seem to make tremendously good sense. I was there all the time, I had the space, I wasn't ready to move to something more manageable, and I knew I could use the company. He came to me and suggested I share the house and land with the shelter and I thought that was a most excellent idea. He told me it would help give me purpose and I believed him.'

'It was very generous of you.'

'I don't know whether it was generosity on my part. It didn't really cost me anything to say yes and I could see so many reasons for it. I thought it would fill some of the holes, add a bit of noise and colour to my life. I rather imagined getting quite involved with the whole thing.' Olive's face clouded over for a second and then, almost as suddenly, it lit up. 'Oh look! A goldfinch!' She pointed to the window, where a jewel-like bird had alighted on the bare thorn that formed part of a thick briar that threatened to ensnare the house altogether.

'Goodness me, he's a colourful chap. Not sure I've had the pleasure of his company before!' Doubler sat still, taking in as much as he could before the bird took flight.

'Chapesse, if I'm not mistaken. It's those seed heads. You've done a great job not deadheading. Keen gardeners are *too* keen sometimes. They cut everything down, forgetting that the seeds will attract a whole host of new visitors to their gardens throughout the lean months. Lovely, just lovely. Well done!'

Doubler beamed, quite happy to allow his neglect to be mistaken for good intention, if these little visitors with their splashes of red and yellow were the end result.

'Charming!' Olive continued. 'Charming indeed. You know that a group of goldfinches is called a 'charm', Doubler?'

'It is?'

'And there's nothing more charming than a large flock of them, performing their aeronautics together low across the land and gathering with a flash of red and gold as they settle on a fence-line. It's a joy to behold.'

Doubler continued to study the bird as it raced to gather fuel, its bright head swivelling constantly, alert to danger.

'A charm of goldfinches. But it's not a 'charm' if it's just the one, presumably?'

'No, there's not much that's charming about a singleton. There's not much point being charming without someone to show off to, is there?'

'But she's a beauty, nevertheless, even with no others to charm.' Doubler reappraised Olive. 'So what went wrong?' he continued. 'You don't seem to be involved in the shelter at all now.'

'I don't know. It started off as I had imagined, but I think very early on, Maxwell must have caught me on a bad day. I have these days, you know. Days where just being alive is a painful process. It's hard to describe and I've never really tried to. If I say I feel sad, it doesn't do it justice. I feel desperate. But when I get one of these spells, nothing has really changed from the day before — there's no trigger or event. I just wake up with the absolute complete certainty that I can't cope. Or worse, I don't even want to try to cope.'

Doubler nodded, recognizing that feeling. 'I've been there myself — or somewhere similar. Mine had a root cause, though, so perhaps was not as debilitating as yours.'

Olive looked so sad at the thought — of her sadness or his, Doubler wasn't quite sure.

'They call it a depression, I think,' she said, still looking out of the window a little wistfully. 'But that's a woefully inadequate word. When I think of the word 'depression', all I can picture is a shallow dip or a low indentation. The mark a finger would leave in dough before it popped itself back into shape. But what I get isn't that. It's jagged and cruel, and I'm so busy trying to throttle it before it throttles me that I often think I'll die trying.'

Doubler nodded in understanding, recognizing the jagged edges of her sadness. 'So Maxwell caught you when you were down? In the chasm, I call it. How did that change things at the shelter?'

Olive leapt on the word 'chasm'. 'A chasm is better, oh so much *better* than a depression! Thank you for that! Yes, Maxwell caught me when I was distraught and I imagine I sent him away with a flea in his ear. I tend to do that when I consider myself unfit for company. He took me at my word. He set about telling everybody that they were not to disturb me, and now they all leave me well alone. At the very beginning, the shelter staff used my dining room as their headquarters. I loved the company. It made the house feel busy and appreciated. But quite soon after that incident, he announced that he was installing the Portakabin so I could have a bit more space. Of course, it was all quite, quite unnecessary. He told me he didn't want to get under my feet or be beholden. Again, he was so persuasive, I didn't really seem to have a say. And now I just hear a bit of your comings and goings. It's not at all what I had hoped for.'

While Doubler's initial reaction was outrage, it was quickly replaced by relief as he saw how easy it would be to correct the imbalance and bring joy and noise back into Olive's life. 'Well, that's so easy to fix, Olive! We can get this sorted out in a heart-beat. Of course you must be involved. It's your land, your stables and your home, for goodness' sake. You can't be our host and benefactor and not feel purposeful. There's no greater purpose, is there?'

'But what about Maxwell?' worried Olive. 'I

get the impression he'd actually rather I kept myself to myself He makes absolutely no attempt to befriend me. In fact, he goes out of his way to avoid me.'

'I'm sure that can't be the case. He's a bit bombastic, it's true, and he's probably a bit of a bully, but underneath it all, I expect he is decent.'

'I don't know. It is only that nice young Derek who always makes sure I'm invited to the get-togethers. He insisted I should come to Mirth Farm for tea. Maxwell kept saying I wouldn't enjoy it, that I might find it too much, with me standing right there!'

Doubler smiled in recognition. 'A very wise woman has explained Maxwell to me. He has what she calls a leader-in-crisis syndrome — he can't quite believe he isn't very important anymore so he likes to exert power over everyone.'

'I am certain that is the case.' Olive laughed delightedly and then leant forward to conspire with Doubler. 'Do you know, I once heard him barking out instructions and thought he might be bullying the student volunteers, so I raced out. But he was talking to the cats! Telling them to wait their turn and expecting them to form an orderly queue! As if you can make a cat do anything it doesn't want to do!'

Olive and Doubler laughed companionably together and Doubler marvelled at his good fortune. He had not sought this sudden intrusion into his solitude, but his life now felt boundless.

Doubler allowed the laughter to reach its

conclusion. He considered the Colonel quietly before adding, more seriously now, 'He's an army man, of course, and a bit old-fashioned. I expect he isn't used to dealing with anyone expressing an emotion. When he caught you on a bad day, he was probably scared out of his wits that he might have to find the right words to comfort you, so he ran a mile.' Doubler assessed Olive, who looked so relieved to have spoken up. Her eyes were sparkling and she looked less hunched with fear.

'I'm so glad I bake!' Doubler exclaimed. 'You're just like that bird — it wouldn't have bothered to stop and investigate the windowsill if I hadn't left some food for it. And if I hadn't kept my pantry full of the promise of cake and scones, you wouldn't have visited me either.' Doubler looked wistful. 'I had to wait a while for that goldfinch.'

Doubler asked Olive, 'Did you ever have a family? I can't imagine you've always rattled around in that big old place on your own.'

'Oh no, we were a large family. I have three grown-up children, two daughters and a son, and they're my pride and joy. The next generation is growing at a rate of knots. Five children between the three of them and more to come, I expect.'

'Oh, but that's wonderful, three children you're proud of!'. Doubler was relieved. After hearing Maddie's story and knowing his own, he didn't want to contemplate more isolation on his doorstep. 'And grandchildren to watch grow. I assumed you were alone in the way I'm alone. That's a delight!'

'Oh, I love them to bits. And they grow so fast!' Olive smiled, but Doubler detected an insincerity.

'But . . . you're not telling me something. You're not being honest with yourself or me. You're lying to one of us, Olive.'

'I am not lying. I couldn't be prouder. They're beautiful children. The light of my life, and the grandchildren, they're just like them. A whole new generation of talented, beautiful people.'

Doubler spotted the inconsistency and voiced it. 'But, Olive, you're not baking anymore. You have an empty house.'

'They're not near enough to pop in for tea. That's the truth of it,' she said, a little too firmly.

'But you do see them? They come and visit? You visit them?' Doubler was grasping for his earlier hopefulness, but he could feel it evaporating rapidly.

Olive confirmed his fears. 'My elder daughter lives in San Francisco, my son lives in Sydney, and my younger daughter lives in Melbourne.'

'Oh,' said Doubler, his optimism crashing down around him.

'Exactly. Not really visiting distance,' said Olive, understating the issue gracefully.

'The ends of the earth,' said Doubler, shaking his head sadly.

Olive felt the accusation and rushed to defend her children and the choices they had made. 'They went with my blessing. The world is so small for that generation. They can up sticks and take root wherever they want, whenever they want. It seemed churlish to hold them back when they all grew up with this overwhelming wanderlust.'

'But the other end of the earth? What were they thinking, leaving you here?' asked Doubler, his incredulity failing to swallow any attempt at sensitivity.

'It's complex. My husband was alive when they left, and at that time we were quite a self-contained unit of two. We had our retirement mapped out. We planned to visit them — perhaps we'd spend as much as half the year travelling, visiting our growing family. But he died quite unexpectedly almost as soon as he retired. And it turned out that I very much liked travelling with him as a companion, but I'm just not so keen on it on my own. I wasn't to know that, was I?'

'Of course not. None of us can prepare for the people we might become. So how often do you go to see them?' he asked, trying to bring the conversation round to something with a more positive note.

'I haven't been,' Olive admitted timidly.

'Never?'

'No. Never.' She looked him in the eye, refusing to be ashamed, but Doubler found her expression impossible to interpret.

'And how often do they visit you?'

'It's hard for them — they have their careers and their families and friends, and they don't get much holiday leave,' she justified, with a flippant wave of her hand. 'Coming here would be an enormous upheaval with their young families.'

'But they *do* visit?' Doubler prompted.

283

Olive hesitated. 'Not yet. But they will. Things will get much easier when the kids get older.'

'But you must miss them horribly!' Doubler exclaimed.

'Yes, of course. But without exception they all miss me horribly, too. I know that. They beg me to sell up and move out to be with them. My daughter in San Francisco has plenty of room and sounds really very keen on having me near. And with two children building their lives and their families in Australia . . . '

'You're tempted.'

'They *try* to tempt me. They promise me a better standard of living, a better climate, better healthcare. They are always telling me how much *better* life would be for me if I were to join them.' She paused before steeling herself to continue. 'But this is my *home*. I'm not unadventurous — I did my fair share of travel as a young woman, and I did plenty of travelling with my husband — but now I'm getting tired. I want to live here and I want to die here. I just want to be with my husband.'

Doubler studied Olive's face, expecting it to crumple with tears, but she was fiercely resolute. 'But your husband is dead and you're alive,' he said gently, looking at this strong woman who had many years, perhaps decades, ahead of her.

'But I'll be dead soon enough,' she said stoically. She shrugged. 'Anyway, they think it would work if I move over there to be with them, but they'd quickly come to resent me. I could lend a hand with the kids perhaps, but I'd almost certainly be a burden. And the older I became and the less I could do, the harder it would be for me to come back here alone. I can't see it working in practical terms. Besides, it does the young good to build their own nests, to find their own style of living. I craved that freedom in my youth, so I have to extend it to them, too, or I'd feel awfully selfish. I left home when I was practically a child. I was married at eighteen.'

Doubler tried to hear the words she wasn't quite saying beneath her blithe dismissal of her plight. He pressed her a little further. 'You might have sought your freedom, but I doubt that involved travelling to the other end of the earth.'

'Will you stop saying that? You're making me feel worse, not better,' Olive joked, but her eyes were full of panic.

Doubler hadn't considered that his role was to make her feel better. In his regular exchanges with Mrs Millwood, they had simply traded stories, taking it in turns to tell each other what was going on or comment on the issues of the day about which they felt most strongly. But he had always taken comfort from their ongoing dialogue, hadn't he? So perhaps that's what Mrs Millwood had been doing all this time: she'd been making him feel better.

'Do you know Mrs Mitchell?' Doubler asked, changing the subject swiftly.

'Of course. Well, certainly by reputation at any rate,' said Olive, relieved the moment of inspection had passed.

'What do you know of her?'

'Mad as a box of snakes, they say,' said Olive gleefully.

Doubler considered this. 'I'm not sure she is any madder than you or me, if truth be told. The three of us — you, Mrs Mitchell and me — we are all in exactly the same boat. We're tied to the land one way or another; our bodies are made of flesh, blood and soil. And our hearts are the same, too. We've all been made lonely by the careless abandonment of our partners — not exactly self-inflicted loneliness, but we haven't made it easy for ourselves, either.'

'Your wife died too?' asked Olive, who had been itching to ask this question since she'd first visited Mirth Farm.

'All our stories are a little different. Mrs Mitchell's husband is still alive, but she rather wishes he wasn't. Your husband died at the most inconvenient time. My wife . . . well, she had her reasons. But the long and the short of it is that the very thing that makes us happy is also the thing that separates us from our families.' He thought about Julian and his contempt for Doubler and his lifestyle. 'I think we are rather lucky to have each other, quite frankly. Meeting you and hearing that you have children who you cherish but can't see . . . That is far worse than my plight. I don't particularly care for my son, and my daughter is very disappointed in me, so not seeing them too often suits me just fine.' Doubler smiled at Olive to show that he harboured no bitterness within this statement.

'So was Tennyson right? I've often wondered. Is it really better to have loved and lost than to have never loved at all?'

Doubler thought about this. 'Mrs Mitchell

loves her children, I think, but they've let her down awfully, so she's very upset with them. All she wants is for her husband to come home. But she loved her husband very, very much and had a long and happy marriage. I don't think she would change a day.'

'You're very good at turning the attention onto other folk, Mr Doubler. But what about you? What about your children? Do they look after you, as they should?'

Doubler stood and looked out of the window, away from Olive. 'As they should? I don't know if they should look after me or not. It's true they don't look after me, but I've never asked them to, so I don't think they've let me down in that respect.'

'But you don't get on with them?'

'I find it difficult to get on with them.'

'Do you want to talk about it?'

'Not really. I'm not ashamed. I'm not embarrassed. It is what it is. But my children made a choice many years ago. After my wife went. They decided I was to blame. Perhaps I was; perhaps I wasn't. But the point was, I was here. I didn't leave them. I didn't desert them. I didn't decide they weren't the life I deserved. I was here for them if they needed me. But they decided to favour the love of an absent mother over the inadequate love of a present father. That's fine — I don't mind in the least — but it was their choice.'

'But they must have been in a lot of pain.'

'Must they?' Doubler turned to face Olive, genuinely curious.

287

'Of course they must. I expect they were devastated, weren't they?'

'I don't know. I find it hard to understand what people think. I would prefer it if they just said, instead. That's why I value the friendship of Mrs Millwood so greatly. She never asks me to try to work it out. Which is just as well really because most of the time I don't seem to have a clue what's going on.' Doubler laughed at himself, realizing he understood very little without Mrs Millwood's valuable assessment and interpretation.

'I knew Gracie Millwood cleaned for you, but I didn't know she was your friend. I was so very sorry to hear about her, Doubler. I gather things aren't looking very good for her. She was such a kind woman.'

Doubler looked sharply at Olive. '*Was* kind? *Is* kind, I think you mean. And she's got plenty of kindness left in her, thank you very much. Mrs Millwood is on the mend,' Doubler said firmly, with no room for further discussion.

Olive looked appalled at her mistake and stammered her reply. 'I'm very glad to hear that, Doubler. I'd listened to some gossip and must have misinterpreted it. But of course you must be closer to the truth. Forgive me. Where were we? We were talking about your children, weren't we?'

Doubler, relieved not to pursue the conversation about Mrs Millwood, tried to explain his situation to Olive as best as he could, knowing he was probably saying much of this for the very first time. 'All I know is that after Marie went,

Julian became very cold with me, very distant. And Camilla? What could I possibly do with Camilla? She needed her mother or some answers and I wasn't capable of delivering either. And she was so, so hard to love. She still is.'

'Because she was cold like Julian?'

'No, because I disappointed her, just like I disappointed her mother. And I still do. Each time I look at her, I see it in her eyes. She wants me to be a different kind of father and I don't know how to be that person. I don't know where she got the idea that the father of her dreams was a possibility. He never existed.'

'But you worked through the most difficult time with them, I assume? Did they eventually come around to you? Time is so often the best healer.'

'No,' said Doubler pragmatically. 'I decided I didn't need them. Their mother didn't need me. They needed their mother. I didn't see a role for me in all of that unholy mess she left. I just let them go and build their own lives.'

'Gosh. You're a bit harsh, Doubler.'

'Am I? Is that what you think?'

'Oh yes. A bit brutal.'

'Oh,' said Doubler, who was quite interested in this revelation. 'I don't really know what was expected of me. I've just stayed here. I got on with my life in the only way I knew. I set about growing my potatoes and I'm still growing my potatoes. My children aren't my legacy. My potatoes are my legacy.'

'Yes, quite, quite brutal.'

'Will you stop saying that?' said Doubler, who

felt he had been very understanding of Olive and her circumstances and that perhaps he might expect similar generosity in return.

Olive continued, 'What do you mean, your children aren't your legacy? I mean, they actually are. They are what you will leave behind.'

'I don't really think of it that way. They're flesh and blood, but I don't see myself in them. When I breed potatoes, and let's face it, I've bred a lot more potatoes than I've bred children, I can weed out the not so good and I can keep producing the good. I've refined and refined; I've had a say in what those potatoes have become. In the meantime, I've been unable to influence my children at all; I see nothing of myself in them. They are not interested in me or my farm, or my life's work.'

'Well, I mean, I'm not being rude . . . ' said Olive, preparing to be rude, 'but it is just potatoes. That's probably not very thrilling to the young. It's hard for the young to get excited about a bit of root vegetable growing in the ground. I mean, can you honestly blame them for wanting to find their own path?'

Doubler cried out in response. 'But what I'm doing here is groundbreaking!' Then, conscious that he rarely spoke of these matters, he lowered his voice. 'I have created a potato that will be hailed as the holy grail of potatoes.'

'Oh, well, that sounds a bit more impressive. The holy grail, you say? Now you've got *me* excited. I could get *excited* about a holy grail. Anyone could.' She thought about this and then backtracked a little. 'But not the young. I'm not sure when they've got all of the world at their feet, not to mention YouTube, they could get excited after all. They probably find the holy grail a bit backward-looking.'

'Backward?' Doubler objected. This was his life's work she was dismissing.

'Well, it's the past, isn't it? Everyone's been looking for the holy grail for ever. It's not going to pay the mortgage or get you a promotion. You can't drive it or go on holiday in it. It's probably not very desirable these days.'

'But it's the holy grail *of potatoes*.'

'You're not selling it to me. Frankly, you've just downgraded it a notch by putting it that way.'

Doubler rarely spoke about his Great Potato Experiment, but he had never felt as challenged about his conviction for the project as he felt now, under the scrutiny of Olive. 'The thing is, I am confident that my patent will be worth an absolute fortune. There won't be a potato grower in the land who won't want to buy my potatoes one day,' he claimed boldly.

'Have you got enough? Can you supply them all? It's supply and demand, Doubler, and it sounds like you'll need a lot if you're going to supply every potato grower in the land.'

'It's not as simple as that. Did you ever grow potatoes on your farm?' Doubler asked Olive.

'We did. But we gave up, to tell you the truth. Sorry to belittle your life's work, but they were a bit of a nuisance. You couldn't grow them in the same soil from year to year; they were prone to disease and pest and blight. That blighted blight!' Olive laughed nostalgically, as if she would trade all the mod cons in the world to return to those days of potato blight.

'Exactly. That's what I'm telling you. I've developed a potato that is resistant to blight. You can grow potatoes on the same patch of land over and over and over again.'

Olive's eyes widened. 'Well, that *is* interesting. I think Don would have been immensely interested in that, too. I seem to remember him convincing me that potatoes weren't worth the bother, but without the blight? We'd probably still be growing them. But I was married to a farmer; we lived on the land; *I'm* interested in that sort of thing. I'm interested in your farm and what you're growing, and I'm interested in the land, like you are. A bit of groundbreaking work in the field of potatoes is *relatable*. But I can see your children running a mile; it's just not very glamorous.'

'I don't do the work to be *glamorous*,' insisted Doubler.

'I know. You did it because you cared about your *legacy*. And that's fine. I'm not going to judge you. I think, if I were to wear a judgemental hat at all, I'd say you've been a tad extreme with your children. I don't think you've applied the 'blood is thicker than water' rule of thumb.'

'No, perhaps not.' Doubler thought about an equivalent rule he could adhere to. 'Perhaps I've applied the 'starch is thicker than blood' rule of thumb.'

'Yes, that sounds more like your approach to parenting.'

'Well, we can't all be perfect parents, can we?'

'No. And our children can't all be perfect, either,' acknowledged Olive sagely, admitting to more than she'd allowed throughout the entire conversation.

Doubler fell silent, reflecting on this reservoir of understanding. Their stories were so different, but the outcome was the same. Neither of them had children who were going to play an entirely satisfactory role in their concluding years. Both of them had resigned themselves to their circumstances with stoicism, but Olive's disappointment was barely disguised. Doubler couldn't help her with the sense of abandonment, that was something he knew too much about for his own perspective to be of any use to anyone else, but he wondered whether he might be able to help her with her empty days.

'I think the team could definitely use you — we're creaking a bit,' said Doubler boldly, knowing that he had made precious little contribution to a team that had yet to welcome him into its fold. 'The animals can certainly use you, and I've got a rather special friend who I think would very much benefit from spending some time in your company. Would you allow me to make an introduction?'

'To your special friend? Why, yes, I'd be delighted. I could do with a friend or two, special or otherwise. Introduce away, Doubler.' Olive eyed up the scones before her, and with a brief glance for permission in the general direction of her host, she helped herself to a third.

# 26

The phone rang shrilly in the sitting room and Doubler answered it anxiously, wondering immediately if the unduly early call signalled a turn for the worse for Mrs Millwood or other such bad news.

Instead, the Colonel's brash bark pierced the air. 'Morning, old man. You've managed to befriend Mad Maddie Mitchell, if my sources are correct?'

Doubler's initial relief was quickly replaced by irritation and he bristled as he answered. 'I've been to see her, yes, and after a bit of a tricky start, we seemed to get on OK. I'm not sure the epithet 'mad' is either accurate or appropriate.'

'Well, this latest episode may well change your mind. But good to hear you've made some sort of breakthrough — that's more than the rest of us have managed. It does mean you're the only man for the job, though. I've probably played the bad-cop role one too many times to be of any help with last night's debacle.'

Doubler's mind raced, recognizing from Olive's description the Colonel's extraordinary ability to bamboozle through an assumption of his own superiority. 'What episode? What happened last night? Not the donkey again?'

'No, not this time. Seems Mrs Mitchell tried to burn her house down.'

'What?' Doubler exclaimed. 'Is she OK?'

'Oh Christ, yes,' said the Colonel with an air of impatience. 'Spectacularly unsuccessful attempt, by all accounts, but the police have been involved and they've contacted social services, so God knows what they'll do with her now. Might be a good idea to pay her a visit?'

'I'm on my way.' Doubler replaced the phone with no other formal goodbye or thanks. He was far too preoccupied with concern for Maddie. With no hesitation and with none of his previous anxiety, he hurried to the garage, desperate to get to his friend before the authorities tied her up in knots.

Doubler expected to find scenes of devastation, a charred roof perhaps or the telltale yellow-and-black tape delineating a restricted area, but Maddie's house was quite intact and she answered the door calmly and with a disarming smile of welcome on her face.

'Maddie, I was out of my mind with worry. Are you OK?'

'Oh, you heard about my spot of bother, did you? Come on in.'

Doubler followed her in and trailed behind her towards the living room. He was aware, immediately, of an offensive, acrid stench that hurt his nostrils. Not sure what to expect, he entered the sitting room, where he found the velour settee stained almost entirely by ugly brown marks and a good deal of sooty mess on the surrounding carpet.

'I must say this is almost a let-down. I heard you'd burnt the house down!'

'Oh, but that was never my intention. Why on

earth would I do that? I was trying to burn the sofa, but it is quite new and covered with this infuriating flame-retardant material. Couldn't get it to go.'

'So I see. What happened? Did you call the fire brigade?'

'No, no need — there was barely a flame, but it seems I triggered the smoke detectors, and when the nice people called, I couldn't persuade them not to come. I had an almighty scratchy voice — this blasted material just sort of shrivelled a bit, but it really stank and the fumes caught me right in the back of my throat, so I think they thought I might be dying of smoke inhalation and sent the firemen anyway.'

Maddie shrugged her shoulders as the two of them examined the sofa. 'They were pretty cross with me. Nice but cross. Then the police were called because, apparently, it is a crime to set fire to your own sofa, and then social services were called, which was a greater problem because they already thought I was daft and apparently no *sane* person sets fire to their sofa.'

'Well, they might have a point, Maddie. What on earth were you thinking?' Doubler, while talking, was tugging open the sliding doors that led to the small patio outside and eyeing up the space beyond.

'Well, I wasn't exactly thinking, was I? I was fed up with the sofa and I wanted rid.'

Doubler, wrinkling his nose, now began to nudge the sofa towards the open doors. It was lighter than he expected, so he was easily able to shove it a foot at a time as he spoke. 'What on earth had it done to offend you?'

'It was mocking me.'

'Well, you've put a stop to that. Good job. It's not going to be mocking anyone anymore, is it? Look at it. It's a laughing stock. Here, give me a hand getting it over this ledge.'

Maddie laughed and made a face of disgust as she grabbed the other end of the sofa and helped Doubler pivot it over the metal frame that housed the sliding doors.

'Oh dear, you must think I'm bonkers. Perhaps I am. I'm just so tired of this blasted piece of furniture being the biggest thing in my life. It's always here, just filling up my vision. I was having a conversation with it, I think, and it's possible that I got angry at it for refusing to answer me. It's just always here, so biddable, so compliant. It's got no get up and go.'

Doubler shoved the sofa out onto the decking and came back inside, sliding the door closed behind him before saying, softly, 'It's a sofa, Maddie.'

'I know. I know *now*. I was confused.'

Doubler looked at the empty space left by the sofa. 'Did you get muddled up with your husband again, Maddie?'

Maddie looked indignant. 'Of course not. Why would I want to set fire to my husband? I'm not mad.' She stared intently at the sofa, as if for an answer. 'I can't remember what I was thinking. Perhaps I decided it was pointless. Yes, that must be it. A sofa for two has no purpose here, does it?' She softened as she turned her attention from the sofa to Doubler. 'Trying to burn it was silly, though, wasn't it? Oh, what a fool I am.'

Doubler took Maddie by the shoulder and steered her to the one remaining armchair in the room. He used a trace of pressure to encourage her to sit, and then he bent down to look her in the eye. His gaze was searching as he asked, a little hesitantly, 'I can understand you becoming confused, but you didn't want to hurt anybody, did you? I mean, setting fire to your sofa seems a bit of a dramatic response to a failure to respond to you.'

Maddie thought carefully. 'Dramatic for a husband, obviously, but not for a sofa.'

'I think you have unrealistic expectations of your sofa, Maddie dear.'

Maddie looked around the room sadly. 'You know what kills me in this place, Doubler? It's the winters.' She paused. 'Ironic, isn't it? My boys told me they couldn't stand the thought of me suffering another winter at the farm, but they can't have realized how important those dark months were to me.'

Doubler nodded emphatically, empathizing immediately. 'Well, winter is a blessing, isn't it? I mean, it's hard if you've got live-stock — you've got to keep everyone fed and watered, despite the elements — but winter is the farmer's respite, isn't it!'

'Yes, exactly. Those early evenings were such a blessing — you'd just have to return to the house as soon as it got too dark to get anything done outside. And, of course, if you'd prepared sufficiently, you could comfortably live off the riches your own effort provided.'

Doubler agreed. 'When you've worked hard all year, those late mornings really are a bit of a treat, aren't they? The lie-ins! Nothing much to do until it gets light! But I think that's the old way, Maddie. I don't think farmers need to wait for sunrise now. Their tractors are fitted with powerful lights and operated by computers! They can work twenty-four hours a day nowadays.'

'More fool them! Winter's for putting on a bit of fat! Both on yourself and on your animals. It's when we used to rest. I did all my reading, all my learning in the winter, and a good deal of that was in front of the fire. In the summer, when it's light for eighteen hours, you work for eighteen hours, don't you?'

'Agreed. I have never taken any heed of clocks going back or forward. And I'm still the same today. I'm outside with first light, and I come inside when I can no longer see my hand in front of my face. Though now I'm getting on a bit, I seem to need so little sleep that I lie in bed waiting for the dawn.'

'Well, there will be plenty of time for sleep when your time's up, I suppose.' Maddie looked outside at the dull morning sky. 'But now? It's a joke. My house seems to be in charge of providing a constant, neutral season throughout the year. Everything is thermostatically con-trolled. It's comfortable, but perhaps it's *too* comfortable. My feelings are numbed; it's hard to take pleasure without some contrast to bring it into focus. The clocks move back and forward automatically; the boiler is set to produce the right amount of heat regardless of the weather;

it's all very *efficient*. I'm on mains gas, too — I don't have to watch out for a low tank of oil. I don't even get to decide whether I should call the fire brigade. The smoke detector does that for me apparently. Shouldn't complain really. I feel such a horrible person for moaning to my sons. There are people who would give their eye teeth for such a comfortable retirement . . . Nice house, nice neighbourhood, money in the bank, pension coming in.'

'And yet?'

'And yet I'm no longer a person. I have no *point*. When I lived off the land, I always felt so busy and useful. Nothing much happened without some physical effort on my part. I lived and breathed that farm. I inhaled and exhaled with the seasons. And I was always content. Sometimes I burst with happiness, not often but sometimes. And sometimes I despaired, too, at something I couldn't solve on my own. But my general state was one of contentment and I think that's all anyone should wish for.'

Doubler stood up and stretched his back. 'Contentment is underrated.'

'By the young 'uns, definitely. My boys would look at contentment with disdain. They pour scorn at people who reach what they call their 'comfort level'. I kid you not. As if reaching a level of comfort is equivalent to failure.'

'And yet they've tried to provide a comfortable environment for you, haven't they? Isn't that exactly what they set out to do by moving you from the farm to here?'

'I torment myself with this argument. But was

it for me, or was it for them? I fear it was for them. A slightly dotty mother in a decaying farm probably felt like a lot of hard work ahead. And they got to show off their skills by negotiating with developers and selling the farm. They divided it up into plots. It felt unnecessarily violent, but they were certain it was the best solution for me financially.'

Doubler thought of Julian, which prompted him to ask, 'Did they pocket the cash?'

Maddie looked shocked. 'Heavens, no! They bought annuities apparently.'

Doubler looked dubious. 'They sound useful.'

'I believe they are. They provide the income I live on. But I spend almost nothing. And money seems to come in and out of my account without me lifting a finger.'

'Lucky you! I'm beginning to think your tragic life sounds quite enviable.'

'What about you? What do you live on, Doubler? You're my age and still working your socks off. Do you have a retirement plan?'

Doubler smiled. Maddie sounded so astonishingly sane. 'Of sorts, yes. It's perhaps all a bit far-fetched, but for the moment I make a tidy sum from my vodka production and, like you, I require very little income. The truth is, on the side I produce a very desirable gin and I trade that for all my groceries. Even my log pile is kept full in exchange for a good supply of the finest.'

'Goodness me. You *trade*. You *barter?*' Maddie sounded horrified.

'I do. That's the polite description for it.'

'Is it even legal?'

'I don't think so. Probably not.'

'Ahh well,' said Maddie with a pious smile.

Doubler examined her closely. Only a moment ago, she had seemed so together, but now, as she gazed happily at him, he wondered just how coherent her thoughts were.

'What are we going to do with you, Maddie?'

'I don't know. I'm desperate. I need to do something. I need to escape, but I don't know how. The truth is, if it wasn't for Thomas still being alive in that place, I'd top myself.'

Doubler had been pacing a little, but this stopped him in his tracks. 'You mustn't think that way!'

'Why on earth not? My useful life is over and now it's just a waiting game. I'd like to hurry it up.' Maddie looked at Doubler and blinked slowly a couple of times. 'I think about smothering Thomas with a pillow sometimes.'

Doubler rushed to her side once again. This time, he knelt down and took her hands in his. 'Maddie, you must be careful. If people hear you say that, they really will lock you up.'

'But we are both so *hopeless*, the two of us. If he died, I could die and I wouldn't be forced to spend the rest of my days arguing with a sofa.'

Doubler looked at the silent sofa outside. It was drizzling slightly now and he wondered if a sofa had ever looked sadder. 'Or a donkey?' he asked, helpfully.

'The donkey was certainly a better conversationalist than the sofa, I'll say that for him.'

'Lucky for old Percy, I reckon. Imagine what would have happened to him if he'd not given a good account of himself.' Doubler nodded towards the glass doors and the sorry scene beyond. 'But in all seriousness, we are going to have to do some very fast talking with social services, and your family perhaps.'

'Oh, the boys won't be any trouble. I'm here out of harm's way. I can't see them giving me any bother.'

'I wouldn't be so sure. They're not bad people, I'm sure of that. But if they're told they have to make full-time provision for your care, what happens next? It would not surprise me if you've drawn a bit of attention to yourself with this latest stunt. I'm going to have to think long and hard. In the meantime, don't do anything. Don't light a match, don't top yourself, don't smother your husband and don't steal a donkey. You've got to promise me that you can behave. Give me twenty-four hours, but if anyone calls to see you, anyone at all, you're to phone me immediately.'

Doubler scoured the room for a piece of paper and pen, eventually finding one in the kitchen next door. He wrote his home number down and tucked it under the telephone.

'Immediately, you hear?'

'Yes, sir.' Maddie grinned a little too cheerfully.

# 27

'I too have had a very productive morning, Mr Doubler.'

Doubler had recounted the tale of Maddie Mitchell to Mrs Millwood and he was now preparing to speculate upon any potential ramifications of this latest development. He had been anxious to update Mrs Millwood as he was confident that Mrs Millwood would have an opinion regarding Maddie's mental state. But Mrs Millwood had her own news to share, so Doubler stopped trying to talk and listened instead.

'Betty, who I had really become quite fond of, died this morning, Mr Doubler.'

'Betty?' asked Doubler, alarmed. 'I've not heard of Betty. Who is Betty, and where does she fit in within your circle of friends?'

' "Who *was* Betty?" don't you mean? Betty was my neighbour, here at the hospital. And a good companion she was, too. She was a little older than me but was quite, quite determined to recover and live for another decade or so. Nobody could question her will to live, but whatever higher purpose decrees these things thought better of it and she just popped off.'

'Well, I am very saddened to hear that, Mrs M. I am sorry you've lost your new friend just when you'd got to know her.'

Mrs Millwood sighed. 'She was a lovely lady.

Very gentle. I'm sorry too. I really came to know her quite well. That is to say, I knew enough to know I liked her and that I was unlikely to discover anything to make me change my mind.'

'And have you got a new neighbour yet?'

'Of course! Enshrinement is not built into the schedule around here, and quite right too — there are plenty of other lives to be saved.' Mrs Millwood dropped her voice a little. 'But as yet the curtains are still closed round the new incumbent, so it will be a while before we know if Betty has a worthy successor. This one will have a lot to live up to.'

'Well, I'd rather you didn't get too attached to the comings and goings of your ward, Mrs M. I don't want you settling in. You're to get yourself home as quickly as possible, right as rain — that was the plan.'

'I'm having to build a little bit of flexibility into the plan, Mr Doubler,' answered Mrs Millwood, revealing nothing in her voice. 'And while it isn't wise to get attached to anything or anyone in this place, I might as well make the most of what I'm given.'

'Of course, Mrs M. That's something you're extremely good at.'

Mrs Millwood continued with her news. 'Betty has a sister, Mr Doubler. She arrived just after Betty had popped off. She'd visited every day and they were extremely close, so it's a great shame that she arrived to find her sister had just gone. But I suppose we can never know when a conversation is to be our last. It's a good reminder to always say something nice to the people you love when you say goodbye. You wouldn't want any regrets in that area, would you?'

'And did Betty and . . . '

'Maureen.'

'Did Betty and Maureen have any regrets?'

'Not of the conversational sort. But nevertheless Maureen was inconsolable and she ended up sitting beside my bed and sobbing her heart out. My own visitors arrived and I had to send them off with barely a hello or a goodbye because poor Maureen was in such a state.'

'She lost a sister she loved. She must have been heartbroken,' Doubler mused, wondering if his two children would ever have such a close connection.

'It was both more and less complex than that. It turns out that the two sisters were a bit of a double act. They had complementary skills. Maureen loved to knit, just like I do, but strangely, and this seems a bit bizarre to me, but who am I to judge . . . ?'

'Not you, Mrs M.'

'I try not to. The bizarre thing is that Maureen had never learnt to *cast on*.'

'To do what?' asked Doubler, his brain scanning for references to the term and drawing a blank.

'Those are the first stitches you knit, Mr Doubler, when you start a new project. You use one knitting needle and your fingers to get the first stitches started. But for some reason, she'd never learnt for herself, and because she'd never had to do it, she'd come to believe that she didn't have the *knack*. Everything she'd ever knitted, Betty had always cast on for her.'

'And was that a regret, Mrs M?'

'It was a *huge* regret. Maureen believed she'd never knit again, because how would she cast on without her sister? I wondered, for a while, whether this was the type of sadness that she might like to carry around with her for a while, but I had to weigh up the options quickly. After all, Maureen is getting on a bit and with time not on her side, it seemed very tragic to me that she might never knit again now her sister had died. But I showed her how.'

'And did she have the knack?'

'For the first couple of tries, she simply refused to believe she had the capability. But I think she was just being stubbornly loyal to the memory of her sister. We all like to think we're indispensable, don't we? And perhaps she felt she owed that to Betty.

'But I explained to her, as kindly as I could, that knitting just isn't a two-person job. Sometimes we need somebody to complete us — we don't feel whole without them — and it is quite conceivable that Maureen will never feel complete without Betty by her side, but that sort of companionship is more a spiritual require-ment and much less about wool and needles.'

'Were you able to teach her eventually?'

'Not without quite considerable delving. It transpired that, despite her lack of skill in the knitting department, Maureen was more capable than Betty in all sorts of areas! Maureen was the much better cook, and Maureen could drive while Betty had never learnt. Once I knew this, I was able to explain to her that it had probably been very important to Betty that she believed Maureen couldn't manage without her, but that now that Betty had gone, there was nothing to stop Maureen learning for herself. Maureen became really quite determined after that. In fact, she had such a grim look of resolve, she appeared to be possessed.'

'And she learnt to cast on?'

'Yes, like a demon! She was quite shocked at just how easy it was!'

'That *is* interesting, Mrs Millwood. And what did you learn from that, do you suppose?'

'I learnt that sometimes two people are necessary to complete each other but it might be more complex than at first glance. Maureen thought she needed Betty to cast on. But I think that more than that, Betty needed Maureen to need her.'

Doubler thought about his lunches with Mrs Millwood and how much he needed her at the table to feel complete. He very much hoped that theirs was a spiritual connection and not the wool-and-needles type.

'And what did *you* learn from your conversation with Maddie Mitchell today, Mr Doubler?' asked Mrs Millwood, echoing Doubler's question.

'Maddie Mitchell needs her husband to complete her, Mrs M. And everything else in her life is just a reminder of that fact. She's not mad. She's not cruel. She's just lonely.'

Mrs Millwood's response was quiet, almost a

whisper. 'I am proud of you, Mr Doubler. We've both learnt a lot today.'

# 28

Small pale buds, easily mistaken for droplets of water, were poised on the bare branches that marked his path. Beneath his feet, the heads of hopeful bluebells jostled for space with the earlier, feistier narcissi. Doubler walked the boundaries of the western fields and marvelled at the many signs of spring that competed for his attention. It was still cold, but there was no longer the threat of something still colder in the air. In fact, the only promises being made to him were of warmer, longer days and of the green growth that would soon fill his fecund fields with a whole new generation of life.

Doubler knew that he had not been able to see very clearly for a number of years. There had been darkness behind his eyes that obscured his perception. This cloak ranged from the pitch-black of coal to a dense grey fog depending upon his mood, but it was always there, narrowing his field of vision and forcing him to squint closely at the things he felt he could control — those subjects he understood with absolute clarity.

But in recent weeks, the veil had gradually risen, and while it hadn't been banished completely, it had at least been replaced by something less opaque through which he could see further into the future and beyond his own immediate horizons.

Today, Doubler was experiencing a lucidity that now made all the answers obvious, even those to questions he hadn't meant to ask. He could see a clear path to his happiness, and this was as easy to pick out as his own chalk drive in the winter moonlight.

As soon as he returned to the farm from his rounds, he called Maddie Mitchell. The conversation was an unwavering, one-sided affair. Not so much a discourse as a set of easy-to-follow instructions.

'It's a beautiful day, Maddie. We're going on an outing. Get your glad rags on.' He smiled as he listened to the barrage of questions fired down the line. 'Half an hour tops, Maddie.'

He knew this was another, quite different version of himself. This was neither pre-Marie nor post-Marie. This was Doubler today and he felt determined to enjoy himself enormously.

He left Mirth Farm with an impish look of resolution etched on his face. He had his cap pulled down low to give him a little protection from the elements, and as he climbed into the Land Rover and gunned it into life, he repeated little mantras over and over to himself.

The truth was, he felt *courageous*. He was leaving his house yet again and he felt increasingly confident that he wouldn't be letting anyone down if he failed to return. He knew, rather, that he'd be letting people down if he *didn't* leave his home, and it was with this sense of purpose that he drove down the steep hill, taking each bend in his stride as he left his property to head first for the new housing development that was Mrs Mitchell's unwanted home.

He drove quickly to Maddie's road, driving past row upon row of characterful homes he had barely noticed in his hurry last time. He rounded the corner into Laurel Drive and drove slowly down the cul-de-sac. He did a quick calculation in his head as he passed a road called Sunrise Avenue, rather hoping it faced east but somehow doubting it. Looking for Maddie's home, he peered at each of the house names as he drove slowly by. The pristine homes were called Brookview and Lakeside, Meadow Charm and Oakdene. Doubler supposed that the homes were built on meadowland, surrounded by oaks, and perhaps there was once a lake, fed by a babbling brook. But the names seemed wistful and full of longing rather than celebrating a glorious past. Doubler refused to allow this to make him downcast and wondered if the irony of his own farm's name had been noticed by Mrs Millwood in Doubler's darkest days.

Soon he found Mrs Mitchell's neat house, and coming to a jerking stop outside it, he felt that his ancient Land Rover with its rugged, expedition-ready tyres seemed entirely the right vehicle for the outing he had planned. He leant on his horn and Mrs Mitchell appeared at her door almost immediately, sporting a bright wave and a worried frown.

'Well done. You're all ready for me, then?'

'Oh yes, this is quite the adventure. I've been fretting since you called. I'm not used to going out to visit, but here I am, in your hands.' She clambered up into the Land Rover beside Doubler.

'Good, good. We haven't got a long journey but make yourself comfy.'

Doubler, now in the role of carer and custodian, felt a further surge of confidence, and as he swung the old car out from the relative calm of the housing estate into the bustle of the town's one-way system, he felt something akin to joy. He chatted to the car under his breath and coaxed it up hills and round sharp bends, making noises of encouragement, while Maddie Mitchell clung to her seat, bolt upright, unsure whether to scold Doubler for his sudden recklessness or admire him for the hitherto unexpressed bonhomie.

'Nearly there!' Doubler shouted above the roar of the engine. He pulled into the rugged track of Grove Farm, saying to the car, 'This is what you're made for, old girl.'

Maddie Mitchell, recognizing the drive, squealed at Doubler.

'You're bringing me to see Percy? Is that what this is all about? A trip to see the blasted donkey? Can't say I'm thrilled, Doubler. Can't say I'm thrilled.'

'Oh, you can say hello to Percy if you must, but let's not rush that, shall we? You've got a little work to do to regain his trust, but as it happens, we're not here for the donkey. There's somebody else I'd like you to meet.'

Doubler stopped outside the farmhouse and helped Maddie down from the car.

'Are you expecting us?' he asked Olive as the

front door swung open.

'Of course. Let's put the kettle on, shall we?'

Doubler held the door open for Maddie and followed her towards the kitchen. He kept up his cheerful patter, aiming to put the two women at ease and dismissing entirely his own tendency towards anxiety in the company of most people. 'The house smells lovely! Have you been baking, Olive? Olive, this is Maddie Mitchell. I expect you know each other, don't you?'

'Pleased to meet you,' said Olive, turning as she reached the kitchen to extend her hand.

Maddie returned the handshake briefly and with the lightest of touches. She was anxious, wrapping her cardigan closer round her in a bid to find comfort and protection in this unknown environment. While a little suspicious of Olive, she was intrigued by the farmhouse, a building she had seen many times but had never dreamt of entering. She looked around, taking in the detail in much the same way Olive had shown an appreciative interest in Mirth Farm.

Olive chatted companionably, putting everyone at ease. 'Funnily enough, I don't think we've ever met, have we, my dear? I don't know how not, really, two farmers' wives in this small community. Should have bumped into each other on plenty of occasions. But I don't think we did, did we?'

Although Maddie might have struggled to articulate the sentiment, she had felt defensive and inadequate, even a little awed by the moment, but being folded so neatly into an identical pair with the words 'two farmers' wives' had reset the balance, making her feel the equal of this woman. She answered curiously, deciding to admit that she knew of Grove Farm and its farmers. 'Other side of town, two different schools for our children. Yours were St Joseph kids, were they?'

Olive nodded. 'That explains it. Different schools, different churches, different pubs, too.'

'And ours was just a small concern. Not on your scale.'

'Ah, but they'd have known each other anyway, wouldn't they, your Thomas and my Don? They'd have met, no doubt. The farm folk always tended to stick together; regardless of size, they always seemed to lend a hand to each other. They had their own network, their own community, didn't they? Bound by the butchers and the feed merchants they shared, no doubt.'

Doubler let Olive fill the silence with her chatter and enjoyed watching Maddie thaw as she got her bearings and began to settle down.

They sat round the small kitchen table and Olive poured tea, still talking, still filling the silence.

'Yours was a smallholding, was it, Maddie dear? I suppose there wasn't much call for our men to meet if your Thomas wasn't off to the farmers' market. That's where my Don could be found most weekends. But still, a smallholding shares all the same challenges, doesn't it?'

'Oh yes, but we only really grew what we needed. Kept ourselves to ourselves. I don't think we were unnaturally antisocial, mind. I think we just had very full lives. It will keep you

316

busy that lifestyle. There's always something to be done. Sometimes there's *too* much to be done. People think it's a life to envy, but really it's just a peasant's life. I often felt like I was living in the Dark Ages.'

'Oh, I know. It's hard work for sure. Looking after livestock, dealing with dead stock and the stockpot in between! It's not a life for the faint-hearted, that's for certain.' Olive trailed off as she looked out of the window.

'We had a lot of land once, but by the end we were only in the arable end of the market. That gave us the richest pickings. We weren't big enough to be of interest to the supermarkets, and the bureaucracy was beginning to get out of control. But we sold a bit of land off just before Don dropped dead. It was our retirement plan, that windfall. The idea was, we'd sell enough to lighten our load but still keep a good buffer of farmland around us. It was going to pay for our travel and whatnot. A few treats as we got older. That was the idea, anyway.'

'But it's still a big spread up here. Plenty of land to keep you worked off your feet, by the looks of it?' Maddie, too, looked out of the window, assessing the scope of the land not in monetary terms but in physical effort.

'We're not big enough these days to be viable is the truth of it. A little under a hundred acres we've got now. But we'd have had five times that land once. Still, it's nice. I like to be able to walk until I'm tired without ever leaving my boundaries. That's a privilege, I think.'

Maddie agreed, nodding her head eagerly.

'You're so right. Ours was a much smaller place, but we used every inch of it, and if you walked round the perimeter, you certainly knew about it. Now my garden out the back is smaller than this kitchen. Barely enough for a bit of veg, but even that is out of the question — it's all put to stone and decking.'

Doubler, who had been enjoying listening, and had barely spoken a word, chipped in with a laugh, 'Decking? What have you got there, a garden or a boatyard?'

Maddie laughed a little too. 'I know. The decking is good for the snails and that's about it.'

'And sofas, Maddie. I've heard decking is very good for sofas.'

Both women laughed, though Olive cast her eyes down briefly, unsure whether she was supposed to know about the sofa incident.

Maddie Mitchell quickly returned to her former, sober conduct. 'But the idea was it was low maintenance. My sons thought of everything when they bought the place.' She considered this further and continued, 'You know, if they'd been really smart, they'd have bought me something *high* maintenance. They should have bought me a small, narrow house with lots of steep staircases and a long stretch of lawn that they could have planted with a particularly vigorous grass that needed mowing every day. That would have finished me off much sooner and they'd not have had to worry about me anymore. Without exhaustion or wear and tear to kill me off, I can't see me popping my clogs anytime soon. Unless I die of boredom, which is a distinct possibility.'

Doubler, finding this rather too close to home, and anxious that the melancholic train of thought might impact on Olive, tried to steer Maddie off the subject of their mortality. 'Oh come, come. There's way too much talk of death. I brought you here to take tea and talk of happier things. How's Percy, Olive?'

But Maddie had made a realization, new entirely or certainly never expressed out loud, and she desperately wanted to air it before it disappeared from her reach. 'But death is the conversation, isn't it? It's not just the elephant in the room; it's a bloody enormous thing in the corner with huge ears, a trunk, a halo and wings, and it's looking at its watch and tapping it impatiently. It's there, death, always hovering nearby. You can ignore it, but it's not going to go anywhere.'

Both Olive and Doubler laughed, rather pleased with Maddie's passionate outcry, but she silenced them with a frown and a shake of her head.

'It's all right for us, as we face it, particularly if we're sitting around twiddling our thumbs, waiting for it to happen. But what about our nearest and dearest? Nobody can plan for anything, can they, if they've got elderly folk to take care of? They can't possibly know when we're going to succumb, which is pretty inconsiderate of us, all things considered.'

Doubler chuckled. 'Ha! You're not wrong there! My son, Julian, is desperate to see the back of me. He's convinced I'm wasting the financial opportunity that Mirth Farm should afford him and he can barely disguise his impatience. The thing is, he's well into his thirties now, but I've got a reasonable chance of living for another couple of decades, so it's going to be a long old wait. And he's not going to want to live in Mirth Farm when he's an old man! He's already far too used to the soft life. It's for that reason and that reason alone I'm absolutely determined to carry on farming up there for as long as possible. I'm going to live a ludicrously long time just to piss him off. I'd like to still be going strong when he's senile himself. That would really amuse me.'

Olive was watching Doubler intently, storing some of this troubling information away to examine more carefully later on. But for now, she joined in with Doubler's flippancy. 'Well, it's very likely that you'll keep going for a good while, isn't it? It's a healthy lifestyle you've got up there. All that oxygen and gin.' She smiled at her two guests and shook her head slowly. 'Look at us, three poor old souls and not a second-generation farmer among us to pass our love of the land on to. It's bad luck, isn't it? What are the odds, do you think?'

Doubler did a rough calculation in his head, seeing the generations of potatoes spreading out on a root system in his head. 'Slim odds, I'd say. Seven children between us and not one of them wants what we wanted at their age. Assuming there's a fifty-fifty chance of each one wanting to follow in our footsteps, then that's a one in a hundred twenty-eight chance that none would. Poor outcome, I'd say.'

Maddie, unimpressed, asked, 'Was it something we did? Maybe the farmer's life just didn't look very glamorous or appealing to the next generation.'

Olive thought about this intently, a look of fierce concentration etched on her tired face, and a huge wave of disappointment washed over her, bathing her in a sadness born out of an irrefutable understanding. 'Our children just never really had their toes in the soil. We didn't raise them on the land; we raised them in a three-bed in West Mead Park. So it's no wonder that they wanted to spread their wings, don't you think? It's easy living, yes — a small, neat house to keep can certainly be appealing when you're raising a family — but it's claustrophobic too, isn't it? They all grew up and wanted to get as far away from here as possible. We were tenant farmers for a few years when the kids were growing up, but we didn't actually buy the farm until the last one was away at university. It was Don's dream, always, to return to the land. It's how he grew up.

'But it's not how *they* grew up. So there's nothing to bind them to this. They didn't grow up looking out of the window at these hills, this view. They grew up in front of the telly, looking at *that* view. And the view on the box is so much bigger; the horizon's so much further away. They looked at their screens and that was their landscape, the whole of the rest of the world. They grew up staring at that as their vista and they saw that the possibilities were endless, so off they went. In pursuit of something they'd been promised by everyone except for their mother.'

Doubler looked at Olive sympathetically. 'It's tough, though, isn't it, after you spent all your life caring for them.' But he could have been talking about his own or Maddie's plight.

'That's true, and then almost as soon as the kids left, one by one, to go overseas, I spent the following years caring for my parents, and then Don's too.'

'And now you're on your own,' said Doubler, again speaking for all of them.

'Sometimes it does seem a bit unfair, it's true,' Olive concurred. 'But there was no contract, was there? Caring for my children was always unconditional. I never did it in exchange for things they could do for me later in life. Even if I'd known they'd grow up and desert me for the other side of the planet, I wouldn't have stopped caring for them. I wouldn't have changed a thing.'

'And yet I bet that nothing stopped you caring for your own parents out of a sense of duty.'

'Like everyone in my generation, I didn't know any other way. And I wanted to care for them; it made me glad. I loved them very much and I visited often, and one day I went there and they seemed so impossibly frail. Like children themselves, really. They were asking for help, I suppose, but not with words as such — it was the light in their eyes that told me what to do and I followed that instinct without really questioning it.'

'And now your children can't see that you need them in a similar way?' Doubler wanted to help Olive resolve this in her mind, however painful it might be. Within him he was conscious of a nagging kernel of doubt about his own children. Was Julian genuinely trying to help him? he wondered. Perhaps his son actually had his best interests at heart and he'd just assumed the worst.

While Doubler tried to sieve through recent events, Olive still pursued the thought. 'I'm sure they'd know my pain if they saw me face to face. But they're not dropping in on me, are they? We have our times to Skype, and I cherish those moments, but if I'm not feeling up to that, if I'm having one of my turns, I simply don't pick up. Wouldn't want to anyway. And then when I'm back on my feet, I just tell them I was too busy, which of course they love. All my children really want to hear is that their mother has a rich, fulfilling life that doesn't require much of them.'

Olive had tears in her eyes, which she didn't brush away. Instead, she talked through them. 'And anyway, when they're looking at me, they're seeing me on a very small screen. There's no light for them to see or decipher — I don't think that is something that can be replicated digitally. And we chat and we share our news. I talk about the shelter — whatever titbits the Colonel might have fed me that week — and I reassure them every time that they are doing the best thing for their own families. And I fully believe that. They are. The opportunities the world can offer them are so rich and so varied, and it's a wonderful thing that they're tasting its fruits.'

Doubler was still thinking about Julian, wondering if he had such sentiment built into him or if he were truly devoid of all filial duty. 'Do you suppose they fear their old age? They must know that their own children aren't going to be there for them. Their children will run a mile, just like they did.'

Olive snorted in disgust. 'That generation isn't remotely worried about their old age. They don't believe in it. The new church is the Church of Perpetual Youth and they all worship at its altar. Everything they strive for is age-defying, age-defeating, like time is something you can actually wage war against armed only with kale and pomegranate.'

Olive blinked away her tears to study her audience more clearly. 'You think I'm joking; I'm not. They make themselves these drinks every morning of green leaves and ginger. They build in something called 'me-time' into their day and something else called 'self-care', which is the same but they reassure me it is fundamentally different and requires its own allocation of time. They believe firmly that by lavishing attention on themselves, they'll never get old. So why plan for something that is simply not going to happen to you? And if they're not worshipping at the Altar of Youth, they're praying to the God of Cash. Because if you work hard enough and amass enough wealth, you can use that to pay for your care in your old age and once again the next generation are let off the hook.'

'Sounds to me,' said Doubler, 'like they're keeping themselves so busy that they don't have time to face up to their responsibilities.'

'But I'm really not their responsibility, don't you see that? Caring for me as I get older could only ever be undertaken through choice or it would be hell for us all. Can you imagine! Think of the resentment and pain if they were forced, through guilt, to give up their sun-bleached lives for this.' Here, Olive waved her hands not just to take in the room and its dusty floorboards and old, tired bookshelves but the ancient fields beyond and the rolling hills behind these, where the English winter refused to quite let go.

'And careers are so different now, aren't they? The good jobs are all so *competitive*. There was probably a time when you worked your whole life for a company and you were expected to slow down towards the end of your career; you'd even be *respected* for taking a bit of a back seat. But now you move around a lot, moving ever upwards each time. There's this promotion here and that one there, and you're on the treadmill set at the fastest possible pace with younger, keener, hungrier people snapping at your heels all the time. Just waiting for you to *slip*. You don't give up that chase; you don't duck your responsibilities to your career to take care of your *parents*. Nobody keeps your job open for you while you take a bit of time out, and the time could be indefinite, too, couldn't it? Whether we like it or not, we are all living longer and longer. I could drop dead tomorrow, but equally I could still be alive in twenty years. Maybe even thirty, perish the thought! How do your kids know what they're signing up to? They can't put their own lives on hold for mine and then risk not being able to live theirs at all. No, this is progress, and progress doesn't allow for the modern family to hold themselves back by caring for each other.'

Doubler was torn between giving Olive the freedom to air these strong feelings and lightening the atmosphere for the sake of all of their sanity. He was unsure whether Maddie was equally moved by the subject: she'd been a little detached from the conversation for a few minutes.

'What do you think, Maddie?' he ventured.

This stopped Olive in her tracks; she'd been pacing the floor, drinking her tea, looking out of the window as she talked, answering these questions that she hadn't dared ask herself before. And now she was so certain that she was right, pleased and proud to have made the decisions that liberated her children from her care, she realized there was another woman in the room who could have been quite offended by the stance. She knew from Doubler that she'd had a difficult relationship with her children recently.

Maddie shrugged, looking quite dispassionate. 'I think you're right. Completely right.'

'You do?'

'Yes. I'd have made the same decisions. You're not being entirely selfless, you know. If you wanted to make your children feel really good, you could sell up here and invest a fraction of the value of this place in a modern condominium near one of them. Then they wouldn't have to live with those pangs of fear and guilt that they probably deal with from time to time. But you've done the right thing by staying put. By choosing a life you know with your dead husband rather than a life you can't know with your living children. That seems like a thoroughly reasonable decision to make and I applaud it.'

'Well, thank you, yes. It's crushingly lonely at times, but you're right — I wouldn't leave Don. Not now. Not after all we went through together to be here.'

Maddie nodded knowingly. 'Take my sons, for example. You see, they can sleep easy at night. They tell their friends that they made completely the right decision. I know they do. I've heard them telling the doctors. They sorted our lives right out, got my Thomas into care, got me into a manageable house, something easy to look after. I have to be very careful not to show any sign of deterioration. I take care never to even wince when I stand up in front of them for fear that they'll have me in a bungalow before I know it. Or worse.'

'Oh, that would be no good at all. Where would we be without the stairs? Without going up to bed?' Olive, in contemplation of living in a single-storey building, shuddered, certainly incapable of comprehending the 'something worse' that Maddie alluded to.

Doubler, too, imagined life without the slow pace of his morning descent in the half-light, still asleep as he grasped the bannister but fully awake by the time he stepped off the final tread into the cool hall. He couldn't consider any other awakening.

'Quite right,' he said, quietly grateful for his home and his independence.

'But you see, my sons made these moves without ever stopping to ask me what I wanted. They did it without consulting me and told me they wanted to spare me the pain. The truth is, I hate the house. I hate its wall-to-wall carpets and its wipe-down surfaces; I hate the self-cleaning oven and the decking in the garden. I miss my dirty fingernails and the ache you have when you come into the house at the end of the day. It was only that *ache* that made me sleep. I slept like a baby up at the farm, but of course I don't sleep at all now. How could I? I'm never tired.' Maddie looked to be on the verge of tears as the realization of the dullness of her every day hit her as if for the first time. Though, of course, in reality she was stuck in a dreadful daily cycle of denial, realization, horror and decline.

She continued, 'I'd so love to feel tired again. I'd love to feel so exhausted that it's all I can do to crawl upstairs — yes, *upstairs* — to get into bed. And I'd love to leave the curtains open so that however deep I sleep, however far I travel in my dreams, it's the dawn that wakes me up.' She looked at her audience with wide-eyed horror, trying to convey the true awfulness of her life these days. 'I can't even leave the curtains open because there's a street light right outside my bedroom window. And I can't even keep my windows open for the fresh air because — get this — they're not designed to *open*.'

328

'What?' chorused both Olive and Doubler, who were beginning to feel guilty about their relatively untroubled continuation of farm life.

'It's true! I have this special double-glazing that traps the warm air in between two panes of glass and cuts down on my heating bill, but you're not supposed to open the windows. You are only supposed to look out of them. But why you'd bother looking out I have no idea. All I can see is the exact same house staring back at me.'

Olive reached out and put a comforting hand on Maddie's arm. 'But you know you're lucky, too, don't you? And there'd be an awful lot of people envying you and thinking you're a right Moaning Minnie. That development you live on? It's pretty gorgeous by all accounts. Your boys took care of you; they found you an easier life. Probably because of *love* for you.'

Maddie dismissed this with a tight-lipped shake of her head. 'Love? I don't think so. Love goes hand in hand with respect and they never, never asked me what I *wanted*. Not once. Everything they did they did *to* me, not *with* me or *for* me. And yes, I sound ungrateful, because I *am* ungrateful. I had a home and I'd chosen a lifestyle that suited me and I cannot forgive them for ripping me out of that house.'

Olive moved her hand from Maddie's arm to her hand and squeezed it reassuringly as fat tears rolled down Maddie's face.

'Silly me, I'm crying. But I'm not sad. I'm *angry*.'

Olive, also on the brink of tears, comforted her with her own furious version of the same tale.

'You're angry and you're sad and both are fine, you know. I'm angry with my kids, too. I'm angry they left me. I'm angry I don't know my own grandchildren. And I'm angry they've made me have to choose. If I want to see my grandchildren grow up, I have to give up the farm. I have to give up everything I know and love. I don't *want* to do that. And I'm angry that this makes me a bad person somehow, that I'm not maternal enough — after everything else — to want to relinquish it all for some grandchildren I've never even *met*.' Olive paused, again conscious that she knew very little of Maddie and might be causing untold offence. She swallowed loudly before asking, kindly, 'What about you, dear? Have you any grandchildren making your life better?'

'Yes, I have four. And they're dear enough children, but I don't really know how to be a grandmother in that house. I barely know how to be a human being. What am I supposed to do? What can I show them? What can I possibly teach them? I think I would have liked my grandchildren to know the farm. I could have shown them where their lunch comes from. They could have learnt to sow carrots. That would have been enough. I keep some jigsaws for them, but they just put the telly on and we sit and gawp at it together and then they go home. It's no wonder they're not really interested in me. I'm not an interesting person.'

Doubler experienced a pang of guilt and vowed to teach his grandchildren to sow carrots. Of course he must. Society might slip backwards entirely if nobody knew how to sow carrots. By wallowing in self-pity for all these years, he had shunned his responsibilities. The grandchildren should each be able to chit potatoes by now, he realized, but just as he banged the table to draw the women's attention to his terrible shortcomings, Olive spoke.

'You know, Maddie, this is absolutely ludicrous. All of it.'

'It is?' she asked, her bottom lip trembling a little.

'Yes. You're living in a place you hate, waiting to die. I'm here living up at the farm, your idea of heaven, where there are animals to be fed and carrots to be sown. And I'm not going to leave here until I'm carried out in a box, and even then, quite frankly, I'll be kicking and screaming. I'd rather be buried down at the bottom of a field somewhere.'

'What are you suggesting?' asked Doubler, looking from one woman to the other and back again.

'Can't you see? It's obvious. Come and share the workload here at the farm with me, Maddie.'

'Here?' Maddie asked with undisguised horror on her face.

'Well, I know it sounds preposterous, but the truth is, I'm not really equipped to cope here on my own. I was never really much of a farmer, more a farmer's wife. Come and show me the ropes. I want to get my fingernails dirty again too.'

'But you barely know me!' squealed Maddie, affronted more than flattered.

'All I know is my own shadow, and to tell you the truth, I'm sick and tired of it. I just want to start again; I want to do something different with this next chapter. Let's take back control!'

This piqued Maddie's interest. She had been feeling wildly out of control for too long now. 'Is that possible? Aren't we too old?'

'Heavens, no! As far as taking control is concerned, we are in our *prime*. We get to do whatever we want to do for the rest of our lives, don't we? If we have earned anything at all, we've earned that. And you can see your days out sowing carrots if that's what you want.'

Olive could see the light in Maddie's eyes. She could see Maddie imagining this as a possibility, so she pressed on. 'I'm not sure you're equipped to live on your own, either. From what I hear, you're a bit of a liability. But perhaps if we look after each other, we can keep each other out of harm's way.'

'Are you inviting me to visit as an occasional guest, or are you inviting me to come and go as I please? I'm not entirely sure what you're suggesting.'

'Come and go as you please. I've got room for you and your things here, Maddie.'

Maddie fell silent while she focused on the practicalities. She continued to quiz Olive anxiously, her worries visible in the crease on her brow. 'How much room do you have? Will I get under your feet? Will there be space for a few of my things?'

'This place is so big that even with the two of us here, we'll still rattle around.' Olive assessed

Maddie carefully before adding, 'You wouldn't do anything *daft*, would you? You're not going to kidnap the animals or set fire to my farmhouse? You're not actually *mad*, are you, Maddie?'

'I don't know. I don't *think* I'm mad. I think I'm just lonely, but it's quite possible that is driving me a bit bonkers.'

★   ★   ★

Doubler smiled to himself. He had rather hoped when he drove Maddie here that something like this might happen. Recently, everything had seemed possible. But that didn't stop him bubbling over with happiness at the thought that these two women might be able to complete each other.

'Olive, you're an absolute genius. It's not a bad idea, Maddie. You could help each other around the place and keep each other out of mischief. And you'd have Percy right next to you, so Thomas can find him if he does come home.'

'Oh, Thomas would *love* it here. I know he would. What about Thomas, Olive? Could he come here too if he ever gets better? He might make a recovery if he thinks there's some earth to dig.' Maddie hesitated. A stark memory swept in and swamped her mind, drowning the thrill of potential she'd experienced for a few brief moments. 'Percy hates me,' she said quietly, to the table.

'Well,' said Doubler a little crossly, 'you didn't always do the right thing by that donkey, did you? Who wants to live in a garage, for God's sake? You think you suffered moving from the countryside to a housing estate? Imagine the trauma that poor beast suffered. A donkey deserves the earth beneath its feet, that's for sure. But . . . ' he said, softening, 'Percy will learn to forgive you. I expect donkeys manage forgiveness quite well.'

'I don't know about that — donkeys are the silent-suffering types. That donkey will always make me feel guilty. Have you seen the way he looks at me?'

'Well, perhaps he will learn to love you again when you start taking him some carrots every day and stop trying to run away with him,' Olive spoke up, her voice also carrying a trace of admonishment, and Doubler realized that she was not going to be a pushover. Maddie was going to have to earn her keep.

'He was happy the first time I broke him out of the farm, I swear. He trotted down the bridle path like he thought he was going on an adventure. He was an angel.'

'Because he thought he was going home!' Olive tutted. 'He probably thought you were taking him to see Thomas.'

'I suppose he did. Thomas was always his favourite.'

'And instead you locked him in a garage with no light.'

'The garage had a window. I'm not crazy. Though I suppose it was north-facing.'

Doubler nodded sternly. 'Exactly. One small north-facing window does not make for a happy retirement home for a donkey. But you can make it up to him now. Grow him some carrots and then when you go to visit Thomas, you'll have some stories to tell him. You can talk about Percy, about your veg; you can tell him when you've seen the first bluebells of the year, the first swallows, or heard the first cuckoo. Maybe he'll be less miserable there when he knows you're less miserable here.'

Maddie recovered from the scolding quickly and was focusing on the possibility of a clean start. 'It's a very attractive proposition. Taking back control, I love the sound of that.'

'And you'll owe me a favour or two, so in return you can both help me take back control from the Colonel. I'm rather fed up with being cut out of the shelter and what goes on here. It's *disrespectful.*'

Doubler interjected. 'Really, he doesn't want to cut you out. He's just a bit frightened of hysterical women.'

'Hysterical? Me? He hasn't seen anything yet. Let's see how he copes with one hysterical woman and one completely unhinged one. That will give him something to think about.' Olive looked at Maddie and winked, the two of them enjoying the solidarity.

'But two farmers' wives? Will that work?' asked Maddie, running the same thought through her busy, confused mind again and again to try and straighten some of the knots into bits of information she could properly hold on to.

'You were never a farmer's wife; you were always a farmer. And I'd love to learn a bit more.

I stopped learning the day Don died, but there are definitely plenty of things you could teach me.'

Maddie sat up a little straighter, hearing the praise and soaking it up. 'It would be an honour. I'd like to see what I still remember. There must be something useful rattling about in here,' she said, sounding unconvinced.

'I can keep an eye on you, you know, if you come unstuck?' offered Doubler grandly.

Olive laughed. 'I don't think we'll be needing the help of a potato farmer, thank you very much. But you can certainly lend us your tractor from time to time.'

Doubler winced at the thought of letting anyone loose with any of his much-treasured farm equipment and nodded some sort of acquiescence, though he secretly hoped the women would be downgrading their ambitions before he had to do any such thing.

Olive turned back to Maddie, serious once more. 'If we're going to make a go of it, we'll need to be productive — we can't just sit here crying into our tea about our awful families or how much we miss our husbands. We'll do some farming; we will grow a bit of veg; we'll get our fingernails dirty again. That has to be the deal. It will feel more like hard work.'

Maddie's eyes shone at the prospect. 'It will either make me live much longer or it will kill me. But either way, it's better than dying a slow, agonizing death of boredom.'

'Well, I can't see any prospect of us being bored together. I suspect it will be far too much of a rollercoaster. But let's make a pact now that we'll smother each other with a pillow rather than die of boredom.'

Doubler let out a gasp. 'Watch your mouth, Olive. This one will be far too quick to take you up on your offer. You'll only have to yawn once and she'll come at you with a cushion to put you out of your misery. I'd stay alert and keep the two of you busy if I were you.' He laughed, but he fixed Maddie with a stare, who was looking innocently at him, blinking her bright eyes slowly.

Let's hope I've done the right thing, thought Doubler, slapping his hands on his thighs to indicate the end of the meeting.

'I take some comfort from the thought that neither of you will be any *worse* off,' he said, then stood and looked out at the view, a view not as grand or as endless as his own but charming in its own way and undoubtedly an improvement on the laurel hedges of Maddie's own.

The women talked excitedly behind him as Doubler wondered, a little proudly, what Mrs Millwood would make of his meddling.

# 29

The next morning, Doubler awoke with a start, sensing that something was very wrong. Grabbing a fistful of bed sheet in each hand, he sat up, looking wildly around him. The noise of something falling was reverberating in his ears through the silence, competing with his own heartbeat. Certain that a sudden clatter must have awoken him, he listened intently for sounds of an intruder, unable to determine if the noise still echoing in his head was dreamt or real.

After several moments of adrenaline-fuelled panic, he collapsed back against his pillow, realizing that it was the unusual light in his bedroom that had given him cause for alarm. For the first time in over twenty years, he had overslept.

He ran through a mental checklist of anxieties, working one by one through the worries of every day that he automatically focused on as he woke and, ticking each one off, found himself remarkably free of concern. Somehow, the things that usually propelled him out of bed at sunrise seemed less pressing in the context of yesterday's successful introduction of Maddie to Olive. Reliving the conversation, he suddenly felt wide awake anticipating the moment he could relay the day's successes to Mrs Millwood.

He wrapped his dressing gown round him and wandered downstairs, the small guilt at his later

338

than usual start comfortably outweighed by the glow of a good night's sleep. But as he descended the stairs, he caught sight of a brown package on the doormat and cursed himself for his complacency. Peele was back.

Doubler was fleetingly tempted to hide the parcel away in the dresser drawer for another day, but as he passed the telephone, Mrs Millwood's voice seemed to float across the hallway: 'You're a brave man, Mr Doubler.' Emboldened, he took a decisive step towards the door and, picking up the parcel, tore at the packaging.

Inside was a small illustrated book, a paperback guide to English garden birds. A postcard of Hever Castle was tucked inside. Turning it over, he read the note, written in Camilla's careful handwriting.

*Dear Dad, I hope you find this useful for your new hobby. The blackbird, page 28, is my favourite! I used to think they were a bit dull, but there's so much more to them than meets the eye . . . Remind you of anyone?! Loving you always, Camilla.*

*(PS I took the kids to Hever Castle and picked this postcard up for you. Do you remember?)*

He read the message again from start to finish. Dropping the packaging on the doormat, he wandered into the kitchen, where he began to brew himself a pot of tea. He leafed through the bird book while he waited for the kettle to boil. Turning to page 28, he examined the picture of the blackbird. With its bright yellow beak and matching eye ring, it didn't look dull to Doubler. It looked handsome and sure of itself. Who should it remind him of? he wondered. He admired the bird again and ruled himself out. Perhaps she meant herself. Or perhaps she meant somebody else entirely. That husband of hers was certainly dull.

Doubler measured the tea leaves into the pot and stirred them absent-mindedly, trying to recall the significance of Hever Castle. He was sure he must have been there once but was quite unable to dredge the memory to the surface. Was it a good memory for his daughter, or had it been another opportunity for him to disappoint her? Try as he might, he couldn't remember the details, so he deduced that it must refer to a happy occasion, since it seemed to Doubler that the painful memories were so much easier for him to hold on to. Was this the same for everyone? Doubler resolved to discuss it with Mrs Millwood when she called.

When she did call, Mrs Millwood wasn't quite as pleased with Doubler as he had hoped. In anticipation of a thoroughly pleasurable conversation, one he assumed they'd both wish to prolong, he had brewed a fresh pot of tea, laid a tray with biscuits and carried it carefully through to the sitting room. He positioned the telephone beside him and made himself perfectly comfortable while waiting confidently for the phone to ring.

When it did ring, he barely paused to enquire of Mrs Millwood's comfort as he regaled her with the full account of recent activities. 'Who'd have thought it, Mrs M? Me, a matchmaker? And a match of Maddie and Olive no less!' He chuckled happily. 'I do believe they are going to be the most wonderful companions. Oh, I have no doubt they'll get on each other's nerves from time to time, because, let's face it, both of them are equally capable of having their *moments*, aren't they? But I think they'll be able to provide so much *stimulation* for each other. They already sound like a couple who have been married for ever and are very happy to forgive each other's faults because they know the pleasures far outweigh the moments of discomfort.'

Doubler took a generous sip of tea and wriggled himself even more comfortably into his chair, preparing himself to settle into his delighted account of recent events. Mrs Millwood had been waiting for this pause, the first with room for an interruption.

'And how are *you*, Mr Doubler?'

'Me? I'm grand, Mrs M!' he exclaimed, barely drawing breath. 'You should have seen Maddie's face when Olive first suggested she should help her up at the farm. Between you and me, I had hoped something like this would happen, but I had no idea it would be suggested so quickly and naturally. It was priceless!'

'Mr Doubler?' said Mrs Millwood sternly. 'I asked how *you* are.'

'I said I'm quite fine, Mrs M!' Doubler exclaimed, inhaling deeply to carry on with his soliloquy.

'Midge isn't so sure. She's worried about you.

341

And if I'm honest, so am I.'

'Oh, Mrs M! I'm not the one to worry about. I'm fit as a fiddle!'

'Doesn't it seem strange to you, Mr Doubler, that you're running around fixing other people's problems but you're not addressing your own? Because it certainly seems strange to Midge and to me.'

Doubler frowned in response and thought about this before continuing at a pace, 'My own problems, Mrs M? I don't think I have any problems to call my own.' He rushed on blithely. 'Oh, and I've had a heart-to-heart with Maxwell! Who'd have thought it? It's just you now, Mrs M. If we can get you on the mend and home, then I'll be the happiest I've been in decades. Perhaps *ever*. I've not heard a peep from Peele, so I was obviously worrying about nothing. As if that good-for-nothing GM propagator could really be a threat to Mirth Farm. I don't know *what* I was thinking.'

Mrs Millwood had to interrupt again.

'You sound cheerful enough, it's true. But you and I know what you've been through and I have to be certain that if I'm not there to keep an eye on you, you can count on people who are capable of looking out for you for the *long* term. And that won't be Olive or Maddie — they've got quite enough on their plates by the sounds of it. And it won't be the Colonel, of that I'm certain. Midge is very fond of you, but I can't ask her to take you on — it wouldn't be fair.'

'Take me on? I'm not a *project*, Mrs M.' Doubler's mood plummeted as he tried to unpick the many pieces of information Mrs Millwood had just dripped down the phone like dirty water wrung out from a dishcloth. 'And anyway, I want *you* to keep an eye on me, and *I* want to keep an eye on *you*. The way it's always been,' Doubler said, sulking now his disposition had been dampened.

'Mr Doubler, that's just not practical. Who knows how long I will be around for? I was your only *reliable* company up at Mirth Farm, so if I'm not there, I can't imagine what will happen.'

'But you *are* going to be here, Mrs M. When you're right as rain. That's what you promised.' Doubler would have liked to stamp his foot to deliver the message with the added truculence he felt it deserved, but instead he slumped back in his chair, the fight dissipating before he'd found the energy to convincingly summon it.

'You are, aren't you?' he asked in a quiet voice.

'I'm doing my best, Mr Doubler. God only knows if that will be good enough. But I will make you a promise that I *can* keep. I promise you the first thing I do when I'm allowed out of this place is head on up to Mirth Farm for a spot of lunch.'

Doubler perked up, drawing himself tall in his chair again. 'You promise?' he said, allowing hope to creep into his voice.

'I *will* promise. But I want you to do one thing for me first, with absolutely no fuss.'

'Anything. I'll do anything,' he said, his mind racing ahead, already planning the meal he might prepare for a recuperating patient. Not sandwiches this time. Not sandwiches ever. 'Fish pie,'

343

he muttered out loud, while meaning to keep the thought in his head.

'Whatever I say,' said Mrs Millwood, impatiently now.

'Of course. Anything. I promise.'

'I want you to speak to your children and tell them what's on your mind. I want you to talk to Camilla and clear the air, and I want you to talk to Julian and be honest with him. No more bottling things up in that potato-filled head of yours. No more skirting round the important issues. They're grown-ups now, so let them share some of the burden that rattles around and keeps you awake at night. You don't need to protect them anymore — it's time they protected you.'

'Oh,' said Doubler, surprised. 'I was rather hoping the promise would be around pigs. Or chickens. I would have said yes, you know.'

'Well, Midge *will* be glad to hear that, but let's not give you any further responsibility for living things until you've learnt to speak your mind to your nearest and dearest.'

Doubler thought about the commitment he was being asked to make and felt a shadow of fear cross his mind as he wondered what was driving Mrs Millwood's urgency. But she'd promised him she'd be back at Mirth Farm, hadn't she?

'I trust you, Mrs M. You're right surprisingly often. It used to be that I'd turn to Mr Clarke for any help I needed, but it's definitely you these days, Mrs M.'

'Well, that is a turn-up for the books,' said Mrs Millwood, laughing. 'I'm a better friend to you than a dead potato farmer? Goodness me, I *am* flattered.'

Comfortable that he could ask her almost anything now, Doubler launched straight in with a troublesome thought. 'Mrs Millwood, would you be flattered to be compared to a blackbird?'

'Well, of course I would. Have you *heard* a blackbird sing?'

'The song isn't the issue. Anyone would be flattered to be considered as melodious as a blackbird.' Doubler tried to organize his thoughts. 'You've tasked me with clearing the air with Camilla. I don't know where to start.'

'Open up a dialogue, Mr Doubler. That's all I'm suggesting. Open up a dialogue and if there are words to be said, they'll be said. Words have a habit of being spoken.'

'But she'll want to speak about the *past*, Mrs M. And what if my memories of her childhood aren't the same as hers? What if I've misremembered? Then what?'

'In my experience, our memories rarely tally. The events are the same, but the way in which they're recorded depend entirely on your frame of mind at the time and what you've done with those memories since. If every time you dig a memory out to examine it, you file it in a different place, it can soon become distorted.'

Doubler was entirely satisfied with this. It seemed very likely that a good memory might have been refiled as a painful one because of other events that had happened in between.

'You might be right, Mrs M. Perhaps there are different ways of remembering the same things.'

And, satisfied he had Mrs Millwood's full attention once again, he resumed his stories of Maddie, Olive and the Colonel, making absolutely certain that he didn't skip a single detail.

# 30

The following morning, Doubler sat by the phone trying to convince himself he had the courage to pick it up and dial the number he'd written out carefully in front of him. He still wore his coat and his flat cap from his morning rounds, determined to use the momentum he'd found when walking in the clear air of spring's first promise.

Several times he picked up the receiver and then let it fall back into its cradle. He knew he had to do this for Mrs Millwood, but the confidences he'd recently shared with Maddie and Olive also replayed themselves in his head. Their tears of lonely accord solidified the thoughts planted so certainly by Mrs Millwood and it was the common ground they all shared that finally compelled him to dial the number.

'Camilla,' he said, as he heard her voice.

'Dad? Is everything OK?' his daughter asked with undisguised anxiety.

'Yes, everything's fine, thank you. I just thought I'd check in with you and see how you're doing. How are the kids?'

'Fine?' Camilla said uncertainly.

'And your husband. Darren? How is he?'

'Fine?' Camilla said.

Doubler could feel her assessment of him crackling down the wire.

Doubler paused. How was it possible that

initiating a conversation with his daughter could be so very difficult? He thought of the ease with which he and Midge were able to interact. He ploughed on.

'Thanks for the bird book, Camilla. That was a thoughtful gesture.'

'I hope you find it useful. There were so many to choose from, it was somewhat mind-boggling. It might be a bit basic, but I can always get you something more sophisticated for your birthday if you'd like.'

'Oh no. This one is grand. I think I will be doing well if I learn to identify half the birds in there. It should see me out, I think.'

'I'm glad you've got a hobby, Dad. It's about time. Julian's convinced you're going crazy up there all on your own.'

Doubler gave brief thanks in his head for the introduction of Julian into the conversation, allowing him a smooth segue. 'I'm glad you brought up the subject of your brother, Camilla. Julian is after my car, it seems. Thinks I'd be better off with something a bit more practical. 'Nippy' was his exact word, I think. He was going to do a swap and take the Land Rover off my hands, but it turns out that my old banger is worth a small fortune.' Doubler paused to allow Camilla to digest this news. 'That *was* a surprise.'

Camilla expelled an exaggerated sigh. 'Jesus Christ, Dad. Julian wants your car precisely *because* it's worth a small fortune. You do know that, don't you?'

'Ah,' Doubler said thoughtfully, allowing the

silence to engulf them both. He carried on bravely. 'The thought had occurred to me, but only very briefly. You think he knew what he was doing, do you?'

'Of course he knew what he was doing! Julian is nothing if not very calculating. He's not exactly known for his spontaneous generosity, is he?'

Doubler was shocked at the sheer speed of Camilla's conclusion.

'Oh,' he said.

'You can't be remotely surprised, Dad. It's not the first time he has done this sort of thing. Remember when you gave us Mum's wedding rings? He got the wedding band. I got the engagement ring. He made me swap with him, telling me it was for sentimental reasons, and then he went and sold the solitaire immediately. The one he allowed me to have in exchange was almost worthless, apparently.'

'Well, that sounds rather manipulative, if you ask me,' Doubler said, wondering if this was a story he had been told and, if so, why he hadn't retained it.

Camilla laughed down the phone. 'That's a bit of an understatement. I didn't really mind. It was just nice to have something of Mum's; I was never that fussed by the value of it. And I probably prefer wearing the band. But I didn't much like him assuming I was too foolish to notice what he was up to.'

'No, no, of course not.' Doubler felt a small ripple of solidarity, which while not invited, was not altogether unpleasant. 'Nobody does.'

Doubler continued carefully, 'Would you mind me asking, Camilla, when you discovered his duplicity, did you have it out with him?'

'No. And that's not the only time he's acted entirely selfishly. But this family is fractured enough, Dad. I don't want to add to it. I figure that he needs to feel in control of us all and that helps him come to terms with his demons. We all have to find our own way of dealing with life, don't we? Who am I to judge?'

'And what would you recommend I do about this car business?'

'I don't know. It's entirely up to you, Dad. Personally, I'd probably just let him do what he needs to do. He's a very unhappy man and perhaps allowing him to think he's got the better of us from time to time will make him feel a bit less cheated by life.'

'You really think that? You think I should let him take my treasured car and swap it for a modern *runaround*?'

'Well, no, of course not. Not if you love your car.' Camilla bleated her response, unable to hide the anguish this conflict was creating within her.

'What are you advising, Camilla? I'm asking for your *help*.'

'But you've never asked for my help before, so I'm not very practised at giving it. You always give the impression you don't need anyone's help.'

Doubler paused and said quietly 'Perhaps I do, but perhaps I never realised that until now.'

Camilla softened. 'Julian is complicated. More

complicated than me, I think. Me? I just don't like confrontation. All I really want to do is keep the status quo and hold my family together.'

'In a way that I didn't manage to hold our family together, you mean?' Doubler said, allowing himself to imagine what it must have been like to be the daughter left behind.

'Oh, Dad. You did a fine job raising two teenagers, which can't have been easy. You did your best to replace Mum, and you made sure we didn't go without any of the basics our mother wasn't there to give us. But perhaps somewhere along the way, in trying to be a mother to us, you weren't always quite there as a father to Julian. Perhaps that's what Julian missed out on.'

'And you really believe that? You think I made him what he is today? The kind of man who would *cheat* his own father?'

Camilla, distraught by the offence she'd caused, backtracked immediately. 'That sounded harsh, didn't it? I'm sorry, Dad. No, I don't mean that. You really did do your best.'

'I'm certain I *tried* to do my best, but I'm equally prepared to admit my best was inadequate.' Doubler thought about his son and the man he'd become. 'But I'm not quite prepared to let Julian off the hook as easily as you are. He had a tough start in life, agreed. I wasn't the role model he would have liked, fair enough. I disappointed him generally, granted. But does that mean we should both accept his poor behaviour? Will he go through life being a thoroughly nasty piece of work on the basis he didn't have the perfect childhood? Shouldn't somebody mention to him that cheating and lying is not really *on*?'

'That's *your* job, Dad, not mine. I'm not interested in getting involved in any of it. He's just my brother, and he's the only one I've got. And besides, I can't remember him being any different. If you want to start giving him a bit of fatherly guidance now, that's entirely up to you, but just don't pick a fight at our family lunches. I'd like my children to grow up with some positive values.'

'Like Hever Castle?' Doubler ventured, hoping his hunch was right and that it was a positive memory for Camilla.

'Exactly!' Camilla exclaimed. 'Carefree family time! Every child deserves that, don't they? I know I made a right old fuss at the time. I thought I was too old for that sort of trip, and Julian was vile all day, wasn't he? But I realized much later how much effort that must have been, to take us on an outing so soon after Mum had gone. I know what you were trying to do: you were trying to make sure our childhood hadn't finished overnight, and that was a good thing to do, Dad. It can't have been easy.'

Doubler closed his eyes and images began to filter through. Linking arms with his daughter as they walked in step across a huge expanse of lawn. Running through a maze, crouching and hiding, laughing breathlessly while waiting to pounce on Julian.

Then standing in a queue in a draughty cafe, dropping a tray of tea and sandwiches, biting back tears. The burn of pitying and accusatory glances from the mothers of family groups as he sat alone at the table, two plates of food untouched, Camilla and Julian having lost interest in lunch. Snippets. Nothing more than snippets. But if Camilla remembered it as carefree family time, then who was he to dispute her record?

Doubler pondered this. 'How do *you* cope, Camilla? What's *your* way of dealing with life? What about *your* demons?'

Camilla let out a shallow laugh. 'I'll let you know when I've worked it out, shall I?' She thought about her father's question and matched his inquisitive tone with a pragmatic response. 'I suppose I try to create as stable an environment as I can for my own kids. I try to let them see the positive bits of my own childhood so they'll grow up carrying the very best of Mirth Farm in their hearts before they learn the painful chapters, because there's plenty of time for all of that.' Her voice trailed off. Then she added, 'I try really hard not to disappoint my husband or my children.'

'Oh,' said Doubler, swallowing loudly.

And then, as if reeling off a list of pre-prepared answers, 'And I try to forgive my mum.' She said this with surprising sure-footedness, sounding to Doubler every bit like somebody who might yet come to forgive her father.

# 31

The doorbell rang and Olive hurried to answer it. 'Come in, come in,' she said as she flung the door open, causing the Colonel to take a step backwards in alarm, treading on the toes of Derek, who stood, as usual, just behind him.

'We are in the sitting room today. Go on through.' Olive ushered the Colonel in and gave Derek a reassuring squeeze on his arm as he passed, which Derek found, contrary to Olive's best intentions, somewhat threatening.

The Colonel was flustered by the relocation from kitchen to dining room, and after a series of rapid calculations, he deftly framed his retreat. He made it quite clear from his reluctant gait that he was prepared to loiter in the hallway rather than submit to any unscheduled change of venue, and to demonstrate his lack of enthusiasm for this new arrangement, he hung back while he worked out how best to take control of the situation. (Sometimes, he was thinking, irritably, it would be nice if people did what was expected of them.) Olive was behaving in a manner that was quite unlike her, and rather than trying to engage him in conversation right there, on the threshold of the sitting room, she forced him through the doorway with a playful shove. The Colonel, discombobulated by Olive's uncharacteristic confidence, was further alarmed when, as he reluctantly entered the room, he came face to face with Mrs Mitchell, who was sitting in a comfortable chair in the corner with the newspaper folded neatly on her lap.

'This is a surprise, Olive,' he said over his shoulder in the general direction of Olive, who was busy hanging up Derek's coat. The Colonel hugged his own jacket to him for fear that Olive might forcibly remove it and prolong his stay.

'You mean Maddie? Isn't it just lovely? I'm so enjoying the company.'

The Colonel turned his back on Maddie and dropped his voice, though not to an inaudible level. 'You'd better not be taken in by her. This is a risky game you're playing. She'll be off with the donkey the minute you turn your back.'

'I don't think so. There's no need, is there?' Raising her voice, Olive directed her question towards Maddie.

'No need for what?' said Maddie, looking up somewhat innocently from her paper, but her eyes were twinkling and she was suppressing a smile that betrayed some sort of collusion with Olive, though neither Derek nor the Colonel was quite sure, when revealed, what shape this conspiracy might take.

'The Colonel here thinks you'll be running off with Percy the minute I turn my back, but he's worrying unnecessarily, isn't he, dear?'

'I can see Percy whenever I wish now, which I have to say makes him considerably less appealing. But if Thomas ever does come home, at least he will know where to find us both.' Maddie nodded her head with satisfaction and returned to her newspaper. Only a repeated light touch to her brooch betrayed any anxiety as she appeared to busy herself with the day's news.

'Sit down, gentlemen. Make yourself comfortable. I'll fetch the treats. We've been baking, haven't we, Maddie?'

'Well, you've been baking; I've been observing. I'm hoping to learn a few tricks, though. Never too old to learn a new hobby.' Maddie was giving a very good account of an elderly innocent bystander, but neither the Colonel nor Derek was fooled. The Colonel narrowed his eyes as he watched her, and Derek smiled, fascinated and somewhat bewitched by the transformation.

Olive stopped before she left the room to address them all. 'That Doubler's a charmer, isn't he? He's been spending a little time here, helping to get Maddie settled in and teaching us both some of the basic principles of baking. You'll be the lucky testers today, trying out some of the delicious cakes we've been perfecting. Paula and Mabel were here only yesterday and they certainly seemed to approve. Frankly, you're lucky there's anything left for you to sample.'

'There is a piece of the lemon drizzle left for the Colonel, isn't there? I do hope so. That quite stole the show.' Maddie sounded genuinely anxious, but Olive had already disappeared in the direction of the kitchen.

Derek pulled up a chair to sit near Maddie.

'Well, this is a bit of a change, Maddie. I hadn't heard the two of you were friends now.'

'I'd say it is a bit of a change. Poacher turned gamekeeper,' the Colonel muttered, resigning himself to his fate and sitting down heavily in a chair on the far side of the room.

'Do I take it you're up here often, Maddie?' Derek probed.

'I am spending most of my time here. I've slept here five nights on the trot. I now consider this my home.' Her lip wobbled as she spoke the word and she blinked sternly to arrest the threat of a tear. She continued, the emotion high in her voice, 'I can't believe my luck. I have to pinch myself every morning when I open my eyes.' She faltered, choking back the tears. 'You know what I see when I first wake in the morning?'

Derek looked towards the window, imagining waking at the farmhouse. 'I imagine it's a stunning view. What do you see? The fields? The trees? The sky?' He smiled at her warmly. 'Tell me.'

'The view is marvellous, of course, but the first thing I actually see is a little patch of mould and this old, old water stain on the ceiling in the corner. I look at it and I know I'm back in a living, breathing home again, a house that will let the elements in but will throw a warm blanket over you if you get too cold. I lie and look at that water stain and think of the stories the ceiling has to tell and I'm almost deliriously happy. I feel like I've escaped from a nightmare.'

Derek looked at Maddie earnestly, wondering whether it was actually possible to find delight in a mouldy ceiling, but her eyes were shining and there was no trace of the scowl that everyone at Grove Farm had become so used to.

'I'm the luckiest woman on the planet,' she added emphatically.

The Colonel studied her carefully. 'Good God, Maddie Mitchell. I expected you to be locked up and instead you've found a whole new freedom.'

'Oh, I'm not off the hook yet. I think there are a few people looking for me. Doubler is very kindly trying to calm everyone down. My boys think I've been kidnapped, the police think I'm trying to avoid arson charges, and social services think I'm a threat to society. It's not all plain sailing.'

'I should think not. There's a reason there's a structure in our society, Maddie. You can't go stealing donkeys and setting your house on fire and not expect to face the consequences.'

Olive walked in for this last comment. 'Enough of that. Maddie is living consequence-free today and she's loving it, aren't you, dear?' She set a tray down proudly and started to pour tea.

Derek whistled appreciatively at the spread before him, and the Colonel acknowledged begrudgingly that this was an improvement on the custard creams.

'We are so loving our new life. I might have been sitting on all of these acres for years, but it turns out I really know astonishingly little. Maddie is making me think about the land and what we might hope to achieve here, given our considerable limitations. It turns out that she's the real farmer around here, and in the meantime lovely Doubler is teaching me how to be a farmer's wife.'

'Lovely Doubler? When did that miserable old potato farmer become 'lovely Doubler', for goodness' sake?' The Colonel rolled his eyes, nonplussed.

'Seems to me like you've both entirely reinvented yourselves,' commented Derek, delighted though still baffled. 'I must say it all seems a bit sudden.'

Olive spoke for them both. 'It was sudden, wasn't it, dear? It was Doubler who introduced us. Maddie had got herself into a spot of bother and Doubler knew I was deathly lonely up here, so he thought we might be good for each other. When we met, it just seemed to make the most perfect sense. I was going to go crazy up here alone. I think I was already about eighty per cent of the way to craziness, if truth be told.'

'Ha!' exclaimed Maddie in delighted recognition of her own plight. 'And I was already one hundred per cent certifiable!'

'And so we put our heads together and decided that twenty per cent sanity between us was better than nothing.'

Their laughs were similar, Derek noticed, like the oldest of friends.

'But seriously,' said Olive solemnly, 'I am by nature a *carer*. That's all I've done with my life. I looked after my kids, my husband, my parents, his parents and then suddenly, completely to my surprise and at great consequence to my health, I found myself completely alone.' She looked at the Colonel with wide eyes. 'With nothing to look forward to from one day to another. That's why when you talked to me about taking some space up here for the animals, I was *delighted*. That's why I agreed so *readily*. I thought it would help deal with my isolation and give me a sense of purpose. But it didn't turn out that way, did it? Quite frankly, you've ignored me from day one. It's like you're here, but you're not here. The sound of your cars coming and going with no one bothering to stop in and say hello makes me feel lonelier than if you weren't up here at all.' This was said without a trace of accusation; Olive was just setting out the facts as she had observed them. It wasn't self-pity she displayed but, rather, she seemed pleased with her careful analysis.

Derek was appalled and grasped her hand. 'Oh, Olive, we do try to stop in once a week to say hello, and we do our best to keep you updated, but if we've been neglecting you, we can certainly drop in more often if you'd like. I had no idea you were suffering so.'

'No, no, this is all my fault,' said the Colonel, who, within the folds of the large armchair, looked smaller than usual.

'Yes, Colonel, it *is* your fault,' said Olive, though merely agreeing and still with no hint of hostility in her voice. 'You talked me into this because it suited you, and the minute you'd got yourselves established here, you abandoned me.'

The Colonel looked disappointed. 'That wasn't the intention. But if that's the outcome and that's how you feel, then I must take full responsibility for it. In my defence, I thought we were a burden. You made it very clear to me that our presence was causing you distress, so I felt we must give you some space.'

'The space wasn't yours to give me, with all

due respect. I already had space in buckets.'

'But you expressly told me to leave you alone. I remember this very clearly. Derek, back me up. Olive here told us to get out of the house, didn't she?'

Derek started to answer, but Olive silenced him with a raised hand. 'I was having a bad day. I remember that conversation. I wasn't up to company and I couldn't cope with your constant questions.'

'Well, exactly. That was all I responded to. I wanted to respect your request for privacy and we did everything we could to make ourselves scarce.'

'It's regrettable that I sent you away. But that feeling, the feeling of not coping doesn't happen very often. The minute I felt strong again, I tried to engage with your activities here, but you cut me out from that moment on.'

'That's right,' added Maddie, nodding encouragingly. 'You made her feel more isolated than ever before.'

'Goodness me, Olive, how long have you been feeling this way?' asked Derek, wondering at his own complicity. He was starting to feel slightly sick at the idea that while noting the Colonel's bullying tendencies, he had done little to defend or protect Olive.

'Since the beginning,' said Olive with a matter-of-fact shrug.

'I feel terrible,' said Derek.

'I feel terrible,' said the Colonel at almost the same time.

'We feel terrible,' they both echoed.

361

The Colonel stood up and started to pace; his whole frame appeared to have diminished with remorse. 'No, really, I must try to correct my misdemeanours. I misjudged the situation. I misread the situation. And I didn't show good leadership.'

'Doubler says you're not good at dealing with hysterical women,' said Maddie, quite kindly.

The Colonel stopped pacing and frowned at Maddie. 'Doubler is out of order making such bold statements. He knows nothing of me or my ability to cope with hysterical women.'

'Did he say that, dear, or did he say the Colonel is no good at dealing with women of *any* temperament?' Olive asked Maddie, as if the Colonel had shrunk into nothingness and could no longer hear them.

'No, no, he was very specific. He definitely said that hysteria wasn't the Colonel's forte.'

Derek laughed loudly and the Colonel raised his voice to talk over the noise. 'Do you mind, ladies? I am still in the room.'

'Oh goodness, I am sorry, but perhaps you'll get a glimpse of what it feels like to be in a room with you. I speak, or at least I try to speak, but you prepare to leave as soon as you arrive. It's *disrespectful.*'

The Colonel, who had just resolved to leave, chose instead to settle back in his seat and he looked at both women boldly, as if to urge them to do their best.

Derek spoke instead. 'While we might not like to hear it, Olive has made a very fair point, Maxwell. We don't tend to drop in to report until last thing on a Friday and it often feels a little rushed. It's her farm, after all.'

The Colonel tipped his head to one side, allowing Derek to make his argument. 'That's a reasonable comment. We ought perhaps to meet more regularly. Would that help?'

'That would be a start,' acknowledged Olive.

'But it's not enough, is it? Not to make up for being ignored all this time. I wouldn't have it, Olive. I wouldn't stand for it a minute longer,' urged Maddie, her eyes beginning to narrow with distrust at Olive's hasty submission.

'I don't think you get to speak on the matter, Maddie. As far as I can tell, you're practically a fugitive, so the less we hear from you, the better,' objected the Colonel.

Olive was quick to interrupt him. 'No, Colonel, that won't do. You won't speak to Mrs Mitchell like that, not in my house. She's here as my guest and she will be treated with the proper respect.'

Derek intervened, emboldened by the metamorphosis of the two women. 'What can we do to make it up to you, Olive? I feel terrible that you feel used when you've been so generous to us all.'

Olive studied both men carefully and folded her arms resolutely. 'I want a fresh start, gentlemen. Like the fresh start that Maddie and I are having. Like the fresh start Doubler is making for himself. Doubler says he's reinventing himself as a *father*. Shows you are never too old.'

'OK, you get one. You get a fresh start. You'll

be welcomed into the team as one of us, we'll have more regular meetings, and we'll have them for longer — we can get into much greater detail. Will that help?' pleaded Derek, realizing he was speaking for the Colonel with no interruption.

'I don't want Olive settling for less than is her due,' said Maddie, her steely determination not remotely diminished by Olive's more conciliatory stance. 'I think she should be in charge. She should be the president.'

'President? Do we need a president? All feels a bit overblown,' said the Colonel, wondering what would happen to his carefully crafted hierarchy if Olive were to suddenly be promoted from obsolescence to omnipotence.

'There's always a president,' insisted Maddie.

'Olive as president is an excellent idea. I think it will help lift our ambition, make us think a bit bolder. More structure and accountability is an excellent idea, Maddie,' said Derek, seeing this step as the first in many towards rearranging the universe in a more equitable form.

Olive was beaming. 'I'm rather chuffed, I must say. President! I've never been *president* of anything.' She sat down heavily, as if overcome by emotion. 'Thank you, Maddie. That was a very sweet suggestion. And thank you, Derek. You've always been very kind to me and I greatly appreciate it. And, Colonel, I'm sorry if I've had my occasional bad days, and I'm sure they scared you a little. There's nothing quite like an out-of-sorts woman to scare the living daylights out of a repressed gentleman like yourself.'

The Colonel opened his mouth to object, but

Olive hadn't finished. 'Now, while we are at it, there's something you can do for Maddie too.'

The Colonel looked exhausted. 'You two are a bit fierce today.'

'To tell you the truth, I feel bolstered. I haven't been part of a couple for a while and I love it, I must say. Having to look out for your other half is part of the fun, don't you think? I rather hope that together we will be *formidable*.'

'I fear you might well be. But I don't know what more I can do for Maddie. I've been getting her out of scrapes for years. You think I've been disrespectful, but who do you think takes Maddie back to her house every time she turns up here trying to steal — yes, *steal*, that donkey? And who has convinced the owners of the tractors, horseboxes and vans she's commandeered not to press charges? Who do you think has even had a quiet word with the *police* to make sure they don't arrest her for any number of crimes that might ordinarily carry a stiff sentence? Like driving without a licence, breaking and entering, hijacking, stealing . . . Who exactly do you think has been watching her back all these years?'

'I'm sorry,' said Maddie quietly. 'I've been rather a nuisance.'

Olive got to her feet and went to stand by Maddie in solidarity. 'Well, we're both very grateful for the help you've given her in the past, but it's more of your powers of persuasion we need. Doubler and I were talking and we think you'll probably need to get a bit involved to get Maddie off the hook again.'

'Well, I'll have a go — one more time can't do any harm — but it's not just the police and the fire services she's upset this time. It's social services, and who knows what they will make of this? I can have a try, but if they think she's not fit to live alone, I can't imagine there is anything much I can do to help.'

'Well, that's not the point, is it? She's not living *alone*. She's with me up here and we are going to take full responsibility for each other's welfare and we'll see how that goes. It might be utter chaos, but we can cope with that. The last few days have been chaotic, but they've been my happiest in recent memory. We had a cooked breakfast this morning! But it's not social services we're concerned about. It's the sons.'

'Yes, Olive's quite right — they're the ones who will have me locked up.' Maddie looked fearful as she spoke.

'Don't be so melodramatic,' chided the Colonel. 'Your sons are not going to have you locked up. They think the world of you and I have absolutely no doubt they have your best interests at heart.'

'They're very cross with Doubler and they think Olive here might have enticed me to join a cult.'

'A cult? God, this would be the strangest cult on the planet. A terrifying network of two old women and a donkey. I'm not sure you're going to attract many followers.'

'I'm not an old woman; I'm the newly appointed president of a registered charity.' Olive sounded both affronted and dignified.

'Quite so. Well said,' said Derek, who hadn't enjoyed a conversation as much for a very long time.

'Nevertheless, I don't suppose it would be very difficult to persuade them of the merits of the arrangement,' sighed the Colonel, knowing he had some convoluted discourse ahead of him.

'Exactly. What possible harm could come from it?' asked Olive innocently.

'I hope everyone will agree it's for the best. I would be happier, less of a burden to my family, and it's a lovely place to bring the grandchildren. I'm going to sow carrots with them.'

'We're planning a veggie patch, aren't we, dear?' said Olive.

'So, you want me to talk to your boys, get them to see sense?' The Colonel addressed Maddie.

'Yes, they're good lads, sensible lads. Then they can talk to social services,' said Maddie happily.

'And social services can talk to the police,' suggested Olive.

'Who'll have a kindly word with the fire services,' added Derek.

'Well, good Lord, I hope you know what you're getting yourself into, Olive. She's a live wire, this one.'

Maddie looked up brightly, colouring a little. 'Thank you, Colonel. That's the nicest thing anyone has said to me for the longest time.'

Olive stood up. 'This has been an excellent meeting, gentlemen. But we can't sit around here all day chatting — we've got things we should be seeing to. You can let us know how you get on with the sons next time we meet.' She led the Colonel briskly towards the door, turning to give Derek a big pantomime wink and blowing him a kiss.

Derek hugged Olive briefly to him before Olive ushered them both out of the door. As Derek and the Colonel left, Olive was already turning to Maddie to plan their next escapade.

# 32

The rain had been relentless, thundering noisily against the roof tiles during the night and continuing to drive hard against the north-facing windows of Mirth Farm throughout the morning. Small pools of water had collected on a number of windowsills where the old wooden frames had been unable to prevent the water from finding gaps to breach, and a wide puddle lay just inside the back door where rainwater shed by Doubler's boots and coat had pooled.

Doubler put his still-damp raincoat on over his waxed jacket once again and, pulling the hood tight, rushed across the yard to carry on with his work there. Despite the torrent, he stopped to raise his eyes to the dark sky above him, giving thanks for this cold, cleansing rain, which would wash Mirth Farm clean and help him prepare the land for the year ahead.

Doubler was hopeful, and with hope came an appetite for new projects. The first of these was beginning to take shape and was already starting to fill in the blanks of his future. He had begun to experiment, and having taken delivery of five sacks of barley in exchange for a single bottle of Mirth Farm gin, he had since spread the wet grain out to germinate. Now, cocooned in the shed, with the noise of the raindrops amplified by the corrugated-iron roof and further by the cavernous space below, he was admiring the green malt and pondering the list of steps he would need to take to turn this into something altogether more interesting. As he contemplated the mess on the floor all around him, he became aware that the noise of the rain hammering on the roof above him had been replaced by the sound of banging. He followed the noise round to the side of the garage to find Midge, a yellow rain hat framing her face, banging a nail to join two pieces of wood.

'Oh, hello!' she said brightly from under her hood, as if undertaking a DIY project on somebody else's property without permission was the most normal thing in the world. 'I thought you were at the shelter this morning. I was hoping to get this done before you got back. It was meant to be a surprise.' Midge grinned happily while attempting to dry her face with her sodden coat sleeve.

'I *am* surprised, so that part of your plan worked,' said Doubler, studying the embryonic project in front of her. Not even a skeleton had emerged, just a pile of pre-cut pieces of wood and some two-by-four planks, which Midge was now wielding with considerable ease and confidence.

'Don't tell me. Your dad liked carpentry.'

'Actually, no. This is all me. It's something I quite enjoy as a hobby.'

'Your talents never cease to amaze me. I don't suppose you'd care to let me in on the secret, would you?'

'Ah, I thought you'd have guessed immediately. I'm building you a chicken house. Not from scratch,' she said apologetically. 'I bought a kit. But I'm going to build a chicken run round it so you don't have to have the birds free range if you're worried about them pecking your potatoes.'

'That's probably the least of my worries right now.' Doubler's voice trailed off. 'Tell me, do you do this a lot?'

'Assemble chicken runs? Heavens, no. This is my first.'

'No, I mean build projects on other people's land without consulting them beforehand.'

'Ah yes, I rather skipped that obstacle. I spoke to Mum about it and she felt that when it came to the crunch, you'd find a heap of last-minute reasons not to keep chickens. She figured it might be better to take the bull by the horns. We concocted this plan together, or more accurately, this is Mum's plan. I'm just the labourer, working to her specifications.'

'That sounds plausible. And neither of you thought a quick chat with me might be polite?'

'Oh, absolutely. We both agreed that we should definitely talk to you first, but then we reasoned ourselves out of it. We decided the risks outweighed the benefits. We figured you'd have less of a reason to object if the henhouse were already assembled.'

While they spoke, Midge consulted a diagram and continued to work on the frame of the small house.

'It's an ark,' she said nonchalantly.

'Good. If it continues to rain for forty days and forty nights, I shall be able to float away in it.'

'Not that kind of ark. At least, I don't think so. Besides, if the valley floods, you'll be fine up here, I should think. You might as well stay put. I don't know where you think you'd go in an ark.'

'True,' agreed Doubler with a shrug of his shoulders.

'Providing you don't mind living on potatoes.'

'Heavens, no, I wouldn't mind in the least. I've been living on potatoes for decades.'

Midge reached for another piece of plywood and slid it into position before picking up her hammer and tapping another nail into place. The henhouse was starting to take shape.

'And at the rate you're working, I shall have eggs to eat by the time the rains stop.'

'That's the spirit. Rather than focusing on the fact that I'm trespassing, focus on the goals in sight. I'm sorry if you think we're taking liberties, but Mum got very excited when I suggested you ought to keep chickens and the plan just seemed to develop from there. We considered converting one of your existing buildings to make room for hens, but Mum felt it would be a much bigger concern to you if we started moving things around.'

'You really don't have to apologize. I'm actually very touched. Honestly.'

Midge looked up and smiled, reaching for another piece of wood and popping a couple of nails between her lips while she lined up the next addition to the structure.

372

'I miss your mum terribly,' said Doubler, out of the blue, his voice almost inaudible under the noise of the rain drumming on the roof above.

Midge spoke through one side of her mouth, the nails still held in place. 'I know you do. I think she misses being up here, too. She certainly worries about you. This plan cheered her up no end. She thinks the hens will be great company for you.'

'I'm sure she's right. I'm sure you're both right. Although, I shall be expecting an awful lot from them if they're to step into your mother's shoes.'

Midge removed the two nails from her mouth while she thought about this. 'Nobody is expecting them to take the place of Mum, but still, it must get very lonely up here sometimes.'

'It used to. I seem to have no end of visitors these days. It's all I can do to find five minutes' peace.'

'Sorry,' said Midge, as she worked. Though she didn't look apologetic at all.

'It's wonderful having you here. You remind me of her so much.'

'Thank you. I shall take that as a compliment, especially given that you think so highly of her.'

'Oh, I do. I think very highly of both of you. You're both amazing.'

Doubler consulted the plans on the ground and found the next piece of wood Midge would need. 'Here you go,' he said, just as she reached for it.

'You know, Midge, there's an awful lot to do up here. There are the potatoes, of course, and the housework. It's a little bit too much for me, if I'm honest, so if you're ever stuck for work or need a bit of cash, I could find you something to do at Mirth Farm.'

Midge laughed. 'Bless you, Doubler. You're very sweet.'

Doubler looked embarrassed.

Midge reassured him with a bright smile, while explaining, 'But I already have a job.'

'You do? I'm sorry. How silly of me. I rather thought that as you were free to pop up and take on this sort of project, you had a bit of time on your hands. I am so grateful for all your help. I just didn't want to take advantage by not paying you.'

'I understand. No need to apologize. No, I normally work full time, but I've dropped down to three days a week so I can spend a bit more time looking after Mum. I'm keeping an eye on her place too.'

'You're an angel. Helping me out can't have been part of the arrangement. This really is above and beyond, you know.'

'It's not what I envisaged, but I made no fixed plans. I wasn't sure how I'd be of help to Mum and I expected her back home by now, so I thought I'd be with her there, helping out. But with her still at hospital, I've more time than I expected. And as far as helping her is concerned, it seems that looking after you is her greatest priority.'

'Gosh. That's kind. So, what sort of work do you do? Something practical, I imagine,' he guessed, as Midge wriggled some pieces of wood into place to get a snug fit for the roof.

'I work as a solicitor.'

'Oh,' said Doubler, unable to think of a more intelligent response.

'I'm a partner at a firm down in the town. There are four of us. We've worked together for a number of years and they're a good bunch. They couldn't have been more understanding when I said I needed to take a bit of time off.'

Doubler spoke while he processed this information. 'You are a constant surprise to me, Midge. I had no idea you had such an important job. I feel even more embarrassed that you're helping me now.'

'Help comes in all sorts of shape and sizes. I love doing things with my hands and I don't get that much of an opportunity. This is fun for me. I suppose you assumed that as Mum is a cleaner, I would have done something similar?'

'No, of course not. And I don't think of your mum as a cleaner. Not that there's anything wrong with being a cleaner, of course,' he stammered, mortified that he had indeed assumed Midge's work would be manual, not cerebral.

'Your mum must be very proud of you!' Doubler exclaimed, as though the thought had only just occurred to him.

'I suppose she is, yes.'

'But she doesn't show off about you,' he said, wondering out loud why not.

'No?'

'No. I had no idea that you had such a success-ful career. I am surprised she didn't mention it.'

'It doesn't surprise me in the least. She wouldn't show off, would she? That's not really her style. And I know that she doesn't believe that my accomplishments are her accomplishments.'

'Ah, but there's a contradiction within that.'

'Is there?'

'Yes, if she really felt your accomplishments were not of her making, she would be able to talk about them without showing off. If she were a boastful woman, she would only be able to talk about them if she felt your success was a reflection of her. And vice versa.'

'If you say so,' said Midge, sounding unconvinced.

'I do say so. She must be extremely proud of you and doesn't want to show off. That seems likely.'

'You might be right. She's a very humble woman. I don't think she even thinks it is possible that her genetics could have contributed to what I have become. Of course, the way I see it, she was a huge role model for me.' Midge looked at Doubler, her eyes shining with pride. 'She worked incredibly hard; she made a number of sacrifices.' Her voice trailed off as she thought of her mother's many struggles. 'I think she thinks of herself as an evolutionary stepping stone. Her role in life was simply to enable me.'

Doubler nodded. He could imagine this of Mrs Millwood. But he was still puzzled. 'So what do you think is her reason for keeping your success quiet from me? We talk about *everything*. Our conversations are very *open*. But she's never breathed a word about you being a *solicitor*. A solicitor in the town no less! And it's not like I haven't needed one of those from time to time over the past few years. I'm baffled.'

'Do you think it might be out of respect for you?'

'Respect?'

'She knows your children are a disappointment to you. Perhaps she doesn't want you to feel further let down.'

'But my children's *careers* aren't a disappointment to me! My son is wealthy and successful. I have absolutely no idea what his *purpose* is, but he seems to have achieved financial success and he is very pleased with himself. My daughter has not had a career, but that has been her choice. She married a man with traditional values.'

'Traditional values?' asked Midge, her eyebrows raised as she searched Doubler's face for explanation.

'Wrong words. Woefully outdated ideas. That might not be what I wanted for her, but she has made a series of personal choices that have led her to her current role. I am not disappointed in my children's careers. But of course I have been a great disappointment to them in a number of different ways.'

'I'm sorry you struggle with them. It must have been hard raising them on your own, and harder still not having a bond that reflects that effort.'

'Much of the raising was done by their mother. By the time she was gone, all I had to do were the finishing touches, but even so it appears that I didn't do a very good job.'

'You kept them fed and watered, and you got them out into the adult world. That *is* the job. That's all you have to do. And to tell you the truth, it doesn't matter how much love there is, children are always pre-programmed to abandon their parents. By not being that close to them, you've probably saved yourself a bunch of other disappointments.'

'That's one way of looking at it, I suppose. It's a shame, though, that it went wrong. I'd like to have been a better father. They just never gave me a chance. The minute Marie went the way she did, they blamed me. Of course, they couldn't blame themselves — that would be self-destructive — but I've always wondered why they couldn't blame her.'

'Too painful for them?'

'Possibly. But actually, Julian just decided it was my fault without any real investigation into the cause. He believed I drove her to do what she did and he's never allowed any room for doubt.'

Midge responded in a matter-of-fact voice, 'Our parents make us. That's the truth of it. We either like where we've come from or we resent where we've come from. But we can't change it. We can embrace it or we can turn our backs on it. Your children blamed you and turned their backs on you and that's probably to protect themselves from greater pain. I think Mum probably saw your pain and felt she didn't want to draw attention to your differences. She and I have always been very close.'

'Julian is embarrassed by me. He believes he

should have been entitled to a better start in life than the son of a potato farmer. It offends him.'

'That's a very harsh judgement. I can't imagine being ashamed of my mother's work. I'm proud of her. Mum didn't have the opportunities I had, but she is very, very bright and she demonstrates that in a number of ways. Sometimes I hate the fact she goes out and cleans houses. I think she deserves more. But the truth is, she is an independent woman. She has raised her family and held it together despite Dad's early death. And besides, she likes looking after you.'

'We're a good team, your mum and I.' Doubler thought some more. 'So, tell me, when I have a legal problem, is it you she consults? She always says she'll ask an expert.'

'Me or a lawyer friend of hers. I suppose she's got plenty of people she could ask.'

'It's just I have some papers I was going to show her the day she became ill. I've been meaning to tackle the issue, but to my shame, I've done absolutely nothing with them . . . '

'What sort of papers?'

'Peele, the potato farmer who owns the land around mine, has written to me a number of times. He frightens me a little bit, but I'm not sure why. He wants to buy this place and he's used quite a lot of threatening language . . . ' Doubler trailed off, looking embarrassed.

Midge was frowning and, guessing why, Doubler pre-empted her objection. 'I suppose this is the sort of thing I should share with Julian or Camilla. It seems silly that I haven't, but I have a feeling that Julian might be behind the offer. It's only a suspicion, but I seem to remember that Julian and Peele play golf together, and I've noticed that Julian takes an unhealthy interest in the worth of this place. I sound like a paranoid old fool, but it's entirely feasible they're in cahoots. Would you have a look? Would that be a huge imposition?'

A deepening frown furrowed Midge's forehead. 'It would be my pleasure.' She looked up at the darkening sky. 'Looks like the rain is coming through again. Let me finish up here. You go and put the kettle on and find us something to eat while I work up an appetite. And then let's have a look together.'

Doubler turned quickly and headed indoors. His mind raced anxiously through the contents of his pantry, and by the time he reached the kitchen, he was already focused on impressing Midge with the best possible version of a Mirth Farm lunch.

# 33

Doubler's relationship with daybreak had shifted. When Mrs Millwood had first stopped visiting, the hours after awakening each morning had been as fallow as his winter fields and as fruitless, too. But now he could rely upon his daily updates from Mrs Millwood, he clutched onto the promise of the next call with such a tight grip that nothing else could force its way to the front of his mind. After each call, he felt temporarily sated and could undertake other distractions that required more of him, but in the early hours of each day, his anxiety could only be quelled with physical labour.

Doubler had always been a hard worker, but now he awoke with a burning energy that was almost impossible to vanquish even with labour. He was up at first light to pace the fields furiously. This morning, he had woken with single malt whisky on his mind and had carved out a pocket of time to sketch out the requirements for his latest project. He was certain that he needn't use any newfangled equipment, reasoning that anything good enough for a fifteenth-century monk was probably good enough for him, but still, his list was extensive and he wondered whose help he might need to call upon. He worked on the project urgently, but then, everything he did, whether baking or polishing or stacking bottles, was fuelled by an unprecedented gravity that delivered such great efficiencies that all he actually achieved was to perpetuate the time during which he had nothing to do but wait.

After his morning's burst of activity, in which he achieved everything he had set out to achieve, he now sat, deflated once more, with his binoculars on his knees, a pile of unopened books beside him and the crossword puzzle already completed with the same joyless proficiency that had conspired to slow time to an agonizing crawl. When he compulsively raised the binoculars to his eyes, it wasn't with the expectation of seeing anything new: he had looked a thousand times to no avail. But here was a car, edging slowly through the gate. And a quick flick of the binoculars to the left revealed a second vehicle following closely behind. He looked at the number plate of the leading car and wrote it hurriedly in the margins of the crossword, but even as he wrote it, he knew instinctively that this was the conclusion of a project, not part of something ongoing.

These were the visitors he had been so certain would come. Recently he'd banished the thought of them in light of more pressing concerns, but they were here now, of that he was certain.

The first car, a shining black Range Rover, glinted in the sunlight as it pulled forward. The second car, a similarly sized vehicle, followed so closely in the wake of the first that Doubler couldn't have read the number plate if he had tried. Together, as though joined, the cars snaked up towards Doubler. He held his breath, and his organs and senses responded by shifting within him. His heartbeat thudded in his ears, his hollow chest banged painfully in his stomach, and the adrenaline that had replaced his blood now coursed through his veins, but his knees trembled so violently the flight his brain screamed for was foiled.

As he lowered his binoculars, a wren flitted past the window; its unmistakable flicker at ground level caught his eye. He drew himself upright and left the safety of the sitting room to meet his foe face to face. He thought about collecting his shotgun on the way, but that would have meant unlocking the great sheds, and those he definitely wanted to remain closed to prying eyes.

It was after eleven o'clock and there was already as much heat in the sun as the day was going to muster. Doubler took strength from the minimal warmth and tilted his face upwards to breathe it in, inhaling deeply to calm his nerves. He walked round to the front of the house and planted his feet as firmly as he could while he awaited the arrival of his visitors. The pose he aimed to effect was that of a man with a shotgun readily available.

The black cars snarled round the final corner and slunk into the yard, coming to a stop only a couple of metres from Doubler. The heavy doors swung open, claiming their right to dominate in a world full of thinner, tinnier car doors. Each assertive clunk was accompanied by a cacophony of beeps and flashing lights. Instructions to their witless drivers? Doubler wondered.

Peele was the first to slither from his vehicle. As he rounded the car, Doubler assessed him. The visitor appeared to be wearing an undertaker's coat, and the dark tie he wore added to the sombre image. Doubler steadied his breathing as best he could, but the portentous imagery seemed deliberately threatening.

'Doubler? I'm Peele. Legion Peele, your neighbour.'

The second visitor, a smaller version of Peele, had joined them and now slotted into place beside his boss but merely nodded. This gentleman didn't need to be introduced apparently, as if he existed solely as an adjunct to Peele himself.

'I know who you are, Peele. I've been up at this farm the best part of forty years. You get to know the comings and goings of your neighbours.'

'I can imagine. This is quite a vantage point you have up here.' Peele looked around him appreciatively, his eyes appearing to flick about like those of a tailor measuring a bespoke suit.

The nebulous man next to Peele barely moved his eyes away from Doubler.

Doubler felt strength in Peele's overt admiration of his farmstead and this manifested in a flush of defiant confidence. 'I don't believe I've seen you about,' Doubler said, forcing the second man to meet his gaze. The rigidity of the ground beneath Doubler, the weight that held Mirth Farm aloft, seemed to seep fortitude through the soles of Doubler's feet. He wriggled his toes in his wellington boots to anchor his feet more firmly still. He held his hand out, forcing Peele's companion to break ranks and step forward.

'Jones,' said the man, but he gave Doubler nothing more. He was clearly a cipher in his own mind, too.

'You've received my letters, I hope?' said Peele, once Jones had stepped back to resume his subordinate place.

'Yes, indeed. Three of them.'

'It's normal practice to respond to communication, Doubler.'

'But not obligatory. I didn't have much to say, and nor did I invite the communication in the first place.'

'I made a very generous offer to purchase your farm. It sits right in the middle of my land and I don't like unfinished business. I don't think I can make it much clearer to you, Doubler: I'd like to buy this place.'

Doubler remained standing, grateful that his knees had not yet let him down.

Peele pressed on. 'The offer carries an excessive premium. You won't get another like it.'

'I don't need another offer. Mirth Farm is not for sale.'

'Everything has a price.'

Doubler considered this seriously, looking beyond Peele, towards the magnificent view. 'Not everything. I can think of a number of things that can't be purchased. A sunset, a cooling breeze, the beat of a skein of geese as they pass low over the brow of this hill.'

Peele looked impatient for the first time,

though his eyes remained devoid of light whether he smiled or frowned. Doubler was unperturbed and prepared to continue with his list.

'Good health. That has no price. Money may improve your odds, I suppose, but you can't buy a life free from illness.'

'That's very true, and a good reminder that you're getting on, Doubler, and who knows what the years ahead will spring on you. You've done a great job managing as you do up here, but this farm is going to be too much to handle soon. You'd be far better off taking my offer and settling down to a more comfortable retirement. Accepting my offer will make you a wealthy man.'

Doubler frowned and looked at Peele closely. 'You sound just like my son. He said the same thing, word for word.'

'Julian? He's a sensible young man. We are members of the same golf club and see eye to eye on a number of matters. He's going to go far, that one. But I can't see him following in your footsteps. He's not a potato man like you and I.'

Doubler, who had been standing stock-still, as if on guard, allowed his shoulders to drop a fraction as he reassessed Peele. Was it possible that he and this man had something in common? Was it possible that they were different iterations of the same thing, united by a shared passion? It was as statistically likely, he supposed, as he and his son having nothing in common despite their shared DNA.

'He most certainly isn't. You consider yourself a potato man, do you?' Doubler scanned Peele for traces of earth in his fingernails or on his shoes or trouser cuffs but found none.

Peele interpreted the appraisal. 'I might not look like you, and my farming methods may be very different, but we are the same. We are both after exactly the same thing. Excellence in our field. From what I hear, there's no doubt that you are an expert — perhaps world class, I'm told. I might have more land than you, and I expect my yields are higher, but I have no doubt that you're the superior technician. I'm sure there is a great deal you could teach me.'

Doubler puffed up a little. The knowledge that somewhere in the valley below people might be discussing him and referring to him as a world-class expert filled him with pride. Peele recognized the shift and seized the opportunity.

'May I come in and talk to you?' Peele hesitated. 'Privately.' Peele gestured to Jones with an almost imperceptible tilt of his head and the henchman turned to go and sit in his car. Doubler was impressed by Peele's control of the man and found himself using a similarly low-key gesture to beckon Peele as he led him to his kitchen.

'What a kitchen!' Peele said, looking around at the ancient fittings. 'It's a museum piece.'

The comment was devoid of praise, but Doubler mistook the incredulity for admiration.

'Thank you. It's all pretty much as it would have been when it was originally built, but it's a living house, Mr Peele, not a museum. It functions admirably and rarely lets me down.'

'Please, call me Legion.'

'It's an unusual name. I've never met another. A family name, is it? Sit down, Legion. I'll put the kettle on.'

'It was my grandfather's name. Quite rare, yes, but it's probably not as unusual as Doubler.'

'That's not my given name — it's one I picked up along the way.'

'A potato reference, I assume?'

Doubler shrugged. He felt Peele's eyes on him as he filled the old tin kettle at the tap and lifted the ancient copper lid of the Aga. A splash of water landed on the hotplate and sizzled in a frenzied burst of steam and Doubler felt proud of all of it: the house, its view, the kitchen and the Aga that only he really understood.

Doubler knew that to retain any equipoise, he would need to give the impression of a man just as busy and important as his visitor. 'I've not got much time to spare — I've a hospital visit to make — so I'll get on with a task or two while we talk, one potato farmer to another.'

'Ah, you're off to St Anne's? Wonderful hospital. Full of admiration for the staff. My mum died there, but the nursing staff couldn't have been kinder.'

Peele's words jolted Doubler, who harboured a deep hope to visit Mrs Millwood but until this exchange hadn't considered there might be a greater urgency than his own impatience. Doubler's hand shook a little as he lifted the now-steaming kettle away to fill the pot he'd prepared. He didn't want to contemplate the possibility of any *deadline* in that place.

'It's hard, getting on a bit,' said Peele, from his

position at the table.

Doubler assumed Peele had mistaken the shake in his hand for something degenerative and responded with affront in his voice as he set the pot and cups on the table. 'I've still got my health, Mr Peele, and I expect to hang onto it for a long time yet. I'm in the fresh air most of every day, and I work as hard now as I did in my twenties. That should keep me going, though there seem no end of people who want to get shot of me.'

'I was talking about myself, Doubler. I find it increasingly tough to cope with the change that's essential if you want to keep on top of the latest techniques. The world moves so quickly. I can barely keep up.'

Doubler looked at his visitor, who must be younger than him by a good twenty-five or thirty years. 'I've always been quite happy to let it move on without me, thanks very much.' He took from a drawer two white tea towels and spread them on the butcher's block. He then removed a number of heavy steel-bladed knives from the knife rack in front of him and laid them out gently on the prepared cloths.

Peele watched him carefully while he talked. 'That's tempting, I know, but us farmers are being systematically squeezed out. Imports are cheaper; other countries have different priorities. There was a day when all the potatoes grown here were British, but that's not the case now. There are potatoes coming in from all over. The imports chase the price down and make it far harder for people like you and me to compete.'

Doubler appeared not to hear him but lifted from a pot of water a stone he'd left to soak. Flicking the excess water from it towards the sink, he then began to sharpen the first knife with steady, slow strokes.

Peele took a sip of his tea and continued, 'Scale is essential — it's the only way forward. You need to have the capacity to produce enough of your crop to influence change. You've got to have a sufficiently loud voice to lobby government. I spend at least a day a week in London talking to the people who can help ensure that potato farmers like us will be around to hand over a robust business to our children.'

Doubler winced, briefly interrupting his meticulous work, and Peele recognized the transparent honesty of his response. After this hesitation, Doubler resumed his knife sharpening, raising the angle of the blade back to a carefully maintained fifteen degrees.

'Well, I suppose it's a little different, isn't it, if the potato line is going to end with you? If you're not intending to pass your business on to your children, then I suppose it's a legacy you're looking for, rather than a viable business, is it?' asked Peele, assessing Doubler carefully.

Doubler was uncertain if this was a rhetorical question but contemplated it seriously.

He and Mrs Millwood had often discussed his legacy. But was it because he had no great expectation for his children that he had been chasing his research so doggedly? Because he knew the line would end and wanted to leave something behind that he could be proud of?

This train of thought felt new to Doubler. He asked himself some more questions, keen to lock these into his conscious mind for thorough examination. Would most parents be satisfied simply with the continuation of their own genetic line? Could that ever be enough? What had motivated Mr Clarke? Doubler couldn't answer this last one with any certainty, but he bet it was excellence in its own right rather than paving a path for the evolution of his own DNA. He felt impatient to ask Mrs Millwood. She would be sure to have an opinion.

'You're perceptive, Mr Peele. My legacy is important to me. I am motivated by the work of the great potato men who came before us, and if I can make just a fraction of the impact they had on our field, then I will die a happy man.'

'I admire that, Doubler. That's very refreshing, and I expect people like you are few and far between. But we are not so different. You crave some sort of recognition for your work; you're not without ego. I too am looking to make a mark and I maintain that to be influential in our world is simply not possible without scale.'

Doubler laid the sharp knife down carefully and picked up the next, preparing to repeat the process.

Peele raised his voice a notch, tired of talking to Doubler's back. 'There's a gadget for that, my friend. It's called a knife sharpener. You could have those all done and dusted in just a few moments.'

'Oh, I'm not averse to a modern gadget,' Doubler said sincerely, but still with his back turned. 'This *is* a modern gadget. I've used this one for a number of years. Before this, I'd always keep my eyes peeled for the perfect stones on the drive. They'd turn up with surprising regularity. You'd scan the same patches of ground day in, day out and then one day — hey presto! the perfect stone for sharpening. Who knows where it would have been hiding beforehand, invisible one day, in plain sight the next.'

Doubler turned round and smiled generously, but the smile didn't quite reach Peele; it rested somewhere just behind him as if there were another person in the room.

'I'm very much in favour of this newfangled whetstone. Very pleasing it is. But really, any stone will do. Ultimately, all you're doing is angling the stone to remove very small particles of metal.'

'But think of the time you could save with the electric equivalent!' Peele insisted.

'I don't suppose you'd save much. I look after my knives very well, so they only need sharpening every couple of months, and each one takes just a few minutes. I probably spend — what, an hour and a half a year sharpening my knives? How much of that time is your gadget going to save me, Mr Peele, and what exactly would you have me do with the saving? Boil an egg?' Doubler chuckled, delighted with himself and wishing Mrs Millwood could be at the table, listening in.

There was a long silence in which Doubler continued to sharpen the blade before stopping, quite suddenly, and turning to face Peele.

'My bet,' Doubler said boldly, 'is that my influence will be longer-lasting than yours.'

Peele was a little taken aback but smiled politely. 'You're arrogant! I like that about you.' And then he added, pointedly, 'It means there's a bit more to you than some have led me to believe.'

Doubler narrowed his eyes as he considered this. 'You mean Julian.'

'Yes, he was certainly of the opinion that you had very little ambition, but from the rumours I've heard, that doesn't seem to be the case, and you're certainly acting like a man who is pretty confident of success within his own lifetime.'

'Julian has absolutely no idea what I'm up to here.'

'Well, perhaps if you entrusted him with some of that knowledge, he'd be more tempted to follow in your footsteps.'

'I don't think he'd have the temperament. This isn't a quick game; this is a life's work.'

Peele was now puzzled. He was not a man to take an uncalculated risk. He had been investigating Doubler's business for a number of years and had made his offer for the farm in the certain knowledge that he had enough on the man to use a blunter instrument if necessary.

'Your life's work is behind you, Doubler. You've proved your point, and you've been a true innovator, too. But it cannot continue, and why should it? There's nothing more for you to do.'

There is plenty for me to do, thought Doubler. He mentally scanned the checklist of the 't's that needed crossing, the 'i's that needed dotting.

Above all else, he required his official validation before he could rest. How far away was that? Weeks? Months?

The waiting was tiresome, but Doubler was confident that once he'd received validation from a global authority, great commercial success would follow swiftly. Doubler had relied on Mrs Millwood to find a solution that would protect him from exploitation. He trusted Mrs Millwood. And once she'd explained to him the benefit of attaining watertight accreditation from an institution of international renown, he believed he could trust the Indians, too. Their reputation for bureaucracy and dedication to process felt reassuring to Doubler.

But now, this interloper, his competitor, was implying that he knew what Doubler was up to. All he would need to do would be to take half a sack of chitting potatoes from one of Doubler's sheds and he could steal the advantage, steal his legacy.

'There are no runners-up in this game — just winners and losers — and there are small-time producers like you going out of business every day.' Peele interrupted Doubler's thoughts, alarmed at the distance Doubler seemed to have travelled with his eyes.

'My farm isn't under threat. Only by you, and you sound like you want to lend a hand, so I should be able to sit comfortably, shouldn't I?'

'You're the second-biggest potato grower in this county, but your capacity is a fraction of mine. I employ the latest technology, the best minds and the biggest workforce. I am at the cutting edge of this industry and still it is tough for *me* to make economic sense out of the business. I struggle. So it must be a whole lot more precarious for you.'

'It's not precarious. My business is sound.'

'But your yields must have been devastated last year — we had the worst conditions since records began. I've got the benefit of big commercial partners who rely on our crop, so they'll take everything I produce, and the contracts I have are enough to paper over the cracks. But you can't possibly produce enough on a good year, so how on earth do you manage in a bad one? You must have creditors banging down your door.'

Doubler was conflicted. The syrupy tone conveyed concern, sympathy even, but he could detect the challenge, and still Peele's eyes were devoid of light. There was defiance there, undoubtedly, and Doubler felt compelled to defend his honour. He was, after all, a hugely successful potato grower on the verge of such groundbreaking innovation that he might be propelled into the ranks of the potato greats. He also made money: his pursuit was not academic alone. His commercial enterprise was not conventional, and some of it was potentially not even legal, but he had no debt, no mortgage and endless resource with which to maintain his lifestyle. All of this rattled around in his head, desperate to take shape into boastful words, to prove to the interloper that he was superior in every way.

Doubler met Peele in his dark, cold eyes.

'I get by,' he said, swallowing the crowing claims that clamoured to be heard.

'My offer could be your salvation. No more sleepless nights, no more early starts. You could start to take things a bit easier, relax.'

'For what? Why would I want to relax? To die, do you mean?'

'To enjoy your retirement,' said Peele, exasperated. 'You will achieve more success through a sale to me than anything you can accomplish as a farmer. That's the truth. Sell up, slow down and enjoy some time with your children and grandchildren.'

Doubler laughed at this as a notion and wondered what Mrs Millwood would have to say on the matter when he shared the conversation with her later. He could already imagine her praising his courage.

'My mind's made up, Mr Peele. I'm very happy to see my days out here, thank you very much. Shall I see you out?' Doubler, with uncharacteristic assertiveness, removed Peele's half-full cup of tea and sloshed it into the sink in a symbolic purging.

Peele stood up and shook his head slowly to demonstrate his pronounced disappointment. Together they left the kitchen.

# 34

The golf club had recently undergone a major refurbishment, with the aim of achieving a reassuring balance of modern, clean lines while still appealing to its traditional clientele, who found comfort in the familiarity of a gentlemen's-club aesthetic. The net effect, a marriage of red velvet and brass-rimmed peepholes, had resulted in an unintentionally burlesque, nautical motif that was quite incongruous with the countryside that surrounded it. Fortunately, the tight-clipped greens and surprisingly sandy hollows that pock-marked the golf course provided a buffer that allowed visitors to acclimatize as they approached the clubhouse, leaving the memory of the flinty downs long behind them.

Julian felt very much at home at the golf club. He wasn't quite as comfortable as in any one of his favoured haunts in London, but his presence in the country, his 'retreat from the madness', as he liked to refer to it to his banking colleagues, was an important accessory. It wasn't unusual for men of Julian's type to hover close to the region they grew up in while simultaneously detesting the things that reminded them of their humble beginnings and Julian had fallen into this habit. He was spending an increasing amount of his free time circling the potato farm, like a shark trapped in shallow water.

Julian was an ambitious man whose desires

could only be sated by wealth and whose contentment could only be expressed through the pursuit of yet further wealth. The golf club was a haven for Julian. While ambivalent about the benefit of the sport itself, he got a unique pleasure from bumping into old friends, a measure through which he could assess his own progress by noting the inferiority of their coats or postcodes.

And yet, since a seed had been sown for Julian to own his very own piece of the county, he somehow couldn't shake the idea that without it he wasn't quite successful enough, and, further, he had come to believe that a second home in the countryside might make him feel less resentful of the many hurts and betrayals he'd been exposed to, not least of all the degrading knowledge that he could never escape the fact his father grew potatoes for a living.

He had met with Peele twice to strike a deal around Mirth Farm. That morning, they had taken their negotiations one step further, out onto the golf course itself.

They had played an even-handed eighteen holes and had each allowed the other to believe they could have played better if they'd chosen to. Now, they were walking slowly back to the clubhouse, punctuating their walk with conversation, hoping to settle the matter before sharing a polite drink in the plush bar.

Julian got quickly to the point. 'I understand you've been up to see the old man. How did you find him?'

Peele's face lit up, much to Julian's surprise.

'It's an incredible place, Mirth Farm. What a view! And your dad's an interesting chap. I rather liked him. From what you told me, I'd assumed he might be a bit of a dullard, but there's much more to him than I expected. He's bright, isn't he?'

Julian shrugged non-committally. 'But was he acting strangely, do you think? A bit unhinged?'

'Well, he's certainly something of an oddball, just as you warned. But on reflection I'd describe him as resolute, determined and of sound mind.'

'You got the right address, did you?' Julian laughed loudly, but the sound was hollow and barely masked his irritation. He pursued the conversation. 'But you did make an offer?'

'I reiterated the offer I'd made in writing, but I'm sorry to report he was determined not to sell at any price. I don't believe he can be budged from that position either — he just didn't seem very interested in the money.'

'And you think that's the action of a rational man, do you?'

'No. His refusal to negotiate is the act of a fool — he'll never get another offer like it.'

'Exactly. He's almost incapable of making a clear-headed decision. He doesn't really know what's good for him. And he must have seemed a bit odd to you, surely. I mean, the two of you might both be in the same line of work, but you couldn't be more different, could you? You, one of the best business minds in the county, and him, still running the farm like it was the 1930s.'

'He is curiously old-fashioned, agreed. And I suppose his mind can't be as sharp as it was.

He's a proud man, that's for sure, and I expect it is pride that keeps him going. But his age is showing. He was easily distracted, and during our conversation he became vague, drifting off on a tangent. It almost felt like he was listening to other voices — either in his head or in the room. It was alarming at times. It felt like there were more than the two of us in the conversation.'

Julian was immediately bolstered by the criticism of his father. 'You're right he's not all there. It's a terrible shame. But he's been through a lot over the years and I suppose it's taken its toll.'

'Your mother?' Peele ventured, keen to get the official verdict on this source of much local gossip and speculation.

'Quite,' said Julian, closing the door on the trail with a definitive slam. 'But you definitely mentioned an actual sum?'

'Yes, I put it all in writing. But I am not sure you can do anything more about it. I've reasoned with him. I've been generous. Money isn't going to talk, so we might have to wait it out. Though, like you, I'm not a fan of that. What's his health like?'

'Strong as an ox. No, no, waiting isn't an option.' Julian shook his head slowly, refusing to believe he couldn't outwit his father. 'Tell me, Legion, just how badly do you want the farm?'

'I need it. You know that. I've been very straight with you. Mirth Farm sits right in the middle of my land and I can't do a blasted thing. I can't change the access road, and moving traffic around, particularly the heavy vehicles, adds a cost I can't afford in today's market. This is a commercial conversation we're having. I want to extract greater efficiencies and I'm scuppered unless your old man plays ball.'

'And you're still prepared to honour my cut as agreed?'

'Yes, I'm a man of my word. But a cut of nothing is nothing, Julian. You'll need to make this happen yourself. I'm afraid I've tried and failed.'

Julian looked beyond Peele and squinted his eyes almost shut for greater focus. 'I've got another plan, a bolder plan, but it's going to take considerable sacrifice on my part. Carve me out a couple of acres on top of the bonus we agreed and I'll make it happen.'

Peele looked appalled. 'I can't do that, Julian.'

'Of course you can. You said it yourself — a cut of nothing is nothing. Look, Legion, I'm your only route to securing this land. If I'm unsuccessful, then you lose absolutely nothing; the status quo remains the same. But if I'm successful, you gain Mirth Farm and get the access routes you want and there are no further obstacles in your way.'

'Two acres, you say?'

'Yes. I don't particularly mind where. Somewhere near the main road to town will be fine. I fancy a project in this neck of the woods, and once Dad's gone from the farm, I'd like to keep a bit of my home for the sake of my mum's memory.' Julian fell silent and looked at the ground, pausing for long enough

401

to allow his words to sink in.

Peele put a hand on Julian's shoulder. 'Of course. I understand completely. You've got it. Two acres plus your bonus. You know I'm a man of my word, but nevertheless, I'll get my lawyer to draft a simple agreement to make sure we all know where we stand and then it's all down to you. As you say, I lose nothing if you're not successful.'

Julian looked back up at Peele and nodded. Unable to conceal his smile entirely, he allowed a little of it to escape as a lopsided smirk. 'Very good. Let's go and seal it with a glass of something, shall we?'

The two men walked companionably towards the bar.

# 35

Doubler had a lot of catching up to do with Mrs Millwood and he launched into their conversation, eager to share his news.

'Peele had the *audacity* to turn up in person at Mirth Farm — and in a Range Rover of all things. There was a time that a visit like that might have sent me hurtling back into the chasm, but I feel much more confident now I have your Midge on my team.'

'I'm so glad. She told me she was helping you out.' Mrs Millwood's response was quiet, but Doubler could hear the pride in her voice.

'Your daughter is an *angel*. I gather she's been incredibly busy with this Peele business and I rather think she's got her teeth into it. She seems to think she's onto something.'

'I doubt Mr Peele is Midge's type. She'll enjoy taking him on,' said Mrs Millwood, relishing the idea.

'And Midge isn't the only one going into battle. The Colonel has taken on Maddie's family *and* social services. They've come up with something called a *care plan* apparently.'

'Ooh, a care plan sounds useful. We should all have one of those, shouldn't we?'

'As far as I can understand, Olive *is* Maddie's care plan, which certainly lets everyone else off the hook. I'm not sure how the Colonel negotiated that one. But at least they didn't put Percy in charge.'

'The Colonel can be surprising. If I know him, he'll have offered his own services to keep an eye on them both. He's not all bad,' said Mrs Millwood, the affection evident.

Doubler murmured his agreement as he thought of the many long conversations he'd had with Maxwell. 'You're right. I owe him a favour. Perhaps I owe him a whole *case* of favours. I'll make sure he's looked after at the next bottling.'

Mrs Millwood laughed happily. 'My sources tell me you'll be owing a few people some favours. I hear *Olive* is now helping Midge with her Peele investigations.'

'Goodness me. Is she, now?' Doubler dwelt for a moment on the consequence of kindness. 'I was always quite proud of not having to depend on anyone, but asking for help isn't as awful as I'd imagined.'

Doubler went on to bring Mrs Millwood up to speed with his conversation with Camilla.

'That sounds extremely *healthy*, Mr Doubler. Her memories are very different to yours — perhaps you've been a better father to her than you've given yourself credit for.'

'I don't know about that, but there is probably still time left to be a better father now.'

'And how are you going to do that, do you suppose?'

'I shall try my hardest to ask the right questions.'

'That sounds very sensible, Mr Doubler. And what about your son? Do you think there is

404

scope for you to be a better father to him, too?'

'He is on his way here to talk to me. He says he has something on his mind. But I have something on my mind, too, so I shall try to get that off my chest first.'

'It will do you good, Mr Doubler, to speak your mind. Just remember, our children are not a product of ourselves. Sometimes they're just the way they are.'

'They are just a sequence of DNA, Mrs M.' Doubler pronounced this as if he were reciting it without fully believing the sentiment.

'You sound very thoughtful this morning, Mr Doubler. Is there anything else on your mind?' Mrs Millwood probed gently.

Doubler did have something else on his mind. A letter had arrived, addressed to him in bold, loopy handwriting and decorated with a cascade of Indian stamps. The letter was now sitting in the very same dresser drawer that housed much of his unfinished business. It was not a lack of courage that prevented Doubler from opening the envelope, of that he was sure, but, rather, a growing certainty that the contents of the envelope might inform Mrs Millwood's legacy as well as his own. And Doubler wasn't yet certain that the confirmation of Mrs Millwood's legacy would provide the motivation she required to get her out of that place and back among the hale and hearty.

'No, Mrs M. I'm right as rain. I need to have it out with Julian, but once I've done that, I shall be able to think more clearly. Perhaps we can speak later? He's due any moment.'

405

'Off you go, and don't forget — I may be incapacitated, but I'm with you every step of the way.' Mrs Millwood's voice was quieter than usual and there was a solemnity there that Doubler hadn't noticed before.

'Thank you, Mrs M. I'm counting on that,' he said, resolving to be strong enough for the two of them.

Julian arrived shortly after Doubler had hung up the phone and, unusually for Doubler, he wasted absolutely no time making his guest comfortable or offering refreshments. He led the way to the sitting room, avoiding the kitchen altogether, and his son followed, stooping under the door lintel, unaware yet that this conversation was not going to be the one he'd expected to have.

'Julian, sit down. Let's talk about money.'

Julian smiled broadly and produced an exaggerated exhalation, delighted that his father had pre-empted what might have been a difficult conversation. 'Excellent, Dad. About time we had this chat. What's he offered?' His eyes darted around the room as if he could assess the sum from the lay of the furniture.

'Who? Peele? No, Julian, I'm not talking about selling the farm. I'm talking about money *problems*.' Doubler batted Julian away impatiently as he sat down in his chair. He pulled the telephone an inch or two closer to him, as if to settle Mrs Millwood comfortably too.

Julian looked at his father and ran a hand through his hair, the incredulity etched on his face. 'Dad. You don't have money problems.

You're sitting on an absolute pile here. A goldmine. Sell up and you'll never have to worry again. This is exactly what I've been trying to tell you.' Julian smiled in an attempt to offer reassurance and Doubler learnt in that moment what a snake might look like if it chose to smile just before it struck you.

'I'm not talking about *my* money problems; I'm talking about *yours*.' Doubler wriggled more comfortably into his chair and glanced pointedly at the other seat beside the empty fireplace, hoping Julian might follow suit. The fact that his son was so much taller than his father put Doubler at a considerable disadvantage when it came to this quite carefully planned confrontation, and the fact that his son had chosen to accentuate this height difference by remaining on his feet meant that Doubler felt entirely *wrong-footed*. He was pleased, therefore, to see from the colour rising in Julian's cheeks that he had rattled him.

'Me? You're joking! I don't have money problems. Life's pretty good. My bonus last year was a record for the department. I'm certainly not the one with money problems.' Julian's face sneered quite naturally, so now, as he tried to arrange it into a look that conveyed an extra measure of contempt, it twisted grotesquely.

'Then why on earth,' said Doubler, with a deliberate pause for effect, 'would you use deceit to try to extract my car from me?'

'Deceit? To extract your car?' For a moment Julian was genuinely puzzled, but quickly his eyes narrowed as he realized what his father was alluding to. 'Careful, Dad — you sound unhinged. I was just trying to help. Look, I don't like the idea of you being stuck out here on your own. I thought I'd try to make life a little easier for you. Can't a son help his dad these days without being accused of deceit?'

'That's complete and utter *bollocks*, Julian, and you know it. You failed to mention, when you offered to swap my car for a Clarins, that my car is worth a *fortune*.'

'It is? I had no idea. And Clarins is a make-up brand, Dad. Swapping a car for a lipstick *would* be deceitful of me.' Julian rocked back on his heels and laughed at his own wit. He remained standing, his hands clasped behind his back.

'Once again that's complete *bollocks*, Julian,' Doubler said, mustering as much imperiousness as he could dredge up from within the folds of his comfy chair. Doubler enjoyed the sound of the word 'bollocks' even more the second time he used it. 'You knew exactly what you were doing when you offered to take my car off my hands, and worse, you made me believe you were capable of kindness.'

'I don't know what you're talking about, Dad. Seems to me you're suffering some kind of breakdown. A breakdown with paranoid tendencies.' Julian smiled, delighted by his diagnosis. 'I suppose it's to be expected, being stuck up here with no friends for all these years.'

'This is not about me or my friends. This is about you and your money problems. I am your father. You can trust me. I am trying to *help* you, Julian.'

'I do not have money problems.' Julian, who stooped habitually as if there were a low and exceedingly sharp object dangling just above him and threatening to stab him at all times, straightened himself up and clenched and unclenched his fists. The gesture wasn't threatening — he didn't look like he might punch his father — but his knuckles were white and his cheeks were pink, and these two colour alterations combined to suggest he might soon implode.

'But why would you go to such surreptitious lengths to defraud me of my car? A car I like very much and one that is perfectly adequate for my needs?'

Julian sighed dramatically, impatient now with his father and no longer interested in denying his deception. 'Because, as you patently know, Dad, the car is worth a small fortune and it is wasted sitting rotting in your garage.'

Doubler looked seriously up at his son, nodding at the truth spoken. 'That's fine, and I agree it shouldn't rot in the garage. That it's worth so much money is rather a shock to me. But why, if you don't have money problems, would you not just tell me it's worth a bob or two? Why wouldn't you let me decide for myself whether to sell it or not? You're pretty intent on me selling the farm — why didn't you just urge me to sell the car, too?'

Julian tipped his head back and stared at the ceiling as if looking for a less obtuse audience among the old oak rafters.

'Because, Dad,' he said, lowering his head and

gaze with exaggerated torpor, 'it's wasted on you.'

'What is? Money? This house? The car?' Doubler was enjoying himself enormously. He had rehearsed this exchange in his head many times, and as he felt no great affection for his son, he felt no real responsibility for the way in which he delivered it or the way in which it was received. His son was nothing like him, so his behaviour couldn't very well reflect badly on Doubler. There was no betrayal here; it was just what he would have expected.

'Yes, all of it. It just seems wasteful. I could make so much more money out of it.'

'But why? For what? Are you in debt? Do you have a gambling problem?'

'No, *Dad. Jesus.* I just like making money. I'm good at it. I don't like seeing the opportunity go to waste.'

'But it's *my* car. It's a *good* car. It's the only one I've ever owned. Has the car really wasted its opportunity? It's fulfilling its purpose right here and you seem intent on turning it into a commodity.'

'It's not a commodity, anything but. It's a 1949 Series 1 Land Rover with all of its original features in perfect nick. And I've got a very keen buyer lined up.'

'But it's not yours to sell! I'm trying to find some sort of reason, some sort of justification for your subterfuge. Tell me you're in debt or have got another money issue of some kind. Then I can help you. I can give you money. You don't have to go to such tortuous measures. If there's no reason, then perhaps . . . ' Doubler looked around the room for inspiration and found it in the cold, empty fire grate. 'Perhaps you're just a bit of a shit.'

Julian physically recoiled, taking a step back in shock. 'Dad! This is quite outrageous! And that is absolutely no way to talk to your son.' Julian paced the room, his angular form jutting and posturing but, in its awkwardness, completely unable to naturally assume any dignified pose of superiority.

'But, Julian, you have just tried to con me out of my car. That is absolutely no way to treat your father. It's only just dawning on me, and I don't know why it's taken so long for me to figure it out: you are a bit of a shit.'

Julian stopped in front of his father's chair and leant down over him, exhaling heavily through flared nostrils. Doubler could feel the heat of his hatred. 'One, I had no idea you knew anything about cars. The fact you knew it was worth a fortune and you were still prepared to let it rot in a farm building just confirms how little head you have for money.'

Julian straightened himself up again, glaring angrily, searching for a second reason for his indignation. He found it and delivered it triumphantly.

'Two, making money is in my bones. It's what I do and you should give me a little credit for it.'

Doubler was interested in this twist. Should he be able to credit his son with some level of ingenuity? Had he failed to recognize a skill within him? 'What exactly do you *do*, Julian?'

411

Julian snarled his answer. 'I work for a bank. I make them a pile of cash.'

'Mm, yes.' Doubler wondered whether this was something he already knew. Had he ever asked? Perhaps not. 'Do you love what you do?' he enquired gently.

The word 'love' looked for a second as if it might stop Julian in his tracks, but he carried on blithely. 'It has its bonuses. I'm good at it, but it's an extremely stressful way to make a living, so there needs to be good compensation, and it certainly delivers that. I earn a fortune.'

'Why is it stressful? What do you worry about?' Doubler was genuinely curious, wondering whether his son shared the same feeling of unfathomable dread he experienced each spring just before the first shoots of green appeared.

Julian's eyes looked off into the middle distance, capturing the feeling in an attempt to do its impact justice. 'When a deal goes well, there's no greater high. But if a deal goes bad, if I call it wrong' — he paused for dramatic effect — 'it can cost the bank a fortune. It's terrifying.'

Doubler imagined the terror, trying hard to understand it and relate it to any of his own experiences. 'But nobody's going to die, are they? I mean, if you just don't turn up for work, nobody will *suffer*. You might make less money for you or for the bank. But then again, if you don't turn up for work and you escape a wrong call, you won't lose as much money as if you'd turned up. Either way, if you don't turn up, there's no actual pain or hardship. Is that right?'

Julian was demonstrably flustered. 'Are you mocking me? I'm proud of my achievements. I've created something out of nothing, which is more than you can say for this old place and your blasted potatoes.'

'Well, as you say, I've sat twiddling my thumbs for the last forty years and the two things I own, my car and my house, are now apparently worth a fortune without me lifting a *finger*. Perhaps it might be the same for you? If you did *less*, you might make *more*. You'd suffer less *stress* certainly.' If Doubler had smoked a pipe, he would have tapped it. He appeared contemplative, but inside his heart was racing.

'You really are the most frustrating old man. This farm is worth a ton of cash and you're going to watch the opportunity sail by. The value of that car is about to go through the roof and you're once again going to blow it. And where then is the result of your hard work?' Here, Julian painted quotation marks in the air, making him in Doubler's eyes look even more childish than usual.

Doubler drew himself up in his chair. 'My business is in good shape. In fact, I too seem to have done rather well for myself over the years. I certainly won't go hungry, and I've got the finest roof over my head that I could wish for. And I'm busy working on my legacy. We should all try to leave one of those. But like you, Julian, what I *do* doesn't particularly matter. If I die tomorrow, nobody will suffer.'

Julian sneered. 'Is that the only way you can value a success, Dad? I don't think you'll find it's a particularly useful currency.'

'Perhaps you're right. But I can't help wondering about our *worth* as individuals as a measure of a life well lived. There was this man — '

'Oh God,' Julian groaned. 'Your damned potato hero. I know, I know — without him we wouldn't have chips. What a tragedy.'

'Actually, I wasn't going to mention Mr Clarke, though I think you'll find that the contribution he made to the planet was significantly greater than chips. No, no, I was thinking of a chap a dear friend once told me about.'

Julian groaned again and, finally, collapsed his tall frame into the chair opposite his father. He slumped low in the seat, stretching his legs out wide in front of him. The move wasn't so much one of defeat, more a vivid illustration of the enormous boredom he was about to suffer. He ran both hands through his hair and then rubbed his face and eyes dramatically as if to ward off a deep stupor.

Doubler continued, untroubled by Julian's pantomime, 'A neurosurgeon, he was. A *brain* doctor. My dear friend saw a documentary about him and we talked at length about that level of personal accomplishment. What struck my friend was how the surgeon, throughout his career, *cycled* to work in the mornings. On a *bicycle*! Even in the snow! He was such a good brain doctor that he used to travel to one of the old Soviet Bloc countries to perform terrifically complicated surgeries and there would be queues and queues of people who had travelled for days to see this chap. And he'd do all of this work voluntarily instead of going on holiday. And then he'd come back home and carry on operating on people who would die a horrible death if it weren't for him.'

Doubler continued, still unbothered by the curled lip of his unimpressed audience, 'What struck my friend, quite profoundly, I recall, was that *bicycle*. 'If I let a man into my brain, picking through my memories and my abilities, I'd want him picked up from his home in a bloomin' chauffeured car.'' Doubler laughed at the memory of Mrs Millwood's words, repeating them as he'd heard them. ''Meanwhile, it's the bankers and the lawyers in their flash cars barging him out of the way. How could they possibly know that this man on a bicycle had the power to save their lives?'''

Julian, exasperated, started to pat his pockets for his car keys, making it clear he had no wish to continue this conversation. Doubler chuckled a bit, his eyes misting up a little at the memory of Mrs Millwood's outrage.

'What on earth are you rabbiting on about, Dad? I literally have no idea what you're talking about. You're losing the plot, old man. Hearing voices, are we?

'I don't know what it can be like being stuck up here on your own day in and day out. Something makes me think your dear friend doesn't even exist. Do you have any friends, Dad? Any at all?'

Doubler stopped chuckling and looked sombre.

'Yes, son, I am beginning to believe that I do.'

Julian looked around at the room, for signs of these friends. Finding none, he smiled a little sadly at his father and stood slowly to his feet.

'You talk about a thriving business. I see no evidence of that. You talk about your friends. I see no evidence of those either. You have a massive opportunity to release equity from this old place, just at the time you ought to be considering downsizing and preparing for the final years of your life, and you're refusing to entertain the idea in a manner that is frighteningly reckless. I do fear for you, Dad. I fear you've lost the ability to make these important decisions on your own, and I think it's time I stepped in and managed your affairs before you do something disastrous. In fact, Dad, I'm not going to sit and watch you fail. I'm going to take steps.'

'Steps, son? You're going to take steps?' Doubler arched his eyebrows, inviting his son to elaborate.

'I can't sit here passively and watch you ruin your life and my inheritance. Where did it all go so wrong for you, Dad? When did it all start to unravel?'

Doubler considered the word 'unravel'. Things had indeed unravelled. But now, a tightening in his stomach, a sickening, gripping, throttling of his lower intestine suggested a *ravelling*.

'And you're so weak, so passive, so detached, Dad. I don't want to become like you. I want to be a man of action: decisive and certain. Which is why I must intervene. I will be doing it *for* you.'

Doubler looked at his son and didn't know whether to pity him or pity himself for raising him. 'You ask me where it went wrong, Julian? But what exactly do you mean? How are you judging my success? What do you even know of my affairs that allows you to be the arbitrator?'

Julian threw his hands in the air in an exaggerated movement. If he could have stamped his feet like the small child he was about to recall, he would have. 'I remember clear as a bell you telling me you planned to be the biggest potato farmer in the land. 'In all of the land' you said! I remember it like it was yesterday, though it was well before Mum left. You had so much drive, such great ambition. You wanted to be the biggest and nothing was going to stop you! I believed in you then, Dad. But look at you. You let Peele beat you at your own game. You sat back and you watched him buy everything around you, and you're marooned here now, with no prospect of expansion. You've been outmanoeuvred time and time again. I find it sad, Dad, to watch you slowly fail. You're like a scorpion surrounded by a circle of fire, about to sting yourself to death.'

'Scorpions,' said Doubler, in a voice that oozed patience while belying his subterranean tremor, 'don't do that, incidentally. They are immune to their own venom, and it seems unlikely that any creature could have survived hundreds of millions of years of evolution with a suicide-inducing fear of fire. It's a myth, I'm

417

afraid, but an evocative one, and you used it colourfully, so let's allow that inaccuracy to pass, shall we? Your memory fails you, Julian. I never, ever set out to be the biggest. My stated intention was to be the *best*.'

'Dad, you're a *potato* farmer. I don't think you can be the best without being the biggest, so you really are clutching at straws. There are no prizes for runner-up in the game of life, Dad.'

'Do you know, Julian, as hard as it might be to get your tiny little brain engaged in the facts, it is just possible that I am already *certifiably* the best. It is entirely possible that I have won in the game of life. Certainly in the potato leagues.'

Doubler got up and went to the dresser; he opened a drawer and retrieved the large white envelope. He came back to his chair, the prize clasped on his lap. He glanced at it, stroked the writing absent-mindedly and turned back to face his son.

'You know of Schrodinger's cat, I presume?'

Julian sighed impatiently and looked at his watch, neither admitting to his ignorance nor denying it.

'I am, as we sit here, both a failure and a success in equal measure. At least, as long as this envelope remains unopened. It is fair to assume that I exist in both states.' Doubler sighed to himself. 'But I wonder, going back to what you said earlier, about measuring your own success in monetary terms. I don't think money *can* be a measure. It is, after all, worthless in its own right. There must be something else to hold you accountable when the day of reckoning comes.

418

Money can't be the determining factor. It just doesn't *matter* that much.'

'This is exactly what I'm talking about, Dad. Your blatant disregard for financial affairs is bizarre. You may well be a farmer, but to be a successful one these days, you must have commercial instinct, and you seem to singularly fail in that department. What's *wrong* with you?'

'I set out, Julian, to live a *consequential* life. And I think, in regard to this pursuit, irrespective of any external authentication that might or might not be recorded here, in this envelope, I consider myself a success. Or at least not a failure.'

'How do you deduce that, Dad? On what measure have you succeeded, if money is so uninteresting to you?'

'I set out to be the best potato farmer in the land. That was my purpose. My goals were a little different; those I have revised and revised over the years. I am confident I have achieved many of my goals, but it is quite possible that I have also achieved my purpose within my lifetime. But if I'm not quite there, then I am satisfied that I have made positive strides in the right direction. I will have travelled a little further down the path in *pursuit* of my purpose. And if nothing else, I might have made it a bit easier for someone else to finish off what I started. It is entirely feasible that somebody might find a small reference to my work in, I don't know, a farming journal or perhaps my obituary — depending, of course, on who writes that — and something they read will pique their interest and they will pick up where I left off. Who knows, it might well take another lifetime to complete what I have begun.'

'What are you talking about? You plant potatoes. Nobody is going to carry on with your work, Dad. You're not inventing a cure for cancer.'

'No, no, I'm not. That I wish I could do and I would give everything I have to deliver *that*. But I am talking about my scientific endeavours, what we like to call my Great Potato Experiment. I'm talking about research I've been undertaking for several decades.'

'Ah, the pursuit of the academic! Otherwise known as living life with your head in the clouds. That explains a great deal. I met types like you at university. Poor as church mice, all of them, and as far as I can tell, not an original thought among them! Completely unemployable, of course.'

'I don't think I could disagree more.' Doubler felt the ravel tightening.

'So, Dad, let me check I've got this clear in my head. You've researched potatoes, and whatever it is you may or may not have learnt about potatoes, you believe it's important enough that somebody, somewhere will find your work and continue it? I hope you're not counting on me! What are the chances of somebody stumbling across this work, Dad? Sounds pie in the sky to me.'

'It's not that pie in the sky. I've submitted my findings formally. My research is well documented and recorded. I have not left it to chance, and to be fair, credit must be given where credit is due. I didn't start from scratch. I simply picked up from where another gentleman left off. He's not with us now and I stumbled across *his* work, so I don't think it's that far-fetched for somebody to stumble across *mine*. And it's easier now, isn't it, to record your achievements and to leave a permanent mark than it was for my predecessors. That's progress, at least.'

Doubler thought hard. He had been determined that Julian should be asked to face up to his shortcomings as a son, but instead had been invited to contemplate his *own* life. These thoughts were not alien to him — he considered them often — but he'd never spoken them out loud. 'But if I die today, I think, yes, I led a useful life. Can you say the same thing? If you died tomorrow, Julian, can you honestly say the same thing? What will they say about you, Julian? 'Oh look, he made money and now he's dead'?'

'Frankly, a swift death feels appealing right now. If I die tomorrow, at least I will be spared the crumbling decline towards senility. I don't know where you think you have achieved success by any measure at all. You drove your wife to despair, robbed your children of a mother and fell into some sort of self-indulgent breakdown, and since then you've wasted your life harvesting potatoes while the risk-takers around you have used a combination of wits and technology to leave you for dust. And you're proud of that little list, are you?'

'Well, I rather hope you won't be penning my

eulogy, Julian. The way you tell it isn't perhaps the way I want to be remembered.'

'And who is going to bother to remember you, Dad? You've not exactly endeared yourself to your grandchildren. You and I are virtually estranged. Your daughter is in perpetual crisis because she's weak, just like you. She's weak. And she's married an even weaker man. Jesus Christ. God help us all. Those genes do not bode well for her sprogs.'

'You know something of genetics, do you?' asked Doubler.

'You know what, Dad? You really are a miserable old sod, aren't you.' This was positioned as a statement, not a question, and the tone suggested a world-weary wryness.

'Me? Miserable?' Doubler thought about recent events and wondered when, among all of them, he'd been even a little unhappy. He laughed, in surprise as well as delight, as he realized how very happy he had become.

'Miserable and mad,' muttered Julian, disgusted by his father's pleasure.

'Do you know what, Julian? Right this minute I am miserable. Yes, I really, really am. But I don't need a psychoanalyst to delve into my sadness for me. The correlation is glaring. My misery happens to coincide entirely with your visits. The rest of the time, I'm almost deliriously happy.'

Julian snorted. He was angry. 'You're not happy, Dad. You're tucked away up here, almost unable to take care of yourself and certainly no longer able to make sane, rational decisions.

422

What level-headed adult refuses an offer of that size? That's not just your money you're chucking away, you know — that's our inheritance. Your grandchildren could certainly do with a little bit of that for their education, and by robbing them of what is rightfully theirs, you're simply proving your irrationality.'

'Why on earth would I want to pay for your children's education? You're making an absolute fortune, you tell me. And besides, they're *your* children — I educated mine and a fat lot of good that did me.' Doubler choked back a sob that had appeared unannounced in his throat, startling him with its vehemence.

He composed himself for a moment before continuing with resignation in his voice, 'I suppose I've failed as a parent. All I've done is raised a woman who daren't speak out for fear of causing disappointment to those around her and a nasty piece of work I am ashamed to call my son.'

Julian began again his ritual of clenching and unclenching his fists. 'You always act like you raised us alone, but it's Mum's memory you're besmirching every time you insult me or my children. You should be ashamed. By treating us as badly as you do, you insult her memory.'

'Oh, Julian. You are incredibly screwed up. The fact is that we all tiptoe around the subject as though your mother is dead, but she isn't, is she? Quite frankly, I wish she *had* died. If she had died, you'd be telling me to get on with my life, to get out and play bridge or hang out with the other lonely folks. But the truth is that your mum left the two of you as well, didn't she?'

This swung in the air between them like a wrecking ball.

Doubler wondered whether he should backtrack, as he always had in the past. He'd get to this point, he would start to say the unsaid, and then he'd see the pain and he'd swallow it for them. He'd take their pain and make it his own. He'd tell his children how much she loved them but how she couldn't cope with life and had to start afresh in order to live at all. He didn't know any of this for a fact, and he didn't believe it, but as a father, it wasn't his job to layer more pain on top of the pain they'd already suffered.

Julian looked at his father coolly, relaxing into a well-trodden trope, saying what he'd said every time they'd ever tried to talk about it. 'I respect the choices my mother has made. She is a strong woman who did what she had to do to save herself. And it wasn't us she had to leave — she left you and the mud and the potatoes. She's found herself there and I am happy for her.' He swallowed loudly and stared at his father with challenge in his eyes, but Doubler doubted his defiance.

'But, Julian, she never, ever looked back. She didn't send for you; she didn't ask after you; she didn't say she wanted you or missed you.' Doubler wanted to stop himself, but something about Julian's snide condescension propelled him forward.

'Because you drove her away, Dad. Mothers don't leave their kids without a very good reason. She had to escape to save herself and she had to make the ultimate sacrifice.'

'The ultimate sacrifice, Julian? She's not a martyr. She's in bloody *Spain*. Not the other side of the world, is it? It's hardly *inaccessible*. She's teaching yoga by day and helping her fella run his bar in the evening, and you know what, Julian? She hasn't lived in torment for years. She hasn't struggled to breathe or to live. She hasn't wanted to *die* from sadness. No, that was my life without her, not her life without me.'

Julian snorted his disbelief. 'You didn't struggle to live, Dad — you just got on with your potatoes. They were the only things that mattered to you.'

'That's what you saw, Julian, because it's what I wanted you to see. I got on with being a dad in the only way I knew how. I carried on as normal because that felt like the best possible way for you to finish off your childhood. I learnt to cook, Julian, so you would both eat. I learnt to clean so you would have clothes in your drawers and clean sheets on your bed, and yes, I sowed and harvested and nurtured my potatoes because there lay my salvation, deep in the earth all around us.'

'Great job rewriting history, Dad. You barely batted an eyelid when she left. And truth of the matter is, Dad, if you had enough courage to admit it, you wish she'd taken us with her.'

Doubler looked at his son with incredulity. 'Is that what makes you so angry, Julian? You can blame me for all sorts of things, but don't blame me for *that*. Of *course* I wish she'd taken you with her! I could have coped with that. I

425

wouldn't have had to look at the pain and fear in your faces every morning you woke. I wouldn't have had to deal with your nightmares and Camilla's constant sobbing. I would have suffered, yes, but it would have been my suffering alone, not the suffering of two children who had lost the heart and soul of the family with no word of explanation.'

'I was there, Dad. You didn't suffer.'

'Is that what you think? Let me tell you what actually happened, Julian. I came home to find my wife gone. All of her clothes, all of her personal effects and her passport, all gone. Her bank account had been emptied. It looked organized, it looked premeditated, but it was so *unfeasible* that we all feared the worst. For twenty-six days the police looked for her. I drove around hospitals; I even went into a morgue to identify a body. Her parents thought she had taken her own life. I thought she'd been *taken*. I kept this from you because I had nothing to tell you other than 'She's gone but I have no idea where.' And then, twenty-six days later, I received a package from her lawyer. She was living in Spain; she was filing for divorce; she was not seeking any custodial consideration. She had returned her wedding rings. That was it. But I couldn't grieve then, could I? She hadn't died — she'd simply resigned from her post without notice.'

'I know all of this, Dad. My point is, you didn't suffer. You made her leave and you didn't have to pay the price.'

'I lost my wife. My children lost their mum. I

426

couldn't allow myself anything as *indulgent* as suffering. I looked after you and I suspended my grief until Camilla had followed you to university. Only then, when I drove back to an empty Mirth Farm, did the grieving begin. Only then did I fall into the blackness of the chasm that then became my world. I'm only just recovering now, Julian, and if you failed to see that, I did a better job than I realized.'

Julian, nonplussed, continued to sneer. 'And you think that any of that is comparable to losing a mother?'

'No, Julian, I don't. I don't pretend to understand what that feels like. But you didn't *lose* a mother, Julian — she *abandoned* you. 'Loss' does not cover it, and it makes it sound like something rather careless that we were all responsible for. 'Oops, we *lost* her.' No, we didn't *lose* her. It was not an accident. It was a *choice*. It wasn't a spur-of-the-moment thing.

'And now she's married and living the life that she *chose*. She chose not to come back when you left home. She chose not to be a grandmother to your children. She's not there knitting scratchy jumpers and baking Christmas cakes. She has never shown one iota of interest in you or me or the grandkids or my potatoes. She's having the time of her life and wearing *culottes*.'

The phone rang beside Doubler, making them both jump.

Doubler grabbed at the receiver and covered it with his hand. 'See yourself out, Julian. I must take this call. It's important.'

Julian looked momentarily baffled but quickly

shrugged as if waking up from a heavy sleep and loped off, shaking his head in confusion.

'Why, hello!' Doubler exclaimed loudly, well aware that these would be the words ringing in his son's ears as he slammed the door behind him. In fact, Doubler rather hoped his son might be loitering just outside the kitchen door to hear the next exchange.

'Very much as we imagined. No plausible explanation, no defence. You'd be proud of me — I called him a bit of a shit. *Twice.* And I don't think he disagreed.'

Whatever Mrs Millwood's response was at the end of the phone caused an uproarious laugh from Doubler, who gasped between outbursts loudly enough to smother the sound of Julian's car as it sprang to life and reversed at speed out of the yard.

# 36

The Colonel had been vague about his reasons for a visit. Doubler, despite feeling pressurized by the many new responsibilities he seemed to be shouldering, made it known that he would be welcome to return to the farm at any time, and to prove the point, he'd laid out tea and cake.

From the moment of his arrival, it was clear that the Colonel was uneasy. He sat down for a few minutes, stood up again, paced the room and then returned to his seat. He stared moodily at his cup, started to speak, stopped himself and then concentrated furiously on his tea once more.

Doubler sat beside him. 'You know I'm a busy man, don't you, Maxwell? If you've got something on your mind, you're just going to have to spit it out.'

The Colonel looked embarrassed. 'Of course. Forgive me. I'm glad you could make the time to see me. I'm in a spot of bother, but I'm not finding the conversation as easy as I expected.'

'What's on your mind? The gin? I've told you I'm going to do my best. I'll have a better idea about capacity in due course.'

'No, it's not that. Well, at least, not directly, though it is related.'

Doubler, with nothing at all to fear from the Colonel, did his best to put him at ease. 'Be straightforward — it will be so much easier on both of us.'

'I'm not very well versed in this man-to-man stuff. Not my style. But I feel compelled to speak to you after our last chat. Do you remember? You talked about past and present, and autumn and hope, and, you know, all that fortune-telling stuff. You were very direct with me. You told me I should go home and value the people around me. I think you were implying I could be a better husband. I've come for advice in *that* department.'

Doubler felt himself redden almost immediately and he stammered his reply, mortified that the Colonel might think he was equipped to offer counsel. 'Oh, that's completely out of my league. I've accomplished one or two things I can be proud of, but being a good husband absolutely isn't one of them. In fact, I'd urge you to steer clear of my advice in all matters pertaining to personal relationships — things won't end well for you if you take a leaf out of my book.'

'On the contrary, you're just the man for the job.' The Colonel stiffened, taking comfort from Doubler's discomfort. He took a deep breath. 'My conclusion, and the matter on which I'm seeking advice, is that I believe I must learn to bake.'

'To bake? You want to learn to bake?' asked Doubler with barely disguised incredulity.

'Yes, and I thought you might be just the man to teach me.' The Colonel did his best to exude some sort of dignity.

Doubler laughed, a rich, hearty, satisfying, unrestrained bellow of pure pleasure, amplified by shock. 'I must say I didn't see that coming. What on earth brought that on?'

The Colonel exhaled dramatically, shaking his head to convey his utter despair. 'My wife is so bloody *capable*. There's not much she can't do. I look at what she undertakes during an average day and marvel. Meanwhile, all I seem to do is get under her feet. It's as if I can't even find a place to stand without being a nuisance.'

'And you think baking will help how?' said Doubler, mystified.

'The women at the animal shelter are so full of you and your blasted *cake*. 'Oh, Doubler's scones!' 'Doubler's lemon drizzle cake!' 'How did Doubler get his icing so smooth?'' The Colonel's voice was mocking, almost contemptuous.

Doubler was delighted. 'Glad to hear it. I think most of the time they think I'm a blithering idiot. I'm rather chuffed.'

'I never knew baking was a *virtue*. I mean, if my men could hear me now.' He hung his head in shame.

Doubler shrugged. 'Everyone loves to eat, and most people appreciate the efforts of a half-decent cook. It's a skill acquired that is rarely regretted. But I'm not sure of your motives. Do you want Paula and Mabel to *admire* you?'

'No, good heavens! In fact, I'd much rather they never heard of this. I want them to remain a little bit afraid of me, as they are now. But I wouldn't mind my wife thinking I'm good for *something*.'

Doubler thought about this and imagined the consequences of the Colonel taking on this new hobby. Something wasn't quite right with the image, but he was unable to articulate his misgivings. 'You know, I fear you're barking up the wrong tree.'

'No, trust me, I've thought about this a great deal. Paula and Mabel seem to forgive your considerable faults for the promise of a Victoria sponge. Perhaps Kath might feel the same about me?'

'Let's have a think about this before you don your pinny.' Doubler remained quiet for a couple of minutes while the Colonel continued to shift uncomfortably in his seat.

'Tell me something,' Doubler said eventually. 'Does Kath cook?'

'Oh yes, yes, she cooks like a dream.' The Colonel nodded enthusiastically, animated by the thought.

'And she bakes, does she? She makes a cake or two?'

'Oh goodness, yes. I don't see much of it — she thinks it's bad for my health — but she bakes these marvellous tray things for her charity dos and all manner of sponges and such for the WI. She makes it look so blessedly easy too.' He cut a slice of cake in front of him, as if the memories of his wife's cooking were making him hungry.

'Interesting,' said Doubler thoughtfully, watching the Colonel eat.

'You don't sound convinced,' answered the Colonel, through a full mouthful.

'I'm just thinking.' Doubler pondered some more, uncomfortable but unsure why. He leant back in his chair and closed his eyes, blocking out all distractions while he conjured up an image of Mrs Millwood and imagined having this very conversation with her. Suddenly, it seemed much clearer.

'Are you trying to impress your wife, Maxwell? Or *compete* with her?'

'What are you saying? I want her to be pleased with me. I thought if you could give me a few lessons, on the q.t., I could go home and do something surprising that she might admire me for.'

'But think about it. You would be treading on her *toes*! Going into the kitchen and baking in the room that she has had to herself all these years? Sounds like a recipe for disaster.' Doubler, convinced now that he was right, waved a fork in the Colonel's face. 'She won't admire you — she'll resent you!' Doubler laughed gleefully. 'She might even *hate* you!'

'I don't find this hilarious, so I'm rather surprised you do, old man. I came for help and you seem to be hell-bent on humiliating me. I'm disappointed, Doubler. I believed we might be friends.'

'We are friends! Look at us! We're having an honest conversation and I'm giving you my advice in a no-holds-barred way. I'm rather pleased with myself. You came here looking for a way to be helpful, and here I am being helpful myself. I've surprised myself, I really have.'

'But you're not being helpful. You've laughed in my face and vetoed my brainwave. I have nothing left to offer. She'll hate me if I do nothing; she'll hate me if I do something. I can't win.'

'Of course you can. You just need to plan this like you would a military campaign. You can't simply wage war on your wife — not in an area in which she's demonstrated a strong command.'

'What are you suggesting?'

'What *doesn't* she like doing? I mean, you paint her as an exemplar of virtue, but there must be areas or tasks where you could lighten her load and make a positive contribution.'

'I have absolutely no idea what she doesn't *like* doing. I haven't asked. She appears to be good at everything. Terrifyingly efficient.'

Doubler thought about his own hobbies and his many conversations with Mrs Millwood on this matter. He took a deep breath. 'What I do know is that baking is very rarely undertaken if you don't absolutely love it. It's not something that anybody *has* to do; they do it because they want to. It might be to give other people pleasure or it might be that the process of baking is therapeutic for them. But nobody has to bake as a chore. My suggestion to you is that you surprise her by taking a *chore* off her hands. That sounds more strategic to me.'

The Colonel looked very put out. 'But it doesn't sound nearly as much *fun*. I rather fancied myself as a baker. It's logical, isn't it? Weighing and measuring, following some rules.

And then — hey presto! I'm winning again!'

'Ah, you see, you do want to compete with her. But my recommendation is that you impress her instead by doing something that doesn't make you the star of the show. Do something else, something less *glamorous*.'

'Like what? Breakfast?'

'I'd keep clear of the kitchen altogether if I were you. You can't have got to such great heights in your career without being quite good at practical matters. What are you good at?'

The Colonel was not forthcoming.

'What about machinery? What's the most complicated piece of machinery you've ever interacted with?'

'As a young man, I liked to tinker with engines. Rebuilt a couple in my time. I've got an engineer's brain, so I'm extremely comfortable in that arena.'

'Marvellous. So you could strip down an engine and reassemble it?'

'I'd be rusty, but I should think so.'

'Then I've got the perfect job for you. The laundry. You might be able to tackle that.'

The Colonel's eyes widened in horror. 'The laundry? I'm not equipped. To tell you truth, that machine scares the living daylights out of me.'

'Well, in my opinion, a washing machine is much less daunting than an oven. And both are less daunting than a car engine. If you can strip down a car engine, you can certainly programme a washing machine. Start with that if you want to make a contribution. I'll show you the basics so you don't make a complete fool of yourself, though every model is a bit different. And then I'll show you how to iron your own shirts. That *will* be impressive.'

'Ironing isn't for . . . '

'For what?'

'For officers.'

'You're not an officer. At best, you're second in command of an army of two. Your reality now, Maxwell, is that your job is that of a husband, and if you can't pull your weight, you're not a terribly good one. Master the washing and the ironing, and see what Kath makes of that.'

The Colonel, while disappointed, felt he must pursue the panacea he'd come for. 'Do you think it will do the trick?'

'I can't guarantee it, but the little voice that sometimes whispers terribly good advice in my ear tells me yes, it will impress her. It will knock her socks off, I suspect. And it might even free up some time so that you can do a bit more together.' Doubler thought about this and added, a little doubtfully, 'Assuming that's what Kath wants.'

'I've always rather fancied bridge.'

'Perfect, and if neither of you has ever played, even better — you can learn together. You'll have to trust each other implicitly.'

The Colonel, whose eyes had shone for the briefest of moments, clouded over again. 'Ironing. Who would have thought I'd have to stoop so low?'

'It's still a skill, just not one you've acquired yet. Learning a new skill is never stooping low; in

436

fact, you'll find it stretches you. I bet you're terribly good at it.'

Maxwell helped himself to another slice of cake, looking at it a little resentfully. Doubler left him to eat it while he disappeared into the pantry, shutting the door behind him. When he emerged again, Maxwell's plate was empty. Doubler placed an unlabelled bottle of clear spirit next to it.

'Is this what I think it is?' the Colonel asked hopefully.

'Yes, sir. Think of it as your reward for services yet to be rendered. Let's get to work and teach you the basics. Then you can go home and help your wife, Maxwell. She'll thank you for it. Try a sip of this served ice-cold both before and after your renaissance and see if it changes the impact the flavours have on your outlook. I'd be interested to know.'

Doubler set about demystifying the secrets of the washing machine to a retired Colonel to whom the gadget had only ever been a curiosity at best. This was an area of speciality for Doubler, and this lesson, which required accuracy, attention and a good head for logic, was one he relished as an opportunity to display his considerable insight. He set about with some rigorous training that encompassed the basics of interpreting a label and intermixing a load, and he finished his masterclass with a special lesson on interrupting a cycle to remove delicates before the harsh spin cycle could do its damage on sensitive fibres. As he worked, explaining the principles of the machine in front of them and testing his pupil to ensure the knowledge was being retained, he thought of his imminent telephone call. Mrs Millwood was going to be delighted with this story, he thought, as he talked enthusiastically about tolerance and leeway when separating colours and whites. Throughout his lecture, he was bubbling over with excitement as he framed the telling of it in his inner dialogue. In fact, he was so carried away he sent Maxwell home in rather a hurry, with his mind reeling at the complexity of the subject.

# 37

Julian spied Peele and made his way purposefully towards him, his hand already outstretched and his face attempting to approximate a smile. From the corner of his eye, as he crossed the busy carpet, he noted two women sitting in the adjoining booth. They were nursing hot chocolates piled ostentatiously high with whipped cream and he winced visibly, wondering how on earth this could represent progress.

'Legion.'

'Julian.'

The two men sat, consulted a menu and ordered themselves their drinks while attempting small talk. They were evenly matched both in status and degree of awkwardness around other men, so both visibly relaxed when they finally parked their trivia and moved confidently towards the business of the day.

Julian opened the conversation with a sad shake of his head. 'Good God. He really is mad.'

Peele laughed. 'You've not been successful either? I told you he wouldn't budge.'

'I don't need him to budge. He's certifiably mad.'

Julian looked at Peele earnestly. 'I've taken advice from a doctor and a lawyer, and they both agree with me. Of course, it's not a surprise he's had another mental breakdown, given his history, but he's frail now, less able to cope with his mental health issues all alone up there. I've been advised to seek power of attorney and have got the ball rolling. My doctor is convinced by my account of my last visit that Dad is displaying signs of schizophrenia, so we all agree that it's for the best that I intervene formally. I might even be able to get him sectioned if I can demonstrate he is a danger to himself or to the community. It shouldn't be difficult. Like you said, he's hearing voices. He isn't of sound mind. And turning down your offer is proof of that, wouldn't you say?'

Peele looked uncomfortable. 'I'd certainly agree that he seemed confused, but it feels quite drastic. I'd like to complete this purchase and have him feel good about it. Perhaps I could offer him a bit more and see if that tips the scales?'

Julian was nonplussed. 'Assuming that increase comes out of your margin, not mine. I'm not going to help you push this over the line for a penny less. If we go down my route, I'll be looking for your help. I'll need somebody to act as a witness and he gets no other visitors up at Mirth Farm, so there's nobody to vouch for him either way.'

Peele nodded slowly. 'I'll do what I have to do when the time comes, but let me up the ante first of all. It won't impact the deal I offer you. I'd just like one more try to let him do this willingly. Though I'm still not convinced he'll bite at any price.'

Julian fixed his eyes on the ceiling above him, as if the blinking fire detector held the answer to all of the world's problems. The fingertips of each hand met in an arch while he considered the proposal. He needed to make enough cash out of this deal to build a decent-sized pile, but, more significantly, he would have a reasonable piece of land earmarked for him. That would be worth a fortune one day. Better now while the property valuations were up in the air. There was so much uncertainty until the exact route of the train line was confirmed. But one thing was for sure: if you owned the land, you held the keys to power.

He nodded and was just about to acquiesce when a disturbance immediately beside him distracted him. It was one of the blasted women on the next table, making a frightful ruckus. Julian turned to see what the commotion was and was horrified to see the younger woman physically restraining the older. The younger woman was dressed in country tweeds of a style that probably hadn't been seen for thirty years, while the older woman was decked out in some frightful parody of a woman golfer's outfit. The colours were garish and clashed. It was almost as if they'd dressed to fit in while clearly having no concept of the etiquette required. He turned back to Peele, rolling his eyes in disgust, but heard his name so turned sharply back.

'Julian,' hissed the older woman once more. She was trying to fight her way clear of the booth, but the younger woman held on to her sleeve while imploring her to calm down.

'Sit down, Olive. This isn't the *plan*.'

'Oh, but I am going to *sock* it to them.' As if to

demonstrate the physical lengths she would go to to settle her score, she shrugged off her cardigan, leaving it in Midge's hands. Midge was both appalled and amused, and throwing her hands up in the air in exasperation, she turned to watch the fallout.

Olive now stood squarely between the two men, unsure of which to feel more contempt for. She settled on both.

'Well, you're a despicable pair.' She said this with a controlled disgust that might have been quite chilling if it hadn't been for the yellow Pringle jumper and the red tartan trousers she had bought in a charity shop in an attempt to blend in with the golfing community. To complete her integration, she wore a cream knitted beret with a central pom-pom, which had slipped forward over one eye during her struggle with Midge, giving her a rakish look that was quite at odds with the visceral contempt she now oozed.

While Olive continued to assess the pair, Peele motioned to the barman, who nodded and picked up the telephone for help. Peele turned back to Olive with a polite smile on his face.

'Can I help you?'

'Well, yes, you had better do exactly that.'

'And you are?'

'I'm none of your business. A *nobody*. Think of me as an *imaginary friend*.' Olive was rather pleased with this. She felt both sinister and disarming. 'I've sat here listening to the two of you plot and scheme and talk about that dear, dear man as if he is some sort of bumbling idiot, but I'll tell you this for nothing — he's smarter than the two of you put together.'

Peele tutted, exuding condescension, which dripped from his lips like oil. 'Listening to other people's conversations is terribly impolite.'

Olive now turned to face Julian directly. 'So is trying to diddle your father out of a fortune.'

Julian took a sharp inhalation, outraged. 'I am doing no such thing and you're very wrong to meddle. I'm simply acting as a middleman. I'm trying to help my dad realize the value of his property while he still can. I'm actually doing him a favour.'

'By taking a cut of the sale value? You call that a favour? Well, I wouldn't like to get on the *wrong* side of you.'

Julian sighed dramatically. It wasn't the first time his interpersonal relationships had been questioned and he wasn't remotely perturbed by the accusation. 'Don't you worry your pretty little head about these matters. They are strictly between my father and me.'

'Oh, so he knows you're negotiating a piece for yourself, does he? He knows that you're having clandestine meetings behind his back? He knows you're planning to stitch him up and sell his house from underneath him?'

'Calm down. You're being hysterical.'

'Hysterical? You think this is hysterical? You haven't seen *anything* yet.'

Just as Olive was settling into her role (one modelled, she hoped, on a barrister from a daytime courtroom drama she had long admired), the bartender and one other man, a janitor or gardener perhaps, crossed the bar to stand on either side of Olive. They had approached with the intention of using force, a rarely executed perk of the job, but on arrival they realized that the subversive was really quite elderly and, despite her outlandish clothes, rather dignified too. They hesitated.

A little nervously, Peele addressed the bartender. 'This woman is causing a disruption to the club, and as a member I'd like her evicted.'

Olive scooped her hat off her head and used it to wipe her brow in one deft move. She gave her sweetest smile to each of the men beside her in turn while physically faltering. The bartender reached out to steady her and she clung onto him gratefully. In this moment, she had recruited them to her team and she was now bolstered by her own small unit of security men.

'I have a slight weakness in my heart,' she said, patting herself on the chest. 'Nothing serious, but stress or confrontation can aggravate my condition. Give me a moment, gentlemen. I'll be out of your hair in no time. You can stay to keep an eye on me if you'd like.'

The bartender moved a fraction closer, affirming his commitment to act as a supportive pillar. Any hint of a threat posed by this diminutive woman in her outlandish garb had long since dissipated. And besides, the bartender, a hub in the club's wheel of gossip, was riveted. He had never quite taken to Julian, who acted like a rich man but was neither generous of spirit or tips. An invitation to see this played out was intriguing.

Olive felt further emboldened. 'Julian, you're not getting off that lightly. You think you're smart, don't you, pulling the wool over your dad's eyes? But I'm sorry to say this one is smarter than you.' She pointed at Peele.

'Don't be daft, woman.' Julian was prepared to accept any claim of duplicity, but he was outraged that anybody would claim that this potato farmer was smarter than him.

'Oh, but he *is*. You think you're doing this clever thing, stitching your dad up for a few quid. But he's so, so far ahead of you he's taking the mickey.'

Peele frowned and addressed the bartender. 'Gentlemen, with all due respect, I don't pay my membership fee in order to sit and listen to slander. Have the woman escorted from these premises. I assume she's not a member, so I don't even know what she's doing here.'

'We are guests of a member and well within our rights, thank you,' Midge called out from the comfort of her ringside seat.

'That's quite true,' confirmed the bartender. 'They've been signed in by the same member every day this week. I believe he's just having a round.'

'Indeed he is,' said Olive, turning to the bartender collaboratively. 'Good of him to allow us access to his private club, but he's got absolutely no *bottle*. An army man — would you believe it? — but he says his days of engagement in battle are long over. Every day he's scuttled

445

off to play golf the minute we've got here.' She now turned to the gardener, giving him a disarming smile. 'Look at me. I'm a golf widow. Well, not a widow. A golf *cuckold*. Well, that's probably not quite accurate either. I'm a golf *stooge*.'

She turned back to her prey, a glint in her eye. 'You are trying to diddle your father out of a few quid, but in the meantime, this man is trying to diddle you *both* out of a fortune.'

'He is?' asked Julian, frowning, looking at Peele for explanation.

'My friend Midge has been doing a bit of research into Mirth Farm. She's another of your father's *invisible friends*. Your father was sensible enough to share your letters with her, Peele, and it turns out there's quite a conspiracy going on here. There's a . . . What's the word again, Midge?'

'Covenant,' said Midge with a slightly apologetic smile.

'That's right. Mirth Farm has a covenant on the surrounding land that prevents any of it being sold for development.' Olive leant round the bartender to look at Midge. 'Am I getting that right, Midge?'

'That's it. You've got this, Olive.'

'If Peele here buys Mirth Farm, he can build property from here to kingdom come. He can do whatever he wants, but without owning Mirth Farm, he's stuck with a big patch of nothing.' Again Olive looked to Midge for confirmation. 'Have I missed anything?'

'No, that's the gist. But I don't think that

Julian here should underestimate the value of the land for future property development. The local council has already granted an off-the-record approval to Peele. My sources say he's been given a nod and a wink. That's right, isn't it, Mr Peele?'

Julian looked apoplectic. 'Is this true? You're planning to develop the land?'

Peele shrugged, as though this were obvious. 'You can't have been blind to this. I was giving you a piece of land to develop yourself. I wouldn't be able to do that without a relaxation of the covenant.'

'You *bastard*!'

Peele shrugged again. 'I'm no more bastardly than you. Or perhaps you're worse. Mine was motivated entirely by a commercial opportunity, whereas you wanted to profit from stitching up your dad. Really, who's the bastard in this scenario?' Peele looked up at Olive for her official verdict.

She sided with the potato man. 'I agree, Mr Peele — Julian takes the biscuit. Screwing your dad is really below the belt. I don't think I've ever seen *worse*.'

'And, according to Mrs Millwood, he was trying to diddle his dad out of his Land Rover the other week! The nerve of this man. He was trying to take a classic car off his dad without telling him it was valuable,' Midge added to Peele, further building the case against the son.

Peele looked disgusted. 'That's pretty low, Julian. Do you have any personal morals at all?'

Julian spluttered, outraged, 'You're trying to

447

be high-handed with me? You were prepared to con me out of my inheritance, out of land worth an absolute fortune. You were being deliberately obtuse. You were going to fob me off with a two-acre plot and a five-bedroom house when you knew all along you were going to build a fucking city. I'd have built my dream house and you'd have immediately invited *suburbia* in.'

Peele was unblinking in his own defence. 'I offered you a deal that you accepted happily. You negotiated further terms in your favour and I accepted those. In the meantime, you were prepared to have your father sectioned, removed from his home by physical force if necessary, just so you could get your hands on a bit of cash.'

The bartender was gripped and watched the insults trade back and forth with the intensity of a tennis coach at a tournament final. Neither player seemed to have the upper hand; indeed, the only person who seemed confident of an imminent victory was the ball girl, who having got the game started with such aplomb, now looked rather pleased with herself, though utterly exhausted.

The bartender took Olive firmly by the elbow. 'Why don't you have a seat? These two will be at it for a while, I suspect — you can watch from the sidelines and sit with your friend. Can I fetch you something to settle your nerves? A splash of whisky, perhaps?'

'Heavens, no. I don't think I'd cope with a whisky — that's a nightcap, not a daytime drink. My very good friend recommends gin and tonic for teatime. He's right more often than not.

Would you mind, dear?'

The bartender hurried off to fetch a couple of medicinal drinks while Julian and Peele traded insults.

Before pouring the drinks, the barman spoke in a low tone to the gardener. 'Stick around. We might need a hand after all,' he said, nodding in the direction of Julian, who was standing up, his white knuckles resting on the table in front of him.

# 38

'Mr Doubler, I've got goosebumps.' Mrs Millwood was speaking softly into the phone, almost whispering.

'What's troubling you, Mrs M?' asked Doubler, holding the phone to his ear with both hands, straining to hear her.

'It's like I'm getting visitations from apple growers from the past. They're *haunting* me.'

'Are you all right, Mrs M? You sound distraught.'

'I am a little. Distraught but excited. I'm *tingling*.'

She didn't sound excited; she sounded exhausted to Doubler. 'Go on?' he asked tentatively, a little frightened of what he might hear.

'I'm not wasting my time while I'm here — I've been busy researching and you'll never guess what I've turned up. I've found *another* nineteenth-century pioneering apple grower called Mary Ann. Though this one is M-A-R-Y Ann and the other one is Ann M-A-R-I-A. But still, what are the odds, do you think?'

Doubler tried to do the calculation in his head, but he didn't have the raw data. To provide an answer, he needed the probability of being called Mary Ann or some combination of those two names *and* the probability of becoming an apple grower. Even without the numbers at his fingertips, he calculated the outcome to be substantially less than one in a billion. And then there were other factors for Doubler to consider: her gender, the historical context. Digits flashed past his eyes.

'I'll have to come back to you, but no less than one in a billion, I'd imagine.'

'Exactly.' Mrs Millwood stopped to cough. The sound was muffled, as though she had covered the phone with her hand. When she spoke again, she still sounded frail. 'I think it's more than a coincidence, I think it's a *sign*. I'm being drawn to these pioneers and they're making me think of *you* and *your* legacy. How would you feel, Mr Doubler, if a few years after your death, Mr Peele gave *his* name to *your* potato?'

'It would be a disaster,' Doubler said frankly. 'And notwithstanding the injustice, Peele is a terrible name for a potato.'

'It would be a disaster, I agree, though in reality it wouldn't undo your *consequence*. The legacy would still be there, your hard work would still have changed the fortunes of potato growers around the world, but it would be sad to think that nobody would ever know it was you! It would be known from here on in as Peele's potato. Would you be able to rest in your grave, Mr Doubler?'

'Heavens, no. I can imagine dedicating eternity to putting a new, resistant, deadlier blight back into the soil to finish off Peele's potato once and for all. I'd scupper him from beyond.' Doubler's confidence began to wane.

'But I can't really see Peele usurping me posthumously, can you? Is this a serious concern of yours?'

'Well!' said Mrs Millwood conspiratorially. 'I didn't think so until I started to delve into the histories of the many fascinating women pioneers of the apple world. I was researching one of your favourites, the Bramley. I reasoned that if I investigated an apple cultivar you held in higher esteem, you'd take my findings more seriously. And that is exactly what happened to *her*.'

'Who?'

Doubler had to wait for Mrs Millwood's answer while she coughed again. Once she'd recovered enough to speak, she croaked the name. 'Mary Ann Brailsford. The Bramley was *her* discovery — she is solely responsible for its existence — but shortly after her death, a neighbour granted rights to reproduce the tree in exchange for giving it *his* name. By all accounts, it should have been the Brailsford. The apple was her legacy. She never even knew . . . '

'That feels fundamentally wrong. I'm so sorry,' said Doubler, apologizing to all woman-kind on behalf of all mankind.

'At least Granny Smith had sealed her legacy. She never knew the scale of it — she was dead before her apple reached fame of *global* proportions — but billions of people around the globe know her name today, and every year tens of thousands of people flock to a festival that honours her memory. They might not know it but they're celebrating her *legacy*. It's still astonishing to think of the impact she had on the world. Though her apple has been claimed by the Australians, Granny Smith was just a simple girl from *Sussex*.'

'This is important information. We will consider this when naming *our* potato, Mrs Millwood, and from now on I shall call the Bramley the 'Brailsford'. The Bramley is dead to me,' said Doubler enthusiastically.

'Me too!' agreed Mrs Millwood gladly. 'And, Mr Doubler?' she added, after a short hesitation.

'Yes, Mrs M?'

'It was probably just a slip, but you said *our* potato. It's not our potato really, is it? It's *your* potato. I wouldn't want to be like Mr Bramley, the self-serving neighbour, stealing your limelight.'

'Oh, it is most definitely our potato. I simply couldn't have grown it without your help. Potatoes need the rich, dark soil, it's true. That was *all* me. But they need light, too, Mrs Millwood. You provided the light. I would have died in the chasm without you, and our potato would have died as well.'

'So I shall have a legacy, Mr Doubler?'

'Indeed it would seem so.'

'That's thrilling, Mr Doubler, because I have been a bit troubled by my lack of legacy.'

'Oh. That sounds like my influence,' said Doubler guiltily.

'Entirely yours, yes. Once, I wondered whether Midge might be my legacy, but I've been thinking about it and I believe you're absolutely right. A child is just a sequence of DNA; they

453

cannot be your legacy. Their achievements must be their own, just as they must take responsibility for their own failures.'

'That sounds very like something I would say. Midge is exceptional — you can be proud of her — but no, she can't be your legacy.'

'But sharing a tiny part of your legacy might feel like compensation. I want to leave *something* behind.' Mrs Millwood fell silent for a while and Doubler, used to these contemplative pauses, waited for her to speak again while trying hard not to imagine where Mrs Millwood might go.

After a few moments, Doubler interrupted his own thoughts, unhappy with the direction in which they were travelling. 'I am very happy to share my legacy with you, providing, Mrs M, that you are prepared to share some of yours with me.'

'But I don't have a legacy to share, Mr Doubler,' worried Mrs Millwood.

'Oh, but I think you do. Your kindness is your legacy and I have had a very small part in ensuring it continues beyond you, beyond me, by passing it on. If between us we can make a dent in both the potato blight *and* the blight of cruelty, then won't we have done well for ourselves!'

'I am not sure kindness can be a legacy, Mr Doubler, but I'm very happy to share it with you. I've always thought you ought to have a plan B, Mr Doubler, just in case the whole potato thing doesn't work out.'

Doubler thought about this. His legacy had always been everything to him and yet he thought now that he might be quite content just to share a bit of Mrs Millwood's kindness for a few more years.

'Mr Doubler,' said Mrs Millwood, barely denting the silence.

'Yes, Mrs M?'

'Perhaps you might like to visit me in hospital. You could read to me.'

'I'd like that very much,' said Doubler, his heart racing at the thought.

'I'm not at my best, Mr Doubler.'

'I quite understand. You've known me at my worst, Mrs M. I think we can both see beyond our darkest days.'

'Very well, Mr Doubler.'

'I'll pop in tomorrow, shall I?'

Mrs Millwood made a smallish sound that Doubler interpreted as agreement, and after hanging up the telephone, he got to work writing a list of the most important things he felt compelled to share with her in person.

# 39

It was a new-found confidence that propelled Doubler towards decisive action on the day of his hospital visit. Things were definitely looking up.

Doubler had made friends, which had come as a very great surprise to him, and the more he got to know them, the more he valued the company of Olive and Maddie. He enjoyed the knowledge that he was the catalyst for their friendship, but he knew that the real credit belonged to Mrs Millwood. It was clear that Olive and Maddie were grateful to him for his role in their union, but now they needed very little help maintaining their friendship, so they had already forged ahead to their next chapter with no trace of nostalgia. Doubler had been relegated to the position of any other visitor to Grove Farm.

And he'd become close to Midge, who he thought was an angel, just like her mother. Midge had spent some time on the papers he'd given her and had apparently even been involved in some type of confrontation with Peele. She said he didn't need to know the details — much of it had been very unsavoury — but suffice to say, she said, Peele would leave Doubler and Mirth Farm well alone now.

Doubler had still failed to open the institute's letter that would let him know, definitively, whether the organization deemed his results a success. Instead, he'd resolved to allow Mrs Millwood to read the letter first. After all, this was to be their shared legacy. Doubler assumed that Mrs Millwood would then call upon Midge to read it, digest it and help them with the next chapter of his life's work. He rather hoped it would be a short chapter. An epilogue, perhaps. But for the time being, Doubler was in no hurry to discover the institute's findings. He had more urgent matters to deal with.

Doubler had arrived nervously clutching all of the things he felt sure would make Mrs Millwood most amenable to the suggestion he had resolved to make. He had packed the basket carefully, with mounting anxiety, as he placed the treasures one by one in the darkness of the wicker.

A tired nurse showed Doubler to the patient and closed the curtain quietly round them for privacy. Doubler, momentarily startled by the intimacy of the space, cautiously pulled a foam-seated chair a little closer to the side of Mrs Millwood's bed. They sat in companionable silence for a while as he poured their tea. Doubler had bought a thermos — two, in fact: one for the tea and one for the milk.

'I've taken the liberty, Mrs Millwood, of bringing you a bone-china cup,' Doubler said as he handed her some tea.

'I don't think that was necessary, but it will make a nice change. Thank you.'

'Tea just tastes *better* from bone china,' he said, holding his empty cup up to the light. 'See that, Mrs Millwood? That's how you can tell it's the real thing. The light shines right through it.'

Mrs Millwood barely glanced at the demonstration, but she smiled nevertheless.

'Though I'd know by the taste alone, I think. Or certainly by the sound a teaspoon makes when it falls against it.' To prove his point, he flicked his fingernail against the rim of the empty cup and listened attentively. 'No sound like it.'

Mrs Millwood looked at the cup in her hands. 'Why is it called 'bone china', Mr Doubler? Would that be the colour?'

'It's made from bone,' Doubler said nonchalantly.

Mrs Millwood looked more closely at her cup with distaste on her lips. 'Actual bone?'

'Yes. I believe at least thirty per cent of the china must be derived from bone to achieve the qualities you are looking for.'

'Oh,' said Mrs Millwood with concern. 'Poor old Mabel. Best not tell her.'

Doubler poured his own tea and took a sip. 'What would Mabel have to say about bone china?'

'She thinks extremely highly of it — she has her very own bone-china teacup in the office. But she's thinking of becoming vegan. I would think bone china is against the rules of veganism, wouldn't you?'

'The strict ones, certainly,' said Doubler vaguely, veganism not being one of his areas of expertise.

'There's no other type. Vegans by their definition are strict. I believe *strictness* is written into their constitution. Nevertheless, even marginal vegans must surely frown upon bones being used in their tea services.'

Mr Doubler thought about this as he took a sip of tea. 'I won't tell Mabel if you don't, Mrs M.'

He noticed that Mrs Millwood was barely touching her tea, but she seemed very content to be holding it, as if the warmth alone would deliver sustenance. He drained his own cup and, wiping it, replaced it in the basket.

'I'm not up to much, you know, but I wouldn't forego the ritual of a cup of tea. Thank you.' She handed the cup back to him and he winced as he noticed her translucent, bruised skin. He placed the full cup beside her bed, not wishing to draw attention to her shocking lack of appetite.

'Well, it's not quite a home brew, but I've learnt to make a decent cup from a thermos. I'll often pack myself one up if I'm going to spend a long period of time in my barn. The secret is the milk. Don't mix it in the flask.'

'Is that right? I'll take your word for it, Mr Doubler. There's not much you don't know about these things.'

'Once you've let a flask of tea spoil, you can never quite get rid of the bad taste. Always keep the milk separate. That's my advice. And never lend a flask.'

'I'll keep that in mind.'

'I mean it. A flask is like a toothbrush. Yours and yours alone. You want to know what's been in your flask. You don't want any surprises.'

'Same with a toothbrush, Mr Doubler,' Mrs Millwood chuckled.

He studied her carefully. She was lying back against the pillow. She was pale and much thinner than he remembered. This realization gave him a tightening in his heart. She was relaxed, though. Her eyes were half closed, and she wore a gentle smile on her lips, the echo of her recent laughter. She looked *receptive* to Doubler.

'Mrs Millwood,' he began gently, 'you have a period of tremendous recovery ahead of you. I think . . . I believe you will be incapacitated for a long time.'

'Who knows?' Immediately alert, she propped herself up on her elbows in defiance. 'I'm strong as an ox really but just weakened by my environment. When I go home, things will quickly improve and I'll be up on my feet in no time.'

'That is as may be, but nevertheless I'm going to make a suggestion to you, Mrs Millwood, if I may. I think you should come home with me and recuperate at the farm.' Doubler was rather hoping that this bold statement would lead naturally to a period of contemplation while Mrs Millwood reconciled herself to the idea. But instead she shook her head vigorously.

'At the farm? That sounds like all sorts of hard work, Mr Doubler. No disrespect.'

'Oh no, I'm not suggesting you have to do anything there. I have that quite under control. I find I am more than able to manage it myself — it just takes a good degree of organization and planning. The house is spick and span really. But I miss your company and I think you might make a speedy recovery there.'

'It sounds far-fetched to me, Mr Doubler. Where would I sleep?'

Doubler paused. He pictured the dark recesses of the bottom of the wicker basket he had carried carefully from the car and he focused his mind on the small jewellery box he had tucked in there earlier. Underneath the tea, underneath the flowers, underneath the box of homemade shortbread, underneath the unopened letter from the Institute of Potato Research and Development in northern India.

'I would like you to consider moving into the farm with me. I mean, I'd like you to live with me.'

'To live with you.'

'Yes, as my wife.'

'Your wife! Oh, Mr Doubler, you're having me on, surely!' Now Mrs Millwood sat bolt upright. Her raised voice was shrill but carried no weight, so failed to catch the attention of the other patients or visitors in the ward. It seemed to Doubler that the universe had the ability to shrink very small.

Nevertheless, he lowered his voice, encouraging Mrs Millwood to do the same. 'No. I have never been more serious in my whole life. I miss you. I miss you every single day and I want you there beside me. I want to take care of you.'

'Are you sure you haven't lost your mind? What do you really miss? My cleaning? A bit of idle chit-chat on our lunch break?'

'No, the cleaning is taken care of. The idle chit-chat? It's irreplaceable. I miss it more than you can possibly imagine. I had no idea how full my life was until your absence emptied it.'

'That's a very nice thing to hear. But our conversations are still available to you. Haven't I proven that these last few weeks? We must have talked most days. And what about all the new people in your life? You really don't need to go marrying me. It seems a bit drastic.'

'It's not drastic. I've thought about this a lot. Non-stop, in fact.'

'Well, I suppose that puts me at a bit of a disadvantage. I haven't had time to prepare in the way that you have. You're a little ahead of me in your thinking. Perhaps you need to give me time to catch up? How long exactly have you been thinking about proposing to me?'

Doubler considered this. How long? The thought had preoccupied him so greatly in recent times that he couldn't recall when it wasn't the first thing he thought about in the morning and the last thing he thought about at night. 'Do you know, I couldn't say. For ever, possibly. At least three months.'

'Well. It would be only fair to let me have some time to get used to the idea.'

Doubler searched her expression. Her thoughts were far away. Perhaps she had already begun to get used to the idea. Some time to catch up with him was probably a reasonable request. His eyes drifted to her bedside table. To the little paper cups with her medication measured out.

'No. I don't think so. I don't think we have time on our side. I can't guarantee that I won't just drop dead while I'm waiting for you to get used to the idea, and you're certainly looking shaky on the prognosis front. We haven't got time for a long courtship.'

'But we haven't had any courtship at all! It won't just take time. It will take action. You'll need to do all sorts of things to make me want to marry you.'

'Things?' His proposal has seemed so glaringly obvious and now Mrs Millwood seemed to have nothing but barriers for him. He tried to suppress his impatience. 'What sort of things?'

'Romantic things. Long walks by the river.'

'Walks?' Doubler briefly imagined a walk that didn't involve his potatoes. It was an unlikely but not entirely distasteful image.

'And the cinema. We'd probably want to go to the pictures a few times. Hold hands. Check we like the same sort of films. What sort of films do you like, Mr Doubler?'

Doubler thought hard, certain that there was a right answer to this and knowing instinctively that a First World War epic was probably not it. Cinema had never improved upon *The Bridge On the River Kwai* as far as he was concerned.

'I like anything you like, Mrs Millwood. I'd like to sit beside you in the dark cinema and hold your hand. That would do for me.'

Mrs Millwood mulled this image over for a while. It was a good answer.

'And restaurants? We'd need to go to some of those. Romantic ones are best.'

'Well, I am a very good cook, Mrs Millwood. I don't think we'd need to go to restaurants. We'd

463

just find ourselves comparing the restaurant food with the food that I could cook for you and I'm fairly sure it would come up short.'

'But that would be the point.'

'It would?'

'Oh yes! We'd go to a restaurant full of hope and expectation, and then we'd quickly find it wasn't quite to our liking. The decor would be a bit fussy. The staff would be a bit condescending. They'd probably talk loudly and slowly to us.'

Doubler laughed at the idea.

'And we'd spend the entire meal thinking about how much better the food would be at home so that by the time we left, we'd be racing out of there, not even ordering dessert.'

'But eating cold apple crumble from the fridge instead?' Doubler ventured, the image crystallizing in his mind's eye as he spoke the words.

'Exactly! And that wouldn't be the end of the experience either. We'd tell our friends; we'd talk to each other about it. For years we'd be saying, 'Do you remember that time we went for that romantic French meal in that fussy restaurant and the staff thought we were simpletons?' And then we'd laugh. And nobody else would find it quite as funny because they'd have to have been there.'

Mrs Millwood thought a little more; her eyes shone.

'And then there would be other occasions. The time we went for a fancy supper in that ponced-up pub everyone was talking about.'

'And we didn't like the food?'

'We never even got to taste the food. There was a power cut!'

'There was?'

'Yes, and while everyone else waited patiently for the power to come back on, we scuttled out of there, giggling our heads off, and went to the chippie and got to the front of the queue before anyone had even realized they weren't going to ever get served in the pub.'

'We did?' Doubler wondered at this moment whether Mrs Millwood was describing an event that had happened to her in the past, it was so vivid as she described it. But she didn't look wistful; she looked excited; her eyes were bright.

'And then the pub we stopped at after a long, wet walk and you insisted on showing them how to serve a ploughman's. We thought the waiter was going to get angry and throw us out.'

Doubler half smiled here, more certain that this was a memory they could create together but realizing, with a dash of shame, how annoyingly *certain* he must seem at times.

'And did he throw us out?'

'No, love. The owner of the pub recognized you as the best potato grower in the county and gave us our lunch on the house!'

'Oh good. Well, that seems like a nice story to tell again.' Her use of 'love' was not lost on him, but he let it float in the air like a bubble, not wishing to try to catch it for fear it would burst.

'So, cinema and theatre. Music and food. That's what we want from our courtship.'

'And how long will all of this last, do you suppose?'

'The courtship? Oh, heavens only knows! You can't predict these things, can you? However long it takes for you to pop the question and for me to say yes. And in the meantime, we'll have enjoyed all of these things together and we'll have created the memories that will sustain us when we're not quite feeling up to making new ones.'

Doubler was doubtful. 'It feels like a long shot.'

'No! Not at all! We'll probably love the same things. We've got a lot in common. I'll tell you who would be delighted. My daughter, Midge. She's grown very fond of you.'

'Likewise. She's been a great help. More useful than my own daughter in all of this.'

'What would your son think?'

'He'd think you were a gold-digger. After my potatoes.'

'A gold-digger? Me? Besides, that old place is not exactly gold. But it's a happy home and that counts for more than all the gold in the world.'

Doubler thought about the offer he'd turned down. Quite a lot of gold under the circumstances.

'But then,' Doubler said, with certainty, 'he'd look at your recent health worries and figure you wouldn't be around for long and then he'd relax a bit.'

'He would? Well, that's pretty poor behaviour from my son-in-law.'

'I know. Turns out he's not a very nice person. Got that from his mum. But then we'd have a

466

huge amount of fun proving him wrong and outliving them all.'

'We don't want to outlive your grandchildren. That's not something to wish for. We'd not have our own teeth.'

'True, and some of those grandchildren are OK. I think you'd like them. There's always hope for the next generation. Kindness can be a recessive gene, I'm sure.'

While Doubler spoke, Mrs Millwood was reaching awkwardly into the bedside cabinet to retrieve her wool and needles. She pulled the partly knitted blanket out first, smoothing it and allowing Doubler to admire the work.

'Oh blast,' she said, collapsing back into her pillows, exhausted. 'It's all got into a bit of a tangle.'

Doubler leant down and pulled out the balls of wool; four different hues, all required at the same time, had wound themselves into a fantastic mess of colour. 'Let me,' he said. 'You rest.'

Doubler calmly set to work unravelling the wool to the point that each pile could sit independently and then set about winding them back into neat balls that Mrs Millwood could use more easily. He was happy in his work, sorting out her little problems, tugging gently at the small knots and tangles. Mrs Millwood didn't quite sleep but lay gently back with her eyes half closed, letting Doubler take charge for a while.

Doubler admired the knitting; the complex pattern was beginning to emerge, though she had a very long way to go before it could be called a blanket. He stretched it out so it formed an extra layer of warmth on top of her pale blue hospital blanket and she gripped its upper edge, pulling it even closer. Mrs Millwood was still resting very quietly. Doubler emptied his basket carefully, arranging the flowers beside her in a jam jar he'd brought for the purpose. He put the tin of shortbread beside the flowers, hoping they might tempt her to eat. He hesitated when his hand felt the jewellery box. He took it out gently and prised the lid open. The pretty ring shone softly.

'I think I'll leave this here, if you don't mind — let you look at it while you get used to the idea. I'll only forget it in the basket and it's precious to me: it was my mum's.' All of this he said quietly, almost to himself.

Doubler wasn't sure if Mrs Millwood was awake to hear him, but she answered equally quietly, barely more than a whisper, and her eyes remained closed and her breathing shallow. 'That's probably a very good idea. I will certainly look at it. And maybe I won't need all that much time at all. Who knows how long any of us have? That's something you learn when you hang around in this place. But just to be prudent, we'd better get working on those memories quick sharp.'

'And this,' he said, with a nonchalance he didn't need to feign. He tucked the unopened letter from the institute under the biscuit tin. 'You can have a look at this when you're feeling up to it. When Midge is here.'

Mrs Millwood said nothing and her eyes remained closed.

'It's not the priority, Mrs M. If you've only got energy for one thing, use it to get accustomed to my proposal. That's the priority.'

Mrs Millwood smiled weakly but still her eyes remained closed. Doubler's heart tore and soared and tore again.

'Cheerio, then. I'll pop in the same time tomorrow, shall I?'

Mrs Millwood didn't answer. Her hands were still lightly gripping her knitting wool, as if she were frightened somebody would wrestle it from her while she slept.

Without looking back, Doubler walked softly away.

# Acknowledgements

Snatches of conversation overheard in passing (often in the most incongruous of surroundings) find their way into my head, take root, and eventually weave their way into their very own tales that will of course end up bearing no relation whatsoever to the eavesdropped snippets I first heard. Nonetheless, I'm hugely grateful for the inspiration provided (however unwittingly) by a proud farmer in the queue for the abattoir; an objectionable young man with absolutely no discernible scruples (who set my mind whirring about the occasional impossibility of familial love); and my gorgeous sister Pippa and her husband Al, whose chat over breakfast planted the very first seed for this book.

This book is entirely fictional, of course, and sadly so are both Doubler's blight-beating potato and his gin with its magical properties. However, the book is peppered with non-fictional characters whose consequential lives have impacted many of us.

John Clarke OBE has not gone unrecorded by history. He received many prestigious awards in his lifetime and his home, Innisfree, was awarded its blue plaque in 2013. John Clarke is used here to provide the foundation for Doubler's work and the motivation that inspired Doubler to believe he might leave a legacy. You will discover here nothing more than the bare bones of

Clarke's endeavours but if you're interested in knowing more, you'll find a much fuller account of his life and work within the pages of Maurice McHenry's book *John Clarke a Potato Wizard*. There is now a festival in Northern Ireland celebrating the undisputed grandfather of the Maris Piper and whilst the number of attendees doesn't yet match those that flock to the festival that celebrates Marie Ann Smith's 'Granny Smith', perhaps it's only a matter of time.

Mary Ann Brailsford planted the seed of the first recorded Bramley apple tree, but she was not an apple grower; at the time she was simply the child of a mother who encouraged such activity. In memory of both Mary Ann and her mother, Elizabeth, we shall always call the Bramley 'the Brailsford' in our house.

A neurosurgeon is briefly mentioned in a conversation between Mrs Millwood and Doubler. She is of course referring to Henry Marsh, whose beautiful and humble memoir, *Do No Harm*, serves as a thank you letter to all those brave and skilful surgeons who live consequential lives every time they go to work.

The Central Potato Research Institute of Northern India exists. I saw a sign for it, fleetingly, from a bus window as I wound my way up a steep hill heading towards Shimla, but whether or not they would have been the right institution to pronounce on the validity of Doubler's discovery, I have no idea. I'm guessing they would.

And finally, my thanks to my gorgeous husband Jon, and my fabulous children, Eoin,